Also by Carolyn Brown

Lucky Cowboys
Lucky in Love
One Lucky Cowboy
Getting Lucky
Talk Cowboy to Me

Honky Tonk
I Love This Bar
Hell, Yeah
My Give a Damn's Busted
Honky Tonk Christmas

Spikes & Spurs
Love Drunk Cowboy
Red's Hot Cowboy
Darn Good Cowboy Christmas
One Hot Cowboy Wedding
Mistletoe Cowboy
Just a Cowboy and His Baby
Cowboy Seeks Bride

Cowboys & Brides
Billion Dollar Cowboy
The Cowboy's Christmas Baby
The Cowboy's Mail Order Bride
How to Marry a Cowboy

Burnt Boot, Texas
Cowboy Boots for Christmas
The Trouble with Texas Cowboys
One Texas Cowboy Too Many

What Happens in Texas
A Heap of Texas Trouble
Christmas at Home

Love Drunk COWBOY

CAROLYN BROWN

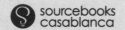
sourcebooks casablanca

Published by Sourcebooks Casablanca, an imprint of Sourcebooks
P.O. Box 4410, Naperville, Illinois 60567-4410
(630) 961-3900
sourcebooks.com

Originally published as *Love Drunk Cowboy* in 2011 in the United States of America by Sourcebooks Casablanca, an imprint of Sourcebooks.

Printed and bound in Canada.
MBP 10 9 8 7 6 5 4 3 2 1

For Todd and Amy Morgan

CHAPTER 1

THE LANIER GUT WAS NEVER WRONG.

Austin Lanier didn't need a deck of tarot cards or a psychic to tell her something was fixing to twist her world into knots. She looked behind her... Nothing but willow trees with new mint-colored leaves dancing in the spring breeze. She looked ahead... Nothing but the muddy waters of the Red River.

The antsy feeling causing all the hair on her body to tingle might be the fact that she was about to sift her grandmother's ashes into the dirty brown water. At least, the old Red flowed gently as if it had no place to go and all year to get there, like an elderly retired man sitting on the porch in his oversize rocking chair and watching the cars go by on a lazy summer day. Later, when the spring rains came, the river would change to a rebellious teenager, rolling and spinning out of control, rushing to its destination at a breakneck speed.

But that day it was as peaceful as Austin Lanier was agitated by the inner turmoil that crept up on her unwanted and unexplained. She stood on the sandy bank, and Pearlita Richland handed her the wooden box. It was about the size of a shoebox, only heavier. Austin held it close to her heart in a hug, but it didn't hug back and it didn't laugh like Granny Lanier. Was this all there was to life? Joys and sorrows reduced to a box full of gray ashes.

"Even though I don't agree with this, it's what she wanted so it's the way we'll do it. So goodbye, my dearest old friend. You hold a place for me on your park bench up there until I finish what I'm doing down here," Pearlita said.

She was eighty-three, the same age as Austin's grandmother, and they'd been friends from the time they started school back in the Depression years. Pearlita was a tall, lanky woman who still stood proud with her head held high and her back ramrod straight. She had gray hair cut in a no-nonsense style that required nothing more than washing and towel drying. That day she wore her one pair of black slacks and a black sweater reserved for weddings and funerals. She'd left her black shoes at home and worn her old brown cowboy boots since she was going to the river.

Austin opened the box and was amazed at the ashes inside. That fine dust couldn't be her grandmother. She'd been a force that never succumbed to age, even in the end.

"She told me that old age wasn't for wimps," Austin said as she held the box out over the water and slowly poured it into the muddy waters of the Red River. Tears streamed down her face and dripped onto her favorite black power suit: tailored slacks, a fitted jacket over a black silk camisole, and black spike heels. The moment the ashes were out of the box, she wanted to wade out into the muddy water and gather them all up to hug one more time. She didn't care if she ruined a pair of expensive high heels in the sand or if the suit would have to go to the cleaners when she got back to Tulsa.

"Living isn't for wimps, no matter what age you are," Pearlita said. "Now we are supposed to watch the ashes disappear and then go to the Peach Orchard for lunch. When we get done, you'll need to start sorting through things at her house. Want me to help?"

"Thanks, but I can do it. I'll call if I need help." Austin watched the river carry her grandmother away.

It wasn't right. There should have been flowers and a casket and weeping, and it should have been done six months ago when she died. She deserved a twenty-one gun salute, even though she wasn't military, and then they could fold up that Superman cape Austin always thought she wore and Austin could frame it in a special box with the big S right on top.

She should've invited Rye O'Donnell, her grandmother's elderly neighbor, to come to the river with her and Pearlita. Even though Verline had told them exactly what she wanted, Rye should've been there. He loved Granny too.

Austin had been talking to him once a week during the past six months since her grandmother died. He'd been her neighbor for several years, plus her best friend, and he'd looked after things after Granny died. There wasn't much to be done since Verline had taken care of everything beforehand, but Rye had kept an eye on the house until Austin could find a couple of weeks to come to Terral to sell the watermelon farm. Maybe that was why her stomach was tied up in knots. She had to meet the elderly gentleman sometime, and he'd be disappointed that he wasn't asked to come to the river.

"My cell phone number is on the front of her refrigerator. She could spout off my regular old phone number from the first time we got party lines, but this newfangled cell phone stuff was almost too big of a trick to teach us old dogs. You take all the time you need here, Austin. I'll be in the truck."

A thousand memories flooded Austin's mind all at once, none of them more than a brief flash. Granny Lanier in her jeans and boots making biscuits before daylight or thumping the end of a watermelon to see if it was ripe or demanding that Austin make her bed every single morning when she came to visit for two weeks in the summer. When the memories played out and there was nothing but the cooing sound of mourning doves in the distance, Austin looked out at the Red River and couldn't see the faintest bit of ashes left. She brushed the tears from her cheeks with the sleeve of her black suit and headed toward the pickup truck where Pearlita waited.

That sinking feeling in her gut said there was more trouble hiding nearby, and in the distance she heard the engine of a truck.

Dust boiled up behind Rye O'Donnell's truck like a billow of red fog. He pushed down harder on the gas pedal, fishtailed the truck when he made a hard right, then another quick turn to the left, sliding into the driveway and throwing gravel everywhere. He bailed out of the truck, slammed the door, bypassed the porch steps with one leap, and shed his dirty work clothes on the way to the shower.

Every time Granny Lanier got a new picture of Austin, she'd hauled it out for him to see. He'd talked to her once a week for the past six months on Thursday night. After he'd assured her that the house and land were fine, the conversation had usually centered on Verline Lanier. He'd missed the old girl horribly and looked forward to talking to her granddaughter, but seeing her on that riverbank had been... Well, hell, it had knocked his socks off.

He took a fast shower, lathered up his face, grabbed his razor, and nicked the dent in his chin. Grabbing a small piece of toilet paper and plastering it down on the blood bubble, he kept shaving, but he couldn't erase that shit-eating grin looking back at him in the mirror.

He finished shaving and peeled the paper from his chin, slapped on his best shaving lotion, and even used a comb rather than his fingers on his black hair. It only took a few minutes to jerk on a pair of starched jeans, a fresh shirt, and his Sunday cowboy boots.

From the time he'd parked the truck until he was back in it, ten minutes had elapsed, but she'd already be at the Peach Orchard. He and his one hired hand, Kent, had been working on a tractor all morning. All that had held it together the previous summer were baling wire, cheap used parts, and cussin' that would fry the hair out of a frog's nostrils. There didn't seem to be any more cheap parts and the baling wire had all rusted. The only thing left was cussin', and even that wasn't working that day. He'd been hot, sweaty, and hungry when he went to the river and had no intentions of cleaning up in the middle of the day until he saw Austin.

Seeing her in person made his heart do crazy things in his chest. Things he'd never felt before.

He hit the speed bumps in front of the school too fast and thumped his chin on the steering wheel. The nick started bleeding again, and he'd forgotten to put a clean handkerchief in his pocket. He slowed down to a crawl and pulled down the visor to look in the mirror. Luckily, there was a paper napkin from the last Dairy Queen trip in the console, so he dabbed at the cut while he drove to the highway and turned south toward the Peach Orchard.

Kent leaned on the rear fender of the old ranch work truck in front of the café and raised an eyebrow when Rye brought his truck to a stop. Kent had a cigarette smoked down to the stub and put it out on the heel of his boot when Rye parked beside him.

"How did it go? I was about to give up on you. Guess you liked what you saw if you got all cleaned up just to meet her. What are you grinning at? I washed my face and hands with one of them wet-wipe things Malee uses on the boys. Do I still have dirt on my nose or something?" Kent asked.

"Your face is clean, and everything at the river went just like Granny Lanier wanted it. Pearlita brought the ashes and Austin scattered them in the river."

"She see you?"

"Who? Granny or Austin?"

"Either one," Kent answered.

"Austin didn't. Granny probably did and is laughing."

"What'd she look like?" Kent asked.

"You've seen her pictures." Rye couldn't think of a damn thing to erase the silly grin from his face.

"That's not what I asked. A picture is just a likeness. Real people have dimension. Why are you smiling like that? What's the matter with me?"

Rye poked him on the shoulder. "Nothing is the matter with you. Dimension? I didn't know you knew ten-dollar words."

"You are avoidin' a simple question and you got all spruced up, which means you liked what you saw."

"Let's go eat some fish. I'm starving," Rye said.

The restaurant was packed full of people. He and Kent walked past the U-shaped cashier's bar and through a door into the dining room on the north side. The noise of several conversations and the smell of frying fish filled the place. They settled into chairs at the table beside the last booth on the west side.

"You look like you put in a morning. What can I get you?" the waitress asked. Her face looked like the bottom of a dried-up creek bed after a drought, but her green eyes were bright and sparkling.

Rye removed his cowboy hat and hung it on the back of his chair. He'd seen Austin when he first walked in the place and was glad that there was a table close by her booth. Damn, she was even more beautiful up close. He should've introduced himself right away, but he couldn't force words out of his mouth.

"It's been more than just a morning," Kent said.

"What's done got you two all in a tizz?" Pearlita asked.

Rye looked at Pearlita but his eyes were on Austin. "Well, I'll be danged. I didn't recognize you without your hat and boots."

Pearlita stuck out a foot. "Look more familiar now?"

"Yes, ma'am, you surely do. And you are Austin?" Rye stood up and extended his hand. "I'm Rye O'Donnell."

Austin was struck mute. That couldn't be Rye. The Rye she expected was at least seventy years old. She'd talked to him every week on Thursday for the past six months. Well, almost every Thursday. A couple of times he wasn't home on Thursday night and at least twice she had to be out of town on business, but they'd talked and he was supposed to be old. Granny had said he was her good friend and a little younger than she was. Hell's bells, that didn't mean early thirties and it didn't mean sexy cowboy handsome.

She put her hand in his, and pure old sexual heat created sparks that danced around the café. "It's nice to finally meet you in person."

"Yes, it is." Rye held her hand a few seconds longer, brushing her palm with his thumb and squeezing just a little bit, unconsciously wanting to take her home with him and never let her out of his sight. "I guess you took care of the burial this morning?"

"We did," Pearlita said. "I'll never understand why she wanted it done on Friday before Easter, but we did it the way she wanted."

"She'd be pleased." Rye sat back down at his table, not three feet from Austin. He knew he was staring, but he couldn't stop and he couldn't think of a thing to say. On Thursday nights they'd talked for ten or fifteen minutes, and he'd never had a problem with words. But sitting so close he could reach and push that errant strand of dark hair back, his mouth was so dry that he felt like he'd eaten a sawdust sandwich laced with alum. His palms were clammy, and he was damn sure glad he was sitting down or his knees would have failed him and he'd have fallen flat on his face right there in the café.

"I hope so. Six months is a long time to wait," Austin said. The gut that did not lie twisted up like a piece of sheet metal in a Category 5 tornado. Her hands trembled, and the place where his thumb had grazed her palm was hotter 'n hell's blazes.

His mossy-green eyes—rimmed with the heaviest lashes she'd ever seen on a man—were undressing her right there in the café in front of Pearlita, the customers, and even God Himself. Pure animal sexuality exuded from him in those creased jeans, cowboy boots, and a green-and-yellow-plaid shirt. Austin still couldn't believe he was Rye and kept stealing long, sideways glances his way. Damn! She should have known a man with a voice like that couldn't be seventy!

"What'll you cowboys be havin' today?" the waitress asked.

"Fish, full order, and sweet tea," Kent said.

"Double it," Rye said. He didn't want to think about food, eat food, or do anything but stare at Austin. Stare, be damned! He wanted to do a lot more than devour her with his eyes. The palm of her hand was as soft as gentle rain on his callused thumb. He wanted to slide into the booth beside her, sink his face into that thick, black hair, and see if it was as soft as her fingertips.

The waitress nodded and disappeared through the door into the kitchen and promptly returned with four glasses of sweet tea, putting two on Austin's table and the other two on Rye's.

He drank long and deep and turned toward the booth where Austin and Pearlita were. That's when she noticed the barbed-wire tattoo circling his left bicep right below his shirtsleeve. She blushed when she realized she was staring at the tat. She shut her eyes and suddenly there he was in her imagination without a shirt, his belt buckle undone and showing a fine line of dark hair extending downward, and a big smile on his sexy face. She opened her eyes with a snap to find him grinning at her. A slow, heated blush crept into her cheeks.

"So you are here for a couple of weeks?" He knew the answer to the question because they'd talked the night before, but he couldn't think of anything more intelligent to say.

"That's right." She blinked and stared at the menu on the far wall.

He did the same. A grown man didn't look at a woman from behind a willow tree on the banks of the Red River and know in an instant that she was his soul mate. That wasn't just bullshit, it was insanity.

He tried. He really, really tried to keep from looking at her. But it was impossible. When he looked up, she was talking to Pearlita so he stared until she shifted her gaze and caught him. Then he blinked and asked Kent if he thought they could find a tractor part up in Ryan at the feed store.

His dark-green eyes and the way he looked at her set Austin's nerves on edge. God Almighty, what was wrong with her? She'd never reacted to a man like that in her life, and he was a cowboy with a tat on his arm. Her mother would stroke out if she called home and said she was panting after a cattle rancher in Terral, Oklahoma, with a tattoo of barbed wire around his arm.

When she jerked herself back into the conversation with Pearlita, the woman was saying, "Me and Verline met in here once a month for dinner, and we usually sat right here in this booth and talked about everything that had happened in Henrietta and Terral since we'd last seen each other. We talked about my niece, Pearl, and you, and what you were both doing these days. I've missed your grandmother terrible these past six months."

Rye leaned across the space from the table to the booth and said, "Are you really going to sell the watermelon farm? There'll be lots of folks interested in Verline's property. It's prime watermelon ground, but I'd like to be first in line to buy it if you decide to sell."

"I haven't made a solid decision about the farm," she said.

Dammit! We've talked on the phone for six months. Why didn't you mention wanting to buy my land during those conversations? And why in the hell didn't you tell me you weren't an old bowlegged geezer who walked with a cane?

Not a single woman had ever affected Rye like Austin Lanier. He'd ridden bulls and broke broncs and had the scar on his left hip to prove it. But he'd never had a reaction where he couldn't stop smiling, and his mind raced around at breakneck speed trying to figure out a way to ask her out on a date. The breeze from the air conditioner blew a strand of hair across her face, and he had to hold the tea glass with both hands to keep from reaching across the space and pushing it back just so he could touch her again. His hand tingled just from thinking about how that silky strand would feel as he rubbed it between his fingers and how he would touch her earlobe with his fingertip and then run his knuckles down her jaw and…

Whoa, cowboy! Slow that horse down, he thought, shaking his head quickly to bring himself to his senses and then shifting his gaze to Raymond Jones, who was heading right toward them.

Raymond removed his hat, lowered his head reverently, and stopped at Austin's booth. "Miz Lanier, I was sorry to hear about your granny. We miss her around these parts. We'll really miss her come Sunday. She was the one who made sure the Easter egg hunt took place every year. She sure got a kick out of it."

Austin looked up at an older man in bibbed overalls and a chambray work shirt. His big ears hung too low on his head, and he had wispy gray hair that barely covered his round, pink head. When he smiled, his teeth looked like a picket fence that a tornado had wrecked.

"Thank you. I miss her too."

"Raymond, you old codger, I thought you died years ago." Pearlita laughed.

"Naw, but it's my turn. Me and Verline had us a bet going. She won because she said she'd go before me. We was almost the same age, but she always told people that I was only six days younger than God and would outlive everyone in the whole town of Terral. I wisht she woulda had a fun'ral so I could go and pay my respects. Still don't seem right for her to just be gone."

"Me too, Raymond," Pearlita said. "But I'm thinkin' when I die I might just do the same thing Verline did. It was simple and there wasn't a bunch of foo-rah around the whole thing."

"Not me. If there ain't nobody left to sling snot over my dead body, then I'm leaving it in my will to pay a bunch of women to come and moan and groan. I reckon if there's enough noise made about me passin' down here on earth, maybe Saint Peter will hear it and think I done some good while I was here. Might give me a fightin' chance at gettin' through them pearly gates," Raymond said. Austin stole a glance at Rye while Raymond and Pearlita were discussing their funerals. He was staring at her again but quickly looked away when she caught him. Could it be that he was as surprised at her as she was with him? What had Granny Lanier told him about her? What had he expected?

"So how long are you stayin' in Terral, Miz Austin?" Raymond asked.

She looked up at him. "A couple of weeks. That should give me enough time to clean things out and put the place up for sale or get an auction ready, shouldn't it?"

"Verline had her affairs in order. She was that kind of woman, so I reckon you could probably do the whole thing over the phone with her fancy-pants lawyer out of Wichita Falls." He bent down and whispered, "I know he's fancy-pants because we use the same man."

"So do I." Pearlita nodded. "And he'll be coming around in the morning at ten to discuss what she's done with her affairs. He acts all prissy, but he's a damn good lawyer and I'm sure Verline did everything possible to make it easy on you."

Austin raised an eyebrow.

Pearlita reached across the booth and patted Austin on the hand. "Verline gave me my orders when she first found out about the tumor. They were to pick up her ashes, go with you to scatter them on Easter weekend even if it was a year away, take you to lunch right here at the Peach Orchard, and tell you the lawyer was coming the next day. Now the responsibility falls on you when I die. You have to do the same for Pearl since Verline died before me."

"You are going to live forever," Austin told her.

"I'm plannin' on it. But if I'm wrong, you are supposed to take care of things for me. I'll call you when I get to feelin' poorly."

Raymond waved at a rancher at another table, patted Austin on the shoulder, and was already talking to the newcomer as he walked away from their booth.

The waitress brought their orders of fish and set a plate of homemade tartar sauce, sliced onions, pickles, and bread in the middle of the table for them to share.

"Want me to put you back some pie?" she asked.

"Save us two pieces of lemon. You do like lemon, don't you?" Pearlita asked.

"If it's like Granny's, I like it. I don't like that canned crap," Austin answered.

Rye chuckled.

"What's so funny?" Austin asked.

How was it that she'd looked forward to talking to him on Thursday night, and now that he was close enough that she could smell his aftershave lotion, she couldn't think of anything to start an intelligent conversation?

His eyes sparkled even more. "What you said. That sounded just like Granny Lanier. She didn't like that canned crap, either, only she called it the real thing, not crap."

"It's real, made from scratch this morning," the waitress said.

"Then save us two pieces," Pearlita said.

"And save us two pieces," Rye said.

"I don't like lemon," Kent told him. "Save me a couple of slices of German chocolate."

Austin looked past Rye at his friend but was fully aware of the cowboy still staring at her from his peripheral vision. Kent was shorter than Rye, less muscular, more sinewy, and had a thick mop of sandy hair that curled up on his shirt collar. The bottom part of a Celtic cross tattoo showed on his upper arm beneath his T-shirt sleeve. His face was slim and his nose almost feminine. His eyes were soft green and his smile genuine. Not one thing about him set her in an emotional tailwind like looking into Rye's green eyes.

A vision flashed through her mind of Rye lying beside her, both of them wrapped up in satin sheets in a fancy hotel, her hand gripping that muscular bicep, and she could almost feel that intriguing tattoo burning against her palm as she dug her fingers into his hard strength. She gasped. Where in the hell were such thoughts coming from? Austin wasn't a hussy. She was a professional woman with a responsible career. She was being groomed to take over the operations department when the boss retired, and she'd worked her tail end off for five years for a chance at that position. And a department head didn't undress a man with her eyes, no matter how sexy he was.

It would have helped if Granny had told her exactly what Rye looked like in even one of the many conversations they'd had or if she'd shown her a picture of him. She'd never once mentioned that he was handsome and muscled up like a bodybuilder. Or that he had amazing deep-green bedroom eyes and hair that cried out to have Austin's fingers tangled up in it. That brought on another vision of him all sweaty and hot, tangled up in sheets with the top half-naked and a fistful of that thick dark hair in her hands as he nibbled on her earlobe and whispered sweet hot words in a breathless Texas drawl.

Sweet Jesus, what is the matter with me? Sure, he's ruggedly handsome as hell, but that doesn't give me the right to think such thoughts. He started it by looking at me like he did. If he'd kept his eyes to himself, I wouldn't be having naughty notions.

Austin had always pictured Rye with gray hair and a bushy mustache. Granny had said that he was a younger man and damn fine looking, but she was eighty-three and her version of younger didn't mean thirtysomething. Now Austin understood why she was so happy when she got off the phone with him each week and why she looked forward to their conversations. She'd thought that he sure had young ideas when she talked to him, but then Granny had been ageless too.

"You got a pretty big job ahead of you," Rye said. "I'm right across the road so I'll be glad to help."

His deep Texas drawl was enough to cause her bikini underwear to start to inch down toward her ankles. She had the urge to reach inside the waistband of her slacks and give them a jerk to remind them that there was no way she was letting a cattle rancher get under her skin or in her pants.

The waitress set two plastic baskets of food in front of Rye and Kent, and they settled into it without talking. Rye kept his eyes on the fish and fries but continued to steal microsecond glances at Austin, burning real-life pictures of her into his brain. Later he'd get them out, shut his eyes, and play them over and over again.

Austin ate her fish and let her eyes wander to the barbed-wire tat. It fascinated her, and she had to hold her hands tightly in her lap to keep from leaning across the space and touching it to see if it was prickly.

What would it be like to have those big arms around her? Why a barbed-wire tat? And why on his left arm? Did he have any more artwork scattered on his body? If so, where was it?

The waitress made a pass by their table. "Anything else I can get you?"

"Ketchup. This bottle is dry," Pearlita said.

The waitress reached across Rye's table, stole the full bottle, and set it between Pearlita and Austin.

"Thanks," Pearlita said. "They don't make anything like this up there in Tulsa, I'll bet."

"Aw, they've probably got anything a body would want up in the big city," Rye drawled.

"Not this good," Austin admitted. Sure they were sitting so close that she could see that little dot on his sexy chin where he'd cut himself shaving, but he kept talking across the distance like they were sitting together. Maybe that was the way they did things in Terral.

"I love fish but Momma hates the smell, so we never had it. When I get really hungry for it, I usually just grab some at Long John Silver's, but it's sure not this good," she said.

"Verline loved fish. I guess you know there wasn't any love lost between her and your momma," Pearlita said. "Woman stole her only son away from the watermelon farm. I told Verline that Eddie never did intend to make a life in Terral, Oklahoma. The day he left for college up in Stillwater, I was out at his car when Verline remembered something she had forgotten. She ran back into the house to get it, and I asked him what he was going to study at school. He grinned at me and said that he was going to go into business because he wasn't going to spend the rest of his life wiping sweat and plowing watermelon fields. She always thought he'd change his mind, but after he met Barbara up there at OSU, I knew he'd never come back to Terral."

Kent finished his food and had drunk three glasses of tea before Rye finally pushed his basket back. "Well, it's about time. I'd begun to think we were goin' to laze around this café all afternoon."

Rye stood up and settled his hat back on his head. Walking away from her wasn't going to be easy, but she'd be across the road and he vowed that he would be spending more time over there.

Austin was near six feet tall with her high heels and she seldom looked up at any man, but when she watched him put on that hat, she could've sworn there was seven feet of cowboy standing in front of her. "I'll be around if you need anything," he said.

"Thank you, Rye. I'll call if I do. I have your number," she said. She wanted to say more but her brain wouldn't work when her eyes were glued on that tat.

"Nice to see you again, Miz Pearlita. Tell Pearl to come see me and the wife when she comes to visit," Kent said.

"I'll do it but I don't expect she'll be comin' around for a while. She chased through for a night last week, and I probably won't see her again until Christmas."

Austin wasn't a bit surprised that Rye swaggered or that his jeans fit snuggly over a damn fine-looking rear end. Not since the initial shock of seeing he wasn't an old man had worn off, anyway.

"Like what you see?" Pearlita asked.

Austin spun around so fast that it made her light-headed. "Yes,

I do. I wonder where on earth the owner found so many branding irons to hang on these walls."

"He didn't. The ranchers brought them in along with the brands on the wooden pieces above them. I'll have to tell Rye that you were interested in using one on his ass," Pearlita teased.

"Why in the world would you say that?" For the second time that day Austin wished she could grab the words, douse them in ketchup, and put them back in her mouth.

"Because evidently you'd like to brand his ass. That is where you were looking."

Austin blushed.

Pearlita laughed. "Eat your fish. You've got a big job cleaning out Verline's house and you will need the energy. She never threw away a damn thing. And now you've got to do it knowing that cowboy with a sexy ass lives across the street."

"Whew!" Austin wiped at her brow. "I got to tell you, Pearlita, that was a shock. Granny never told me what Rye looked like. I figured him for a seventy-year-old cowboy with bowlegs, a gray moustache and hair, and walking with a cane. Came close to giving me a heart attack when he introduced himself. I didn't drool, did I?"

Pearlita had to swallow fast to keep from spewing tea across the table. "Girl, you are just like Verline. I've missed her. We'll have to do this more often."

Austin laughed with her. "I don't know if my poor heart could take it if every time we eat here I get a shock like that."

Pearlita poured ketchup over the top of her fries. "Rye lives in one of them big double-wide trailers right across the street from Verline's place. The old house on the property finally got too worn out to put a patch on, so he tore it down, used what lumber wasn't termite-infested to build a hay shed, and bought him a trailer. Put it right where the old house used to stand. I guess it had something to do with insurance, but he said it was so he could run across to

Verline's when he smelled the cinnamon rolls cookin'. She loved that boy like a son. Sometimes I think he became Eddie in her eyes. He moved up here the same year Eddie died, and they had a grandma-grandson thing going from day one. She should've told you all that instead of letting you believe he was an old man."

Austin dipped a piece of fish into the best homemade tartar sauce she'd ever eaten and bit into it. "Yes, she should've. I bet she's laughing her butt off right now. Tell me more about this thing with Granny and Mother. I know Mother hates this place, but I had no idea that Granny wasn't too fond of her."

Pearlita swallowed a bite and said, "Your mother was a city girl. By the time she finished college, her parents were ready to retire. Your mother and Eddie married right after they graduated from college, so her parents bought them a house in Tulsa and gave them both high-powered jobs. They taught her and Eddie about the car dealership for a couple of years and then gave them the business and retired."

"That explains a lot," Austin said.

Pearlita nodded. "Well, darlin', I've got a one-thirty appointment at the hairdresser's to see if she can get the yellow out of my hair without making it blue, so I'm going to scoot on out of here. You give me a call if that house overwhelms you, and I'll bring a couple of scoop shovels and a box of heavy-duty garbage bags."

Pearlita motioned for the waitress and handed her a fifty-dollar bill. "You settle up our bill and put the rest in your pocket."

"Thank you!" The waitress gasped at the huge tip.

Pearlita stood up and patted Austin on the shoulder. "Verline gave me that very bill when she got sick and said for me to keep it for this day. Remember what I said, Austin. I'm less than half an hour away, and Rosa, my hired help, can run the motel if you need me."

"I will, and if Pearl comes around in the next couple of weeks, tell her to drop in on me," Austin said.

She finished every bite of her lunch after Pearlita disappeared, but her thoughts kept wandering back to Rye and hoping that he stayed on his side of the road while she was there. Or she would need one of those big, old adult bibs like they use in nursing homes to catch the drooling.

When she'd finished, she drove through town and out past the cemetery where Granny should have been laid to rest beside her husband but instead she was nothing but bits of ashes floating down the Red River.

When Austin turned right into the driveway, she saw the hired hands gathered around the porch, hats in hands, waiting for their new boss. She took a deep breath and crawled out of her little bright-red Corvette. She had no idea if there were watermelons in the ground or if they were sprouting, and she didn't know anything about farming them. But Rye had told her the crew had arrived from Mexico and was hard at work getting the ground ready to plant.

"Miz Austin, we are sorry to lose Miz Lanier. We didn't even know she had passed on until we got here last week. We could go back to Mexico, but we will stay and keep things going until you make up your mind what to do with this place," Felix said. "This is Angelo, Estefan, Hugo, Jacinto, and Lobo. They are all my kinfolks, and we all have work visas through the summer." He pointed to each man as he introduced them. Angelo was short and thick-bodied with a round face. Estefan was tall and thin with a slim nose and a thin mouth. Jacinto had a shaved head and a tattoo of a rosary on his bicep. Lobo had kinky, curly hair and soft brown eyes. Hugo had a dimple in his chin, not unlike the one on Rye's face.

Damn it! I'm not going to think about the neighbor, Austin thought.

"And I'm Rye," a deep Texas drawl said from the shadows of the porch.

"Rye's been working with us since we got here," Felix said.

"I've met Rye, and I'm glad to meet you all. Since I'm not familiar with what it takes to run this farm, I'll leave it all in your hands, Felix. Is there anything else I'm supposed to know?"

"We get paid on Friday. Miz Lanier writes us each a check and we sign the back. Then she takes them to the bank and sends all but twenty dollars to our families in Mexico. She brings us back each twenty dollars for things we need in the week. Today is Friday, and the bank in Ryan closes at four," Felix said.

"Then I'll find the checkbook first thing and get your checks written. Give me thirty minutes and come back. Is that all right?"

Felix nodded. "That will be very fine."

They walked away speaking in rapid Spanish. Lobo, a tall, thin man with skin the color of coffee with lots of cream, a hook on his pointed nose, and firm, skinny lips laughed and said, "*Rye está hechizado por la morena que todos quieren.*"

Rye took a step out of the shadows and yelled, "I can hear you, Lobo."

Lobo looked back over his shoulder and grinned.

"What did he say about you?" Austin asked. Not one thing about the cowboy had changed. His eyes were just as green in the bright sunlight as they'd been in the dimly lit café and his hair was even blacker. That tattoo beckoned to her to touch it, and she had trouble keeping her eyes off the big silver belt buckle.

Rye wasn't about to tell her that Lobo had said that he was bewitched by Austin. His palms were already sweaty just standing there in her presence. He was more than just bewitched by her. There was an itch so far down in the middle of his heart that there was no way he could scratch it. And the physical reaction quivering behind his Wrangler zipper said he'd best get his mind on ranchin' instead of Austin Lanier.

"I asked you what he said," Austin said.

"I'm sorry. I was translating it from Mexican slang into English," Rye said quickly. He'd deal with Lobo later when he was flirting around with some local chica. The only one of the crew who wasn't married, he was tall, thin, and would be playing in Mexican movies if a talent scout ever visited his village.

"Hey, Rye, *no quiero bronca contigo*," Lobo yelled.

"And what was that?" Austin asked.

"He made a remark about me and then said that he didn't want to get into a fight with me," Rye said with a grin. *Damn!* His face was going to hurt by nightfall if he didn't wipe that constant smile from it.

Austin had sent thoughts racing around in his brain that he had no business entertaining. Someone who worked in a high-powered office in Tulsa wouldn't be staying in Terral, Oklahoma, with a population of four hundred if you counted half the dogs and part of the stray cats running around town. Without them the total was probably closer to 350.

Austin opened the front door and said, "Okay. Guess I should've taken Spanish in college rather than French. Did you need something, or were you just checking up on the hired help?"

"Felix asked me to be here when you arrived. They've been spooked about meeting you for fear you'll decide not to put in a crop this year. It's their means of living for the whole year. They work hard, send their money home, and then live on it until the next spring. They're afraid you are going to tell them to go home, and their families will go hungry this winter," Rye said.

"Well, thank you. Looks like I've got to hit the ground running if I'm going to get their checks written and taken to the bank."

Send them home to starve kept running through her mind. She could never do that. If they knew a year ahead of time there wouldn't be work for them at Verline Lanier's, then they could make arrangements elsewhere. But how could she run a watermelon farm and work in Tulsa at the same time?

"I've got to go to Ryan to the feed store and tag agency. I'll drive you up there," Rye said quickly.

Austin nodded before she thought about it because she was worrying with the idea of those men and their families going hungry all winter.

"Okay, I'll go get my truck and come right back."

CHAPTER 2

AUSTIN INHALED DEEPLY BEFORE SHE OPENED THE FRONT door into the small white frame house and went inside. She hadn't been there since her grandmother died back in the fall. There had been no need. The tumor wasn't something they could surgically remove. She'd opted for no treatments and taken her last six months with no chemo. They'd talked every Thursday night and she'd visited Austin twice, both times in Dallas when Austin had trips there.

She'd decided early on how she wanted things done. No funeral. Cremation. No fuss and no need to come to Terral. Pearlita would keep the ashes until Easter. Verline died on a Thursday and Rye had called. He and Austin had talked every week since then, and that had filled the space when she normally talked to Granny. Except Austin thought she was talking to a much, much older man all those months.

The windows had been opened, and cool spring breezes pushed the lace curtains out away from the window in the living room. The house had been built the first year Verline and Orville got married back in 1947 and reflected the simplicity of the times. The living room took up the first quarter of the house with a bar separating it from the kitchen. A short hallway to the left had doors that opened into a small bathroom and two equal-sized bedrooms. The washer and dryer were in the garage off the kitchen. It had been years since there was enough room out there to park a car. Now it housed the overflow of Verline's love for pure old junk.

Austin turned around slowly and took in every nook and cranny filled with stuff. Getting through it all would take every waking hour for the next two weeks. Maybe she should have taken her mother's offer to come and help her. Barbara would have gone through the place like a whirlwind, and in two days it would have all been relegated to the trash bin. Austin wanted to take her time and make decisions about what to keep and what to toss.

"Granny was a junkie of the purest kind," she mumbled.

Granny's business desk was in the corner of the living room, back behind the recliner that faced the small television set. A letter bearing Austin's name rested on top of a business checkbook, lying in plain sight on top of an antique desk. The oak chair squeaked when she sat down as if it realized the wrong woman was using it. She recognized the spidery handwriting on the letter as her grandmother's and held the letter to her chest before she opened it and read.

Hi, honey,

> *If you are reading this, then my ashes are floating down the Red River and I'm already sliding down a rainbow or chasing raindrops. I'm writing this today because I know the time is nearing. Don't know how, but it is, and I don't want you to cry for me, Austin. Just pick up the reins and run this old ranch like it was the love of your life, and it'll give back to you a hundredfold. The lawyer will come soon and you'll see just how prosperous good, old hard work will make you. But in case you need to take care of business before he gets here, the checkbook will tell you what I pay the hired hands. Felix will tell you how we do business. Rye will help you with anything he can. He's a damn fine young man, and he's been good to me. Do whatever you want with the farm and the house. I'd love it if I could see what you decide, but I trust you to do what's best for you. Remember I love you and the times we shared were the highlights of my life… Granny*

Austin wept until she got the hiccups. She finally got it under control enough to look through the checkbook, find the amount owed each hired hand from the previous summer, and write out six checks, but when she signed the last one, she swallowed hard past the lump still in her throat. Verline Lanier had lived in this little house, less than half the size of Austin's Tulsa apartment, for the majority of her life. She'd lived in Terral all eighty-three years. Could Austin really sell a lifetime to strangers looking for a good deal at an auction?

"They wouldn't even realize how many hours Granny spent sitting in this creaky old oak chair or why there's a chunk out of the corner of the desk."

Austin rubbed her upper arm at the memory of the summer when she was running through the house and stubbed her toe on a throw rug. It sent her flying into the desk, knocking out a chunk of wood and putting a gash in her arm that required five stitches at the Nocona hospital emergency room. Granny hadn't even told Barbara and Eddie about it until it was time to send Austin home. The scar was barely visible, nothing more than a tiny white line that showed up when she had time to get a tan. Barbara had said her daughter would never go to that godforsaken place again, and Eddie had said it wasn't any big deal. Barbara had asked him what he was going to do the next time when it scarred Austin's face.

Austin's father had said that they'd hire a damn good plastic surgeon if that ever happened. She didn't even know what a plastic surgeon was and wondered that day why a doctor would ever work on plastic people.

She went from the desk to the kitchen. The sink was on the right-hand side with a window above it looking out over acres and acres of freshly plowed earth. Cabinets running the length of the west wall with the bar made an L-shaped leg. The refrigerator was on the east wall: one of those old rounded-top things that Granny said was irreplaceable because it didn't circulate air like the new ones, therefore it didn't circulate odors. Trash can to the right of the refrigerator. Granny said that way the icebox, as she always called it, hid the ugly thing from anyone sitting in the living room. A sugar bowl, salt and pepper shakers, and a bottle of pepper vinegar were arranged in the middle of a chrome-legged table with a red top. Four red padded chairs were pushed up under the table. A ceiling fan above the table was turning, slowly stirring the breeze from the windows into the kitchen.

Red-and-white-checkered curtains hung on the window above the sink with matching ones on the window of the back door that led out into the garage. Austin stared at that window for a long time, trying to figure out if they'd built the garage years after they'd put up the house, since the door had a window. Probably so, since Granny would have needed a place to store her extra stuff after a few years of marriage. She'd always had a penchant for keeping every single thing that came through the front door.

Austin started a pot of coffee and opened the refrigerator to find it filled with crates and crates of eggs. She counted twelve with two dozen eggs in each one. That was twenty-four dozen eggs. Why on earth would there be more than two hundred eggs in the refrigerator?

"Easter!" she moaned.

Granny always ordered eggs for the hunt. She'd gotten them from Martin's Grocery down past the school. It was the only one in town other than the Mini-Mart, a convenience store that also sold gas and diesel.

"What am I going to do with all these eggs? And why are they here? Granny's been gone six months. Surely she didn't order them before she died. I'll call Pearlita and see if she knows who will take them off my hands tomorrow, but right now I've got to go to the bank as soon as my hired hands get in here and sign the checks." She talked to herself as she listened to the gurgling sounds of the ancient percolator.

Her grandmother had hated the newfangled drip machines and had said that they were the beginning of the ruination of decent coffee. Give her a good percolator and plenty of strong, dark roast coffee to go in it, and they could take all the fancy machines at Walmart and bury them in the nearest landfill or cram them up their asses. She didn't care which just so long as they didn't expect her to use one of the gadgets.

A gentle knock on the door brought Austin back to the present. She motioned for Felix and the other men to come inside. They lined up right inside the door, hats in hands, and waited. She brought the checks over to them and handed Felix the ink pen. He went to the bar and laid his check down, signed the back, and left it lying. The rest of the men followed his example just like they did every Friday.

"Would you all like a cup of coffee? Will the bank know the right place to send the money?" Austin asked.

"We are fine, and Miz Verline always took care of it for us so I hope they know what to do," Felix said.

"Okay. I want you guys to know that I'm not sure what I'm going to do with the place, but I appreciate you staying on until I get it figured out. I gave you each a ten-dollar raise. Do you want that brought to you or sent home?"

"Please bring it back to us. Our families will be looking for a set amount. We will take care of the rest and thank you," Felix said, then fired off rapid Spanish to the others.

"¡Este padre!" A wide grin split Lobo's face.

"He says that's awesome." Rye walked right in without knocking. "I forgot to tell you about the eggs I put in the fridge this morning. The grocery store called yesterday and said they were there. Granny had ordered them six months ago so I picked 'em up and stored them in her fridge. Didn't have room in mine. We'll color them tomorrow. I'll be here early. What time do you get up?"

Felix headed toward the door. "Lots of cháchara." He motioned at all the knickknacks sitting everywhere on every single flat surface in the room.

"What?" Austin asked.

"*Cháchara*. Junk." He waved again at it all.

"You got that right." She smiled. "I'm going to the bank now. I'll be back as soon as possible."

"*Sí*. We can take the pickup to town for food when you get back, yes?"

"Did Granny let you do that?"

He nodded and wiped his eyes. "Yes. Once a week on Friday night we go to town and buy food."

"Then that's fine."

"We thank you, Miz Austin," Felix said.

"How long have you been working here?"

"Forty years. My father was here before me. Estefan and Lobo are my nephews."

"Then you knew her well."

He nodded and said on his way out the door, "Miz Lanier was a great lady even if she did like the *cháchara*."

"Are you ready?" Rye asked.

She picked up the checks. "What makes you think I'm going to dye Easter eggs tomorrow? I've got enough to do without that on my plate too. You can come and get them in the morning and do them yourself, but not before ten."

Rye didn't argue but held the door open for her. Her heel sank into the dirt when she stepped off the porch, and he quickly slipped an arm around her waist to keep her from falling. She looked up with those big, round blue eyes, and he had to stop himself from kissing her right there. It was a crazy feeling: If the woman were drugs, he'd be addicted the first time his lips met hers.

"That was almost a disaster. I guess high heels aren't any good on a watermelon farm, are they?" She blushed.

"Guess not." He grinned.

But if they make you fall into my arms, then by all means wear them every single day. I'll take a chance on the addiction.

He drove back into town, past the cemetery, the watermelon shed, the grain elevator, the school that had had a much needed facelift, the Baptist church on the left, the community center beyond that with the old boarded-up Methodist church on the next corner, and then the funeral home. On the right was the Church of Christ and the grocery store, then a building that Granny said the Watermelon Jubilee crew had bought to rent out for special occasions like birthday parties and baby showers, and then the Mini-Mart on the left facing Highway 81, with a fire station, a car fixing place, the telephone company, and a café in between. When he reached the highway, Rye turned right and pointed the car to the north.

"It hasn't changed a lot since I was a kid," she said.

"People move in and move out. Population stays about the same."

"Didn't there used to be a grocery store on the other side of the street? Somewhere about where the fire company is now?"

"That's right. When I was a kid, my folks brought us over the bridge to the Fourth of July festival. Terral always had the best fireworks show in this area, and there was a store there that still sold penny candy and put it in a little brown paper bag."

If he didn't look at her, he felt like they were back on familiar ground. Talking about things like they did on Thursday nights, but one glance and *poof!* Every intelligent thought slipped right through his mind and he wanted to touch, taste, and feel. All of which would most likely bring about one reaction and that was a solid slap on the jaw.

"I was here one time for that. We sat in lawn chairs up by the Methodist church and I got all sticky eating cotton candy," she said.

She looked out the side window at the cattle, the fields of

alfalfa, and the barbed-wire fence. It was easier if she couldn't see him; then he was the same man she'd pictured to go with the voice on the phone. An elderly gentleman who was kind enough to oversee her grandmother's place across the road. How in the hell had she not realized from his deep Texas drawl and his laughter that he wasn't seventy years old?

He was tempted to drive slower so he could keep her beside him longer, but the nine-mile trip to Ryan went fast even at the speed limit. He turned left at the flashing light, made a U-turn at the end of the street, and parked beside the bank. "Here we are. If you'll wait at the drugstore over there on the corner across the street, I'll pick you up there when I get my feed and tractor oil."

He opened his door but she shook her head. "Don't get out, Rye. I'm able to open a door and shut it all by myself. I'll get my business done and then wait for you at the drugstore. Do they still have a soda fountain?"

He nodded. "Probably in the same place at the back of the store as it was last time you were here." He was disappointed. He'd wanted to help her out of the truck so that he could touch her again. Maybe it had been like a flash in the pan: instant, fiery heat that burned itself out in a few minutes.

The heat in the pickup came close to blowing the windows out, so it was not a flash in the pan, he thought as she slid out the door.

"Then that's where I'll be." She slammed the door shut and walked across the sidewalk into the bank.

He watched her until she was inside the bank and slapped the steering wheel. If he'd parked a half a block away, he could have watched that cute little fanny a helluva lot longer.

The lady who waited on her knew exactly what Verline did on Friday with the checks and the transaction went smoothly. She put a twenty and a ten-dollar bill in each of six bank envelopes and handed them to Austin.

"We all sure do miss Verline. We always looked forward to

seeing her on Friday afternoon. She was an institution in this county and a pillar down in Terral. You going to sell the farm or run it?"

"I'll probably hang on to it until the end of the season so the hired hands won't be without work."

"You are a good woman. I see a lot of Verline in you."

"Me? Granny always said I looked exactly like my mother."

"Not in your looks as much as your actions. You move like Verline. She was tall like you and you have her smile."

"Well, thank you. I take that as a compliment."

"It's meant as one," the teller said.

The drugstore hadn't changed a bit since the last time Austin had been in it, and that had been at least fifteen years before. She'd gone there for ice cream with her grandmother the last time she came for a visit. That would have been when she was fifteen. After her sixteenth birthday, her mother and father decided that she would work summers at the dealership. She missed Terral the first year but soon her life was so busy that the years slipped by quickly. She always managed a couple of days at Christmas and maybe two or three scattered quick visits throughout the year, but never a long visit again.

She went inside to find that it had changed very little. The pharmacy part of the store was still at the back on the right-hand side with the soda fountain on the left and a few scattered tables and chairs. A couple of elderly ladies were sitting at one table and waved at her.

"You'd be Verline's granddaughter, I bet," one said loudly.

Austin nodded.

"Come on back here and let us buy you some ice cream. We used to meet with her on Fridays right here."

"I'm Austin Lanier, and you are?"

"I'd be Molly and this here is Greta." The one with the bluer hair pushed a chair back. "What kind are you eating?"

Austin sat down. "Chocolate and a cup of coffee for afterward. She talked about you two when we visited on the phone."

Greta held up two fingers. "We sure do miss Verline. We looked forward to our ice cream Fridays with her. She'd tell us stories about the watermelon farm, what all you'd said on Thursday night when you called, and then we'd bitch and moan about our families."

The lady set a cup with two enormous scoops of chocolate ice cream in front of Austin and patted her on the shoulder. "I loved your granny. She was an independent old gal."

Austin picked up her spoon. "She did things her way right up to the end. And we did what she wanted even though I'd have liked a real funeral."

"It's best to do what she wanted. That way there'll be no regrets. I'm making a pot of coffee now. I'll bring out three cups when it's finished."

"Verline did do things her way," Greta said.

Austin changed the subject. "I'm going to have to run an extra hour tonight to get all these calories off my thighs."

"Ah, honey, you got Verline's genes. That woman wouldn't fatten up if she ate six pounds of bacon and a gallon of ice cream a day. She was slim her whole life." Molly giggled. "Y'all ain't built for fat cells. But I am. I got a right good relationship goin' with my fat cells. They're happy as sailors in a whorehouse when they hear me orderin' ice cream, and I'm happy to keep them that way."

Austin giggled. "Tell me stories about Granny, since you knew her so well."

"Honey, we could make your hair stand straight up like them punk rockers on the television set, but we made a pact with her long ago that what got discussed in the drugstore stayed in the drugstore. We growed up down in Terral with her and Pearlita. Pearlita married and she and her husband built a motel over at Henrietta because he worked on the railroad part time. Them two never did have no kids but Pearlita took a big shine to one of his nieces who was named after her. You know Pearl. She used to come up to visit when Verline got you in the summertime for those weeks. Then me and Molly, we moved to Ryan when we married, so that kept all four of us pretty close together. We know too many secrets to tell anything much in one Friday afternoon, but if you was willin' to meet us here about two o'clock every Friday, we might forget that we promised we wouldn't tell secrets," Greta said.

Austin raised an eyebrow. "Y'all wouldn't be tryin' to keep me in Jefferson County, would you?"

Both of them nodded emphatically. "Verline said once you come back and got a taste of farmin', you'd stay. We're just hopin' to make sure you get a good taste."

"Why?"

"Because that's what Verline wanted. She always wanted Eddie to love the farm like she did. You know your grandpa wasn't worth a damn on the farm. He was smart as a tack when it comes to investin' money but it was Verline who liked farmin'. He wanted to move into a house in town when he got that job for that company that took care of other people's money up in Waurika, but she wouldn't have no part of it," Molly said.

So that's where Dad got his business savvy and his distaste for farming, Austin thought.

"She said that she made the money and he took care of it. Then he died and she kept doin' what she liked and bringin' in the crops," Greta said.

No wonder she and Mother didn't get along. They are just alike.

"You met your neighbor, Rye O'Donnell, yet?" Molly asked.

Greta fanned her face with the back of her hand. "Now that's a man with a future. Let me tell you, if I was fifty years younger I'd done already have him corralled up in the hayloft and you wouldn't have a sinner's chance in heaven of takin' him away from me."

"Ah, Greta, you never would've had a chance with him. He's like Mark Chestnutt sings about."

Austin cocked her head to one side. "What is it that Mark sings about?"

Greta's eyes lit up. "He talks about something bein' hotter than two rats in heat inside an old wool sock. That's the effect all of those O'Donnell boys have on the women." She lowered her voice and her chin and looked up over her wire-rimmed glasses. "Personally, I always thought Rye was the prettiest one of the lot."

"That's pretty hot. There's more of the O'Donnells?"

Greta nodded.

Rye whistled all the way to the feed store and told the man there to load twenty gallons of tractor oil into the back of his truck.

"What's got you in such a good mood today? You break down and buy a new tractor or what?"

"Nothing." Rye grinned.

"Boy, it's either a new tractor or a new woman. Ain't nothin' else can put a look like that on a man's face. So is it a John Deere or what's her name?" the old fellow asked.

Rye's face lit up even brighter just thinking her name and visualizing her big blue eyes and the way his hands felt when he kept her from falling.

"Might as well spit it out, son. You sure didn't look like that the last time you came in here all serious. Matter of fact, I ain't never seen such a spring in your step."

"I just met her. Don't want to jinx it by talkin' about it."

"I knew it was a woman. A new John Deere might put that look on my face, but I'm forty years older 'n you. I'll tell Randy to load up that oil and you'd best get on home to her. Don't be lettin' her out of your sights now," he said as he walked back through the store and told his son how much tractor oil to put in the bed of Rye's truck.

Rye signed a ticket and started whistling again before he made it to the feed store door. Damn, she was pretty in that suit, but he bet she'd look like a rodeo queen all dolled up in jeans and a pair of boots. Or a model from Victoria's Secret in a cute little sky-blue silk nightgown with those skinny straps and her dark hair set loose to fall down to her shoulders.

That last visual was set firmly in his mind as he drove past the drugstore, made a right-hand turn, and was three miles down the road toward Terral before he remembered that she was waiting for him at the drugstore. He whipped the truck around in the middle of the road, stomped the gas pedal, and was driving eighty miles an hour when he looked up and saw the flashing lights right behind him. He stomped the brakes, came to a sliding stop in the parking lot of the tiny used car business not two blocks from the drugstore, and slapped the steering wheel.

"Shit! Shit! Shit!" He pushed the button and his window rolled down.

"License and registration, please," the officer said.

Rye pulled out his wallet and opened the console to find the papers. He handed both to the highway patrolman and waited.

"Mister O'Donnell, do you have any idea how fast you were driving?"

"Yes, sir, I do. It was stupid but I was supposed to pick up my..." *Damnation and hellfire, what do I call her? My friend? The woman in the sexy silk nightgown in my dreams?*

"Yes?" the patrolman asked.

"I brought a lady friend to town, and I forgot her and left her at the drugstore. When I realized what I'd done, I was hurrying back to get her," Rye explained. Even in his ears it sounded stupid.

"I'll be right back." The patrolman carried Rye's license and registration back to the black and white car with the lights still flashing.

Rye tapped his foot. He set his jaw and ground his teeth. He rolled his eyes.

Austin was going to be furious that he'd forgotten her. She'd never go anywhere with him again. Granny Lanier would haunt him forever.

"And shit! I forgot to buy feed too," he mumbled when he looked over his shoulder and saw the oil but no sacks of grain in the back of the truck.

The patrolman took his own good time returning, and even when he was beside the truck, he held the papers in his hands for a full minute before passing them back to Rye. "Mister O'Donnell, I ran your license and you haven't had a ticket in the last three years. Since you were distracted and there were no other cars on the road, I've written you a warning, but the next time you're doing eighty down this road, I will write you a ticket. Is that understood?"

"Yes, sir, and thank you," Rye said.

"Go on and get that woman. You're probably going to be in more trouble with her than a speeding ticket would be anyway." The gray-haired fellow chuckled and walked back to his car.

Rye tossed everything over into the passenger's seat, looked both ways, and pulled back out on the highway. He drove very slowly to the flashing red light, made a left, and parked right in front of the drugstore. He quickly put the registration in the console and his license back in his wallet. When he got out, that silly grin plastered itself right back on his face!

"Well, I do declare, speak of the devil and he shall appear," Greta said when Rye walked into the drugstore. "And ain't he pretty?"

"Shhh. You'll embarrass Austin," Molly said.

"Hello, ladies, warm day, ain't it?" Rye said.

"Afternoon, Rye. What brings you to town? And yes, it's a warm day but it's goin' to get really hot here real soon." Greta pushed her ice cream dish back. "Summertime, it gets hotter than Lucifer's tail feathers, Austin. By then you'll be wearin' Verline's old overalls, and they'll feel right good especially if you roll up the legs up above your knees."

"What makes you so happy today? Warm weather?" Molly eyed Rye.

The tips of his ears turned red and he felt the heat, but he couldn't think of an answer.

Greta looked at Molly.

Molly winked at Greta.

Austin could figure out what was going on between the three of them, so she spoke up. "I know about southern Oklahoma in July."

And this other heat that gets me from the inside out every time I'm in Rye's company is something that overalls won't fix.

"Well, if you stay on, anything under a hundred degrees from the end of July to the end of September means we done got us a cold snap," Greta said.

Molly slapped Greta's arm. "Don't be scarin' her away."

Greta grinned. "Don't drink the water then. If you ever do, you'll be doomed forever."

"Why's that?" Austin asked.

"Tell her, Rye," Molly said.

"It's magic. If you drink the water in Terral, you won't ever be happy anyplace else."

"I drank it when I was a kid and it didn't affect me. I even took baths in it." Austin smiled up at him, careful to blink when she looked down so her eyes wouldn't fixate three inches below his belt buckle.

"You ready?" Rye asked.

"I am. Felix and the guys will be waiting to go to the store. Next week I'll buy the ice cream." Austin stood up.

Rye escorted her to the front of the store with his hand on the small of her back. After the shock in the café and the jolt when he caught her when she stumbled, he wasn't a bit surprised that his palm felt like it was on fire. Or that the only way he wanted to move it was further down to cup one cheek or up around her shoulders to hug her close to his side so that he could feel more of her body next to his.

"Well, I'll be damned," Greta whispered loudly. "She didn't say he'd brought her to town."

"Shhh," Molly said. "They'll hear you."

"You are right on time. We'd just finished our ice cream," Austin said.

Rye's grin got bigger.

The DJ was rattling on about it being Good Friday when she got into the truck. The Friday before Easter, the day she was to toss her granny's ashes into the Red River. Why on earth had Verline wanted it done that way and in that manner?

She looked around at the town, a little bigger than Terral but not much. Her mother said the first time her father, Eddie, brought her to Ryan, she thought all the history books in the world were wrong. The world was not round. It was flat and when they left Ryan they drove off the edge, landed in hell, made a left-hand turn at the *Welcome to Terral* sign, and drove another two miles out to the place where he grew up. Barbara said that she felt like she'd landed right smack in the middle of a *Hee Haw* set that day.

"I need to run back by the feed store," Rye said. He didn't dare go home without the grain or Kent would never let him live it down.

"Okay," she said. "Must've taken awhile at the tag agency?"

"You know how those things go," he mumbled. No way was he telling her that he hadn't even gone to the tag agency. He still had two weeks before deadline on the pickup tag so he'd take care of that another day.

Her cell phone rang when they were backing out. "That's my mother. How far is it to the feed store? I can tell her to call back."

"No need. It's not two minutes from here. You can visit while I run inside and take care of things," he said.

"Hello," she said.

"Is it over? Are you okay?" Barbara asked.

"It is and I am. I've got a six-man payroll that I'm taking care of today. Tomorrow I meet with the lawyer and start packing."

"I don't envy you that job. Verline never threw out a thing. You'll probably come across school papers that your dad colored when he was in kindergarten down there. God, I hate that place."

"Well, stay in Tulsa, and I'll take care of it."

"That house is as old as God. I swear it is and she wouldn't move up here even when she got sick. I offered to take care of her, hire the best nurses, send her to a specialist, and have the tumor removed, but she'd have no part of it."

"I know, Mother. Granny did things her own way right up to and including the funeral."

"Well, if it overwhelms you, I'm just a phone call away."

"Thank you, and I'll remember that. I may just pack it all up and put it in a storage unit, then go through a box or two a month until it's all done. That way I won't have to make decisions right now."

"You were always organized. Gotta run. It's payroll day here too."

"'Bye, Mother."

"That was quick." Rye backed the truck up to the feed store so loading would be easier.

"She just wanted to be sure everything went as planned. I told her that it had."

As planned, he thought. *Not one blessed thing has gone as planned today. From the time I hid behind the willow tree and watched you dump those ashes into the river, my whole life would make Katrina look like a summer rainstorm.*

"I'll be right out," he said and disappeared down the side of the truck into the store.

The two big glasses of iced tea at the café and the cup of coffee she'd had at the farm plus the two cups she'd had after her ice cream while she talked to Greta and Molly hit bottom, and Austin needed to find a bathroom. She opened the door, slung her long legs out, and walked inside where Rye was signing a ticket on the counter.

"Do you have a restroom I could use?" she asked.

An elderly man looked up at her. "Yes, ma'am. Right back down that aisle and to the left."

His eyes widened and he looked back at Rye, a silly grin on his face. "Is that what made you forget to buy your grain?"

Rye nodded.

"Well, son, I reckon you done good to remember what your name was when you signed the tickets. I ain't sure I could if I had that a-waitin' on me."

Rye chuckled.

"John Deere don't make nothin' that looks like that. You better keep her in your sights real good or some other old cowboy will boot scoot her right out from under you," he teased.

"Yes, sir," Rye said.

By the time she was finished and had walked back to the front of the store, the feed was loaded and Rye was leaning on the side of the truck waiting for her. She and the older gentleman exchanged waves as she left.

"You need anything else before we go home?" he asked.

Home? That sounded strange. Terral wasn't home.

"Not a thing," she said.

The wind kicked up a minor dirt storm right outside of Terral, and by the time they reached the farm, it had blown enough red dirt around that her cute little Corvette looked like it had gone through the Great Depression Dust Bowl days. She jumped out of the truck and headed into the house as fast as she could in three-inch spike-heeled shoes.

Rye was right behind her. "We've got to get the windows down or there'll be dust in everything. That stuff can get into the smallest cracks. Don't worry. I'll take care of them. I know which ones

I opened to air the place out for you." The minute he was in the house, he was chasing from one room to the other slamming down windows.

"I wondered if they'd been up all week." She brushed a coating of something resembling rust-colored baby powder from the front of her black suit.

"House smelled all musty when I came over this morning. It's been shut up for six months, and other than me comin' by last week when the guys came from Mexico, no one's been inside," he said as he shut the final window in the living room. "Didn't think about a dirt storm."

"Well, shhh…crap! My suitcases are in the back of my car. Do you think the dust got in them?"

He held out his hand. "Give me your keys and I'll go bring them in for you."

She fished around in her purse until she located them and put them in his hand.

He had to control his breathing when her fingertips touched his palm. *Dammit!* He was thirty-two years old, not sixteen. He'd been in love. He'd had girlfriends and serious relationships. What was it about Austin Lanier that built a fire in his gut?

Austin removed the envelopes from her purse and laid them on the bar. Then she went to the window and watched his fine-looking rear end as he hurried to her car in the dust storm. If he'd walked into her oil company, a dozen women would have hog-tied him and carried him off to the nearest broom closet. That brought on a jealous streak that wiped the grin off her face and replaced it with a frown. Sure they'd talked lots of times, but she'd only met the man that day. She had no right to be jealous. Maybe he had a girlfriend, a fiancée, or maybe he was just being nice to her because he'd loved her granny like his own grandmother.

He set her suitcases inside the door and shut it behind him, went to the thermostat on the wall, and adjusted it to blow cool air. "It's too warm with the windows down. We usually have to use the air conditioner a few hours about this time of year. I still got feed to unload so I'll be going. Oh, I put the dye for the eggs up on the refrigerator in case you want to do some tonight. But I bet you are too tired to mess with them, aren't you?"

"I told you I'm not dying eggs. Not tonight or tomorrow."

"See you later," he said.

She opened her mouth to argue more, but he was gone before she could get a word out. Mumbling all the way about Easter eggs, she hauled her suitcase down the short hallway to her old bedroom. Nothing had changed. It still had a twin-sized bed pushed up against the east wall, a dresser on the west wall, and a fluffy pink rug between the two. A picture of Eddie when he graduated from Terral High School was framed and took center stage on the dresser. One of him and her mother on their wedding day was on the left and Austin's senior picture on the right. More than a dozen smaller ones were scattered around them. Pictures of Austin at a ballet recital. She picked it up and frowned. She must have been ten because that was the last year she took dancing lessons. The next one she picked up was one of her with her mother and father at her college graduation.

She put the picture back and threw her suitcase up on the bed. In half an hour it was unpacked, her clothes hung up, underpants and pajamas in the one empty dresser drawer, and she was removing her dusty suit jacket that would definitely need a trip to the dry cleaners when she got back to Tulsa.

She heard someone knock on the kitchen door and then Felix yelled her name. She kicked off her shoes and padded barefoot through the living room.

"Hello, come on in. I was in the back of the house. Here's your money." She picked up the envelopes on her way to where he stood just inside the door and handed them to him.

"Could I get pickup keys too?"

She unhooked the keys from a rack at the end of the bar.

"Not those. That is Miz Lanier's fancy new truck keys. The ones on the other side with the red key chain is the old work truck."

She replaced the keys and picked the other set off the rack. "Where is this new truck?"

"She keeps it in the shed behind the house. The old work truck is parked in the backyard. It is so old the weather and dust storms don't do much damage."

"Why don't you just keep those keys while you are here? That way, if you need something from town you can go get it."

"Thank you." Felix grinned.

———————

She really meant to take a quick bath in the big claw-footed tub but when she sank down in the warm water, she groaned and leaned her head back on a rolled towel. She'd forgotten how well her body fit in the tub and just how deep it was. She shut her eyes and a picture of Rye appeared instantly. She snapped them open so fast she swore she could hear the pop.

She was not going to think about that man even if he was the best eye candy she'd seen in months. She lazed in the water until it went cold, contemplated letting part of the water out and refilling it with hot, but didn't. She stepped out and wrapped a big, white towel around her body. She dried her hair, brushed her teeth, dressed in a pair of soft knit pajamas, and opened the door to her grandmother's bedroom but couldn't make herself go inside. She had at least five hours before bedtime, and she could get a lot done in that time, but she was mentally exhausted. She couldn't face packing a single box or going through even one dresser drawer that day. All she wanted to do was curl up in an easy chair and shut her eyes. On Thursday she'd call the old man, Rye, like she always did, and they'd have their usual conversation. But a quick reality check told her that nothing was normal and wouldn't be again. Granny was gone. She wasn't coming back. Rye wasn't an old man. He was a helluva sexy cowboy.

Tomorrow after the lawyer came and went, she'd get serious about the business of packing up Granny's things. She'd done enough for one day. She went to the living room, turned on the television, channel surfed until she found reruns of *NCIS*, and settled into the worn recliner where her grandmother had always sat.

Kent left at five thirty but Rye worked until dark with Austin on his mind all evening. He finally got the tractor in running order and drove his old work truck back to his house. When he removed his shirt and tossed it at the dirty clothes hamper, he realized he hadn't changed clothes after he'd driven Austin to Ryan. His favorite Sunday shirt now had big, round ugly oil stains all over the front. He looked down at his jeans and groaned. They'd come from the cleaners just last week and hadn't even been worn until that day. Now they had grass stains on the knees, oil on the hip pockets where he'd wiped his hands, and a nice two-inch tear down the thigh.

His best boots had weathered a dust storm, waded through a feed lot and the pasture, as well as kicked the tractor wheel more than once. It would take a week to get them back to the shine they'd had that morning when he put them on to go to the cafe.

"What was I thinking?" he said.

He went to the window in the kitchen and looked out across the road at the little white house. The blue light flickering from the living room said that Austin had the television on. What was she watching? Did she like old movies like he did? What would it be like to share his oversize recliner and a bottle of cold beer with her while they watched a movie?

He stood there for a full ten minutes before he went to the

kitchen and opened the refrigerator. He pulled out a container of leftover lasagna, put it in a pan and slid it into the oven, turned the knobs, and headed for the shower.

It took awhile to get all the oil and dirt from under his fingernails and three shampoos before the water ran clear out of his hair. When he finished, he wrapped a towel around his waist and padded back to his bedroom in the far left corner of the house. He pulled the blinds up and looked at the house across the road again. She was still watching television. Had she fallen asleep?

"It's only eight thirty," he said. If he dressed in a hurry, would it be too late to run over there with the lasagna? There was plenty for two, and she probably hadn't had anything since ice cream in the middle of the afternoon.

He grabbed a fresh pair of jeans from the closet and tossed the towel in the corner. He pulled a knit shirt over his head and took off for the bathroom to see if he needed to shave again. The plague of having dark hair was that a man's beard was also dark, and either he looked scruffy or he shaved every day…twice if he wanted to impress a lady.

He had his nose right up next to the mirror when he got a snoot full of smoke. "The lasagna!" he yelled and rushed into the kitchen.

When he opened the oven, a blast of black smoke billowed out and up his nose. He hurriedly turned on the exhaust fan above the stove and opened the kitchen window. So much for taking a late supper across the road. He pulled the smoking pan from the oven and carried it to the deck off the living room where he put it on the picnic table and left the sliding doors open.

He sat down in a lounge chair and put his head in his hands. He'd had more bad luck since he'd met Austin than he'd ever had in his life, and still he could hardly keep from inventing an excuse to cross that road to see her again.

CHAPTER 3

It was Saturday morning, the day before Easter, which fell on the first Sunday in April that year. No matter where Austin was, Saturday was her day to sleep in. She didn't care that research had shown that missed sleep couldn't ever be reclaimed. She put in long, hard hours all week and she slept on Saturday morning. Neither psychological nor physical proof meant squat to her. She didn't care what the specialist in *Vogue* magazine said about the issue or if Professor Know-It-All had proven beyond a doubt that one day of sleeping in did not atone for five nights of working late. Sleeping in on Saturday caught her up on missed sleep, and if she didn't get it, she was bitchy.

The sun was barely up when she was awakened to rattling pots and pans banging in the kitchen. She put a pillow over her head but the sound didn't go away. She groaned, looked at the alarm clock, and sat straight up in bed when she realized she wasn't in her apartment in Tulsa. If that wasn't Granny Lanier resurrected from ashes and come back to life, then whoever was in there had better be able to run fast or else like the sting of rock salt on their hind ends. Because Austin fully well intended to jerk that shotgun from behind the door and start shooting. She didn't bother pulling on a robe or slipping her feet into house shoes but stormed down the hallway muttering curses the whole way.

"What the hell are you doing?" She popped both hands on her hips and glared at Rye O'Donnell. "Do you know what time it is?"

He poured a cup of coffee and set it on the kitchen table. Damn, but she was cute in those pajamas with her hair all tousled. She didn't have a bit of makeup on and yet she still looked gorgeous.

He laid a hand on her shoulder and steered her to a chair. "Drink that. It will wake you up."

A night's sleep hadn't taken the jolt of electricity away when he touched her shoulder. The steam rising up off the boiling eggs was cool compared to his hand and yet he had a deep desire to pick her up, carry her to that big recliner in the living room, and hold her until she woke up.

"I don't want to be awake. I told you I sleep late on Saturday." She grumbled to cover up the way his mere touch made her knees go all weak and rubbery.

She wanted to be grumpy. She wanted to be mad until the next Saturday when she planned to sleep in, but his smile sure knocked a hole in that idea. That and his red-hot touch on her shoulder didn't do a damn thing but make her want to grin back at him. She picked up the coffee and sipped but she was not going to dye Easter eggs. If he wanted those gazillion eggs all colored up and pretty, then he could dye all day. When she finished her coffee, she was going right back to bed.

"I told you that we dye eggs every year for the Easter egg hunt. I promised Granny Lanier that I would keep up the tradition for her and I'm going to, with or without you," he said.

The coffee was just like Granny made and ten times better than Starbucks. The second sip woke her up a little more. She shouldn't finish drinking the whole cup or she'd never go back to sleep, but it was so good she kept sipping. "It's not even seven o'clock!"

"If you'll step out on the porch, there's a beautiful sunrise putting on a show just for you," Rye said.

More than the aroma of good coffee wafted to Austin. He had shaved recently and the aroma of his shaving lotion blended with the coffee smell, and good Lord, was that bacon frying in the electric skillet? A man that dyed Easter eggs, cooked breakfast, and looked like he just walked out of a western movie. It wasn't fair that he lived in Terral and not Tulsa.

"How do you like your eggs?" he asked.

"In an omelet with tomatoes and mushrooms."

"Don't have fresh things in the fridge and the garden won't be ready for weeks so it'll have to be with ham and cheese."

"Why'd you ask if you were going to make them that way?"

"So I'll know next time. Get that smaller skillet out from under the bar, and you can stir the sausage for gravy while I keep the bacon turned."

"This is my house."

He pointed at the bar. "Yep, it is. After today you'll know there are two electric skillets that we use on Easter weekend when we need all the burners on the stove to boil eggs."

She set her mug on the bar and pulled out the small skillet. "Sausage, ham, cheese, and bacon. I'll gain ten pounds on breakfast alone."

"And you'll work every bit of it off on a watermelon farm. Plug that in and crumble the sausage…"

"I know how to make gravy. I don't need a lesson." Her tone had softened and she almost smiled.

His eyes twinkled every time he glanced her way. "Good. The biscuits are already in the oven. Out of a can because my biscuits have to be registered with the police as weapons. Granny never could teach me how to make decent biscuits. If you can make them like hers, we'll go on to the courthouse in Waurika and get married today."

She gasped.

"Don't faint. I was teasing. I'm not in the market for a wife even if it is a sore spot with my family." He said the words but his heart didn't believe them for one minute. If Austin had turned around and said she would marry him right then, he'd have scooped her up in those cute little pajamas and carried her out to his truck before she could change her mind.

Good Lord, what in the hell am I thinking? I'm not ready for marriage. Austin is hot and I'd love to date her, but marriage? I don't think so.

She cut off a fourth of the roll of pork sausage and put it in the skillet, fished an egg turner from the drawer under the bar, and used it to cut the sausage into tiny pieces. Her stomach growled as the smell of the sausage blended with the other breakfast aromas in the small kitchen. On weekdays she grabbed a Starbucks on the way to work and called that breakfast. On Saturday she had a late brunch with her mother at the dealership that usually consisted of a bagel with cream cheese and a cappuccino with skim milk and extra vanilla. It had been years since she'd had a big country breakfast, probably the last time she was in Terral.

Traitor, she thought as she touched her noisy stomach. *One day in this place and you already want to dive right into country eating.*

"After we eat breakfast, that batch of eggs should be ready to put in a sink full of cold water and we'll start the next batch to boiling."

"I told you…"

"I know and, darlin', if you don't get the Easter fever the first time you dip an egg into dye, you can put on them fancy shoes and go on about your business. Granny and I did this every year. Several years ago the folks decided to use plastic eggs and fill them with candy, but not Granny. She said that bunnies didn't lay eggs one day a year to be replaced by store-bought plastic eggs, and as long as she was alive, there would be real eggs. She carried enough clout in town that no one argued with her, but no one would help either so I got recruited. From day one I loved it. I'm doing it this year in memory of her."

"Okay, okay, I'll help. No more guilt trips."

Rye's face lit up when he looked down at her in the close quarters. He raised the fork he was using to turn the bacon and said, "Be it known that this country boy will never buy a plastic egg. He vows to uphold the tradition of the real Easter egg until his dying day."

"We've got a lawyer coming around in a few hours. I'll get him to work up an affidavit and notarize your signature on that profound statement."

A sensitive man with his looks. Just what you've been searching for, young lady.

Austin could swear her grandmother's voice had entered her head, or else the old girl had come back to life and was standing behind her. She looked over her shoulder but the only person there was Rye in his tight-fitting jeans, a three-button yellow knit shirt with a slightly wrinkled collar, and dark hair that needed a trim two weeks before. He really was what she'd been searching for, but why did she have to find him in Terral, Oklahoma, right on the edge of hell?

I've told you all about him for years. Didn't you listen to a blessed thing I said? He's a good, honest man. Verline's voice argued with common sense inside Austin's head.

Austin had said, "We have a lawyer coming." That little word *we* put another big smile on Rye's face as he turned the bacon to be sure it was cooked just right. He stole long sideways glances at Austin as she stirred the gravy, amazed at how comfortable she was in the kitchen. He'd found a woman who set his heart to doing double time, but she was a fancy lady, not someone who'd be at home at a rodeo or riding beside him on a tractor. Now what was he supposed to do and where did he start?

She looks like she's pretty well at home in the kitchen, and that's a plus. He could hear Gemma's arguments. *Come on, Rye. If you don't get married soon, our parents are going to be too damned old to even enjoy their grandchildren.*

Hey, he argued silently with his youngest sister, *it's not written on stone that I have to marry before the rest of you do. Don't wait on me.*

Irish rules, remember. Daddy said we got to do it in the right order, and I'm getting tired of waiting on you. We're all going to be gray-haired and walking with canes by the time you find someone that'll meet the long list of ridiculous qualifications you've got. I wish you'd never gotten that damned tattoo.

He was gazing out the kitchen window without seeing a thing. When he finally blinked, Austin was doing the same thing.

He touched her arm lightly, letting his fingers linger just a beat longer than he should have. "What are you thinking about?"

She looked around quickly to find him staring into her eyes. "What are you thinking about? You were staring out the window all the way to eternity. If you burn my bacon after getting me up before daylight, I'm going to be one upset woman."

"I'm not burning the bacon. I was arguing with my sister. She gets into my mind and fights with me."

"About bacon?"

"No, about Easter eggs."

Austin looked away, poured milk into the skillet, and kept stirring. "I don't believe you. What were you arguing about?"

He avoided the question. "Do you ever argue with someone who's not really there?"

"Sure, I was just doing so with Granny, but I'm not telling you about what."

Rye grinned. "Then I don't have to tell you what Gemma and I were fighting about."

Austin drew down her brows in a frown. "Gemma?"

"She's my youngest sister and even more Irish than the rest of us. Black Irish, Daddy says. We are all dark-haired. Some of us have green eyes like Daddy and some brown like Momma."

"Is Gemma an Irish or Indian name?"

"Irish to the letter. Gemma is number five. Three boys. Me, Raylen, and Dewar. Then Colleen and Gemma makes number five. She's named for Daddy's grandmother." Rye drained the bacon on a paper towel before transferring it to a plate and making an eight-egg omelet in the bacon drippings.

"Did you invite all the hired hands in for breakfast?"

"Nope, I have a healthy appetite. Granny did, too, and since you are her kin, I kind of figured you wouldn't eat like a bird. Don't worry. Anything we have left over, old Rascal will be glad to clean up for us." It felt right to be in the kitchen with Austin. It even felt right to be arguing with her.

"Is that old cat still alive? He must be fifteen years old?"

"Sixteen. He just gets fatter and lazier every year. He'll be on the front porch by the time we finish breakfast. Long about noon he'll move to the shade tree in the backyard and then to the shed after supper."

"Has he turned gray?"

"Around the nose but he's so big and sassy the other tomcats leave him alone." Rye turned the omelet over, loaded it with grated cheese and chopped ham, and flipped it in half.

Austin poured the gravy into a bowl and took two plates from the cabinet. In a few minutes she was sitting at a table that would have put any waffle house to shame. She split open a biscuit and covered it with gravy, cut a fourth of the omelet and slid it over into her plate, and picked up three pieces of bacon with her fingers.

"Crispy."

"You like it floppy?" he asked.

"Oh, no. Granny and I like our bacon crispy, our steaks medium rare, and onions in our fried potatoes."

"Women after my heart." He smiled. "What time is the lawyer coming around?"

"Pearlita said at ten o'clock. How many eggs are in that refrigerator?"

"A helluva lot. We boil four dozen at a time, then we color them all pretty and put them back in the crates. Tomorrow we'll hide them all around the community center. One will be the prize egg. That means whoever brings it to me gets a certificate to go down to Cavender's Western Wear in Nocona and pick out a brand-new pair of cowboy boots."

"How do you know which is the prize egg?"

"We do different things. Sometimes we just write prize on the side with one of the wax pencils that comes with the dying kit, and sometimes when Granny was real spicy, we did it in glitter. I got both up there on the fridge so you can decide this year since it's your first time."

"What on earth made you move to Terral? I thought people moved out of here, not to here."

"Cheap land. My uncle had this property out in west Texas and, when he died, willed it to me. Never had any kids. I didn't want to live out there so I sold it and started looking for a place close to Ringgold. My folks live seven miles across the river. Oklahoma taxes are lower than in Texas, and the land was less expensive. So I got four sections of land, two miles long, two miles wide across the road from here. My folks are seven miles away, two miles south of what's left of Ringgold, so I can see them anytime I want. What keeps you in the big city? You've got a farm free and clear, and Felix and the guys are here all legal and ready to work."

"I like my job. I like what I do, and I'm in line for a big promotion. I'll clear the table if you'll start those eggs to cooling and the next batch to boiling. We might even get most of them done before the lawyer gets here if we work at it together."

She scraped the final two tablespoons of omelet onto a paper plate and added the rest of the gravy on the other side and carried it to the front porch. Sure enough there was Rascal, the big, old black tomcat, waiting patiently for scraps. He rubbed against her leg and purred as loud as a threshing machine until she set the plate down and then he hovered over it, daring even a sparrow to look crossways at his breakfast.

She sat down in the rocking chair and watched the sun going from half an orange to a full-fledged giant Nerf ball as it left the far horizon and took its place in the cloudless sky. Granny used to talk about the Easter snap, a cold spell that usually hit every year on

Easter weekend, but she must've taken it with her on her journey down the river because the day promised to be beautiful with no hint of bad weather.

The peace that surrounded Austin was like a warm cloak on a blustery, cold winter night. She drew her knees up and wrapped her arms around them. Instead of horns honking as people rushed around the city, crickets and tree frogs serenaded her. A dog barked over across the road at a passing truck. The driver stuck his hand out the open window and waved at her. Somewhere down near the river she heard a coyote howl and a boat motor firing up.

It wouldn't be difficult to sit in that rocker day after day and let life pass by in peaceful hours. *In a month I'd be bored out of my mind. But right now after only one day, I feel more relaxed than I have in years.*

"You ready to dye eggs?" Rye asked from the doorway.

"Are they cooled?"

"I put them all in the sink, ran cold water on them, and dumped in two trays of ice. I think they're ready but you might want to get dressed to keep from ruining those cute little pajamas."

She fought the impulse to cross her arms over her braless breasts, even though they were discreetly covered by pink knit and he'd already seen her. Hell's bells, they'd had breakfast together so it was too late to be covering up her boobs now.

"I'll find some work clothes and meet you back in the kitchen." She stood up, raised her arms high over her head, and stretched.

Rye couldn't take his eyes from her. He really needed to step back, but he couldn't move from the spot and she was coming toward the door. When she opened the old-fashioned screen door, he managed to move to one side and she brushed against his side. It took every ounce of self-control he had not to grab her right there in the doorway and kiss the living daylights out of her. As it was, he felt like just the brush of her hip against his was setting him on fire. He cleared his throat and she looked back at him.

"What?"

"Nothing," he lied. He couldn't tell her what effect her body had on him, not after less than twenty-four hours. What he needed was a shot of tequila to calm his nerves and a lime to bite on to wipe the constant smile off his face.

Austin headed down the hallway to her bedroom. She vowed she'd never ever let herself fall for Rye because if his touch was an indication of how hot things would be, one night in bed with him and they'd both burst into flames. How was that man not married? There wasn't a woman on the face of the earth who wouldn't fall backwards on the bed if he so much as laid a little finger on their cheek.

If I don't stop thinking about him, I'm going to need to dip my whole body in that ice bath for the eggs. But I do wonder what a kiss would be like. Would I have lips left after he kissed me, or would they melt right off my face? Hush! I can't go back out there with naughty thoughts like this.

She flipped through the hangers in the closet while she removed her pajamas and put on a bra, but she'd brought nothing to wear while dying Easter eggs. She took a pair of khaki capris from a hanger and had one leg in them before she remembered that they cost too much to ruin with dye. That's when she saw Verline's faded overalls hanging in the closet.

She and her grandmother were both five feet, ten inches, and there probably wasn't ten pounds difference in their weight so the overalls should fit fine. She stepped into them. They *were* comfortable. She found a sleeveless chambray shirt, put it on and buttoned it up the front, then flipped the galluses over her shoulder and fastened them. She rolled the legs up to right under her knees and slid her feet into an old pair of rubber flip-flops she found on the closet floor. Then she secured her shoulder-length hair up into a ponytail and giggled at her reflection in the long mirror. "Farmer Jane. Mother would be appalled. I should have Rye take a picture of me with my cell phone and send it to her. She would either drop dead with a heart attack or fly down here and jerk me back to Tulsa so fast I'd think this was all a dream."

Mismatched coffee cups filled with six different colors of egg dye were sitting on the table. Two crates of eggs were cooked, cooled, dried, and waiting. Rye was working on another crate when she walked in the kitchen. His mind went stone cold dead. Not one word would form and all he could do was stare. Dressed up, she was stunning. In pajamas, she was sexy. In those adorable overalls, she took his breath away.

He started across the floor with a crate of eggs, stumbled, and had to do some fancy footwork to keep from dumping two dozen eggs right at her feet. Only four fell out, but he managed to step on all four in his attempt to get his balance.

"I bet you say you can't dance," Austin laughed. "Only messed up four. That's a miracle." She rolled off several rounds of paper towels and bent down to clean the smashed eggs from the floor.

He started at the back of her long legs but his gaze stopped at her rounded rear end just inches from his fingertips. He was glad he still had a crate of eggs in his hands, or he would have patted that fanny even if it cost him a hard slap on the face.

"I can dance. Want to go honky-tonkin' with me?" He set the eggs down, grabbed the paper towels to help her, bent down, and butted heads with her as she was standing up.

The woman would think he was a klutz. Thank goodness she didn't know about him forgetting to change out of his best clothing. Or that he'd actually forgotten the feed yesterday. Or that he'd come close to burning down the house the night before when he was thinking about her.

He sat flat down on the floor. "I'm sorry."

She joined him, holding her head. "It was my fault. I should've said I was standing up."

"Let me see." He pushed back her hair and checked her forehead with his fingertips. There was the heat again, boiling up from deep inside his body. He looked into her eyes, and time stood still for what seemed like eternity. He knew this was a bad idea but a tractor trailer and a team of six horses couldn't have stopped him from leaning in for that kiss, especially when Austin gulped and then nervously licked her lips. He just about pounced right then, but used every ounce of his willpower to move slowly. He could hardly wait to kiss her, but then the phone rang. He froze, and she stared at him for a beat, but the moment was over so he took a deep breath and sat back.

Austin had wanted that kiss—she was just about drawn to that man's lips like flies to honey—and then the blasted phone rang. She didn't even care if his kiss did melt her lips off her face. She'd hire a plastic surgeon to build her some new ones.

He helped her up with one hand.

She grabbed the kitchen phone on the third ring. "Hello?"

"Is this Austin Lanier?"

"It is. Who is this?"

"Your lawyer. I will be about thirty minutes late. Is that a problem?"

"No, sir. That's fine," she said.

"Then I will see you at ten thirty. Goodbye, Miss Lanier."

She didn't even have time to say goodbye before the line went dead. She put the receiver back on the base and turned around. Rye had cleaned up the egg mess, tossed the paper towels in the trash, and was sitting at the table.

"That was the lawyer. He'll be here at ten thirty instead of ten. He sure was curt. It's been at least twenty years since I've dyed Easter eggs so I'm not so sure I remember how."

"All lawyers are like that, so don't worry about it. Dying eggs is like riding a bike. It'll all come back to you." He had come so close to kissing her that it was scary. A kiss that quick would scare her right back to Tulsa for sure. He had to remember to take things slow. Sure, he had the hots for her but maybe she didn't feel the same way. After all, he was pure country and she was a city girl.

"It is coming back to me right along with the smell. Haven't they figured out a way to make it where you don't have to use vinegar?" She put an egg in a wire holder and held it down in the purple dye.

"Granny said that this kind works better because it sets it better."

"She never was one much for change. This one has color. Now what?"

"Decals or glitter or paint pens. Decorate to your heart's desire."

She picked up a decal of a butterfly and read the directions. She held a wet cloth against the decal and counted to ten using the one-Mississippi method and then gently peeled the paper away to show a lovely yellow and hot-pink butterfly.

"I hope a little girl finds this one."

"If she doesn't, I bet a little boy will peel it and cram the whole thing in his mouth. They have contests among themselves to see who can eat the most boiled eggs. That's something you can't do with plastic eggs."

One second he couldn't talk; the next his mouth flapped like laundry hanging on the line on a windy day. Austin would think he was the dumbest old redneck cowboy she'd ever met up with if he didn't get it together any better than that.

"Do they really have an egg-eating contest?" She dipped the next one into pink dye and affixed a white bunny decal to the side. "I'd forgotten how much fun this is."

"Not a sanctioned egg-eating contest. They don't get a prize for it but it happens every year. Granny thought it was a hoot. Their mommas would have a hissy if they knew, but they hide over behind the stage and lay bets as to who can eat the most in three minutes."

"How do you know so much about it?"

"I watch. One of Kent's boys has won the past two years with more than ten eggs. And that's after a big Easter dinner."

"Good Lord. Ten eggs! Does it make him sick?"

"I don't know what happens when he gets home."

Rye picked up the wire holder and sank an egg down into the yellow dye after he'd drawn a smiley face on the side with the wax crayon. He brought it out and set it on the drying rack for a few seconds and then outlined the smiley face in bright orange with a fine-tipped paint pen.

"So you raise cattle, take care of a bunch of mean old rodeo bulls, and you are an artist to boot. I'm impressed," she said.

"Enough to sell me this place after you get through taking out Granny's personal things?"

She cut her eyes around at him. "Is that what this is all about? Buttering me up to steal the place out from under me?"

"No, this is about Easter eggs. I'm real good at buttering women up, though, if that will work."

"I bet you are, and no, it will not work."

"Can't blame a man for trying. We'd better work faster if we want to get these finished before your lawyer gets here. Granny said he was the fanciest thing in Wichita Falls in his three-piece suits, alligator boots, and driving that Caddy."

"Are you saying I should change before he gets here?" she asked.

"No, ma'am. I think you are sexy as hell in that outfit. Just don't be surprised if he hits on you, and it won't have a thing to do with the money Granny left in the trust fund for you. He's already rich."

"What money? We always figured she barely got by from one year to the next. I mean, all she did was grow watermelons."

Rye chuckled. "I'll let the lawyer explain it all but, honey, raisin' watermelons is like finding gold. She told me part of it but I don't have the whole story. She played her cards close to her vest. Speaking of which, if a couple of old girls from up at Ryan call and want to come down here for a poker game and you need a fourth hand, call me."

"Greta and Molly?"

She grinned and his heart did a flip, skipped a half beat, then raced like he'd run a mile on an uphill slope.

"Don't let those two old gals fool you into thinking they're lousy at poker. Me and Granny played with them about once a month. They'll clean out your bank account and laugh all the way out to Greta's 1958 Chevrolet truck."

Austin's grin widened. Who would have thought those little blue-haired ladies would be crackerjack poker players? Jefferson County was just full of surprises.

Crates of colored eggs lined the bar and the table was barely cleaned up when ten thirty rolled around. Austin pulled the ponytail holder from her hair and shook loose a mane of dark hair to fall around her shoulders. She started toward the front door at the same time Rye headed for the back door. They collided in the middle of the kitchen floor. He wrapped both arms around her to keep her from falling, and she grabbed him firmly around the neck. He looked down into her blue eyes, which were looking up at him.

Once again, time stood still and Rye felt like he was moving in slow motion. He leaned in and she rolled up on her toes. When their lips met, it was like nothing he'd ever experienced before— hot and sweet, brand new and like destiny that had been waiting for him forever, and as he touched the tip of his tongue to hers, he felt his whole body respond with a rush of steaming need and raw desire and heavenly heat. That kiss came close to frying a hole in the kitchen linoleum.

It set off bells in her head and fire down low in her gut that only a romp between sheets could put out, and Austin was not that kind of woman. She did not fall into bed with a man just because he tickled her fancy. Casual sex was for other people; not Austin.

The doorbell rang again, but she thought it was the crazy music in her head. When it rang a third time, she took a step back. "I don't do that. I'm not that kind of woman. I don't kiss a man."

His heart fell to down to the kitchen floor. "You aren't straight?"

"Yes, I'm straight!"

"Then what are you talking about?"

"I'm not loose-legged, Rye. I'm pretty old-fashioned."

"Well, you better get your old-fashioned butt over there and answer the door because I think I saw the shadow of your lawyer giving up."

She took off for the door and Rye slipped out the back door, through the garage, and around the side of the house. He slid down the rough bark of the old shade tree in the backyard and put his head in his hands. He felt as if he'd known Austin Lanier for ten years but nothing had prepared him for the emotional roller coaster set loose in his heart and mind when he saw her in those overalls. Barefoot she was even sexier than she'd been in the fancy business suit down on the river when he'd first seen her and his world tilted ninety degrees to the left.

Austin opened the front door and yelled in a breathless voice, "Are you Verline Lanier's lawyer?"

He was dressed in a three-piece suit that left no doubt that it had not come right off the rack at Sears but had been custom-tailored to his slim build. His light-brown hair was feathered back and his blue eyes luminous behind wire-rimmed glasses.

"I'd given up on you being here."

His smile reminded her of a wolf approaching a helpless newborn lamb. It had none of the warmth of Rye's boyish grin. There wasn't one thing about Mr. Fancy-Pants that made her want to kiss him or even dye an Easter egg with him. She touched her lips to see if they were actually as hot as they felt and was surprised to find them cool.

"My neighbor and I've been up to our ears in Easter eggs.

Granny had already ordered them so we went ahead with her plans." She held the door open for him. "You can set your briefcase on the table. There's only a little bit of stain from the dye."

His nose flared at the old table and the smell of vinegar still in the house.

"Care for a glass of sweet tea or a cup of coffee?"

"No, thank you. I've got another appointment back in Wichita Falls at noon. I'd like to take care of this quickly," he said.

The expression on his face when he looked at her overalls and the dye on her fingers said it all. He thought Granny had been crazy to leave all her earthly belongings to her redneck granddaughter.

She pulled out a kitchen chair and sat down. "I'm sure we can."

"I am Glen Rushing. I've handled Verline Lanier's affairs since she got sick. She wanted me to arrange things so there would be a minimum of fuss for you when she was gone. I thought you were in the oil business in Tulsa."

"Did Granny tell you that? That's what she would have liked for me to be," she said.

The man rubbed her wrong. It wasn't his business if she lived out of the back of a rusted-out pickup truck with a leaky hooch over the bed and counted it a good day when she had bologna sandwiches. Not that she did any of that, but if she had, it wasn't his concern.

He popped open his briefcase with a flourish and brought out several papers. "For the record, I don't usually make house calls. Especially on Saturday, but Mrs. Lanier made me promise I would come see you the day after the memorial. Now to begin with, I need you to sign this paper saying that you will take over her business transactions. That includes the farm and the wine business."

Austin was shocked to know that there was a wine business. She picked up the papers and began to read. In the fifth grade they'd timed her at four hundred words a minute with perfect retention so it didn't take long. The farm, all 1,920 acres, and all the equipment, house, personal belongings, and the crop, along with any other of Verline Lanier's earthly possessions, were willed to Austin Lanier along with the wine business. It took her twenty minutes to read every single paper he put in front of her and sign them. He left a sheaf of original documents for her with instructions that she would probably be wise to put them in the bank deposit box at Verline's bank in Ryan. He turned over the stock portfolio that Verline kept with a company in Wichita Falls and bank statements for the past six months with enough zeroes to stagger Austin.

"And that concludes our business, Miss Lanier. A bit of advice that I hope you won't take the wrong way." He scanned her from bare toes upward across the overalls and chambray shirt. "If you use this wisely, it will support you, your children, and your grandchildren. Mrs. Lanier worked hard to leave this to you. Don't squander it."

"I'm sure I'll take care of things just the way Granny told me to."

"One more thing." He snapped his briefcase shut with a flourish and popped up like a windup toy from the chair. "Did you really read those things, or can you not read and you were putting on a show for my benefit?"

"That is a rude question that I have no intention of answering. Good day, Mr. Rushing." Austin marched to the door and held it open for him.

"You'd be so proud of me, Granny," she said when he was gone. "I didn't pepper his better-than-thou ass with rock salt."

CHAPTER 4

FOR THE SECOND MORNING, AUSTIN AWOKE TO THE SOUND OF pots and pans rattling in the kitchen. The aroma of coffee and bacon blended and floated down the hall, past the bathroom, under the door, and to her nose. She opened one eye enough to see the clock and shut it quickly against the bright sunlight flowing in the window beside her bed.

"Déjà vu," she mumbled and sat straight up in bed, her eyes popping wide open. Was this like that movie she'd seen when she was thirteen? *Groundhog Day* with Bill Murray. In the movie, Bill Murray's character had to relive Groundhog Day every single day until he finally did what he was supposed to do.

Did Terral have some kind of weird power that would keep her on the watermelon farm reliving yesterday every single day? Dear God, was she going to have to dye Easter eggs and put up with that egotistical lawyer every single day?

"If that's the case, then today I'm going to shoot him in the hind end with the rock salt and I'm going to throw all the eggs at Rye. Wait a minute… That means I get to kiss Rye every day too. I'm not sure my hormones can take that every day until I get things done the right way," she kept muttering as she peeked out the door to hear Rye whistling in the kitchen. She belted a pink silk robe over her pajamas and padded up the hallway, hoping the whole time that the stove wasn't filled with pots of boiling eggs.

"Good morning, sleepyhead. I thought the smell of coffee might wake you. I made banana-nut pancakes this morning. Have a seat. I just poured up the last of the batter. We'll be ready to eat in five minutes." He set a cup of coffee before her, kissed her on the forehead, and went back to the stove with his lips tingling and his thoughts going in all kinds of indecent directions and a sudden tightening in his jeans that almost made him groan.

Get a grip, cowboy. You're moving way too fast here.

"Thank you and good morning. Do you make breakfast here every morning?" The red-hot kiss on the forehead sent her into a whirlwind of a tailspin for a moment, but she regained control by concentrating on the breakfast. She was grateful for pancakes and not sausage gravy and biscuits and even happier to see an empty stove.

"No, ma'am. Granny and I only had breakfast together on Saturday. Every other day she was busy raising watermelons and I was busy taking care of a cattle ranch. Except on Easter weekend. We had breakfast both days then because this morning we have to get down to the community center by eleven o'clock and get the eggs hid. We take care of that while all the kids and their parents are in church. Then at one o'clock they all line up. Everett rings a cowbell and the fun begins."

That little robe that barely came to her knees was plumb sexy. Pink was definitely her color. Not black.

"Are you going to put on a pink Easter bunny outfit?" she asked. Now wouldn't that be fun to unzip that fuzzy bunny outfit and run her hands down over all those muscles that bulged his shirtsleeves. And then when she got even further...

That's enough, Austin Lanier!

He wore jeans, but instead of a knit shirt, he had on a bright-yellow-plaid western-cut shirt. His hair still needed a cut, and there was a definite mark across his forehead where his hat had kept the sun from tanning the inch of skin right below his hairline. And he still wasn't an old man. Why in the hell had she gotten that idea fixed in her mind so firmly anyway?

Rye set the platter of pancakes on the table. "Dig in, and the answer to that question would not be *no*, but *hell no*."

Austin piled pancakes high on her plate and looked around for the butter container. Rye handed her a small white pitcher with flowers on the side. She recognized it immediately as the one her grandmother always put milk in when she served coffee to guests.

"I melt the butter, the real stuff, not margarine, in the microwave and then add warm syrup to it. That way you get both together."

She rolled her eyes with the first bite. "Granny didn't teach you to make these, did she?"

"No, Momma did. This is our traditional Easter breakfast."

"She's only…what did you say…seven miles south? Why are you not there for Easter breakfast?"

"Because we hide eggs this morning?"

And I wouldn't miss the fun of hiding eggs with you for anything. Besides, I know how to make banana-nut pancakes, and I love the way you roll your eyes when something tastes good.

"You got a mouse in your pocket? We, as in you and I, are not hiding eggs. I'm working all day in the garage. I spent yesterday afternoon out there and didn't even make a healthy dent. I've got seven huge black plastic leaf bags full of nothing but old medical statements, receipts for electric bills dating back to the fifties, and gas receipts for the vehicles when the price was thirty cents a gallon."

"History is relegated to the trash heap. What a waste."

"I haven't thrown it out yet. You want to haul it over to your place and preserve history?"

"No, thank you!"

"Speaking of trash heap. What do I do with all of it?"

"We can make a burn pile or you can call for a roll-off dumpster to be parked in the backyard. When it's full, they'll come haul it off and bring you a new one if you need it."

"Is there a place in the phone book?"

"Not the Terral book. You would probably have pretty good luck finding one on the internet maybe out of Wichita Falls or Nocona."

"I haven't had time to open my laptop, but Granny didn't have…"

He raised an eyebrow. "Yes, she did. Her computer is in the wine cellar. About all she ever used it for was the wine business, but she's got a wireless connection and she was pretty damned good with the computer."

"Wine cellar?"

"Yes, the wine cellar. Surely you knew that she made wine. It's known all over the South and from coast to coast. You've never bought a bottle of Lanier Wine?"

"First time I knew anything about wine was yesterday when the lawyer mentioned it. I thought it was something she invested in."

"Well, she did invest time and money in it, but she loved making it too. I'll show you where it is if you hide eggs with me and then join me at my folks' for Easter dinner."

"I can find it on my own, thank you very much."

"Oh, really! Well, good luck with that. You've been here how often since you were how old and you didn't even know about it. There's nearly two thousand acres here. Where do you intend to start looking?"

She finished off her breakfast, poured a second cup of coffee, and thought about where her grandmother would put a wine cellar on the nearly two thousand acres of flat land. And where were the grape arbors? She'd never seen anything but fields and fields of watermelons, not a single bunch of grapes. Surely she didn't buy the grapes to make the wine. That didn't sound like Verline Lanier at all. She used to say most of her food came right off Lanier property. Her vegetable garden was big enough to feed half the county, and she had fenced off a hundred acres down on the southeast corner of the land to raise steers and hogs for her meat. The chicken pen was out beyond the shed where her new truck was parked. Guineas roamed the yard and pastures because they ate ticks, and Rascal and his tomcat buddies kept the rat population at bay.

None of that conjured up a vision of a place where she grew grapes or had a wine-making business. Maybe there was no business on the property. Maybe her grandmother just had an interest in someone else's winery and Rye was jerking her around.

He refilled his coffee cup. "Figured out where it is yet?"

"No, but I will."

Even disagreeing with her hadn't made him want to scoot right back across the road and forget all about his new neighbor. Matter of fact, she was kind of cute with her blue eyes all wide and her brow wrinkled. "Might as well go on and get dressed. Wear something casual. We never get all dressed up for Easter. It's just the five kids, Momma and Daddy, and my grandparents who live on the same ranch with them. You'll make a nice even number of ten this year. Course afterwards there's people dropping in all evening, but it's still casual."

"I said I'm not going to hide eggs or go with you. Good grief, Rye, I only met you two days ago. Why would I go home to meet your parents?"

"Because Granny did every Easter, and it'll make it easier if some of her kin is there. We all loved her and now she's gone. And because it's Easter Sunday and that's a family holiday and you shouldn't spend it alone."

And because the last thing I promised Granny Lanier was that when you arrived I'd take care of you. She said you'd have some difficult decisions to make about the farm and that I was to help you through the tough times. And because ever since I laid eyes on you at the river, I can't get you out of my mind. Add the fact that the kiss yesterday knocked the common sense out of me and I want to spend today with you.

"Oh, all right," she said. "Now where is the wine business?"

"I'll show you when we get home tonight."

She popped her hands on her hips and locked eyes with him. "I keep my word, Rye."

He touched the end of her nose with his fingertip and grinned. "I would expect you to since you are a Lanier."

She was sexy as hell and as frustrating as the itch...the seven-year kind with no cure. He wasn't sure he could get drunk enough to take his mind off her, especially when every time he managed to come in contact skin to skin he thought he was going to spontaneously combust.

"Then show me now," she said.

He shook his head. "When you see what she's done, you will want to spend hours there, not minutes. We've got to hide these eggs and you've got to get ready."

"At least tell me where she's hiding a grape arbor."

He ran a sink of dishwater and began the cleanup. "Grape arbor?"

"Wine!" She raised her voice.

Yep, she was cute as a baby kitten when she was angry.

"She didn't make that kind of wine. Lanier Wine has a watermelon on it. She made wonderful watermelon wine. Ever heard that song, 'Watermelon Crawl'?"

Austin was stunned. "There's really such a thing?"

"Oh, yes, and darlin', hers is high dollar and coveted by the connoisseurs all over the world. She had quite a little business going here. I suppose you'll have to apply for all the right licenses to run it in your name now, or maybe she's already taken care of that."

Austin lowered her voice. "She did. I signed the papers taking ownership and all the legal stuff yesterday."

"Well, I expect she's got her recipes hid in the vault."

"What vault? Dammit, but you are frustrating!"

One side of his mouth turned up. He was glad that he'd frustrated her because she'd had the same effect on him since he laid eyes on her. "That, too, is something for later. Maybe we'll even share a bottle sometime. Fifty-five minutes until hiding time. How long does it take you to get ready?"

"Casual?" She sighed.

He nodded.

"Fifteen minutes."

He tossed a kitchen towel toward her. "Then you've got time to dry the breakfast dishes and put them away."

She caught it midair. "And here I thought you'd make someone a perfect wife. Breakfast. Easter eggs, and you wash dishes. But then you blew the whole picture by making me dry the dishes."

"Is that a proposal?"

"Hell, no!"

"Good, because I won't marry anyone who doesn't get down on one knee and who doesn't have a little velvet box with a ring inside," Rye teased.

Austin set her jaw and kept the blush creeping up her neck from materializing on her cheeks. The man was handsome and funny, and his kisses would knock a holy woman off the wagon. Mercy, if he ever showed up at a Sex Addicts Anonymous meeting, he'd break up the whole party. Even a seasoned old gal, who'd been celibate for ten years, four months, seventeen days, and six hours would start peeling her shirt up over her head.

The image that produced made her laugh out loud. Her laughter filled the room like a sweet country song in an old honky-tonk beer joint. One minute there wasn't anything but smoke and conversation, and then someone put a quarter in the jukebox and Blake Shelton was singing "Austin."

"What are you thinking about? You've got a funny expression," Austin asked.

"Austin."

"Yes?"

"No, I was thinking about Blake Shelton's song, 'Austin.' Are you a country music fan?"

She nodded. "I lived in a divided home. Daddy liked country music. So did Granny. Momma liked Coltrane when she listened to music. She's not much for music. I still listen to the old country stuff more than the new because that's what was around. Daddy got a big kick out of that song when it came out since my name is Austin."

"Your laughter reminded me of country music."

She frowned. "How?"

"It's a good thing so stop scowling. When you laughed, I got a flash of dancing to that song in a honky-tonk."

"Can't say I've ever had anyone compare my laughter to that. Momma says I laugh like a truck driver instead of a lady." She hung the drying cloth on the side of the dish drainer. "You can load all those eggs while I'm dressing."

"Yes, ma'am!" He saluted sharply and clicked his bootheels together. "What were you laughing about anyway?"

"No wonder Granny liked you. You're crazy! And I'm not tellin' you what I was laughing about."

"Oh?" He wiggled his eyebrows.

"No, I am not. I'll be back in a few minutes." She hurried away before he coerced her into telling him what had been so funny. She took a quick shower, washed her hair and quickly dried it with a blow dryer, ran the straightening iron over it a few times, and dressed in her khaki capris and a bright-orange knit shirt.

"Eggs are loaded. Is the Easter bunny ready?" he yelled from the living room.

"One more minute," she yelled back, but she mumbled, "If he's really got a pink bunny outfit up there he expects me to wear, I swear I'll find that damned wine-making business all on my own."

She had brought high-heeled shoes and her running shoes from Tulsa. Granny's feet were a size bigger than hers, so she couldn't even tap her closet for a pair of sandals. Somehow rubber flip-flops wouldn't work for a family reunion, and her black heels were still a mess from the memorial at the river. So she pulled out the brown leather three-inch multistrapped sandals and sat down on the edge of the bed.

She couldn't hide eggs in those things. There'd be quarter-inch-sized wormholes all over the community building's yard if she did. And falling into Rye's arms yesterday had proved high heels and dirt did not mix. She picked up her running shoes and shoved her feet into them and carried her heels out along with her purse.

He looked up from the table where he was waiting. "Wow! The Easter bunny is beautiful all dolled up!"

She held up the spike heels. "Not in these shoes but I'm changing after we hide the eggs."

He glanced down at them and imagined her in nothing but those shoes. He shook his head like he was ridding it of a pesky mosquito.

"What's wrong?" she asked.

He thought fast and said, "Gemma will try to steal those from you."

"Thanks for the compliment about being dolled up, but I'd fight Saint Peter for these shoes so she'd better be a fast draw or a real fast runner. Are we ready?"

"Yes, ma'am." He stood up and opened the door for her, wishing she'd worn the shoes in her hand so she'd tumble into his arms again.

His black truck was parked behind her Corvette and she could see dozens and dozens of colored eggs in the bed when she reached the passenger door. He opened it for her and shut it behind her when she was settled into the seat.

"What happens if a bird flies over the eggs on the way?" she asked when he was behind the wheel.

"Granny and I throw away whatever eggs get splattered with bird crap. We always check them and then argue about being wasteful. She says we ought to wipe it off and hide them anyway because the kids would peel them. But my vote goes to putting them in the trash can."

"Yuk!"

"She didn't waste anything. My grandma is like that too. Guess the Depression made pack rats out of everyone."

She was even cute with her nose all snarled up thinking about bird crap on Easter eggs.

"So the Depression is what I've got to blame for that house full of junk," Austin said.

"*Cháchara*!" he said.

"That's what Felix called it. I haven't seen them in two days. This is Easter weekend, but they work on regular weekends?"

"Until noon on Saturday. Then they get their laundry done and on the line to dry. Granny bought a secondhand washer and dryer for the trailer but they don't use the dryer. Felix says it's a waste of sunshine. Sunday they borrow Granny's old work truck and go to church, come home, and rest up for the week. They work from daylight to dark, and you won't find any better or harder workers than that crew."

"You don't have to sell me on them. Granny's told me for years that she had the best crew in the state. I gave them the keys to the truck and told them to use it when they wanted."

"Good idea. I've been telling Granny to do that for years."

"Why didn't she?"

He shrugged. "She liked to be in control. Just because she was getting older didn't mean she wasn't still the boss. They'll be in and out a lot starting Monday. Felix will give you a daily report every evening if you don't go to the fields to help. They've been plowing. Tomorrow they'll start planting the watermelon seeds. That'll take about two weeks. That way the first crop will be ready for harvest, then the next one will be ready in a day or two and right on up the road for three miles."

"How do you know so much about it?"

"Learned it all from Granny," he said.

He drove slowly all the way into town, the trip taking ten minutes when it should have taken three or less. He parked behind the white building across from the school and hurried around the truck to open the door for her.

"What's the plan?" she asked.

"The plastic ones are in the building. Folks put them there before church and leave it unlocked. We'll grab a sack each and start hiding. Save the real ones until the end so we don't step on them while we're working with the plastic."

The community building was a long, white frame structure with two back doors. The one Rye opened and held for her led into a room with a kitchen on the west end and enough tables and chairs to seat close to a hundred people.

The bar closest to the kitchen was laden down with sacks of plastic eggs filled with candy. She followed Rye's example, picked one up, and headed out the door. "What now?"

"Hide eggs."

"Where?" She looked around at the flat yard surrounding the building. The grass was about six inches tall but even that wouldn't provide much cover for brightly colored eggs.

"Anywhere. Over there at the stage is always good. Beside the fence posts. You are a cute little bunny. Hop around and find places. Oh, and remember the little tots hunt over to the east side, the three- to five-year-olds on the west, and the bigger kids in the front."

By the time she finished the third bag, Austin was already out of hiding places and had begun to put two at a time in clumps of grass. When they started on the real eggs, she started putting a real egg in among two plastic ones.

"There's enough eggs here for the whole state of Texas," she said.

"The kids will have full baskets," he said and laughed.

"How many of these things are there all total?" she asked when they'd lined the last six real eggs up around a tree on the east side of the building.

"We usually have about six or seven hundred," Rye said and stepped on two plastic eggs. "Well, shit!"

"No, it was eggs. I heard them crunch under your boots. And that's chocolate on your boots, not shit."

He wiped the chocolate off on the grass and bent over to pick up the shattered plastic. "If it had been real eggs, it wouldn't have made this much mess. What are you grinning about?"

"Nothing. Seems to me like you ought to dye an extra dozen for all the ones you ruin. And your boots look like you've been wading in the cow lot instead of hiding Easter eggs."

She took a step and felt two real eggs squish under her feet.

He brought a trash bag over and picked them up. "You were saying?"

"This place is a like a field of enemy land mines. We'll have to watch every step to get out of it." She started picking her way around eggs and back to the edge of the lawn.

He followed behind her, enjoying the view of her cute little rounded butt and those legs that went all the way from earth to heaven. His mind went into overdrive and pictured those long, shapely legs thrown around his body, with his hands cupping that delectable derriere, and he had to press his lips hard together to keep another shit-eating grin off his face.

"It's twelve thirty. Want to stick around and see the kids find them?" he asked when they were finally out of danger of smashing any more eggs.

"What time is dinner served at your folks' house?"

"Easter is a late breakfast, dinner on the table at two, and eating the rest of the day. We'll have plenty of time. Granny and I always watched the kids."

"Then I'd love to see the kids," she said.

"We'll put the tailgate down and sit on it. That way we can see them. Look, the first ones are already here."

A pickup nosed into a slot in front of the community building.

Austin wondered if the low pipe fence had started out as a hitching rail. Terral had been an up-and-coming town in its day with hardware stores, a furniture store slash funeral home, a dentist, a doctor, two drugstores, the Ash Hotel, at least one lumber company, a cotton gin, and a feed store. Nowadays all that kept a person from missing the whole town were the two big speed bumps to slow down traffic in front of the school.

Austin looked across the street at four little girls all dressed up in their pink-and-white lace Easter dresses and cute white sandals. Pretty soon, a whole bouquet of girls had gathered up together giggling and pointing at the eggs in plain sight. Boys measured their ties against each other's to see which was the longest, and from their gestures, they discussed who was going to fill their baskets first. Rye watched her with amusement, and then she turned to him and he smiled. "Granny and I never hide the prize egg in the same age category two years in a row. It was the three-and-under age group this year. You like kids?"

"Don't know. Never been around them very much. I'm an only child. Dad was an only child and Mother has two sisters, both as career-minded as she is and neither ever married. How about you?"

"Love 'em. I'm the oldest of five and the mutton bustin' at the rodeos is my favorite part. You ever seen that?"

She shook her head. "What is it?"

"The little cowboys riding sheep like the big boys ride the bulls. They wrap a rope around one hand, put the other in the air, and try to stay on for six seconds. It's a real hoot."

"I think I like those prissy little girls better," she said.

"Spikes instead of spurs. That's what Gemma says all time. She says when she has kids she's having a dozen girls to dress up all pretty. I always remind her that she only wears heels part of the time and that she can put on boots and ride a bull as good as I can."

A lady dressed in a bright-red pantsuit and a fellow in cowboy boots, jeans, and a white shirt set about roping off the three areas with brightly colored crepe-paper streamers. When they finished, the lady rang a bell on the porch to get everyone's attention.

The man who'd helped her picked up the cowbell and held it over his head. "Okay, kiddos. On your mark. Get set. Everybody ready?"

Everyone yelled and held up their baskets.

He rang the bell loudly and yelled, "Go!"

It looked like a swarm of bees in a bed of clover as the children took off in a run, gathering eggs into their various colored baskets until they were overflowing.

"Granny got the biggest kick out of watching them. She called them greedy little varmints, but she'd laugh and clap her hands. She especially liked the little ones," Rye said.

A pang of jealousy shot through Austin. Rye had experienced so much more with her grandmother than she had, and she had no one to blame but herself.

He touched her arm. "You look sad. This is supposed to be fun."

His touch sizzled on her skin like cold rain on the top of a sheet-metal roof on a hot afternoon. Damn and double damn! How could her world be turned inside out so much in just two days?

"It really is fun. I was thinking about Granny."

He hopped down off the tailgate and wrapped his arms around her, pulling her so close that she could hear his steady heartbeat. "I didn't mean to make you sad. She loved you, Austin. Talked about you all the time."

She fit perfectly into his arms. Short women made him bend so far that it gave him a backache. The few tall ones he'd dated intimidated him. But Austin was just the right height and had just the right amount of soft curves and sweet scents, and he wished the moment could last forever. He would love to two-step all over a dance floor with her or just stand there and hold her until the sun set that evening. He took a step back before he kissed her right there on the Main Street of Terral and made an utter fool of himself in front of a whole crowd of curious folks.

"You ready to go on to Ringgold?" he asked hoarsely.

She nodded, not trusting herself to say a word. If there was a Holiday Inn in Ringgold she would almost be willing for a side trip on the way, and for a moment she let her imagination run wild with images of tangled sheets and bodies intertwined in ways that made her heartbeat speed up and her mouth go dry and other parts of her go decidedly moist. She shook her head to get herself back under control and sighed. Ringgold had lost half its houses to a fire fifteen years ago, leaving the town with only about a hundred people. And that was raking up everyone and their cousins in a ten-mile radius. No Holiday Inn for her today.

"Are you sure your folks won't mind you bringing in an extra?"

"Honey, everyone in the whole area will stop by sometime today. Friends as well as the neighbors. It's old home week at the O'Donnell place."

"You told me a casual family affair with only ten people," she said.

"That's for dinner. Afterwards is open door and free leftovers."

It took ten minutes to drive two miles south of Ringgold on Highway 81. Rye slowed down and turned into an oak tree–lined gravel lane with a big, white two-story house at the end of the driveway. It had a porch surrounding three sides topped off by a widow's walk at the top with doorways opening out onto it.

"Welcome to the O'Donnell horse ranch."

"Horse?"

"Dad is Irish and loves the ponies. He and Mother raise quarter horses, and my brothers help him."

Austin kicked off her running shoes and slipped her feet into the spike-heeled sandals and was instantly sorry that she hadn't come better prepared. The shoes didn't go with the outfit she had chosen. And she'd forgotten to spray on perfume. Her hair was a fright from hiding eggs, and the majority of her makeup had sweated off.

His touch on the small of her back made her even more nervous when she stepped into a cool foyer. The noise of several conversations going on in a room off to the right made her want to run back to Terral and hide. But she held her head high and fought back another shiver when he escorted her into the living room.

"Rye, is that you? It had better be. I'm starving and...oh, my God." A dark-haired woman stared rudely. "Momma, did you know Rye was bringing someone with him?"

"Is it Ace or Wil?"

"It's Austin," Rye hollered.

"Well, bring him on in and make him known to the family."

Everything went so silent that the flutter of angel's wings would have sounded like shotgun blasts when he ushered Austin all the way into the room.

"Everyone, this is Austin Lanier, Granny's granddaughter."

"Welcome to Easter, Austin. Come on in here and get acquainted." Cash O'Donnell held out his hand and graced her with a broad smile.

CHAPTER 5

"This is my father, Cash O'Donnell, and my mother, Maddie." Rye pointed as he made introductions. "My sisters, Colleen and Gemma, and brothers, Dewar and Raylen."

"I'd be his grandmother, Franny, and this is his grandfather, Tilman," a woman with gray hair said from a rocking chair right at Austin's elbow.

"Now can we eat, Momma? I'm starving," Gemma said.

"It's on the bar in the kitchen. Everyone can help themselves the rest of the day soon as Poppa says grace," Maddie said.

Everyone talked at once as they headed through an archway leading into the dining room and beyond that to the kitchen. Rye steered Austin with his hand still on her back. The house was cool but that spot where his hand rested felt as if someone was holding a blowtorch two inches from it.

Maddie bowed her head but opened one eye a slit to look at her oldest son. He'd been the serious one of the boys, but he had an expression on his face she'd never seen before, not even with Serena, the girl he thought he was in love with back when he was about twenty-one. He was absolutely smitten with Austin Lanier, and Maddie wanted to weep for him. The girl was a high-powered businesswoman who lived in the big city of Tulsa. Rye would never be happy away from a ranch.

Tilman delivered the grace. "God bless the corners of this house, and be the lintel blest, and bless the hearth and bless the board and bless each place of rest, and bless each door that opens wide to stranger as to kin. And bless each crystal windowpane that lets the starlight in, and bless the rooftree overhead and every sturdy wall. The peace of man, the peace of God, the peace of love on all. Amen."

It was the strangest prayer Austin had ever heard, and she looked at Rye with a question on her face.

"It's an Irish blessing that he says every Easter," he whispered.

"Then you weren't kidding about being Irish?"

"Not one bit. Momma is too. She was Maddie O'Malley before she married Dad."

"And we've all got the temper to prove it. And Rye is the worst of the lot. That's why he's not married," Gemma said.

She had black hair cut in short layers that framed an oval face, deep-green eyes beneath arched dark eyebrows and heavy lashes, and a wide mouth. She took care of her short height with a pair of three-inch wedge espadrille sandals on a one-inch platform. She wore a flowing gauze skirt in a splash of bright spring colors and a skintight tank top the same color as her eyes.

Colleen playfully poked her sister on the arm. "He'd be runnin' a close race to you."

Her hair was that strange burgundy color that usually comes out of a bottle but looked totally natural. Her face was slightly rounder than Gemma's angular planes and her lips a wee bit wider. She was a little taller than Gemma, but her bright-red high heels, which matched her cute little capris and western-cut top, put them at about the same height.

"Love your hair," Austin said.

"Looks like it would come right out of a Clairol Nice'n Easy bottle, don't it?" Gemma said. "But it's virgin as the Mother..."

"Don't say it." Dewar pointed.

That he and Rye were brothers was undisputable. They had the same dark hair and the exact same shade of eyes, but Dewar wasn't quite as tall and his face more square. He also sported a deeper dimple in his chin and a scar on his cheek.

"What? I wasn't going to blaspheme. Not with Poppa in the house. He'd bring down lightning to strike me dead. God wouldn't have to lift a finger," Gemma said.

Raylen chuckled. He was the shortest of the O'Donnell brothers; about the same height as Austin. As if God were making it up to him for making him the short straw, He gave him the deepest voice, blue eyes, and thick dark-chestnut hair, colored somewhere between Colleen's and Rye's. He also gave him almost as much sex appeal as Rye and a smile that would cause major global warming.

"We're glad you came today. We've missed Verline. She'd become part of our family," Maddie said. "She was a hoot!"

"Thank you," Austin said.

Maddie didn't look old enough to have five grown children. She had a few crow's-feet around her bright blue eyes, but her chestnut hair was as virgin as Colleen's. She was taller than her daughters and slim as a model. Any twenty-year-old woman would have been delighted to look that good in snug jeans and a western-cut lime-green blouse.

Hell's bells, Austin thought. *I'd be happy to look that good and I'm thirty!*

Maddie handed Austin an oversize paper plate. "Did Rye make an offer for the farm? I told him to talk to you soon as you got into town. He's been wanting to expand for a while, and that would be ideal since it's right across the road."

"Rye did mention it but I'm still thinking about things," Austin said.

"Darlin', Easter isn't the time to talk business." Cash nudged his wife on the arm. "Excuse her, Austin. She's got a mind that never quits. Woman is what made this ranch what it is."

"You got that right," Grandma O'Donnell said from across the bar where she was piling her plate high with ham, baked beans, sweet potatoes, and a corn casserole that looked scrumptious. "Maddie took this old wore-out place and turned it around. I swear that girl could make silk flowers reproduce, and what she can do with horses is a gift from God. She can take a colt that's all gangly legs and turn it into a million-dollar racer."

Grandpa patted Grandma on the shoulder. "Got that from you, sugar."

"Damn right she did. I'm a lucky woman to get a daughter-in-law like her."

Austin wasn't shy about filling up her plate. The banana-nut pancakes had been wonderful, but hiding Easter eggs had used up that energy and she was as hungry as Gemma. If the girl planned on having a piece of the pecan pie on the dessert table, she'd better eat fast because Austin had laid mental claim to the biggest slice.

When she sat down beside Rye at the long dining room table, he raised an eyebrow at her plate. "Need some sideboards there?"

"This is just round one. I like good food, and nothing you say will make me feel guilty," she said.

Raylen slapped Rye on the back. "Met your match, did you?"

"Them Frenchies can't hold a candle to us Irish for eating." Rye's eyes twinkled. He started toward his mouth with a forkful of corn casserole at the same time Austin poked him with her elbow, and every bit of the casserole landed on the front of his shirt.

He couldn't catch a lucky break if he'd been driving a hundred and forty miles down the road in a good tailwind. The one woman he wanted to impress more than anyone in the world, and every time he turned around he was as clumsy as a hippo in ice skates.

"I'm so sorry," she said.

He wiped at the spill with a napkin. "At least my shirt is yellow and it won't show."

"You're a good sport, but be careful what you say about the French, darlin'. I'm only half-French. The other half is pure English, and we can whoop your Irish butt when it comes to eating," Austin said.

Grandpa tapped Grandma on the shoulder. "Aha, she's got spunk, sugar!"

"What'd you expect? She's Verline's granddaughter." Grandma laughed.

"I forgot to get a beer. What would you like?" Rye asked Austin. "We've got Coke, Dr Pepper, sweet tea."

"Coors?" she said. She could count the number of beers she'd drunk in her lifetime on one hand and wondered why in the devil she'd asked for beer when she meant to say sweet tea.

"You bet," he said as he pushed back his chair. It was torture sitting so close to Austin with everyone wedged in so close around the table. His elbow touched hers. His leg brushed against hers. And yet he found himself rushing back to the table so he could sit close to her again.

"Loved your grandma." Gemma was crammed in so close to Austin that their elbows practically touched when they picked up their forks. "I should've sat at the end of the table with this left hand handicap but I wanted to get to know you. I used to tell Verline that I was going to grow up and be just like her."

Austin smiled. "Me too. So she was here often?"

"Every Sunday Rye could talk her out of Terral. She was like an extra granny to us all."

Rye set a can of Coors beside Austin's plate. It was so cold that the outside had water beads hanging on it, and when she popped the top, foam floated out so fast that she had to gulp it to keep it from spilling out on the tablecloth.

"Sassy, smart, and knows how to drink beer. We might keep you," Cash said.

If Mother saw me right now, I'd be casket shopping tomorrow. Beer and paper plates, all the fat and calories in the state of Texas, and a cowboy from Terral flirting with me. I don't know if it's because he wants my property or if he really likes me, but his touch just plain sets me on fire and makes me think thoughts that would make the devil blush.

Austin raised her beer to Cash and smiled. "You'd be paying someone to take me off your hands come morning light."

Rye wasn't surprised by his family's reaction to Austin. She was smart, beautiful, and sassy. That all fit right in with the Irish clan, but they'd have been happy to see him bring a plain, shy woman who was only marginally pretty to Easter dinner. He was thirty-two years old and they'd always kidded that the O'Donnell offspring would marry in the order of their birth.

He'd liked dark-haired women ever since he'd kissed his first girl when he was thirteen out behind the barn after a cattle sale. Her name had been Kaylene Stephens, and her father had bought one of the O'Donnell horses. They lived in Hereford, Texas, and he never saw her again or forgot the way the kiss made him feel.

But that was nothing compared to the delicious taste of Austin Lanier's lips on his, the feel of her soft skin on his palm, or the way her curvy body fit just right all up and down his when he held her close. If kissing had made her knees go as weak as it did his, she would have fallen over backwards on the kitchen floor and taken him with her. Now there was a happy thought.

Maddie looked across the table at her oldest son. "How's the ham?"

"It's wonderful. Watermelon wine?" Rye asked.

"In honor of Verline. It was my last bottle. Are you going to keep making it like she did?" Maddie asked Austin.

Austin shrugged. "Don't know. Didn't even know she made it."

"Well, I hope you do. It makes the best ham in the world. Just pour a bottle over it and put it in the oven. Gives it just the right amount of sweet. I used blackberry wine until she brought me a bottle of hers. Does your mother have a secret for ham?"

"My mother doesn't cook. She has a combination housekeeper and cook. I've never known Bertha to make ham. Mother is very health conscious and ham is on her blacklist, but this is wonderful. You should open a restaurant!"

"Don't give her any ideas." Grandma giggled.

"Maybe I will when I retire from raising horses," Maddie said.

"What do you do?" Gemma turned to Austin.

"I work for Humphrey's Oil in Tulsa. How about you?"

"I'm a hairdresser over in Wichita Falls."

"And I'm a blackjack dealer at the casino in Randlett, Oklahoma," Colleen said. "Sometime you'll have to pop in at Gemma's joint, get all dolled up, and then come over to the casino and win a few dollars at my table. Bet you could find something a hell of a lot better than Rye O'Donnell in my casino. We get some damn fine-lookin' cowboys in there," Colleen said.

Austin smiled. Was Colleen trying to strike up a friendship or trying to steer her away from Rye?

"Want some help over there at Granny Lanier's? She was a collector." Gemma winked and shifted her eyes toward her grandmother.

Austin nodded ever so slightly that she understood. "Thanks, but I'll have to go through it myself to know what to toss and what to pack for storage, but anytime you got a spare hour or two, drop by and keep me company."

"I just might—and don't you roll your eyes at me, Rye," Gemma said.

"You can't see me," Rye protested.

"I can hear it when you roll your eyes," Gemma told him.

Austin giggled. Her childhood had been lonely. Her father had wanted at least two children; her mother wanted none. They had too much wine in Austin celebrating their first anniversary so they compromised. One child. And no more accidents.

Rye poked Austin on the arm, and white-hot heat flooded through him in the form of pure old sexual desire. "What's so funny?"

"All of you. This is fun."

"I'm glad you think so. It's a blistering chore to come down here on Sunday and put up with their sass," he said but his expression didn't back up his words.

"And what do you think it is for us? You're a big blister on all our asses," Colleen said.

"Momma, she's using ugly words at the dinner table," Raylen teased.

"No, she's not. She's speaking the gospel truth." Dewar put his two cents into the mix and the argument was on.

Austin couldn't remember the last time she'd had so much fun on Easter Sunday—or any other Sunday for that matter. She'd polished off a healthy piece of pecan pie and was wishing she had room for another small slice when Grandma stood up and announced that it was pickin' time.

Austin wasn't sure what they were going to pick or if it was time for her to make excuses, say thank-you, and let the family get on with whatever was next for their Easter afternoon. Surely they weren't talking about five grown children hunting eggs out in the pasture! If they were, then someone else was hiding the damn things.

"Music," Rye whispered, his warm breath sending tingles down her arms and putting goose bumps on her scalp. "Grandma likes to do a little playin' on Easter or any other time she can talk us into making music. Out under the shade trees in the backyard. I think it reminds her of when she was young."

Grandma slapped him on the shoulder. "I might be old but my hearing is still good. A woman likes good music; it don't have nothin' to do with her age. And you need to bring that girl around more often. You've smiled more today than I've seen you do in a long time."

"What makes you think it's Austin causing me to be happy? Maybe I just like Easter," he said quickly.

Grandma just patted him on the shoulder and grabbed Grandpa's arm as he headed out the door.

Quilts had been thrown down in front of six chairs under the shade of two enormous pecan trees. Kittens romped and played on the patchwork quilts but scattered quickly when Rye and Austin sat down.

"I'd best sit in a chair today. I can sit down on the quilt without a problem, but gettin' up, now that's a different story." Grandpa pulled an extra folding chair from behind the tree and set it up beside where Austin was sitting.

Colleen pointed at Rye. "You've got a job to do, and it's not sitting there while we work."

"I've got a guest."

"So? Granny Lanier was your guest and you still played. Get on up here. She can hold down that quilt without you."

Two cowboys flopped down on the pallet with Austin and Rye.

The taller one with the light-brown eyes flashed a smile at Austin. "Hey, we'll help hold down the quilt and talk to the pretty lady while y'all play."

The other one nodded seriously at her. "I'm Ace Riley, and that ugly cowboy would be Wil Marshall. He can't help it if he's as ugly as a mud fence covered up in horse apples. Protect your eyes and don't look at him, ma'am. And you'd be Miz Verline's granddaughter? She always did say we ought to meet each other."

Rye bristled at the banter and shot a mean look across the distance separating him and Ace. He would have liked to shoot a fist over and connect with his eye even if Ace and Wil were his two best friends.

Colleen strummed on the banjo. "Come on, Rye. We are waiting."

Grandma pulled up a chair beside her husband. "I'm sittin' this one out. You kids get the instruments warmed up and then I'll take over."

Rye slowly got to his feet and picked up the guitar waiting on the last chair left with an instrument in it, but he kept an eye on his two friends who were busy carrying on a conversation with Austin. Raylen was adjusting the strings on a fiddle. Gemma was playing the Dobro, and Dewar was sitting down with a dulcimer in his lap. And Maddie had a harmonica up to her mouth, running up and down it to get the feel for the right sound.

Rye struck up a chord and they all fell in to begin the back-yard concert with "Red River Valley" and followed that by "Bill Bailey." In the latter, Rye had the lead and made the guitar whine the melody so well that Austin could hear the words to the old song in her head as well as if someone were singing it.

Grandma stood up at that time and kissed Grandpa on the forehead. "They got them all warmed up now, darlin', so I'll play your favorite."

He grinned and she took the dulcimer from Dewar and motioned for him to relieve Raylen from the fiddle and for Raylen to take over for Rye.

"Good grief, can they all play all of those things?" Austin asked.

"No, honey, only Raylen can do it all. The rest are limited to a couple or three each. But Raylen and my sugar can play anything that falls into their hands," Grandpa said.

"We'll be doing 'Rye Whiskey' now and, honey, you'll be sing-ing," Grandma said.

Grandpa nodded.

Dewar pulled the bow across the stings, and the whine of the fiddle stirred something deep in Austin's soul. Guitar music joined him and then the rest of the instruments before Grandpa came right in on cue with the first words of "Rye Whiskey."

Rye held out a hand to Austin. "Walk with me and see the new colt Momma got last week."

"No fair, stealing her away. You know Granny Lanier wanted me to meet her. She even said our blue eyes matched up so per-fect that we'd have beautiful great-grandchildren for her." Ace laid a hand on Austin's to hold her back.

She didn't feel anything but a big, old warm hand: no tingles, no internal fires, no oozy feeling in the pits of her gut. She pulled her hand away and put it in Rye's and there it was: all the blazes of hell!

"Granny Lanier would have shot you on the spot if you'd come sniffin' around the door," Rye said. "She knew you were a bad boy."

"Not me." Wil reached up and grabbed Austin's other hand to keep her from walking away with Rye. "I'm the good boy. You two were always the ornery ones. Austin, I swear I'm the good one and I can prove it. Look at their arms. They're the ones who got drunk and wound up with tats. I was the good one who didn't let them talk me into such a thing."

Austin was amazed. Rye's touch was sending shock waves from her hair roots all the way to her toenails. Wil's was like shaking hands with a new customer at the oil company. She pulled free from Wil's hand and let the jolt of electricity flow through her as Rye pulled her to her feet.

"Yeah, right!" Rye said. "You were too drunk to get out of the back seat and get one. If you'd held your whiskey better, you'd have been right in there with us."

Austin had never had three men fighting over her. It felt pretty damn good even if they were all teasing, but Rye was the only one she had eyes for that day. She didn't jerk her hand free when he laced his fingers into hers and led her toward the barn in the distance. She looked back to see Ace and Wil grinning, Gemma giving her a thumbs-up sign in between strums on the Dobro, and Colleen frowning.

When they reached the corral, Rye popped a leg up on the lowest rung of the white fence and looked out over the mares and their new offspring. Austin leaned on a fence post and watched the long-legged colts romping in the afternoon sunshine.

She could hear music behind her and recognized "Barbara Allen."

"Do they play anything current?"

"Yes, they do. We just play the old ones when Grandma is around. She still likes that kind of music. Isn't listening to the old stuff better than going through dusty old boxes all day?"

Austin leaned on the fence beside him. "Yes, it is. Granny used to have an old fiddle cassette with lots of those songs on it. When

I was little, we'd dance around the living room together. Come to think of it, there was actually room to dance around in those days. When did she start bringing in so much junk? Did you and Granny walk out here on Sunday afternoons?"

He shook his head. "No, she sat on the porch with Grandma and Grandpa and talked politics. If Congress would have come on down here to north Texas and spent the afternoon with them, the whole government wouldn't be in the shape it's in today. They could have solved all the problems and even gotten the country out of debt in one Sunday afternoon. And she always was a collector but after she got the tumor she started hitting every garage sale in the county and always brought home a box of stuff. I thought it was something in her brain. She seemed to get a big charge out of putting it everywhere. I told her once that you would have a time getting rid of all of it, and she told me to mind my own business and stay out of hers."

"Sounds about right. Granny was very opinionated. That's why she and my mother never did get along. They're too much alike."

Rye could have stood right there forever with his left forearm resting on the fence and holding her hand with his right hand. Their fingers intertwined felt so right—there was the heat, the tingle, but also a feeling like their hands were joined together with their souls somehow—like this was meant to be. "I didn't even know your mother was alive. I did know all about her son, Eddie, and her granddaughter, Austin, but she never mentioned your mother."

"That's too funny for words."

"Why?"

"Because Mother still asked about her every week. We have brunch together most Saturdays and I talked to Granny on Thursday nights. Mother always asked how she was doing and what was going on at the farm," Austin answered.

"Why is it that they didn't like each other?"

"Granny never forgave her for taking Eddie away from Terral. Even if he didn't want to come back, it became Mother's fault. End of story."

"I wouldn't like it either if some hussy stole my only chick."

"My mother is not a hussy," Austin said. At last he'd said something that irritated her and proved he wasn't perfect after all.

"Hey, pardon me. I wasn't out to stomp your toes. To each his own and all that shit."

"Apology accepted."

He reached out and ran his knuckles down her jawline, leaving a trail of heat that swirled all the way down to her toes. "You get all tense when you are angry. Anyone ever tell you that?"

"I've been told that my eyes flash lightning bolts." Right then, more than her eyes was hot!

Using the other hand, he cupped her face in his hands and leaned in for the kiss. She shut her eyes and got ready for the shock. His lips moved slowly, drinking in the taste before his tongue teased her lips apart and he made sweet love to her mouth. The tension left her body and the pure raw desire began.

Then all of a sudden he pulled away leaving her panting and her lips suddenly cold—almost bereft.

"What was that all about?" she asked.

"Happy Easter. I'm glad you came to dinner even if my family gave you hell." He struggled mightily with himself not to plunge back into another soul-tearing kiss, but Rye knew he had to stop or else he was going to throw sanity out the window and take her to the hayloft and do a helluva lot more than kiss her, and Austin Lanier deserved better than a bed of hay.

"I love that your family included me in the teasing. I've enjoyed the day but that didn't have a thing to do with a kiss like that."

"I wanted to kiss you all day. You looked so damn cute hiding eggs and sitting on the tailgate watching the kids," he said softly.

"And I thought you were just trying to get next to me to get my watermelon farm for a song and a dance—or would that be a home-cooked meal and a kiss?" she smarted off. How dare he call her mother a hussy! Granted she might be just that, but he had no right to call her one.

"If that's what you think of me, then it's time we go back to Terral. I've got chores to do anyway after I show you the wine cellar." She'd finally aggravated him, and it had only taken a little more than twenty-four hours. He'd known it was too good to be true and that eventually he'd figure out she wasn't as perfect as he'd thought when he finally saw her in real life.

"That sounds fine by me. I'll tell your family goodbye and thank them for the lovely afternoon."

"Don't bother. Just get in the truck and I'll call Momma later tonight." Rye's tone was curt and serious. The smile was gone, and his eyes were dark instead of sexy.

Austin wished she was wearing anything but high-heeled sandals on her stomping journey back to the house. Rye O'Donnell had horse crap for brains if he thought for one minute that he was going to order her back into the truck, leaving his family to think she was too damn rude to thank them. He could drive his sorry ass home alone and she'd walk the whole seven miles before that happened. Her hussy mother hadn't raised a rude child.

"Looks like trouble in paradise to me, sugar," Grandpa said loudly.

"I said I'd call Momma later." Rye laid a hand on Austin's shoulder when he caught up to her. Anger did not take away the jolt of desire brought on by a touch.

She shrugged his hand away. "I'll do my own talking."

"Looks like he really has met his match." Grandma giggled.

"Flowers and candy for a starter, Rye. And follow it up with a nice dinner at the Peach Orchard and a walk down on the river-banks after the stars come out," Ace said.

Rye shrugged and sat down on the pallet. "Where's Dewar and Colleen?"

"Dewar had to go get a guitar pick. Colleen went with him to get something to drink."

Austin smiled at Maddie. "I've got to get back to the house and pack some more this afternoon, but I wanted to thank you for a lovely meal and all the fun. Can I help with anything before I go?"

Maddie hugged her. "No, honey, not a thing. Come on back with Rye anytime. We'll look for you next Sunday."

"Thank you. I'll get my purse from the house."

Maddie motioned with her hands. "Gemma put all the purses on her bed. Upstairs. First door to the left."

When she'd retrieved her purse, Austin went straight for the bathroom. If someone made her mad, she talked to her reflection in the mirror as if she were the therapist and the woman in the mirror the patient. She'd barely shut the door when she heard voices outside in the hallway. She heard her name so she forgot all about the therapist session and pressed her ear against the door.

"He's smitten with her. I've never seen him act like he did today. He can hardly keep his hands off her, and she's not the right one, Dewar. We've got to do something," Colleen said.

"She's not country material, and he's smart enough to realize it."

"But he's never had that look in his eyes. Not even with Serena. Lord, can't you just see her on the ranch? She wouldn't last a week. Rye can't live in a city or work in an office. He's a rancher and a cowboy."

"Don't you like her?" Dewar asked.

"She sees a good-lookin' rich man."

"Colleen, think! She comes from money. She's inherited three sections of land and a wine business. She's not looking at him for what he's got. And he's only known her a couple of days, Colleen."

"He fell hard for Serena too."

"That was ten years ago."

"And he hasn't brought home another woman until now."

Austin wondered who in the devil Serena was, and why it even mattered.

"He should have married Serena," Dewar said.

"He would have but she left him, and this one will too."

"It was that big fight they had over living in Oklahoma and then that other guy…"

Colleen didn't let him finish. "You don't have to remind me. I was fifteen and thought all love ended like in the fairy tales."

"Well, he's a big boy. He can take care of himself."

"They'll fight and his heart will get broken and he'll never find anyone else."

Dewar chuckled. "You don't have to wait on him to get married. That's just a family joke."

"It would take a special man to ever put me in a corral," Colleen said.

And me, Austin thought. *I'd like to walk out of here right now and tell you both that I'm not interested in your brother so you can stop worrying. I like the way he kisses. I like the way he fills out those jeans and the way his shirt is stretched over that broad chest but…* She couldn't think of any buts other than Rye's and the way he filled out those Wranglers.

"Amen to that, sister." Dewar laughed.

"You won't tell Rye that I'm not too impressed with his woman, will you?" Colleen asked as their voices faded.

Austin stepped back and looked at the blushing woman in the mirror. "Don't look at me like that. They were talking. I just listened. So the family is divided in their opinion of the new girl in town. Well, it's a Scarlett O'Hara situation here. Quite frankly, I don't give a damn."

But I do. I loved being here today among all these people. I loved the teasing and the sibling rivalry and all of it. Even if it was a one-day thing never to be repeated, I wanted it to be one of those memories that

I can pack away and get out every so often and think about, and now I've spoiled it with my temper.

She slowly went downstairs and out onto the porch. Grandma was coming in the door so Austin held the door for her.

"Don't hold whatever he said or did against him. He gets them high-temper genes from his dad. That man always did say the wrong thing at the wrong time. It's a wonder he ever talked Maddie into marryin' up with him."

Austin looked at Rye sitting on the blanket with his friends.

"It's the O'Donnell pride," Grandma whispered.

Austin smiled. "Well, tell that proud O'Donnell jackass when he gets finished with his important conversation that I'm walking home."

Grandma cackled. "I'll do that, honey."

She went straight to the truck where she changed back into her running shoes and put her high heels inside her purse. A nice, long jog might work some of the humiliation out of her system.

What were we fighting about other than he called Mother a hussy? It had to have been important but I can't remember. Whatever it was didn't cool the physical attraction one bit because he's still sexy as hell sitting out there with his cowboy friends.

She did a couple of deep knee bends, slammed the pickup door, and took off in a slow run down the lane toward the highway. *I've never felt so stupid or done anything so silly in my life but it feels pretty damn good.*

"Where is Austin?" Rye asked his grandmother when she returned with a glass of iced tea.

"I guess she's gone home. She said to tell you that you are a proud O'Donnell jackass and that she was walking home. I wouldn't date her no more, Rye. She's done lied to you on the first date. She ain't walkin'. She's runnin'."

"Well, shit!" Rye ran to his truck, fired it up, and caught up to her midway down the lane.

"Get in the truck, Austin. It's seven damn miles back home. Stop your pouting and get in."

She shot him her best go-to-hell look and kept running.

He drove another ten yards and hung his head out the window again. "Come on, Austin. You are acting like a spoiled teenager."

She picked up the speed.

She reached the end of the lane and turned left out onto the highway and heard the truck engine stop. She glanced over her shoulder to see him coming after her, making pretty good time in those boots. She put it into high gear and ran faster and then in a whirlwind of motion, he spun her around and threw her over his shoulder. Her butt was in the air. Her legs were pinned down by strong arms, and her head was dangling so close to his rear end that she had a view that made her mouth water. She braced her hands against the backs of his thighs and felt the most amazing muscles she'd ever experienced flexing against her palms. She thought she might pass out right then and there.

"Put me down!" she yelled.

"Yes, ma'am. I will do that as soon as we get back to the truck."

I've never been so turned on in my life.

"You are a jackass," she said.

"Yes, ma'am, it's the Irish. You are a smart-mouthed Frenchie. Hell of a combination, ain't it?"

He turned his head slightly and kissed her right on the fanny and thought he'd die of lust and embarrassment and he'd never be able to face her again. A thirty-two-year-old man shouldn't be carrying a thirty-year-old woman down the road like a sack of chicken feed. And it shouldn't be as intoxicating as a double shot of rye whiskey.

He opened the passenger door to the truck and plopped her down in the seat. She folded her arms across her chest and stared out the window. He got in, fired up the truck, slung gravel when he stomped the gas pedal, and parked in her front yard in four minutes. If there had been a highway patrolman out that Easter, he'd have had a ticket for sure but it would have been worth every dime it cost him.

She opened the door, let herself out, and leaned back inside. "That was uncalled for, childish, and rude. Where's the wine business?"

He pointed at the new truck sitting under the makeshift shed roof. "Pull out her new truck. She built the shed over an old cellar where she keeps her wine. There's a trapdoor under the truck. Pull it up. And I wasn't the only one who was childish."

Austin slammed the door with enough force to rattle the angels out of heaven. She stormed through the house, tossed her purse on the kitchen table, picked up the truck keys, and stomped the whole way to the carport or shed or whatever to hell the thing was called.

Rascal followed her and sat next to the far wall while she backed out the year-old Ford Ranger truck. Didn't anyone in this area drive a Silverado? If Austin had known that Granny was in the market for a new truck, she could have gotten her a fantastic deal on a Chevrolet at the dealership.

Sure enough, there was an old cellar door right there under where the truck had been. Austin vaguely remembered being in that part of the yard and playing jacks with Granny on the concrete top a few times when she was a little girl. She pulled the door up and looked down into the dark abyss. She didn't like basements, dark cellars, spiders, or mice so she stood at the top of the stairs a long time before she took the first step. Nothing squeaked or crawled off the wall onto her leg. The second step built a little confidence but the third one sent her scrambling to the top of the stairs brushing spiders from her face.

"Shit! Shit! Shit!" Feeling like a contortionist, she checked everywhere for a black hairy varmint crawling on her but found nothing. She peeked down the stairs, and sunlight reflected off something dangling in the air at about the third step. She leaned in but didn't take a step and studied the thing until it moved again.

Feeling like a fool, she figured out the wicked thing that had attacked her wasn't a spider but a wooden spool hanging on a long length of twine. She caught the spool on the third step and gave it a good solid yank, and the whole cellar lit up. At the bottom she stopped and stared. It was shiny clean with rows of bottles on three sides and a small desk with a computer right in the middle of the room. She sat down in the comfortable chair and opened the laptop. It came up with a window asking for her password. She typed in *watermelon* but the system refused it. She tried dozens of words, and it refused them all. Standing up and looking around, she tried to think of what Verline would use as a password but nothing came to mind.

She pulled a bottle of wine from the rack. It had a parchment-colored label with a picture of a watermelon entwined with crawling vines and leaves. Lanier Wine was written in fancy script lettering with the year 2006 written down the side. She slid it back into its slot and opened the desk drawer searching for recipes or notes. The first thing she picked up was a small notebook and the first page yielded the password: *Austin*.

The password opened the wine world up to her on a wireless connection. She flipped through folders that were organized beautifully by year, by recipes, and by distributors. Evidently there were a lot of people who loved Lanier Wine.

CHAPTER 6

ON MONDAY MORNING AUSTIN AWOKE TO THE SOUNDS OF nothing in her house.

"Praise the Lord, and I'm not blaspheming, Granny," she said aloud. She hopped out of bed and stuck her nose out into the short hallway. No coffee and bacon aromas wafted down the hallway. No pots and pans rattling or whistling. All of a sudden the house felt very empty.

She made a pot of coffee, stuck two slices of bread in the toaster, and decided to pack Granny's room that day. Daylight filtered through the kitchen window and across the table in a wide streak while she ate a piece of buttered toast and drank two cups of coffee.

She looked around at all the junk and sighed. "Why didn't Granny have a garage sale and get rid of this? I don't know what to keep and what to get rid of."

Your granny was sick and she wanted to leave this world with all her things around her. Look around. A whole lot of this crap is what you bought her because you knew she liked knickknacks. You think she would have given away a single hair from your head that got left behind on the bathroom sink?

Then Austin felt guilty. She finished her toast and wandered into the living room. Used to be there was at least a spot big enough to set a coffee cup on the end tables but not anymore. An anorexic flea couldn't find a place to land if it hopped off Rascal and tried to light on a table. She should have stayed home from the egg hunt and dinner at the O'Donnell's the day before, but that was water under the Red River bridge.

The more she looked around at all the crap, the angrier she got.

There was no way in hell Granny had bought all of that junk. She would have never bought that butt-ugly duck wearing a grass skirt and sunglasses.

A hard knock on the front door startled her so that she sloshed coffee onto her pajama top. She dabbed at it with the kitchen towel on her way to tell Rye that she wasn't interested in anything he had planned that day, but it was Felix and the other five hired hands standing on the porch.

"Miz Austin, I just thought I'd let you know that even though we always plant on the first Monday after Easter, I think we'd best put it off this year because it's going to rain. Weather says we might get up to two inches today and tonight. The seeds would be washed away if we plant now and the tractors would be stuck in the mud," Felix said.

"Whatever you think is best."

"Then we will wait a week. The weatherman says it will rain most of this week. We'll spend our time working in the implement shed getting the tractors tuned up and ready for next week's planting."

"You take care of it. I'll use this week to pack up the stuff in the house, and we'll plant next week."

"You want me to send Lobo in here to help you?"

"No, thanks, I can manage this part."

"Okay, then we will talk each morning and start to plant next Monday." He settled his straw hat on his head and barely made it to the truck before it started to rain.

Austin poured another cup of coffee and started in her grandmother's room. Clothing that she had no interest in wearing went into a big, black garbage bag with a yellow tie on the top. She slapped a strip of masking tape on the outside with a brief description of what was in the bag so she wouldn't get it mixed up with the trash.

She found a half-written letter to her father in one of the nightstand drawers. It was dated fifteen years before and mentioned how proud her grandmother was of Austin's achievements in school that year. She put that in a box with a small snow globe she had brought her grandmother from a skiing trip to Italy and other things too precious to toss out.

The rain subsided and the sun came out in the middle of the afternoon. Austin opened the windows to let the sunshine and fresh air flow into the room. It was near midnight when she shook pillows down into fresh cases and finished remaking the bed. All total, she'd found four hundred dollars in ones, fives, and tens stashed in drawers and coat pockets and stuffed down into boots. She'd have to go through every envelope and shake out every single piece of paper, or she might actually throw away money.

―――――――

Rye stood at the kitchen window and stared at the lights across the road. She was in Granny's bedroom, no doubt cleaning it out in a fit of anger. He'd called her mother a hussy in a joking tone, so why had she taken such offense? He hadn't meant it to start a fight, but she was so damn cute when she was angry.

At midnight the light went out and he picked up the phone and punched in the speed dial to the house phone. On the third ring she picked up.

"Hello?"

"Wishing you had caller ID so you could hang up on me?" he asked.

"You must be psychic."

"Still mad?"

"I'm too tired and sleepy to be mad."

"Good. I'm slated to ride in a rodeo tomorrow night down in Houston. Want to go with me?"

"Rye, I've got to get this work done," she said.

A stone the size of the Rock of Gibraltar replaced his heart.

He'd hoped she'd drop everything and go with him. But that was a fool's thinking.

"I'm leaving at sunup tomorrow morning. Have to be there to check in for the bull riding at 6:30 p.m. If you change your mind, be ready at six. I'm sorry I called your mother a hussy, but I was only joking," he said.

"I'm sorry I accused you of wining and dining me to get my watermelon farm. Be careful and call when you get there." She rolled her eyes. Why in the hell had she said that? She sounded like his mother or, worse yet, her grandmother.

He wanted to dance a jig right there in the kitchen. "I will do that. Good night, Austin."

"Good night." She held the receiver to her ear long after the dial tone said he'd hung up.

At six o'clock the next morning, she awoke with a start and ran to the living room window. Rain was coming down in sheets, blowing hard against the window, but she could still see Rye's pickup as it pulled out of the driveway. She watched until the taillights disappeared and then she brewed a pot of coffee. After breakfast, she started work in the garage. Granny had kept every scrap of paper that her father had ever brought home from school, and they painted a picture of her father growing up.

Austin was having a midmorning break when the phone rang, and she really did wish for caller ID. "Hello?"

"Are you awake yet?" Rye asked.

"Of course I'm awake. I've been in the garage all morning."

"Miss me making breakfast for you?"

She smiled. "My fat cells did."

"You don't have any fat cells." He pictured her in those cute little pajamas and swerved over into the wrong lane. A loud car horn jerked him into the present, and he pulled off onto the shoulder and stopped.

"What was that?" she asked.

"Car horn. Someone was angry at someone else. So what did you find in the garage?" Anything to keep her talking. Her voice was rye whiskey, all fire and warmth with an aftertaste that lasted all day.

"I found four hundred dollars stashed away in the bedroom last night, so now I have to go through everything a piece at a time so I don't throw away money," she said.

"Our grandparents are Depression kids. They hid money because they were still afraid of banks."

"Well, in today's economy, I got to admit I'm about ready to hide it in fruit jars in the cellar too. Where are you?"

"South of Dallas a hundred miles. Got caught in the morning traffic and that held me up but I left in plenty of time to allow for it."

"My cell phone is ringing and it's Mother's ringtone. I'd better go."

"Talk to you later," Rye said.

"Okay. Be careful."

It hadn't been a dial-up-sex call but Rye felt like a teenage boy who'd hacked into the 900 numbers and had free access to them. He went over every word Austin had said all the way to Houston.

Tuesday evening she had to make a run to town for milk and bread and missed his call before he settled onto the bull's back. The bull came out of the chute with both hind legs off the ground, his horns practically touching the dirt in front of him and twisting and turning like a whirlwind. Rye hung on for eight full seconds and qualified for the Thursday night ride, but it was the toughest ride he'd ever done. Not because of the bull but because the whole time he had one hand in the air and the other around the rope, he kept wishing he'd thought to ask for Austin's cell phone number before he left.

He tried calling the house several times but got no answer. He was ready to get in his truck and drive all night back to Terral when at ten o'clock she finally picked up.

"Hello," she said breathlessly.

"Hello," he said in his slow Texas drawl.

"I'm so glad you called. Didn't know if you'd try to call tonight but I hoped you would. I laid the phone down on the kitchen counter after we talked this morning and went to get my cell phone to talk to my mother and forgot about the other phone and the battery went dead. I spent the day cleaning out the garage—and why in the hell didn't you get my cell phone number before you left?" She sucked in a full lung of air and started again. "What if you'd been killed on that bull and why do you ride those mean things anyway and…"

"Whoa!"

"Don't you whoa me, Rye O'Donnell!"

He slapped his thigh and turned around three times in the motel room. She cared enough to worry about him!

"I've got a pen in my hand. What is your cell phone number? I'll program it in and put it on speed dial. And if you were so worried, why didn't you call me?"

"How could I? Granny didn't have caller ID, and I don't have your cell number." Her tone was pure frustration.

"Two things. It's programmed on her phone. Your cell phone is star number one. Mine is star number two. And it's on a piece of paper on the refrigerator. Those last couple of weeks her memory was bad so I wrote it down and stuck it to the refrigerator door with a magnet."

"Well, hell's bells, nobody told me that. How'd your rodeo go?"

"I racked up enough points to ride again on Thursday. I'll be home Friday evening. Want to drive down tomorrow and watch me ride on Thursday?"

"Still got work to do, and I want to look at that wine business a little more. Do you have any idea what she means by fast yeast like for Montrachet? She says in her recipe that watermelon juice has a tendency to spoil before it reaches a preservative level and to use this fast yeast, and I need something called Campden tablets."

"No, but I bet we can find out if we go to her suppliers. She had to have ordered it from somewhere because you sure can't buy anything like that at the grocery store in Terral."

He did a few fast moves of a line dance in happiness. She was intrigued by the wine. Would that keep her in Terral?

"I guess so. And she talked about putting the fresh-squeezed juice in the refrigerator for the first twenty-four hours for the Campden to work. And to never use anything but pure juice. She said some recipes call for water but to ignore them. I feel like I'm groping in the dark but it's all so interesting," she said.

Rye sat down on the edge of the bed. "I've seen her float a hydrometer in the juice to see how much sugar to add. She told me once she had to do it with every single recipe because the watermelon juice was different in every batch she grew. A good wet spring made for better juice. Drought years were horrible."

"Guess I've got a lot to learn," she said.

Wednesday, Austin kept her cell phone with her but by midmorning she'd figured out that she had no reception in the wine cellar so she left the door open and laid her phone on the top step. It rang ten minutes later, and she scrambled up the stairs so fast she didn't even see the granddaddy long-legged spider.

"Hello!"

"Well, that was a spicy greeting. Are you about to get that rat's den cleaned up? Think you can come home a few days early? We could fly to the beach and spend a long weekend together. What do you think?" Barbara asked.

"Sounds like fun but it's not going to happen, Mother. It's coming along but not very fast so I'll be here the full time. Right now I'm in the wine cellar."

"You are where?"

"In the wine cellar. Granny made this wonderful watermelon

wine that everyone raves about. She's got a fancy setup down in the storm cellar. I've been learning about making watermelon wine and, Mother, she's made a small fortune with it."

Barbara laughed. "Well, that's a business you can sell and build a nice little nest egg for retirement. Gotta run. There's a salesman with a question about a used car. Talk to you later."

Austin had barely made it to the bottom of the steps when the phone rang again. She got it on the second ring and answered.

"Hey, what are you doing today?" Rye asked.

"I'm in the wine cellar. I tried cleaning the garage but all I could think about was wine so I've been down there reading over her notes and trying to figure out things. I found a place where I can buy that Montrachet yeast online, and from the looks of it, she bought it in pound packages. And Campden is sodium metabisulfite in tablet form and goes into the juice twenty-four hours before fermentation. It's a process, let me tell you. I can't wait to make my first batch."

"Sounds like you are a fast learner. Granny told me the first time she decided to make a batch, it wasn't any better than glorified Kool-Aid, but you've got a head start with her recipes." He wanted to be next to her, not all the way across the damn state, but if he won tomorrow night, the purse would go a long way toward a bull he had his sights on buying for his own rodeo stock.

"I wish I had some good ripe melons to start on right now," she said.

"Well, darlin', you'll have to wait until the end of June for that. Maybe even the first of July since you're getting a week late start on planting. But they're always ready by July 4 so you should have your hands deep in the juice by then."

It hit Austin right then like a dump truck full of bricks falling on her head that on July 4 she'd be in Tulsa in a new office with a lovely view.

"You still there?" Rye asked.

"Yes, I'm here. I was just thinking."

"Well, go on back to your wine-making business. I'm meeting a fellow with a good rodeo bull for sale for lunch. I'll call you later tonight."

"I'll be right here," she said and hung up with a heavy heart. She went back to the house, made a ham and cheese sandwich, put it on a paper plate with a pile of barbecued chips to the side, and carried it with a can of cold Diet Coke back to the cellar.

It was almost seven when Rye called again, and Austin was shocked to see that it was dark when she hustled to the top of the stairs for the phone.

"Where are you now?" he asked.

"I'm turning out the light and leaving the cellar. Where are you?"

"Fixing to walk into the rodeo and see how my competition looks. If I win the purse tomorrow night, I'm buying the bull. We agreed on a price, and he'll be a great addition to my stock for the summer."

"Purse?" she asked.

"The money for being the best." He laughed. "You ever been to a rodeo?"

"No." She pulled the string on the light and closed the cellar door with one hand.

"What was that noise? Did you fall?"

"The cellar door got away from me," she said.

"First bull is fixing to come out of the chute now. I'll call you before I go to sleep," he said.

"I'll still be here," she said.

How long could she say that? The idea of never trying her hand at watermelon wine was weighing heavy on her mind. Maybe she'd keep the farm and hire a foreman, take the best of the melons to Tulsa, and make Lanier Wine up there.

She carried that idea into the house, but it didn't last until she'd run a bath. "Granny would jinx it and make it all go bad. Then I'd have nothing but gallons of glorified Kool-Aid."

———————

Thursday, Rye called twice in the morning, twice in the afternoon, and just before he got on the bull. Then he called her five minutes later to tell her his score and that things were looking really good for buying the new rodeo bull.

"That's great! So you'll be home tomorrow evening?" she asked.

"That's right, and you'd better be ready to go on our very first real date. How about a picnic down on the riverbanks?"

"What if it rains?"

"Then Chinese and a movie in Duncan?"

"That sounds like a plan," she said.

"I miss you," he said softly.

Why was it that as long as she was talking to him on the phone she was fine? Sure, she visualized his cute butt in those Wranglers and his smile and that dimple in his chin. And she dreamed about him kissing her again and again. But when they were together, she felt like her world was falling apart at the seams. Maybe it was because they'd started out with a phone relationship and that's where she was comfortable.

"You going to answer that?" he asked.

"I'm sorry. I was thinking about that picnic." She told a white lie. "What would you like me to bring?"

"A bottle of Granny's wine. You. A pizza from down at the Mini-Mart. You. Don't bother with napkins. Did I mention bringing you?"

"Why no napkins?"

"If you get pizza on your face or hands, I'll lick it off," he said.

A delicious shiver raced down her backbone and settled low in her gut. "You are a rogue, talking to me like that when I'm more than three hundred miles away."

"You mean you would like it?" he teased.

"Good night, Rye. I'm hanging up now."

She heard his husky voice chuckle as she flipped her phone shut.

———————

Friday morning Austin forced herself to do some work in the garage, but her mind kept going to the cellar and Rye. She'd think about making wine and that would bring on a tasting session with Rye, which would trigger a hot feeling on her lips as she thought about kissing him after tasting watermelon wine. She almost popped the cork on a bottle of Lanier Wine just to see what it did taste like, but she wanted to share that moment with Rye.

After lunch she took a bath, washed her hair, and went to Ryan to cash the hired hands' checks. She'd promised to buy the ice cream that week, and she looked forward to seeing her grandmother's old friends again. They did not disappoint her. They were waiting at the same table when she pushed inside the drugstore.

"Hey, you showed up, which means you stayed a whole week?" Molly said.

"So how are things with Rye? We know you did the Easter egg thing. Verline would've been happy about that," Greta said.

"Haven't seen him all week. We went to dinner at his folks', had us a big old fight, and he left the next day for a rodeo in Houston." Austin pulled out a chair and sat down.

Greta smiled. "I heard that he won the purse. I think it's funny as hell that they call it a purse even though big, old tough men win it."

"How do you know so much about him?"

"It's like this. Oma Fay is Kent's momma and she's Pearlita's cousin so Kent tells his momma stuff and she tells Pearlita and Pearlita calls one of us nearly every day."

"Small towns."

"Yep, don't you just love 'em? What have you got done in the packing area?" Molly asked.

"I got a tiny little dent put in the garage and Granny's room all cleaned out. Y'all know where the nearest Goodwill store is?"

"Sure, but we got a clothes place in our church if you're just wanting to donate them. Bring them next Friday and I'll take them to the church," Greta said.

"Thank you."

"Sure you don't need any help down there? Verline was the worst pack rat in the world. I can't imagine you going through that place all by yourself," Molly said.

"If I could stay out of the wine cellar, I could get more done, but it keeps calling my name. I'd love to try my hand at making watermelon wine."

The waitress set their ice cream in front of them and Austin had her spoon halfway to her mouth when Greta said, "So one week down and you still haven't got a chance to get Rye into bed. That's too bad."

Molly shook her finger at Greta. "Stop it! You'll embarrass her. Besides, I'll bet you twenty dollars she sweet-talks him into the bedroom before she goes back to Tulsa."

"I'll take your bet but she has to be honest with us and tell us that she did or didn't."

"You two are crazy," Austin said and her cell phone rang. She pulled it out of the pocket of her grandmother's jeans and answered it without looking at the caller ID.

"I'm stuck in traffic. An accident happened up ahead. I won't be home before eight. How about I just slap a steak on the grill and we eat at my place?"

"That sounds fine to me," she said. "I'll bring dessert."

"Bring a bottle of Lanier Wine and you can be dessert." He laughed.

"Hold that thought." She giggled as she hung up.

"You are going to lose your money," Molly said. "Was that Rye?"

Austin dug into her ice cream. "It was."

"Hold what thought?" Greta leaned over and whispered.

"He said I was dessert."

"Yep, you might as well pay up now."

Austin smiled. "Who says I'll be honest and tell all? You'd best hang on to your money."

———————

She found a pair of denim capris in her grandmother's closet and a blue-and-white-checkered shirt that she tied at waist level. After trying on four pairs of shoes, she tossed them all aside and wore a pair of Verline's rubber flip-flops. At least they were blue and matched the shirt.

Once she was in the wine cellar, she had no idea what bottle to take. Did she take last year's vintage or 2006, which was the oldest label in the cellar? Since she had no idea which were good and which weren't she picked up a 2006, 2007, and 2008. Surely Rye would know enough about them to pick the right one to complement his steaks.

It seemed senseless to drive such a short distance so she walked down the short driveway and across the road. The first step on his property made her antsy enough to consider turning tail, kicking off the flip-flops, and running all the way back home. They'd talked and flirted on the phone and all was well, but what would happen when he opened the door? She reminded herself that she was thirty years old, but it didn't stop the jitters.

———————

Rye got home at seven o'clock. He threw two steaks into the microwave and pushed the thaw button, rushed to the shower, shaved, nicked himself in that same place he had when he was in a hurry to get to the Peach Orchard to see her the first time, applied cologne, and tried on four shirts before he put on a soft blue-plaid cotton.

He cut up two large potatoes and wrapped each one in a foil packet with real butter, salt and pepper, and a quarter-inch slice of onion, and put them on the grill to cook while he prepared a salad and put it in the refrigerator to chill. He pulled down two plates and carried them out the sliding glass doors to the deck.

The sound of the doorbell made him jump. He rolled his neck on the way through the house, but when he swung the door open, he was tense all over again. She was damn beautiful standing there with three bottles of wine cradled in her arms.

He opened the door. "Come on in. I'm about to put the steaks on. The potatoes are cooking and the salad is chilling. Want me to put a bottle of that on ice?"

"I don't know anything about watermelon wine so I brought three bottles and thought you might help me decide which would go better with supper." She held all three out to him as she stepped inside the cool house. There was no way he could take them from her without brushing against her bare skin.

She managed to keep from visibly shivering.

He wanted to gather her up in his arms and hold her forever, kiss her, make love to her, wake up the next day with her in his arms. But he took the wine and set it on the cabinet and said, "I've got the steaks ready to slap on the grill. Hope you are hungry."

"Starved."

"Make yourself at home."

The awkwardness was back. On the phone they were fine. Off, well, that was a different matter.

Austin busied herself taking a look at the living room. One look around said that Rye O'Donnell was a neat freak. The living room was furnished in mahogany-colored leather furniture arranged in front of a fireplace. Not a speck of dust was visible on the heavy oak coffee tables or the end tables. She didn't even see a skim of dust on the rungs of the oversize rocking chair. No doilies. No frills but good serviceable furniture that begged to be sat on and tables with enough space to set a cup of coffee or tea without knocking over a ceramic duck or elephant. A bar separated the living area from the kitchen, which was spick-and-span. Carpet was a light neutral shade of sandy brown; tile on the kitchen floor and cabinet tops were the same shade of mottled brown. All in all, a man's house.

"Nice place you've got here."

"It's temporary. My goal is to build a big house like Mom and Dad's about a quarter of a mile back on the property by the time I'm forty. Buying a prefab worked at the time and it's serviceable but it's not big enough to raise a family."

"So you're thinking of a family?"

"Sure am. Gemma says I'm grown up enough to start thinking about one. Matter of fact, she's insisting I think about it. How about you?"

"I'm not nearly grown up enough yet, and I don't have younger sisters to pester me about it. Actually, it's the opposite in our family. I've got two aunts who would put out a hit on any man I got serious about."

He raised a dark eyebrow. "Really?"

"No, not really. But they'll be very disappointed if I marry anything other than my career."

"What about your mother?"

"In her words, she doesn't need grandchildren to fulfill her life."

"That's strange to me. I came from this big, loud family. I can't imagine not having one just like it. What about you? Leaving aside your aunts and mother, what do you want?"

"Well, when I grow up..." Austin pondered the issue. "I've been so busy getting to where I am that I never gave it much thought, to tell the truth."

Rye put the wine into a galvanized milk bucket, dumped two trays of ice in on top, and motioned for her to follow him through sliding doors out to a deck. The sun was starting to slide down toward the western horizon, and the new leaves on the elm tree danced in the cool evening breeze.

"Got to take advantage of the pretty days and nights. Pretty soon it'll be so hot that we'll be hugging the air conditioners like them folks who hug trees," he said.

"It's beautiful back here."

The cantilevered deck offered an octagonal picnic table that would seat eight, with a bright-red umbrella tilted just right to prevent the sun from shining in their eyes. Adirondack chairs were placed up close to the grill where the delicious aroma of onions almost, but not quite, obliterated that sex-in-a-bottle shaving lotion he'd used.

"By the way, you look beautiful tonight," he said.

And you smell so good I could forget the steaks and have you for supper, she thought.

"Thank you," she said.

"You like your steak well done or—?" He let the question hang and raised one eyebrow.

"Medium rare. Pink in the middle. Scorched on the outside."

"I like a woman who knows how to eat steak right."

The awkwardness was fading now that they were talking.

"So that's the way you like yours too?"

"Wipe the sorry old slobbers off its face. Shoot it. Slap it on the grill long enough to get a burn mark on the outside and flip it over for a minute, then put it on my plate. And don't be offerin' me any sauces or ketchup to drown it in. I like the flavor just like it comes."

"So you don't marinade it for hours in all kinds of secret sauces?"

"Nope, I just slosh a little watermelon wine on it 'bout the time it gets done and serve it up. If I don't have any of Granny's wine, I pour beer on it. You want a glass of wine while we wait? It won't be real cold yet, but I'll swish it around in the ice a few times. That 2008 bottle is good right off the rack. It's the best she ever made."

"I'd love a glass of wine. I've been waiting for you to get home to taste it. I didn't even know which bottle would be the best or if it went with fish or steaks or what."

He opened a bottle and filled two stemmed wineglasses. "It goes with anything, in my books."

"Wow, all fancy!"

"Don't get too excited. They're plastic and from Walmart down in Bowie. I only have two and they're for special times."

"Oh, so I'm a special time."

He touched his glass to hers. "Yes, ma'am, you sure are. To Austin and her first taste of watermelon wine."

The wine was sweet and smooth with just enough kick to taste good. She finished the first glass and poured another, which was colder than the first. She sipped it while he grilled the steaks and decided that she could probably drink watermelon wine with dinner every evening. It was doing a fine job of mellowing her out.

CHAPTER 7

AUSTIN REACHED FOR THE WINE BOTTLE AND THE SKY TILTED slightly to the left. She'd never gotten tipsy on two glasses of any kind of wine before. Maybe it was because she'd put it down on an empty stomach or drunk it too fast. Whatever, she had to slow down or she'd be more than mellow. She'd be downright uninhibited before the night was out and Molly would win that bet about her sweet-talking Rye into bed.

She stifled a giggle and realized that she was indeed getting pretty tipsy on watermelon wine. She checked Rye's glass and was surprised to see that he was still working on number one. It damn sure wouldn't take much to remedy that.

"Open this bottle, and let's see if it's as good as the last one."

"But there's still some in the other bottle." Rye looked up and realized it was almost empty.

He uncorked the second bottle, downed what was left in his glass, and poured more for both of them.

"Yep, every bit as good."

"I believe you are right."

Would the flirting end with a walk across the road and lingering on the porch after a good-night kiss? Is that what she wanted? Did she really want to start a relationship with Rye?

She was sitting at a picnic table with another glass of sweet red wine in her hand, watching a hunky cowboy grill steaks and didn't know what the hell she was going to do. The wine was heady enough that she wondered what the alcohol content was. One measly glass of any kind of wine had never caused light-headedness before. But then she hadn't eaten since lunch and skipped supper because she'd had ice cream with the girls at the drugstore.

She remembered the hired hands' trailer looking different the last time she came to Terral. It had been faded turquoise and white and not nearly as long. There had been a rattling old air-conditioner propped up on wooden legs that stayed wet from the condensation, and the porch was nothing but a set of wooden steps that were rotting away.

"When did Granny buy the hired help a new trailer?"

"About five years ago. Got it real cheap and had the guys do some work on it when they got here that year. They put on the porch and wanted to dig up a garden out back but she told them that they already took care of her garden and could have anything they wanted out of it. It's got three bedrooms so she put six twin beds in there. The living room has television and a couple of used sofas. They love it."

"Well, this new one sure looks better than that old turquoise one."

I'd rather be talking about you than a used trailer house, he thought. *About you staying and running that watermelon farm. Why didn't Granny Verline prepare me for the way you'd make me feel?*

The steaks put off a heady aroma that made Austin's stomach growl. "Sorry about that. I'm really hungry so don't be thinking you are going to get half my steak. You touch it, I'll put a fork in your hand."

Rye chuckled. "I like a woman who appreciates a good steak. Don't know that I could ever…" He stopped and took a sip of wine. He'd been about to say that he could never fall for a vegetarian.

"Ever what?" Austin asked.

"Ever be a vegetarian."

"Me either. One of my aunts is a vegan."

"How many aunts do you have who'd put out a hit on anyone you got serious about?"

"Two. There were three girls in my mother's family. Their mother was a career woman. She helped her husband, my grandfather, build the dealership. No, rephrase—she built it and he sold cars. She had the business sense and passed it on to her daughters. Mother was the only one who married. The other two are married to their careers."

I'd rather be kissing you or making love to you under the stars than hearing about your fancy-pants aunts.

"And you? You going to grow up to be a vegetarian?"

"Hell, no! I like steak too well to be a vegan. When will it be ready?"

Holy shit! Either Terral or watermelon wine is rubbing off on me! I'm cussin' just like Granny!

"Five minutes. I'll bring out the salad and bread. The potatoes are already done. Would you please refill our wineglasses while I get it on the table?"

He carried out a salad in a clear crystal bowl with a hinged plastic fork and spoon stuck in the middle. "Granny gave me her recipe for dressing. I hope you like it because I've already added it to the salad."

"The oil and vinegar with all the seasonings?" Austin asked.

"That's the one." He put a hand on her shoulder and set the salad on the table. He'd like to forget supper, take her to bed, and touch her body all over at least a dozen times.

"You've got to write it down for me. I love that dressing and never even thought to have her copy it for me."

"It's in her recipe book. The loose-leaf binder up in the cabinet above the microwave where she keeps her cookbooks, all except for her wine secrets. They're on the computer in the wine cellar."

He set a small bowl in front of each plate on the table, opened the grill lid, and stuck a fancy fork in each steak. "Looks done."

"What is that thing?"

"A meat fork. It shows when they are medium rare, rare, or well done," he said. *And if you stuck one in me, it would register off the chart with heat.*

"Handy looking little thing. If I ever buy a house and get a grill, I'll have to purchase one of those."

"You have a house right across the street so I guess we need to make a trip to Walmart and buy you a meat fork."

"You know what I mean."

"So you don't own your home in Tulsa?"

"I rent an apartment."

"I couldn't live like that. All scrunched up with neighbors so close they could hear…" He stopped before he said "bedsprings."

She cocked her head to one side. "Hear what?"

"A beer burp," he said quickly and plopped a steak in the middle of her plate and one on his. Then he shifted foil-wrapped potatoes beside them and made a hasty trip back inside to bring out a loaf of French bread he'd heated in the oven. "It's not homemade. I don't do so well with bread so I just buy it or pop a can open."

"I'm hungry enough that I might even eat the wrapper."

"Well, saw off a piece of that Angus and tell me how you like it."

She cut a bite-sized piece and put it in her mouth. "Mmmmm," she said the whole time she chewed.

The only thing better would be a long romp between the sheets with you. God! Where are these thoughts coming from? I bet they aren't coming from God. More likely from Lucifer who set up shop in my brain from the minute I figured out you weren't a seventy-year-old man with a gray moustache.

"So you like it?"

"It's wonderful. If my aunt ever came down here and ate your steak, she'd convert to carnivores and cowboys."

"Now that's the best compliment I've ever had."

"Oh! My! God! This bread is…"

"Good? Bad? Or what?" He frowned.

"As good as the steak. What did you do to it?"

"That's my secret. I whip real butter, and like the good KFC Colonel does to his chicken, I add herbs and spices. And you won't find the recipe in Granny's cookbooks. I don't give it away."

She blushed. "And what happens if a woman wants bread and you don't want to give it to her?"

"We still talking about this bread?" His grin widened.

"Of course."

"Then I suppose she will simply have to go hungry."

A smile tickled the corners of Austin's wide mouth as she ate her dinner. She chewed slowly even though she was so hungry she wanted to wolf it all down and then fight him for what was left on his plate.

"Tell me how you came to live in Terral, anyway," she said.

"My mother's brother, Uncle Terrance, lived out in west Texas. He'd inherited a farm from one of their uncles back when he was about twenty. Long story short, he was out rounding up cattle one day and was coming down a small rise when his horse tumbled and his foot hung up in the saddle. He couldn't get out and the horse rolled on him. A rib pierced his heart and he died instantly."

"I'm sorry. Were you close to him?"

"I went every summer and stayed a couple of weeks with him. When I was a teenager, I worked summers for him. I was twenty-five when he died, and he left everything he owned to me. I didn't want to live in west Texas so I sold his ranch and used the money to buy this one. There was an old house sitting right here but I tore it down, used the same electric and water lines to hook up my trailer, and moved his cattle all up here."

"So you just raise Angus?" Anything to keep her mind off that broad chest and the barbed-wire tat on his arm.

"That's what I raise for beef cattle. I also ride bulls and keep rodeo stock and in the summer I'm in Mesquite, Texas, every weekend making a few dollars with them," he said.

"Did your Uncle Terrance do the rodeo stuff too?" Keep him talking about cows and bulls. Surely that wouldn't conjure up visions of her cheek lying on that barbed-wire tat.

Rye nodded. "Yes, he did. Only he was a bronc rider like

Raylen. I learned to pick out good bulls for rodeo from him, and he taught me a lot."

"How to make this bread?" She smiled brightly.

Rye's eyes twinkled. "You are a sly one but it won't work, Austin Lanier."

"Never underestimate me, Rye. I'm used to getting what I want whether it's by hard work or plain old good luck," she told him.

"And what do you want?"

"The recipe for what you dose up the butter with for this bread."

"Good luck. You'll need it."

"Fair enough. So you moved here ten years ago. That was when you were twenty-seven. What did you do before that?"

"Rode a few bulls. Finished high school. Went to college."

"What did you study?"

"Agribusiness. Finished college. Spent a year out on Uncle Terrance's place and decided I didn't like it out there. Did a few rodeo rounds, but I'm not as good as Dewar or Raylen. Made a few dollars though. Worked at an agribusiness center in Plano for a year but hated the city and couldn't wait to come home every Friday night. Was saving to buy my own place. Living cheap. Driving an old truck. Then I had the good luck to have a quick buyer on the west Texas property and I bought this place. Not much exciting. Just plain old living. Now tell me about you?"

"You already know about me. Granny kept you well informed. You said so yourself. Why did you choose a barbed-wire tat?"

"It's a long story. Only Gemma and I know the real reason."

She waited.

"Okay. My girlfriend dumped me. I was drunk and I decided to get a tat to remind myself never to trust another woman. On my left arm because that's where the vein is that runs from the finger to the heart according to the old wives' tale about why we wear wedding rings on our left hands."

"Why barbed wire?"

"At the time I decided to stretch barbed wire around the vein so that no woman would ever hurt me again. It was a symbol to never let anyone near my heart again."

"Have you?"

"Not yet," he lied. "How about you? Fellers?"

"A few."

"Serious?"

"A couple."

"Ever lived with one?"

She shook her head. "Never got that serious."

"Why? Are they stupid?"

"I tend to turn men off."

He cocked his head to one side and stared at the beautiful woman sitting across the table from him. Dark hair floating like strands of silk to her shoulders, eyes the blue of a summer sky with thick lashes, lips that begged to be tasted on an hourly basis. Were all the men in Tulsa brain-dead?

She took a deep breath and went on, hoping that she didn't get tangled up in her words. She couldn't remember the last time she'd gotten tipsy and wasn't sure what might happen.

"You'd think I was a blonde. You've heard all those blonde jokes. Well, most men seem to expect that kind of mentality from me. Mindless stupidity. They want a robot that looks like a movie star and performs in the kitchen like Rachael Ray and in the bedroom like a whorehouse madam. By the second date they realize I'm none of the above and they walk me to the door, give me a peck on the cheek, and I never hear from them again."

Rye finished the last bite of steak and asked, "And the two who did call back?"

"One in college. We were in our rebellious years and that was our connection. When I settled down to study for my master's, he went on to the next rebellious girl. The other was a workaholic just like me. We had everything in common on a business plane but no actual vibes on a physical level. You'd make any woman a wonderful wife the way you can cook. You think you'll ever find a woman you can trust?"

"Never know. I might. I did once but Granny was too old for me. She said so herself when I proposed." Rye reached over to a chair pushed up beside the grill and touched a button on the top of a portable CD player. A country piano and drumbeat started; then Hank Locklin began singing "Please Help Me, I'm Falling." Rye stood up and held out his hand. "May I have this dance, please, ma'am?"

"Dinner and dancing too. This *is* a date," she said.

"Yes, it is. Did you have a doubt that it was?"

She shrugged and melted into his arms, her face on his chest where she could hear his heart doing double time. She started with one hand around his neck and the other in his hand. Before Hank finished the first song and George Jones began singing, "Walk through This World with Me," she had both arms around his neck and he had her hugged up to him with his hands on the small of her back. The porch became a dance floor and the deck the best honky-tonk she'd ever set foot inside.

"Where did you find a CD like this?"

"One of those things on television. You know those 'Get this for only nineteen ninety-nine—but wait! There's more!' Well, I ordered this box called *Lifetime of Country Romance*. It's all the oldies."

They danced through another song, and then Willie Nelson began singing "Georgia on My Mind." She and Rye were swaying and moving their feet very little by then. She would have gladly stayed in that vertical position until eternity. It was peace wrapped in wanton desire, heat and angel wings rolled into one.

Rye was afraid to stop dancing for fear she'd go home, and he didn't want to ever let go of her. Willie sang about how an old sweet song kept Georgia on his mind. Well, that CD would always put Austin on his mind. He shut his eyes and inhaled the sweet coconut smell of her shampoo.

"Tired?" he asked.

"Not at all. I haven't danced in years. Is that Johnny and June? I haven't heard this song in years," she said.

"It's 'If I Were a Carpenter.' Someday I'll get the family to sing it and we'll dance on the grass in our bare feet," he said.

His warm breath on her neck weakened her knees and made her glad she could lean on him. "Oh, my Lord, is that Ray Price? Daddy loved him. Momma hates country music so it was a fight in our house. Daddy finally kept his music in the den and listened to it after she went up to bed."

Austin leaned back when the song ended and looked up at Rye. His eyes were all dreamy and soft and she was drawn to them like a moth to blazing flame. It was a dangerous situation and the closer she got, the hotter the fire, but it was so intriguing she had to see what it was all about. Her gaze had shifted to his lips and hers parted slightly just thinking about a long, lingering steamy kiss.

Rye could have gone swimming in her crystal-clear blue eyes. Hell, he could have gone skinny-dipping in them and stayed there until his hair turned gray. He knew he was a goner when he looked at her lips. If it had meant hanging from the nearest oak tree for kissing her, he'd have put the noose around his neck and gotten ready to hear his neck snap.

The kiss was a completely out-of-control wildfire. Austin couldn't hear for the buzzing in her ears. She parted her lips and nipped his lower lip gently, tasting the remains of the steak and watermelon wine. She felt as if she were drowning and couldn't breathe, and she didn't give a damn. Drunk. Sober. Somewhere in between or over the top, it didn't matter. She belonged in his arms and his lips belonged on hers. Simple as that.

Rye's heart was thumping in his ears like a bass drum. His tongue eased past her lips and tasted watermelon wine. It was even headier than what he'd drunk out of the glass. He'd hit the repeat button and the CD started over again with Hank Locklin asking her to close the door to temptation. Well, it was damn sure too late for that to happen. If Austin closed the door to temptation now, he'd kick the damn thing down with his bootheel.

He picked her up like a bride and carried her into the house, where they both collapsed on the sofa. In between heart-stopping kisses, he untied the knot in the shirt and ran his hand up her naked back, hugging her up against him so tight she could barely breathe.

"We shouldn't," she whispered.

"I know," he answered but didn't stop.

His callused hands touching her bare skin caused a flooding desire that she couldn't and didn't want to stop. She didn't care if they shouldn't; there was no way she wouldn't, not at that point. She could feel the heat and hardness of his desire pressing against her belly, and she knew she was driving him as crazy as she felt. Her panties were so wet she wanted to squirm right out of them, and as she ground her hips against him, a moan escaped her lips. In that moment, his bare hand teased its way up her spine and his fingers fumbled with the fastening of her bra.

Her skin was silky satin to his rough hands. In a flash, he understood addicts if they wanted drugs as badly as he wanted to touch every inch of her body. He was unhooking her bra and panting against her throat when the phone rang.

"Ignore it," she said breathlessly.

He tasted her earlobe. "I intend to." She threw her head back to give him access to her throat and felt his tongue rasping against her collarbone as their hips pressed hard against each other.

Four rings later, the answering machine picked up. "Rye, this is Kent. Don't know where you are but I'm about a mile from your house. Two of your rodeo bulls are out of the fence and on the road. I tried your cell phone but it went to voicemail and I left a message. I'll be there in five minutes, so if you're in the shower, get your britches on. We've got to get those bulls in before they get into Miz Verline's garden. Her granddaughter will kill you grave-yard dead, man, if those bulls tear up her vegetables."

Rye groaned and rolled off the sofa. "Damn it!"

"Estefan would kill you if the garden was ruined. Verline's granddaughter would rather kill the bulls." Austin buttoned her shirt, retied it, and stepped out onto the deck cussing the whole way. *Damn it all!* Verline had probably come back as a ghost and spooked those damned bulls so bad they broke through the barbed-wire fence and were swimming across the Red River into Texas. Why would she do that? Bring her to Terral, let her find the wine, and then spook the bulls so she couldn't have Rye?

Rye switched on a lamp and headed down the hall to the bath-room. He didn't even know that she'd unsnapped his shirt until he noticed it in the mirror as he washed his face with icy water. He quickly fastened it back and was in the living room when Kent knocked on the door and popped his head inside.

"Anybody home?" he yelled.

Austin poked her head in the sliding doors. "What shall I do with the leftover salad? Oh, hello, Kent."

"Sorry to interrupt your dinner but there's bulls out of the fence," Kent said.

"I'm sorry, Austin. Just leave it all." Damn, the woman was good. Anyone would think that they'd been on the deck the whole time and he'd come in for a bathroom break.

Austin tried to put an innocent look on her face. "Are you sure? You cooked. I don't mind cleanup. Can I help get in the bulls?"

"Naw, we'll take care of it, ma'am." Kent blushed.

"Okay, then I'm going home. Thanks for supper. Good night," Austin said.

"Good night. I'll see you tomorrow then?" Rye winked.

"I'll be in the fields all day," she said.

"And we'll be fixing fence for sure," Rye said.

Austin kicked her flip-flops off at the door, slid down the back of it, and sighed. Was it the kisses that made her dizzy or the wine or the combination of the two? Whatever had done it, it sure enough had the whole room rolling like one of those little airplanes that takes tourists up for a ride.

Two bulls would be hamburger meat if she had her way right then. "Maybe it was an omen," she whispered into the dark room. "Another five minutes and his house would have been one big bonfire. Kent could have used it to barbecue those two rodeo bulls."

She forced her still-weak knees to carry her to the bathroom, where she peeled off her clothes and giggled. If Verline knew what she'd been doing in that shirt and capris, she would pass little green crab apples. Austin turned on the shower above the old claw-footed tub and pulled the curtain around on the oval rod. She took an icy shower and wrapped herself snuggly in her grandmother's terry robe that hung on the back of the door.

Bending down, she picked up the shirt she'd worn, shut her eyes, and inhaled deeply. Steaks, wine, and his shaving lotion. She held it to her bare breast and carried it to the bedroom where she found Blake Shelton's "That's What I Call Home" on her phone, and waltzed around the floor, eyes shut again, the shirt held close to her chest.

Blake sang about a little house made of nails and wood, a place that he called home. He said it was a place where the world couldn't touch him anymore. She two-stepped to the bathroom and listened to the song again. She sashayed back to the bedroom where she fell back on the bed and curled up with the shirt beside her head on the pillow.

She fell asleep and dreamed of Rye.

It was past midnight when Kent and Rye got the two rangy old rodeo bulls herded into the pasture and the break in the fence repaired. Kent fanned his face with his sweat-stained cowboy hat. Rye leaned against the side of the pickup truck and wiped sweat from his forehead with the tail of his shirt. He caught a whiff of her perfume, something sensually floral that conjured up a vision of a field of white daisies.

"So now that we got them devils where they belong, tell me about your date tonight. Leave it to a bunch of bulls to ruin it for you," Kent said.

"Nothing to tell," Rye said.

"Which means you ain't goin' to kiss and tell." Kent laughed.

Rye shrugged.

"You trying to use your good looks to get at that land, or did you fall for that girl the first time you saw her in that booth?" Kent asked.

"You're as bad as my sisters," Rye said with a tired chuckle.

"You ain't goin' to answer me so I'm going home to get a shower. I feel like it's already July. Them critters can give a man a workout, can't they? And leave your phone turned on. If Tom Walters had been able to get ahold of you, he wouldn't have called me."

Rye swiped at his face one more time and inhaled Austin's scent on his shirtsleeve. He crawled up in the passenger's seat of Kent's bright-red Dodge truck and almost fell asleep before they made it two miles to his house.

"See you in the morning. Evidently we'd best do some more fence repair," Kent said.

"Hey, thanks for taking the call and for the help. Why don't you take tomorrow morning off and we'll start at noon? That'll make up for the hours you spent here tonight," Rye said.

Kent shook his head. "No thanks. I'll use the hours another time. Maybe when Momma needs one of her therapy things down at the hospital or a treatment. I'd rather get that fence taken care of proper than have to put in another night like this. Besides, it's cooler in the morning time."

"Okay, then I'll see you about eight." Rye opened the door and headed for the house with an over-the-shoulder wave.

He stripped in the bathroom, throwing his dirty jeans and socks in the hamper. If Austin had been there when he returned, they'd be showering together. Imagining her in the tight little shower with him caused a physical desire that made him realize he had to rein in his wild thoughts or it would be a long, aching night.

"I'm too tired for more than one cold shower," he mumbled as he washed his hair.

He turned the water off when he finished bathing and wrapped a towel around his waist. He padded barefoot to the kitchen, poured a tall glass of cold milk, downed it all before he came up for air, and then remembered the dishes on the patio.

"I'm too tired to deal with that now," he said. "Damned old bulls, anyway. If they'd minded their business, she would be curled up in my arms and we'd be making love again after a long, long bout of lovemaking."

He tossed the towel into the hamper on his way to his bedroom and fell into the bed. When he shut his eyes, he envisioned her moving slowly around the porch as they danced to the old tunes. He dreamed of the two of them lying on a soft blanket in a field of daisies where there were no phones or bulls to get out of the pasture.

CHAPTER 8

AUSTIN WAS EXPECTING TO PLANT WATERMELONS ON Monday morning so she was surprised on Saturday when Felix knocked on the door as she was having her morning coffee. The sun was barely up and she'd slept poorly, but at six o'clock she'd gotten up and made coffee and eaten a piece of toast.

"Miz Austin, it's time," Felix said.

"For what?"

"The weather is good. The fields are ready and we've wasted five days. We should start planting today even though it's not Monday. The tractors and the seeders are ready but Miz Verline always planted the first seed in each row by hand for good luck. You need to come with us this morning," Felix answered.

"Go ahead, Felix. I've got a ton of work to do in here."

He shook his head. "It's for good luck and a good crop."

"Oh, okay. I'll get dressed."

"Yes, ma'am. We'll wait on the porch."

"How long is this going to take?" she asked.

"All day."

She bit back a moan.

"All day every day this week and next," he said.

"But I've got all this packing to do."

His narrow shoulders drew upward in a shrug. "We usually quit at dark so you would have the evenings, yes?"

"What time do you start?"

"Six thirty."

"So I'd have a little while every evening."

"Yes, ma'am."

She nodded. "Give me ten minutes to get dressed."

She tossed her pajamas on the metal footboard of the bed, donned her grandmother's button-down chambray shirt and overalls, and wished she had a pair of work boots. Her running shoes would have to do since she couldn't wear flip-flops or spike heels to the fields.

She didn't even bother with a brush but finger combed her hair into a ponytail and secured it with a rubber band. She did take time to apply sunscreen to her face and bare arms. Plant the first seed? What exactly did that mean? And what the hell was a seeder?

"You can ride in the front seat with me." Felix led the way to the old work truck where five men sat in the back.

At one time it had been blue but nowadays very little color could be seen among the splotches of primer where Felix had sanded off the rust and sprayed it primer gray. The bench front seat was covered with a multicolored striped serape, and the directional letters on the floor gearshift had long since faded away. But when Felix turned the key, the motor purred like a something new right off the showroom floor.

"You take care of this truck?" Austin asked.

"Yes, I do. Miz Verline trusted me with it when she bought it brand new the first year I came to work here almost fifty years ago. The engine is easy to take care of. The outside, though, it's *hijo de puta*!"

"What?" she asked.

"Son of bitch." He grinned.

She laughed. "I see."

"Miz Verline bought a new one, and now this is the old work truck. But the new one won't ever see the years and miles this one has. It's not built as well. We are here. We start on this end and work our way east toward the hog pens and the garden. A quarter of a mile down the road, a mile toward the river each day is what we like to get done."

He stopped the truck and the rest of the crew bailed. Three

men crawled up into the seats of the green John Deere tractors and fired them up. Austin stood at the end of the freshly plowed field that went toward the river. The furrows were straight as a ruler, mounded up into peaks, reminding her of tiny mountains and valleys.

Felix handed her a hoe handle that had been sharpened on one end. "You will poke a hole in this mound right here and drop a seed in it, then tap the dirt over it with your boot."

That didn't sound so hard. Any monkey could do that job, and it wouldn't even have to be trained. Austin drove the hoe handle down into the earth about six inches and looked up to see Felix shaking his head.

"A watermelon seed should only be planted twice the depth of the seed. That would be less than half an inch." He kicked the hole full of dirt. "Look at the end of the stick. It has a mark on it. That's how deep to make the hole."

She held up the stick and sure enough there was a notch about half an inch up on the pointed end. She carefully poked it to the right depth and Felix handed her a small brown paper bag with watermelon seeds in it. She dropped one and missed, bent over, put it where it belonged, and covered it with a handful of dirt.

Felix smiled again. "You'll get better. Miz Verline could drop that seed and the angels took it right in the hole, then she'd use her toe to cover it up. The seeds are top quality. She said that only the best seed could make the best melons. When we get to the land right behind the house, that's where we use the best of the best. That land is for her wine melons and she told me once that she goes out at night and tells those melons stories."

"I thought she put the wine melons up near the cow and hog lots," Austin said, remembering her notes.

"For years she did; then she decided to move them behind her house just last year. I think she did not have the energy to go that far to tell them the stories. I'll take the next shift on the tractors, but I always walk with Miz Verline and we talk at the beginning of the first day of planting."

"Then that's what we'll do. I want to know all about watermelons. Making wine fascinates me."

"You have to have good melons to make good wine, and that's why the acre right behind her house is for the wine melons."

"Only one acre?"

"One melon makes about a gallon of wine. Now think about a whole acre of melons and how much they would make. Sometimes she would cut open a melon, taste it, and throw it out because it wasn't sweet enough."

Austin sighed. "But I don't know by taste what is sweet enough."

"Rye does. He's been over here when she was throwing them out. He can help you and you will learn fast."

Why did he have to mention Rye's name? It had taken her hours to cool down and even longer to go to sleep. Then she'd slept poorly, dreaming of Rye and waking up wanting to feel his hands on her body, to finish what had gotten started on his sofa.

Damn it, Granny! Did you really have something to do with that?

She'd finished the twelfth furrow and was starting for the next one when he raised a hand. "Not yet."

"Why?"

"Because the tractors have not come back. When they get ready to plant another row, then you can do the next ones. That's the way she did it for good luck. The tractors go down the land, two furrows at a time. Then they come back to us, the same: three tractors, two furrows each. Three men to drive. Two men to walk along and make sure the seeds are falling just right. Sometimes they have to stop and readjust or sometimes the chain doesn't quite cover the seed and they have to do a little bit by hand. Most of the melon farmers don't do that but Miz Verline said that she wasn't paying for high-dollar seed to let it become bird food."

"And this is the way she did it every single year?" Austin asked.

Felix nodded.

"Some of the others are starting the seeds early in greenhouses. Miz Verline said that was crazy so we still do it the old way. Put the seed in the ground and hope for good rain," Felix said.

"Why would it be crazy?"

"The good thing is that you get a two-week jump on the crop if you plant transplants rather than seeds. The bad thing is that when you handle the tiny plant you can bruise the roots and it will die, so you've lost the money on that seed. Or the worst thing is that one plant will get disease in the greenhouse and it will spread to all the rest. Then you've lost many, many dollars in seed and have to go back and buy more."

Austin did the calculations in her head: three hundred dollars an acre for seed. Multiply that by almost two thousand acres and it would become a huge risk for a two-week jump on the crop.

Felix went on. "And you've got to use different equipment to put the plants in the ground than she already owned for the seeds."

"How long until these seeds come up?"

"Ten days for most. We'll see some early ones at six days. But in ten days these will be tiny shoots. Then what we do tomorrow will come up and right on down the land to the end. When we start the harvest it will go the same way. We'll start in this field and work our way down. If me and the boys can't handle the load, we hire young boys from town to help us but most years we have our way of doing things and we don't need extra help."

"When I was little I always came in June and she talked about the watermelon festival or jubilee or something like that in the middle of July. Is that about when you start the harvest?"

Felix nodded and looked at his watch. "There they are. They did good. No trouble on this turn around. The harvest is almost done by the time they have their watermelon party in town. Miz Verline always donated half a truckload of melons for the day.

They give away slices of cold melons all day down in the middle of town. It's on a Saturday, and we go back to Mexico that next week."

The three drivers hoped off the tractors and Felix, Jacinto, and Lobo got on. Angelo and Estefan walked behind the machinery and Lobo went back to the truck. Austin made her twelve holes, planted a dozen seeds, and then sat down at the end of the last row and waited.

Two trucks stirred up road dust when they passed behind her. The dry dust and the warm sun made her wish she'd had the foresight to bring a bottle of water. She wondered what Rye was doing that morning. Was planting pasture grass for bulls as time consuming as getting a watermelon crop in the ground?

"Good morning!"

She jumped and spun around to see Rye walking toward her in long strides. She looked around for his truck but it wasn't anywhere.

When he was close enough that she could smell his aftershave, he stopped and smiled. His grin and bedroom hair that hadn't seen even a good finger combing made her heart skip a beat. He wore a knit shirt that stretched over his broad chest, faded jeans, and a plain belt without a big bull rider buckle. His boots were scuffed and worn and she had trouble keeping her eyes from traveling up and down the length of him over and over again. He was even sexier in his work clothes than he'd been all decked out in starched jeans and dress boots.

"Looks like they talked you into being Granny today."

"I thought you were fixing fence today."

"I always come around on the first day of the planting to watch for a while. Brought you some coffee."

She hadn't noticed anything in his hands, but a small silver thermos appeared out of nowhere. He poured a cup for her and sat down in the dirt beside her. "Things going good so far?"

She sipped. "Good coffee."

A cool morning breeze brushed across her face but her insides were as hot and steamy as the coffee.

He threw an arm around her shoulder and squeezed. "Figured you'd be ready for something. This is boring work but Granny always said it was necessary. If she was out here amongst the hired help, they knew she wasn't afraid to get her hands dirty or to sweat. One year only five could get a visa so she drove a tractor all summer. I tried to get her to let me do it but she told me to go home and raise cows. If I touched her watermelons with the smell of bovine on my hands, it would be bad luck. I'm sorry about last night. I wanted to slaughter some bulls before the night was over."

"So am I."

"Want to take up where we left off?"

He'd heard about soul mates and first love and all that folderol but he'd always thought it was fairy-tale material. It didn't really happen except in old people's minds that were afflicted with dementia and couldn't remember all the fighting and fussing they'd done in their married lives. The way he felt sitting there in the dirt with his arm around Austin changed his mind.

"Right here at the end of a watermelon field?" She laughed.

"Anywhere. Anytime." He grinned.

"I don't think so, cowboy. You are wicked!"

He made tiny little circles on her arm with his callused hand. She'd never realized a rough hand could be so damn sexy.

"You were thinking the same thing I was. I saw it written on your face like those bubble things above cartoon people. So you staying out here all day like she did?"

"I have a poker face. You can't read me that well, Rye O'Donnell. And yes, I'm staying out here all day, and tomorrow and the next day after that. Something tells me that Granny would rather I did this and hire all the packing done. Next time I'm walking behind the tractor. I need the exercise. That'll be as good as a morning run."

He hugged her tightly for a second, then stood up. "Have fun. I'm off to Nocona to buy barbed wire. Need anything?"

She felt empty without his arm around her. "You and Felix would know more about that than I would."

"They've got the garden in the ground, and she has her watermelon seeds sent from a special place. Prepays for them a year in advance so you'll need to find that invoice and talk to them about next year's crop."

Austin nodded. "Where is the garden?"

"Up by the hog lot where it's always been. But she got rid of the hogs and the steers when she took sick. Just take the thermos home with you. Want to grab supper at the Peach Orchard tonight? We could go to Duncan or Wichita Falls, but Kent and I'll be fixin' fence until dark and it'd be late. Maybe we can plan on a Friday date," he said.

"Are you tellin' or askin'?"

He grabbed her hand and brought her fingertips to his lips. "Miss Austin Lanier, would you please have dinner with me tonight and Friday night?"

"That sounds like fun. I bet after today I'm too tired to go to Duncan or Wichita Falls anyway," she said.

The tractors roared into sight and Rye waved at Felix and was gone before the three men slid out of the seats and headed toward the truck which Lobo had pulled up close to where they'd parked. All of them went for the big orange cooler in the bed of the truck and filled a water bottle. They drank deeply and traded places. Lobo got on one tractor, Angelo stayed with the truck, and Felix fell into place behind the tractor.

"I'm going with you as soon as I get these twelve seeds into the ground," Austin said.

"It's a pretty fast pace, keeping up with the tractors," Felix said.

"I'm used to running three miles every evening. I've missed two nights. I need the exercise."

"Then I'll send Estefan to hoe the garden." Felix spoke rapidly in his native tongue to one of the hired hands, who grinned and nodded. Then he yelled at Angelo and pointed east.

"Can I drive the tractor next time?" Austin asked.

"It is your land and your tractor, Miss Austin," Felix said.

They didn't exactly walk but they didn't jog. It was more like a canter that gave Austin more of a workout than any morning run she'd ever done. She was back and forth hopping her six furrows like short hurdles, and Felix did the same on his side. Twice on the mile-long trip out to the end of the field, Austin had to bend over and push a little dirt over a seed. Three times on the way back a clump of hard dirt prevented the chain on the seeder from filling the hole and she had to stop long enough to cover the watermelon seed. When they finished the two-mile journey, she understood why they switched places.

"You really want to drive?" Felix asked.

"I really want a long drink of water and then yes, I'd like to try," she answered.

Felix barked orders to adjust for another driver and told Angelo to leave Estefan at the garden. "He likes it there better anyway."

"Rye said you have planted a garden since you've been here?"

Felix chuckled. "Oh, yes. We do that every year. Estefan likes the garden work. He's like a woman with her kitchen. He doesn't want anyone else in the garden."

"Then leave him there today and I'll take his place. Maybe I won't tear things up too badly on the tractor."

"Just keep the wheels between the furrows. The machinery will do the rest. I'll put you on the middle tractor. Keep pace with the other two and you will be fine."

She thought about Rye as she bounced along in the seat. The man made her hot as hell just throwing an arm around her shoulders, but there was no future in Terral and she really shouldn't encourage something that wouldn't last. But when he was around, she threw caution to the wind like tossing out yesterday's garbage. Her pulse picked up when he was in sight, and when he touched her, she felt like the world stood still.

But what if I don't care about a future? I could have a few romps with the cowboy. I don't have to spend every waking minute sorting through boxes! However, if I did have a romp in the hay with the sexy cowboy, something tells me it would haunt me every day no matter where I was. So it's a no-win situation. How can a woman's life get so mixed up in one week?

"Damn!" She swore under her breath. For a town with fewer than four hundred people, Terral had sure made her life one complicated mess in a short time.

The day went fast and Austin barely had time to wash the red dirt out of her hair before Rye knocked on the door. She wore another pair of her grandmother's capris that night. Red ones this time with a red-and-white-striped knit shirt and red flip-flops. She really did need to go shopping, but where did a watermelon farmer find time for that?

"Don't you look all spiffy," Rye said when she opened the door.

His black hair had water droplets hanging on the long parts that brushed his collar, and his eyes were twinkling. His jeans weren't starched stiff but looked soft and his boots were clean but worn.

"You look pretty damn fine yourself," she said.

"The city girl cusses. Terral water is getting to you. You get the quota in today?" He threw his arm around her shoulders and escorted her, hugged up to his side, to the truck. It brought on the sparks but it also felt natural, as if his soul had found what it had been searching for.

"I cuss in the city, too, so don't blame it on the water. Felix said we did good. We didn't quit until half an hour ago."

He opened the door and she slid into the seat.

"How about you?" she asked.

"Walked five miles of fence and fixed what had to be restrung.

Kent was whining that next time I offered him half a day off he'd take it." He laughed.

He was glad that he didn't have to ride in another rodeo that week and could spend every free minute with Austin.

They sat in the same booth that she and Pearlita had occupied the day they had taken her grandmother's ashes to the river, but they were the only ones in the dining room. Their knees touching under the table created enough sparks to fry the fish in the kitchen. He reached across the table and brushed a strand of hair back behind her ear so he could see her blue eyes better in the dim light.

"I hate to say this but I'm almost too tired to chew," he said with a sigh.

"Me too. How on earth did Granny keep up with all this at her age?"

"She was made of tougher stock. I swear that Depression thing they went through when they were kids made them tough as nails."

The waitress appeared at their table with two glasses of water. "What can I get y'all tonight?"

"A full order of chicken strips and whatever beer you've got that's cold," Austin said.

"Full order of fish and bring us two Coors in the bottle, long-necks," Rye said.

"It's pitiful to be so hungry and not have the energy to chew," Austin said.

"Maybe food will revive your spirits." He wanted more than her spirits revived. He wanted her to be as eager to fall into bed with him as he was with her, but it wasn't happening that night. When it did, it wouldn't be a slam-bam-thank-you-ma'am thing but an evening that she'd remember forever.

The waitress brought their beers and two glasses. Rye tipped his back and drank from the bottle. Austin did the same.

"Damn, that's good," she said when she came up for air.

"After a long day, it's tough to beat a cold Coors."

She looked at the branding irons hanging on the wall. Each had a plaque under them with the brand burned into the wood, showing what it would look like on the cattle. Cowhide fabric covered with clear plastic served as table coverings. A roll of paper towels on each table was used for napkins because most of the greasy food was eaten with fingers. The menu was written in giant letters and hung on the wall on the east and west ends of the room.

Other than the table coverings, the place had looked the same back when she was a little girl and came to visit her grandmother. Back then, the tables were covered in red-and-white-checked oil cloth. It was comforting in an odd sense of the word to find a world where things stayed the same. That must have been what her father was running from, what her mother couldn't abide, and what her grandmother loved. But where was Austin in all that? Was she running from it or toward it?

"Yours up there?" she asked.

"Not yet but it will be someday."

"Why not yet?"

"I haven't brought one in here."

"What's it look like?"

He rolled a paper towel from the holder. "Got a pen in your purse?"

She dug around until she found one with her company logo and handed it to him.

He drew an R with a rocker under it.

"The Rocking R?"

"That's right. It wasn't registered in Oklahoma so it's my brand."

The waitress returned and set baskets of food in front of them and a plate between them with onions, tartar sauce, and bread. "Y'all need anything else, just holler. We still got coconut pie and German chocolate."

Rye looked at Austin who thought about it a second, then said, "Coconut."

"Two of that," he said.

They ate slowly, talked little, but enjoyed every single spark that danced between them that Saturday night. When he took her home, he walked her to the door, fenced her in with an arm on each side of the door, and kissed her hard and passionately.

"Revived?" she asked.

"Not quite, but I'm workin' on it."

She pulled his lips to hers for another searing kiss.

"Picnic on the river tomorrow night? Maybe neither of us will be dog-tired," she said when she broke away.

He leaned in and their lips met again for a kiss that caused fireworks to explode in her head. "Then tomorrow at dusk? What do I bring?"

"Yourself. This time I do the honors," she said.

"I'll see you then." He kissed her on each eyelid, on the nose, and added one more on the lips after each word.

She slept late on Sunday, did laundry in the afternoon, checked the window several times to see if Rye had moved his truck, and finally picked up the phone at two o'clock and called him.

"Are you alive?" she asked when he answered.

"I'm catching up on housework and laundry. Are we still on for the picnic?"

"Oh, yes. What's your favorite dessert?"

"Your kisses," he said.

"Other than that?" A country song called "Long Slow Kisses" by Jeff Bates played through her mind as she waited on his answer.

"Chocolate cake," he said.

"Okay, then chocolate cake and kisses," she said, laughing.

She made half a recipe of chocolate cake, fried a chicken, and made potato salad that afternoon. She packed it, along with a loaf of French bread and a block of Colby Jack cheese, into a basket with two plastic plates, silverware, napkins, and two chilled bottles of watermelon wine. She found a blanket in the top of the closet in her room and tucked it under her arm. When Rye drove across the road, she was waiting on the front porch.

He wrapped her up in his big arms and kissed her when he walked up on the porch. "Staying across the road and doing my Sunday chores was the hardest thing I've done in my life," he whispered into her hair when he broke away from the kiss.

"I've looked forward to this all day too," she said.

He stepped back, grabbed both her hands, and took her in from black flip-flops to cutoff jean shorts, a tied-up shirt that showed skin above the jeans' waist, and cute little black-and-white polka-dot earrings. "You are gorgeous."

"Thank you. Now it's my turn."

She started at his sandals, then moved from jean shorts that grazed his knee and a gray muscle shirt to his freshly shaven face and twinkling eyes to his hair, combed straight back and still too long.

"You are sexy as hell."

He grinned. "Thank you. Never had a woman tell me that when I was dressed for the river, though."

"Well I never had a man tell me I was gorgeous in hand-me-down cutoff jeans and flip-flops," she said.

"Were they all blind or just stupid?"

She laughed and the clouds parted. Rye O'Donnell was in heaven.

He drove to the river and carried the basket to the sandbar. She flipped the blanket out under a weeping willow tree and sat down on it. He dropped the basket and joined her, sitting close enough that their bare legs touched. The sizzle was right there, but Rye felt like they had all the time in the world and there was no hurry at all. They had all night and then some, if he had anything to say about it.

"It's nice out tonight. I'm starving," she said.

He opened the basket and his eyes widened. "Fried chicken, plates, and is that really chocolate cake?"

"From scratch with fudge icing."

"Will you marry me?"

"You're not on one knee and you don't have a ring," she teased, but her heart skipped a beat when he said those magic-sounding words.

She took out the plates, cutlery, and napkins and then the chicken, potato salad, bread, and cheese. She handed him a knife.

"To slice the cheese."

"You remembered everything. This ain't your first picnic, is it?"

"No. Granny packed a picnic of peanut-butter sandwiches and chocolate milk in a quart jar for me and Pearl when we were little and let us come to the river. She sat under the trees far enough away to make sure we didn't do anything stupid like skinny-dip in the river, and we thought we were the luckiest two little girls in the world."

"I feel like that tonight," he said softly.

She looked up in time to see his lips coming toward hers and shut her eyes so she could enjoy every sensation that the kiss would bring. She wasn't the least bit disappointed as he slowly, perfectly pressed his warm lips to hers and pressed gently, gently until she opened for him and their tongues tangled. He ran his hand up her back, and her body heated up twenty degrees.

"Your kisses turn me inside out, but I'm starving," she said.

His eyes twinkled. "Eat for energy for what comes later."

"Something like that." She forked a wing and a leg and bit into the chicken leg while he sliced cheese.

He broke tidbits from a slice and fed them to her, then licked the grease from the chicken from her fingertips, lingering on each one long enough to send electricity all the way down to her curling toes. "That's a wonderful way to eat chicken," he said.

"Even better than the gravy and fries?"

"Better location and I don't have to stop with just one taste. It's like having a one-inch bite of good steak or having a whole one right there on your plate," he whispered.

"So I'm just a chunk of steak?" she teased.

"Darlin', you are..." He paused and kissed her passionately. "There are no words for what you are. God didn't create them yet, but when He does, I'll tell you exactly what you are to me."

They managed to eat their supper between more slow, hot kisses, and then they started on the second bottle of wine. They'd each had a glass from it when the pickup load of teenagers invaded the sandbar right in front of them. The kids had two six-packs of beer and a couple of fishing poles: three boys and three girls who didn't even see Rye and Austin sitting back in the shadows of the weeping willow. The teens pretended to fish but mostly the boys chased the girls in and out of the edge of the water and teased them about going skinny-dipping.

"Ever done that?" Rye asked.

"Not with a boy."

He raised an eyebrow. "Girl?"

"Pearl and I were about nine or ten. We got in big trouble but we didn't have bathing suits on and we wanted to go swimming." She smiled.

"They won't stay long. Lie down here beside me in the crook of my arm. We'll snuggle while they act like normal teenagers."

She plastered herself to his side. He kissed her forehead. She laid her head on his chest. He undid the knot in her shirt above her belly button and made slow, lazy circles with his fingertips on her back. The tension eased out with each circle, and pretty soon she was asleep on his chest.

He smiled and shut his eyes. The kids would get bored and leave soon.

It was three o'clock in the morning when he awoke with a start to find a raccoon staring at him from the edge of the blanket. It had snagged what was left over of the bread and was having its own picnic.

"Hey, darlin', you'd better wake up. It must've been the wine, but we fell asleep and it's only a few hours until sunup." He kissed Austin awake.

"Mmmm," she mumbled. "Did they leave?"

"Hours ago. It's three in the morning."

She sat straight up with a start. "We've got to go home, Rye. I've got to plant watermelons at six thirty."

"I know, darlin'."

"What is that?" She pointed at the raccoon.

"A thief. I'll help you get the leftovers packed up unless you want to leave them for the old boy."

She shook the cobwebs from her head. "That was some good wine."

He tossed everything but the cake out toward the raccoon and repacked the basket. She folded the blanket and they went back to the truck, arm in arm, like an old married couple.

But she didn't feel married. She felt cheated and determined that she wouldn't drink another bottle of wine on a night when she had a chance to make Greta (or was it Molly?) pay up twenty dollars.

CHAPTER 9

BLACK CLOUDS COVERED THE SKY ALL MORNING ON MONDAY. The seeds already in the ground could use a good soaking, but muddy fields would keep them from finishing planting that day. Austin listened to country music loaded on her iPod when it was her turn to drive the tractor from one end of the field to the other and back again. The Judds were telling her about love that morning. She kept time with her thumb on the steering wheel and wiggled her head a few times when Naomi and Wynonna sang about moving the moon and stars above.

She'd made the turn at the end of the field and started back toward the road when her phone rang. She pulled it from the bib pocket of her grandmother's striped overalls, popped the music from her ears, and held the cell phone with one hand while she steered with other one.

"Hello."

"Austin, what is that noise? What are you doing?"

"Planting watermelons. This is my second day. I'm getting the hang of this tractor. I can even turn it around without tearing up half the field."

"You are what?" Her mother's scream made Austin jump, and she had to grab the wheel to keep from swerving out of the ruts.

"I'm planting watermelons. I decided to do this rather than use my time to pack. Just a minute. I've got to lay the phone down to turn this thing around. It takes both hands."

She slipped the phone back into her pocket, turned the tractor around, and dug the phone out again. "Okay, I'm back."

"Have you lost your mind? I swear, the closer a person gets to the Red River, the more brain cells they lose. Get off that tractor and come home. I'll pay someone to go down there and take care of the packing," Barbara said.

"Actually, I'm having a helluva lot of fun. I met this handsome hunk who lives across the road. Remember me telling you about Rye, the older gentleman across the road who I talked to on Thursdays for an update about the place?"

"Yes, what about him?"

"Well, I thought he was old and wondered how in the world an old man and I could talk every week and enjoy it so much. He's not old. He's thirty-two and handsome as hell. He's so sexy, he'd even melt Aunt Clydia's underpants, and I'm not even sure she's straight." Austin laughed.

"Damn it all to hell!"

"Momma, ladies do not swear."

"Well, they don't drive tractors or plant watermelons either. I worked my whole life to keep you out of that place, and all Verline does is die and you get on a damn tractor. If you aren't home by dinnertime, I'm coming after you."

Austin couldn't control the giggles. "Bring some work clothes. You can help plant watermelons. I don't think Granny's overalls will fit you. They're doing a fine job for me. I even wore her capris and a shirt from her closet over to Rye's for steaks, down to the Peach Orchard, and to the river for a picnic last night. He makes this most incredible bread you've ever eaten."

"Are you teasing me?"

"No, ma'am. I didn't bring anything but my spike heels and my running shoes down here. That wasn't too smart, was it? Anyway, my feet are a size bigger than Granny's but she has a whole bunch of those rubber flip-flops that fit me. Are you really coming down here? You'd love it in two days' time. It's so peaceful and you sleep like a baby at night."

"No, I'm not coming down there. I hate that place."

"I did too, but I'm learning to love it. With all this exercise, I can eat like a horse and not worry about my weight one bit."

"Promise me you'll come home immediately. We'll fly anywhere in the world you want to go. Want to go to Paris and shop for next season's clothes?" Barbara's tone softened.

Austin giggled again. "How about we go to Nocona to the western wear store and buy some boots and jeans and throw all our power suits in the river?"

Barbara gasped. "Are you on drugs?"

"No." Austin bit the inside of her lip to keep the giggles at bay. Not unless there was a brand-new drug out there called RO, short for Rye O'Donnell.

"Did you sleep with that cowboy?"

"Not yet."

"Are you coming home?"

"Not until I have to. Goodbye, Mother. Talk to you later." She hung up, finished out the row, and looked up to see Rye sitting on the side of the road in his truck.

"Hey," he called out the window. "I've got to drive to Nocona for some more barbed wire. Want to go with me and have lunch at the Dairy Queen?"

She looked at Felix.

He checked his watch and nodded. "It is dinner and siesta time. We'll start again about two o'clock."

"I'll be back by then." She pulled off her brown cotton work gloves, tossed them on the tractor seat, and got into the truck with Rye.

To Rye she was far sexier with a little bit of dirt on her face than she had been in that fancy black suit the first time he saw her. The woman might shape up to be a farmer after all.

"Well?" she asked. "Are we going or are we going to sit here all day?"

"Sorry, I was admiring the scenery."

She blushed. She'd been afraid it would be awkward between them with fall-out from the almost-sex but it wasn't. She didn't feel like there was an elephant in the truck with them. She glanced at him from her peripheral vision. His jeans had grass stains on the knees where he'd been kneeling to fix fence. His shirtsleeve had a tear up near the shoulder where the barbed wire had won at least one fight. Would that tat keep her out if she decided to make a run for his heart?

She'd never made out with a man with a tat until now. Just looking at the thing was exhilarating. The next time her mother called, she fully well intended to tell her about it. If she was reduced to unladylike cussing when she found out Austin was driving a tractor, just think what kind of words would flow from her mouth when she found out her daughter was having lunch at the Dairy Queen with a rancher with barbed wire tattooed around his arm.

They passed the school on the right. The children were out on the playground, running from swings to merry-go-round and playing chase and tag. Kids were the same at that age, whether they were playing in a schoolyard with five hundred of their classmates or ten.

"What's the school population these days?"

"It stays between fifty and sixty from what I hear from Kent. He's got a first grader and a second grader. Both boys. Wild as Apache Indians."

"That's for the whole school?"

Rye slowed down at the Highway 81 intersection and looked both ways before turning left. "First through eighth grade. High school is bused up to Ryan."

"That's only about seven or eight kids to the grade."

He nodded. "Kent's two are in the same grade. Teacher has first and second grade in the same room. I feel sorry for her. Those two boys could tear up an army tank with a chicken feather."

"I'd like to meet these two wildcats."

"You'd be taking your life in your own hands. Last time they came to my place, even the rodeo bulls were hunting a place to hide."

"Oh, come on, they can't be that bad."

"Invite them to a playday but don't tell Felix. He and the boys will leave you to work a watermelon farm by yourself. I'm telling you, those boys are ornery as hell." He crossed the river bridge into Texas.

"Two mean little boys who could tear up a John Deere tractor with a feather and who make big, old mean rodeo bulls climb trees to get away from them. Maybe those two bulls broke the fence trying to outrun them."

I know they didn't! I'm convinced that it was Granny keeping me from having sex with you. I haven't figured out why yet, but I will before I leave this place.

"I wouldn't be a bit surprised. Those boys probably snuck out of the house and chewed their way past the barbed-wire fence to get at my bulls."

"That's bullshit."

His laughter filled the truck and she smiled. She'd never worked so hard or played so hard in her life, and it felt so damned good. It wasn't going to be easy to give it all up.

They listened to the radio without talking on the twenty-minute trip to Nocona. Rye ushered her to the Dairy Queen with a hand on the small of her back. A thick layer of denim, a cotton shirt, and even cotton underpants didn't keep the touch from sending sizzling tingles up her spine.

"Hey, Rye, heard two of your rodeo bulls got out the other night. They didn't get hurt, did they? I'm bankin' on ridin' one down in Mesquite this summer," a cowboy said as they passed a table with eight chairs around it.

"They was hell to get corralled. Don't know why they broke the fence. Could've been a pack of coyotes feelin' their spring oats," Rye said.

"You goin' to be stingy, or you goin' to introduce us to your lady friend?"

Rye threw his arm around her shoulder and pulled her closer to his side. "This is Austin Lanier. She's been helping get a watermelon crop in the ground. And this is Rick and that other rodeo feller over there is Henry."

"Mighty pleased to make your acquaintance. Lanier? You'd be Verline's granddaughter, right?" Rick asked.

"That's right."

"Your granny was a fine woman. You goin' to keep runnin' that farm, or are you goin' to sell it?" Rick asked.

"Thank you. I haven't decided when or what just yet. Right now I'm just getting the crop into the ground."

"Well, you decide to sell, don't let Rye have it before you talk to me. I'll beat his price by a hundred an acre," Rick said.

Rye shot him a dirty look. "Why would you buy that land? Your ranch is here in Nocona."

"Maybe I want to dabble in watermelons. See if there's as much money in them as Verline always said."

"Lot of work is what there is in watermelons," Rye said.

"Hell of a lot of money in them too. Good crop can bring in a hundred thousand on good ground in a year."

Austin had seen the figures, and Verline's ground beat that most years. By the time she paid her help and paid for machinery upkeep, she still had a nice income. Add that to her wine income, and she made more than Austin did as an oil executive.

"Looks like it's our turn to order. See you at the rodeo. Old Diablo will give you a run for your money," Rye said.

"I'm lookin' forward to it and, Austin, you remember what I said."

Rye steered her to the counter where he ordered a double-meat double cheeseburger, large fries, and a Coke. Austin just told the waitress to double that.

"While you find us a booth, I'm going to wash up," she said. "I came right out of the field."

He nodded and reluctantly took his arm away. He waited to find a booth until she was out of sight, watching her move between tables and catching glimpses of men, old and young alike, staring at her as she passed.

Austin felt Rye's gaze as she crossed the smoking section and went right to the sink in the ladies' room. Knowing that he was watching her put an extra spring in her step and a smile on her face that she was almighty glad he couldn't see. The smile faded quickly when she looked in the mirror and gasped. She hoped she didn't smell as bad as she looked. Dirt on her face. Strands of hair had escaped her ponytail and stuck to a sweaty neck. A rim of dust had settled between the cuff of her long-sleeved shirt and where her gloves had stopped. She peeled off a handful of brown paper towels and did the best she could to make herself presentable. Without a purse, all she had to comb her hair with were her fingers, but she managed to get it all back up in the ponytail.

Her mother would do more than cuss if she saw her daughter out in public with no makeup and wearing running shoes that looked as if they'd never been white with a cute little pink swoosh on the side.

"It's a good thing that six hours separate us right now," she said to her reflection before she left the bathroom.

She found Rye already in the booth, talking across the room to another bunch of men who'd arrived since she left. She slid into her place and took a long drink of the Coke in a Styrofoam cup. It wasn't watermelon wine or even Coors beer, but it was pretty damn good.

"This is Oscar Johnson and his brother, Rich." Rye made introductions. Austin had washed the dirt from her face and redone her hair, but he thought she had been just as pretty with the smudge of dirt on her nose.

"Glad to know you. Knowed Verline my whole life. I was sorry when she died last winter. Heard you might put her farm up for sale," Oscar said.

"It'll be fall at the earliest before I put it on the market," Austin said.

"It's a good farm. Lots of people want that land so you shouldn't have any trouble sellin' it. Well, Rich, you ready to go collect them women at the drugstore? I reckon they've had enough time to have lunch with their Sunday school class," Oscar said.

"If they ain't, then they can gossip on the phone. I'm ready to go home and get these boots off," Rich said.

"I'm wondering why our paths haven't crossed in the past ten years," Rye said when the old fellows were gone.

"Mine and yours?" Austin asked.

He nodded.

"Probably because I only came on weekends in the summer. Granny said you rodeo during that time. I loved Granny and wished she would come to Tulsa to live with us when I was a kid or at least in one of the houses on our block. When the house next door came up for sale, I begged Dad to buy it for her."

"Did you ever learn to like Terral when you came to visit?" Rye reached across the table and took her hands in his. Her fingers were long and slim and so, so soft.

"The summer I was thirteen. Granny and I had so much fun that year that I didn't even care if my friends all got to go to a dude ranch. For the next three years I looked forward to coming to Terral. Then when I was sixteen I got a job at the dealership. From then on, it was hit and miss and for some strange reason, Granny and I got closer with the passing of each year."

She looked around at the decor. Coca-Cola trays were hung on the wall everywhere. She wondered where in the world they'd found so many.

"Did you ever even one time entertain notions of living here?" Rye pressed on.

She shook her head. "My mother would drop dead of acute cardiac arrest if I even thought such a thing. She called this morning. She's ready to fly down here, use Main Street for a runway, and haul me back to Tulsa just because I told her I was driving a tractor."

"Your mother flies a plane?"

"No, Dad liked to fly. She has a stand-by pilot who can fly Dad's plane. It's nothing big. Just a little four-seater but it scoots her around when she has to go somewhere. She hates to drive or ride."

The waitress brought their food. She set a bottle of ketchup in the middle of the table and asked, "Anything else?"

"I forgot to ask for a side of gravy," Rye said.

"Bring it right out."

Austin wrinkled her nose and slipped her hands from his so she could eat. "Gravy?"

"To dip my fries in. I like it better than ketchup. I got a call this morning. They've rescheduled the rodeo board-of-directors meeting in Mesquite for tonight. I'll be gone until Thursday night. It's something I do every year, but I'm so sorry that it's this week. Last week was the rodeo and this week the board meeting and I really don't want to go, Austin. I meet with the Resistol Arena for the rodeo season down there. I supply the bulls for them each year and we have to go over the contracts, meet with the other stock suppliers, and all that stuff. Want to go with me?"

"You know I've got watermelons to plant. Did Granny ever go with you?"

"She always said the exact same thing you just did. 'You know I've got watermelons to plant.' But Gemma and I talked her into going with us to the rodeo pretty often. She was a hoot. You should have seen her the year that George Strait put on the post-rodeo concert."

"She loved country music and George Strait was one of her favorites. Don't tell me she was a groupie and hung on the edge of the stage."

"No, but she bought everything she could from the vendors. While you are going through her things, you'll find a mug, a calendar, a shirt, and every CD they had for sale that night. She said it was the highlight of her whole summer."

Disappointment washed over Austin. She didn't want Rye to be gone three days of her last week in Terral. Hellfire and damnation! If she'd known that, she would have drank less wine and done more than fall asleep under the stars the night before.

Austin pushed the fries to one side and picked up her hamburger. She bit off a piece and changed the subject before the tears welling up behind her eyelids spilled over the dam and wet her cheeks.

"This is so good," she said. "I know it's not socially acceptable to talk with food in your mouth but it really is good."

"Do you like Blake Shelton?"

"I wouldn't know. I've heard him sing but I'm not a groupie-type person for any singer. Why are you asking about him? I thought we were talking about George Strait."

"He's playing one night down at the rodeo this summer. If you were around, you could go hear him in person."

The waitress set a bowl of gravy in front of Rye but didn't tarry. Every table and booth was full and there were people waiting outside the door. Austin wasn't a bit surprised to hear two truckers in the next booth talking about how glad they were they'd gotten in when they did.

"When he played in Tulsa, I went to his concert. Did you know that he has a ranch over near Tishomingo?"

"Had no idea." Rye dipped his fries in the gravy. "Help yourself. Beats the devil out of ketchup."

She did. "Mmmm, you are right. This is good."

"I'll be back Thursday night. Friday is date night."

"Okay." She reached to dip a fry at the same time he did, and their hands got tangled up together. He dropped his potato on the top of her hand.

"Oops!" He picked up her hand and brought it to his mouth where he ate the fry from her hand and then licked the gravy off.

She bit the inside of her lip to keep from moaning out loud right there in the Nocona Dairy Queen. Good God, didn't he know how he affected women? Or how his mouth on the back of her hand made her insides go all oozy and hot? Another minute and she'd have thrown the paper towels and tartar sauce off on the floor and had sex with him right there in front of truckers, ranchers, and even schoolkids on their lunch break.

"It's even better that way. Want to do it again?" he asked.

"I don't think so, cowboy."

"I'm going to miss you like hell these next three days. Seems like everything gets in our way. Bulls, kids, wine," he said softly.

I hope to hell it's not an omen, she thought.

━━━━━━━━━

Rye sat through meetings, signed new contracts, and took tours of the stockyards where he'd be keeping his animals. He had dinner with the board of directors at the club. He called Austin every morning, sometime in the afternoon when he had a break, and at night just before he went to bed. He felt like they were slipping back into the Thursday night telephone world, and he hated it.

He hated being away from her, loved talking to her, and couldn't wait to get home to do more than talk. It was going to take some fancy footwork to keep her in Terral and more than just a few kisses.

If he hadn't been busy from noon on Tuesday until Friday evening, he would have driven back each day just to see her for a few minutes. But finally Thursday night rolled around and he could look forward to the last affair, a dinner at the club with a live band and dance afterward.

He was having a beer at the bar after dinner when a tall redhead perched herself on the barstool beside him. "So what's going on in your neck of the woods?" Delilah McMurry asked.

"Just work," he answered. "I figured you'd sell off the buckin' broncs when you married that fancy-pants lawyer. I was surprised to see you here."

"I started to after last year but caught the husband with those fancy pants at the foot of the wrong bed. Decided I like cowboys better than lawyers after all. Want to come to my room for a drink after dinner? I promise I'm not lookin' for husband number five. The lawyer broke me from suckin' eggs."

"Thanks but no thanks," Rye said.

"What's her name?"

"Who?"

"Rye O'Donnell, I'm not used to men flat-out turning me down. Only reason they do is there's a filly and it's serious. So what's her name?"

"Austin."

"Well, she must be one hell of a cowgirl. Good luck with her. Here comes the rest of the crew. Maybe I'll find a lonesome old cowboy among them."

"Good luck," Rye said.

The days went by like a blur for Austin until Friday when it started raining early that morning. Felix showed up on her porch to tell her that they couldn't plant in the rain and the fields would be gumbo the rest of the day. He said he and the guys would be in the big implement barn down by the hog pens if she needed them. They'd use the day to service the tractor engines and make sure everything was oiled, greased, and ready to go on Monday if the rain stopped.

Austin packed all morning, stopping only long enough to heat up a can of tomato soup and make a grilled-cheese sandwich for lunch. She talked to Rye as he drove home twice during the morning, and he called again while she was eating.

She loved sharing news of the watermelon planting, what she'd found out that day about making wine, and everything in her life…except Tulsa. Neither of them brought up the fact that this would be her last weekend in Terral. She banished that thought and let her mind go to the date they had that night. She'd think about leaving when the time came and not let it ruin today.

After she ate, she took a quick shower, donned her black suit and high heels, and took the time to straighten her hair. When she looked in the mirror, she was looking at a stranger.

"This is the real me," she told her reflection. "I've gotten too damned comfortable in that Farmer Jane look. And I look forward to Rye's calls three to ten times a day entirely too much. Leaving here on Sunday is going to be horrid."

She drove to Ryan in her Corvette, did the banking, and sent the guys' paychecks to their families, put their spending money into envelopes, and made it to the drugstore by two o'clock. Molly and Greta were waiting at the first table beside the ice cream counter. Austin pulled up a chair and slipped off her spike heels under the table. She'd gotten so used to wearing Nikes or flip-flops that the high heels pinched her feet.

"You are still here. That's a good sign," Molly said.

She wore a muumuu-style dress with big yellow roses printed on an electric blue background. Her flip-flops had yellow silk daisies at the top of the piece that went between the toes. Her wispy gray hair had been permed that morning, and Austin could still smell the solution.

"Yes, I'm still here and I love your hair."

"Well, darlin', there ain't much to love these days. It's thin and finer than what grows on a frog's ass but my poor little hairdresser does the best she can. Not everyone can be blessed with beautiful gray hair like Greta. Some of us are beautiful and smart instead."

"Hey, now, just because you got those five hairs on your head to do something today don't give you the right to be sassy," Greta said.

She was as scrawny as Molly was plump. All of her calories and fat grams went into making a thick mop of curly gray hair that looked like a wig. Her face looked like she'd just taken a nap on a chenille bedspread and her mouth was thin but her blue eyes sparkled with mischief.

"If I get up in the morning and my feet touch the ground and I can sit up to the damned table and eat my breakfast, then I've got the right to be sassy," Molly said.

Austin looked at Greta. "What gives *you* the right to be sassy?"

"If I can eat all the rich ice cream I want and not get the walking farts until I get home," Greta said without missing a beat.

Austin giggled. "I'm going to grow up and be like you two."

Molly shook her head emphatically. "Oh, no! You are going to grow up and be like Verline. She was the only one that could keep us from scratching and biting each other all our lives. She and Pearlita stepped between us so many times in our catfights on the playground that we'd have to take off our shoes to count them."

Greta motioned for the waitress. "We're ready to order. I want a scoop of each one. Vanilla, strawberry, and chocolate all lined up on one of them fancy long boat things. Then top it all off with chocolate syrup and whipped cream. No banana."

"I'll have the same with the banana," Molly said.

"Make mine like Molly's," Austin said. "Now tell me more about these catfights."

"Greta picked on me," Molly said.

"I did not! She was a whiny kid that was spoiled rotten at home, and when she came to school, she expected everyone to wait on her hand and foot. I come from a big family of boys and I had to be tough so I never could abide her whining. Good thing she married a man who was half-deaf," Greta said.

Molly pointed a long freshly manicured bright red fingernail at Greta. "Let me tell you about her. She was meaner than a junkyard dog and whopped the biggest boy in the class the first three days of school. After that, nobody picked on her but me. She'd call me a sissy and I'd call her a bitch and the fight would be on. Pearlita would get between us and Verline would hold her back to keep her from killing me. But when the teacher asked us what was going on, we always said it was just a game we were playing."

"Ain't no way I'd be the schoolyard rat," Greta said.

"She tried to get rid of me but I married her brother, and there wasn't a damn thing she could do but suck it up."

The waitress bought their ice cream and set it down.

"Can you hear that singing? It's my fat cells jumping around inside this big, old floppy dress and getting ready for the first bite," Molly said.

Greta picked up the spoon and set about eating. "Austin didn't come in here to listen to us old hens fussin' about the past. She come for advice, didn't you, sweetheart?"

"What?"

"Advice," Greta said.

"About what?"

"You are still here. You've had dinner with Rye and you've been plowing and planting. You've packed a few boxes and you've found her wine cellar, which intrigues you," Molly said.

"How'd you know all that?" Austin's eyes widened.

"Honey, you can't fart in Terral without Oma Fay calling Pearlita and telling her what you ate for dinner, and we talk to Pearlita every night on the telephone. Remember we told you that Oma Fay is Kent's momma and he stops by there on his way home every day to pick up his boys. God, them is some wild kids. If anyone ever wants to bring them to your house, tell them if they do, you're goin' to drown them in the Red when they do," Greta said.

"Good Lord!" Austin shoved the melting ice cream into her mouth.

"Last time I checked He was good." Molly laughed. "So what do you want advice about? Staying? Leaving? How to get Rye to propose?"

"None of the above," Austin said. "Why would you even think that?"

"Look under the table," Greta said.

"What's on the floor?"

"Your bare feet. No hose today and those pretty shoes are hurting your feet after you've got used to work boots or sneakers or whatever it is you wear out on the tractor," Molly said.

"You mean you can't tell me what brand of shoes I wear? Oma Fay must be falling down on the job," Austin teased.

"Some kind of sneakers. I expect they're them fancy kind but Oma Fay didn't know the brand."

"Nike," Austin said.

"Aha!" Greta grinned. "Now we know something that she don't. Tell us more so we won't be the poor white-trash cousins."

"What?" Austin giggled.

"Oma Fay is the queen because she knows more than us. Pearlita is the princess because Oma Fay talks to her because they're cousins. Me and Greta is third in line. So tell us something to make us more important."

"Like what?"

"Well, we know you went to the river with him for a picnic and a bunch of kids came up and you went to sleep. We got that because one of the kids had to take a leak and found you sleepin' and saw the picnic stuff. He's Oma Fay's nephew and he told Kent so Kent could tease Rye when he gets back from Mesquite. We want to know if Rye kissed you yet or if you been to bed with him. That would be a real biggie that them other women don't know because Rye wouldn't tell Kent jack shit," Molly said.

"Good girls don't kiss and tell." Austin played coy.

"We don't give a damn about good girls. Did you sleep with him yet? I'd love to be the first one to know that bit of news. Oma Fay would have a shittin' hemorrhage if we found out when you sleep with him before she does. I bet if you do, you don't ever leave Terral, not even for one day."

Austin fought the grin so hard that her mouth hurt. "I did not sleep with him. But I'll tell you something so you won't be the white-trash cousins. We have a date tonight. We're going to eat Chinese and go to a movie up in Duncan."

"Don't wear that outfit," Molly said seriously.

"What should I wear? I only brought this, two more suits, and some capris," she said.

Greta pointed toward the back of the drugstore. "Go on up the road toward Waurika. Over on the left-hand side of the road is a consignment shop where you can buy some decent jeans and shirts. Might even be able to pick up a pair of broke-in cowboy boots and a hat. Stuff is cheap enough that if you only use it this next week and then trash it, it'll be worth it."

Austin raised an eyebrow. "A consignment shop?"

That's one thing she sure wouldn't tell her mother. If she ever found out her daughter had bought a wardrobe out of a second-hand store she would have her committed for sure.

"Yeah, it's a red barn place. Everyone in these parts calls it the Red Barn, but I think it's got a name like the Country Closet or something like that. I forget what it is in the phone book. I buy lots of things in there," Molly said.

"She could shop in New York City with all the money she's got, but she's so tight, she squeezes her pennies so hard, it makes Abraham Lincoln cry," Greta said.

"Why would I want them big-city clothes? I'm old and shapeless, and I'm damned sure not going to punish my fat cells with a girdle. I burned all my Lycra years ago, and I'll be damned if I go buy another one. Them things weren't nothing but torture. I'm sure a man invented them and the bra," Molly said.

Greta poked Austin on the shoulder. "In our day no self-respectin' woman would be caught at a dogfight without her Playtex Living Girdle. You don't know how good you got it, girl."

"Okay, give me advice, girls. What should I wear tonight?" Austin asked.

Molly laid her spoon down and got serious. "Pair of them hip-slung tight-fittin' jeans, boots, and a knit shirt that's a size too little to make them boobs look bigger and your waist even smaller. A good-lookin' belt with a big buckle that sparkles so his eyes will go to your waist and his hands will itch to undo the belt. Some of them underbritches that wouldn't sag a clothes line even if they was soppin' wet. What do they call 'em, Greta?"

Greta touched her chin with her finger and made a thinking face. "Not bikinis. Thongs! That's it. Sounds funny, don't it, since we call our flip-flop shoes that name. But wear some of them things with a string up in your ass and a little lace patch over Miss Lily."

Austin blushed scarlet. "Over who?"

"That's what we call it because we are too old-fashioned to call it by the name in the medical book," Molly whispered.

"Old-fashioned? You two?" Austin asked.

"We're old and we can say anything we want and get away with it, but some things is too much even for us," Greta said. "Now you've finished your ice cream, so get on out of here and run up to the consignment shop and get yourself all dolled up for the night. I can't wait to get home and call Pearlita and tell her that we know something before she does."

Austin slipped her feet into the spike heels and paid for all their ice cream on the way out of the drugstore. She backed out of the diagonal parking space and drove a block up the street, made a U-turn, and drove back down to the stop sign. She had no intention of going to a secondhand store. She might make a fast trip to Nocona, Texas, to the western wear store if she had time. But when the coast was clear, she turned left toward Waurika instead of the right toward Terral. It was as if her car and her heart were joined together and overrode all her better judgment.

Ten minutes later, her bright-red 'Vette was parked in front of a big, red barn-looking building. She eased out of her car and went inside the store to find racks and racks of clothes. Bewildered, she stared at the whole place and wondered where to even start since she only had half an hour.

"Could I help you, honey?" the lady behind the counter asked. "Jeans?"

"What are you? About a seven?"

"With a long, long inseam."

She pointed to the right. "Racked up by size. Your size will be at the far end. Either try them on or hold them up to your side. Dressing rooms are to the far left. You sure you are in the right place?"

"Molly and Greta sent me."

"Oh! Well, come right on. I'll help you," the lady said enthusiastically.

Half an hour later, there were six pair of jeans, a belt with a flashy buckle shaped like interlocking hearts, two pairs of boots (Barbara would get severe acute diarrhea if she knew her daughter was putting her feet into someone else's boots, but the lady said she knew the woman who'd owned them and they were good), five knit shirts with different screen prints on the front, and six western blouses. One of the blouses was stretch lace and had flouncing ruffles on the sleeves.

Austin almost fainted when the lady added it all up and the total price was less than a hundred dollars. She couldn't have bought the blouse for that amount at the dress shop where she shopped in Tulsa.

"Thank you for all your help," she said as the clerk ran her credit card through the machine.

"Thank you for the biggest sale I've had all day. Tell Molly and Greta hello for me. They send a lot of customers my way. By the way, who are you, so I can tell them that you were here?"

"Austin Lanier. I'm Verline Lanier's granddaughter."

"Oh, my! I sure do miss Granny. She did a lot of business with me. Bought nearly all of her overalls in here. I miss her advice. I'd have left my husband if she hadn't convinced me to give him another chance," the woman said.

"Really?"

"Yep. She said to give him one more chance, and if he went back to drinking, then she'd whip his sorry ass for me. I live between Terral and Ryan. She got me the job working here two days a week too. Verline was a wonderful woman."

"Yes, she was. Thank you for sharing that with me." Austin signed the credit card slip and carried her bag outside. She tossed the brown paper bag into the passenger's seat and giggled. "I'll have to get those fancy underbritches for Miss Lily when I get to a Victoria's Secret, girls. I'm not wearing hand-me-down underpants."

CHAPTER 10

AUSTIN RUSHED HOME, CARRIED HER SECONDHAND CLOTHING into the house, and dumped them on the floor beside the washing machine. She crammed all the jeans inside the machine, added liquid detergent, and turned it on.

Then she paid the hired hands and listened with half an ear as Felix told her the rain was supposed to pass on through that night and the weekend would dry the land out so they could get back to planting on Monday.

Monday, she was supposed to be back at work in Tulsa. She would not think about that. Rye was coming home and she had to be ready for a date with him.

When the washer had finished its cycle, she tossed the jeans into the dryer, reset the washer on delicate, and tossed in the shirts. She was ironing a pair of jeans when her cell phone rang. She fished it out of her purse and answered on the third ring.

"Where were you? I was getting worried when you didn't answer on the second ring. Is everything all right down there in the land that stood still?" her mother said.

"Mother, I can take care of myself."

"Are you on your way home?"

"I'm ironing jeans for a date tonight."

"Don't tease me, Austin!"

"I'm not. Molly and Greta, that's two of Granny's old friends, and I had banana splits at the drugstore in Ryan today, and they told me about this cute little shop called the Red Barn. I bought jeans and boots for tonight's date with Rye. We're going for Chinese and then a movie." She punched the speaker button and laid the phone on the windowsill beside the ironing board.

Total silence on the other end made her think her cell phone had gone dead.

"Mother?"

"I'm here."

"Mother, I'm coming home in a couple of days. Stop worrying."

"You've come so far in your career. I hate to see you throw it all away for a watermelon farm."

Austin rolled her eyes. She hated trying to reason with her mother because the guilt trip would follow and that's what she really, really hated.

"I'm not throwing anything away. I'm going out on a date with a really hunky cowboy. I deserve it after a hard week in the fields."

"I don't have to remind you that you are the only grandchild my mother and father have too. I've made plans for Sunday. We are having a family dinner right here. Both of your aunts are coming and your grandparents. Promise me you'll be here. We're eating at seven. That will give you plenty of time to drive home and get ready."

"I will be there," Austin said but her blue eyes did a double roll.

And her heart took a tumble down past her knees to the floor. Did she really want to go to Tulsa or plant watermelons?

"Good!" Barbara's voice was suddenly chipper. "Your boss came in today to look at a new car for his wife. He mentioned that he's looking forward to retirement in six months and that he knows you will do fine when they promote you to department supervisor. I'm so proud of you. To think my child is going to be in charge of operations at the oldest oil company in Tulsa when she's only thirty. Your grandparents are going to be so, so happy when we tell them on Sunday."

"Mother, I've got to get these jeans finished, and my shirt is almost dry and I have to iron it too. I've got to go or I won't be ready when Rye gets here."

"Enjoy your fling, darlin'. You should have something out of the sorriest vacation of your entire career. See you on Sunday for dinner."

"I told you I'll be there. Stop worrying about me. Goodbye, Mother."

She'd barely hung up when the phone rang again. She pushed the button, left the phone on speaker, and said, "Hello."

"Hi, sweetie, it's Aunt Joan. I'm told we're having a family dinner. Was wondering if you want to go shopping tomorrow for something new to wear to the affair. I hear Neiman's has a sale going." Her voice was almost identical to Barbara's but had a very, very slight nasal twang. All of the Watson girls looked as if they'd been popped out of the same mold: dark-haired beauties with blue eyes and built on a tall, slim frame that was stunning in business suits.

Without even shutting her eyes, Austin could imagine her Aunt Joan in her quaint little two-story house on five acres of prime land in Memphis, Tennessee. She was ten years older than Barbara, which made her sixty-two years old.

"Wow!" Austin said when she realized Aunt Joan was close to retirement age.

"So we'll do Neiman's and have lunch then?"

"No, I won't be home until Sunday. How long are you staying in Tulsa?"

"I'm just flying over for the weekend. Your mother tells me you are taking care of selling your grandmother's farm? Never met her but I'm sorry you've got to waste your vacation time like that."

"Thank you. I'll look forward to seeing you then on Sunday at the dinner."

"What are you doing right now?"

"Ironing jeans. I found this cute little shop called the Red Barn, and it's got really reasonable prices. I've got a date tonight with the hunky cowboy rancher who lives across the street."

"Why are you ironing jeans? Don't they have a dry cleaner in town?"

Austin laughed. "Terral has a population of three hundred and eighty-six at last count. They barely have a grocery store and the school only goes to eighth grade."

Joan gasped. "Sweet Jesus!"

"Take a week and fly into Dallas. I'll pick you up and you can help me plant watermelons. Driving a tractor is a lot of fun and even though you are tired at the end of the day, you'll feel like you've accomplished something."

"Gotta run, darlin'. See you at the dinner. Don't do anything foolish. Goodbye," Joan spoke so fast that Austin only caught every other word.

She'd barely finished ironing the jeans when the phone rang again. Before she answered it, she laid the creased jeans on the top of the washer and jerked the lacy western-cut blouse from the dryer. It looked good enough that she didn't need to iron it, so she put it on a hanger and punched the speaker button.

"Hello."

"Hi. I was about to hang up or leave a message. This is your aunt Clydia. Where are you? Still at work?"

"You know where the hell I am. Mother called, didn't she?"

"She's worried about you. Thirty is a tough age, and you've got this promotion and all the responsibility that will go with it. She's afraid you'll throw everything away on a whim," Clydia said sternly. She was a year younger than Joan but a hundred times bossier and a thousand times more serious. A smile might ruin every Botox injection she'd ever had, and she wasn't taking any chances on that.

"I've got a date tonight with the sexiest cowboy this side of the Red River. He's got muscles across his chest that would make even your hormones go into overdrive, and his kisses are like heaven. When his big, old callused hands touch my bare back, I want to roll over like a puppy and let him do anything he wants to my body." Austin smiled when she heard Clydia suck air.

"What? Are you serious? You are teasing me because you think I'm interfering in your life, aren't you? For God's sake, Austin, you weren't raised to talk like that or…" Clydia stammered.

"Or what?"

"You better keep your goals in your sights and not do anything stupid." Clydia quickly regained her superior status after the stuttering tirade.

"I'll see you Sunday. If I'm smiling, you'll know I got lucky."

"Good God!" Clydia hung up without a goodbye.

"Jesus *is* sweet. God isn't good; He's great. Beer is good. And people are the crazy ones according to that country song I heard on the radio. I'm *damn* glad I don't have but two aunts or I'd never get ready on time," she told Rascal, who had curled up on top of the dryer.

The house phone rang at seven o'clock just as she was slipping her feet into the buff-colored boots she'd bought that day. She reached for it and propped it on her shoulder, hoping she could get rid of whoever was calling quickly because Rye would be there any minute.

"Hello," she said cautiously.

"I'm running about ten minutes late."

Rye's deep Texas voice sent shivers all the way to her toes.

"No problem. I'm just now getting my boots on."

"I was expecting you to have on those high-heeled things, but boots sure does draw up a pretty picture in my head. I can't wait to see you. Be there in ten."

She made one more run to the bathroom mirror to check her makeup and hair and was on the way down the hall when she heard the crunch of truck tires in the driveway. Bootheels sounded on the wooden porch and she swung the door open to find Gemma, her eyes swollen and her face a mess from crying.

"Can I come in? Rye isn't here, is he?" Gemma asked.

"No, but he will be in about five minutes."

Gemma started toward her truck in a trot. "Then I've got to get out of here."

"Hey, put it in the backyard and I'll call Rye. I can put him off for ten minutes," Austin yelled.

"Hey, I was about to put my boots on and come over."

"Give me ten minutes. I had a makeup emergency and I'm not quite ready," she said smoothly.

"Sure thing. Looks like we should've said seven thirty instead of seven." He chuckled. "No problem. We'll have a nice long supper and see the late movie. You don't have to get up early tomorrow, do you?"

She motioned Gemma into the house. "No, but if you don't let me get this makeup fixed, it's going to be a midnight movie."

"I missed you so bad these past three days. Please don't tell me that you turn into a pumpkin after midnight."

"No but my Corvette does if I'm not home. Goodbye, Rye." She put the phone back on the base.

Gemma stopped inside the door and wiped her teary, swollen eyes. "I'm so sorry. I had no idea you and Rye were going out. I just needed a place to go tonight where no one knows about."

"You got ten minutes to talk, and you are welcome to stay here. I just won't be here. Is that all right?"

"It's fine. I could've gone to a motel but I was afraid they'd track me down. You said to drop by anytime. I hope you meant it."

"I did. What happened? Can I make a pot of coffee or get you something to drink before I go?"

"Got a good slug of whiskey?"

Austin pointed to the cabinet. "No, but I've got a bottle of some pretty damn good watermelon wine right there, and you are welcome to it."

"That'll do. Short story is that I've got...had this boyfriend. We've fought before. He doesn't like it when I go anywhere with my girlfriends. I'm supposed to spend every minute with him doing what he likes, which most of the time I don't like. Golf on television drives me crazy. It's not such a short story, is it? Tonight we got into it again when I told him I was going out with my friends for dinner. The last time we broke up, I promised Rye I'd never go back with him because my boyfriend slapped me and Rye wanted to kill him."

Austin patted Gemma on the shoulder and took down a tumbler from the cabinet. "Enough said. Pour this full of wine, and if it doesn't do the trick, pour up a second one. You can hide out here all weekend if you want. There's food in the fridge and more wine on the cabinet. Make yourself at home. You can sleep in Granny's room or on the sofa. Take your pick. The room with the twin bed is mine. Turn off your cell phone, and if you need to make any calls, do it on the house phone. That way no one can track you by your phone. I hear Rye driving up so I'm going out to meet him on the porch."

Gemma nodded. "You are a good woman, Austin."

"Shhh," Austin opened the door and stepped outside. "Hey, right on time. It's been exactly ten minutes and my makeup disaster is fixed."

Rye was thunderstruck by Austin all dressed up in creased blue jeans, a western-cut top that belonged on a country music star in concert, and boots. His eye went from her boots up to the belt buckle that glittered in the fading light of the setting sun and on up past a long, slender neck to the prettiest girl in the county. Hell, she might even be the prettiest one in the whole state of Oklahoma.

"You are beautiful tonight. My vision did not do you justice." He met her at the bottom of the steps and wrapped her up in his arms. How could he ever let her go on Sunday? He wanted to carry her across the road and lock her in his house and flush the key down the toilet.

He tilted her head to the right level with his fist and claimed her mouth in a fierce kiss so full of passion that it set her hormones to humming so loud that her ears buzzed.

Monday! Reality stopped the hum and sent cold chills down her spine.

He broke away and planted a soft kiss on each eyelid, then stepped to one side, laced his fingers in hers, and led her to the truck.

"I missed you, Rye," she said. "And darlin', my vision did not do you justice either."

"Me?" His crazy old cowboy heart swelled up until it put pressure on his rib cage. She'd said that she missed him. "I'm just an old cowboy who drove hard all day and looked forward to a Friday night with a pretty woman."

"So you like a woman in jeans and boots better than one in a dress suit and spike heels?" she asked.

He stopped beside the truck and put a palm on each side of her face. "Darlin', everything I've seen you in so far has looked damn fine. You are gorgeous in a suit, smashin' in overalls and sneakers, and almighty delightful in whatever them shorts are you wore to the river. But in jeans and boots you are delicious lookin'." He brushed a kiss across her lips so light and yet so full of promise that she shivered.

He settled her into her seat and shut the door.

She could see the tail end of Gemma's little truck in the headlights and was glad that he hadn't noticed it.

"Your sisters wear high heels. What's the matter with them?" she asked as he backed the truck up to the road.

"Yep, they do." He headed west, through town to Highway 81 where he'd turn north. "They're half cowgirl and half hussy. See, I called them hussies and I love them so that proves I wasn't being mean when I called your mother a hussy."

"Are you one of those big brother types?"

"I am."

"I bet they just love that."

He reached across the console separating them and laced his

fingers in hers. "Don't care if they love it or not. I'm protective. They were the babies of the family, and Momma said us boys had to take care of them. Colleen has always had her head on straighter than Gemma so I don't have to big brother her as much as I do Gemma."

He drove through town and made the turn north toward Duncan. "Are you hungry?"

"Starving. How far is it?"

"Forty miles."

"Then they'd better double what they put out on the buffet tonight. Did you and Granny ever go to this place?"

He grinned and the dimple in his chin deepened. "Granny hated Chinese food. Her favorite restaurant food was whatever they served out at the Peach Orchard. She did occasionally like a hamburger from the Dairy Queen in Nocona."

Sitting so close that every breath brought her a fresh wave of his shaving lotion, Austin had two choices. Either make him talk to divert her mind from the naughty thoughts dancing around in her head or else flip that console back and slide across the seat and nuzzle her face into his neck. Talking seemed the better choice so she asked, "Why did your parents name you Rye?"

He smiled again and she wished she'd forgotten the questions and done the sliding.

"The story Dad tells is that they had a different name picked out. I was supposed to be Holt after a bull rider they liked. But when she was in labor, Mom kept telling Dad if he'd sneak a bottle of Old Overholt rye whiskey into the room and let her have a couple of shots that the pain would go away. Then they got to singing that old county song, 'Rye Whiskey,' between pains. When I was born, they decided that Rye was a better name for me than Holt."

"So you're named after the whiskey your momma liked, and I'm named after the city where I was conceived. We're quite the pair, aren't we? Hey, that mural on the side of the building there"—she pointed at the end of a big building in Ryan as they went through town—"with the cows and cowboys. What are they talking about? The Chisholm Trail?"

"It's the path the ranchers drove their cattle up through going to Nebraska to ship them off to the East. Came across the Red River and right through Terral and Ryan. I heard in the day that there were lots of banks and brothels in this area. They still have a reenactment every year of the cattle run. They start in Terral and ride horses and herd a few head of cattle up north. The newspapers come around and write up stories and take pictures of the chuck wagons and covered wagons when they head off up 81."

"They go right up the highway? Doesn't that cause problems?"

"Hasn't yet. I've got to stop up at the truck stop outside of Waurika to fill up the truck. You want to grab a candy bar or something to hold you until we get to Duncan?" he asked.

"No, I'm going to embarrass you with how much I eat when we get there. But I could go to the bathroom," she told him. She was surprised that she had said such a thing, but she was as comfortable with Rye as if they'd known each other their whole lives.

It was only a few more minutes before she saw the truck stop at the crossroads in Waurika. Rye pulled up to the gas tanks and she hopped out to run inside. The truck stop had a convenience store on one end with snack foods, drinks, and souvenirs and the other end was a restaurant. Her stomach growled when she smelled the aroma of grilled onions.

"Restrooms?" she asked the lady behind the counter.

She pointed toward the back of the store. "All the way to the back. Women on the right."

"Thank you."

Austin used the restroom, checked her makeup and hair in the mirror as she washed her hands, and was walking back toward the door when she overheard two women talking. One asked the other if she was taking her kids to the rattlesnake festival and said that the armbands were twenty dollars this year.

"Well, when you consider how many rides my kids will whine about, that's a pretty good deal."

Austin made her way out to the pickup where Rye had finished filling the gas tank and waited in the cab. That's when she saw the sign that said "Rattlesnake Hunt."

"What's that all about?"

"This is the weekend for the big Waurika Rattlesnake Festival. It kicks off tonight. They rope off three or four blocks of Main Street and have a big foo-rah."

"Do they have food?"

"Just about any kind you can think of."

"Can we go there rather than Duncan?"

He grinned. "It's noisy, loud, and there's lots of people. It won't be as intimate as dinner and a movie but we can do whatever you like. Ever been to a rattlesnake festival?"

"No, do they have real snakes or what's the deal?"

"For weeks locals hunt the snakes and bring them to the festival. There are prizes for the biggest snake, the most pounds, and the most rattlers. There'll be pens of them so you can see them and vendors where you can buy fried snake. Want to taste it or change your mind and go for Chinese?"

"I want to go to see the snakes. Is it like a circus?"

"More like a miniature state fair. Ever been to one of those?"

She shook her head. "Rides?"

"Lots of them. Think very small amusement park."

"Ferris wheel?"

He started the engine and turned the truck around. "Yes, ma'am."

They passed several city blocks of garage sales before they turned right onto the street that had been barricaded off for the festival.

One woman's junk is another woman's treasure.

She'd heard her grandmother say that lots of times and wondered if Verline's treasures came out of places just like she was seeing. The woman had enough money to build a brand-new fancy house and have a decorator flown in from New York. She must have loved her little house with all its junk because that's where she wanted to finish her life and that's exactly what she did.

Rye nosed the truck into a scarce parking spot. "Look like something you'd be interested in?"

"No, thank you. There's twice as much in Granny's house as whatever they are selling in their garage sales."

"I wasn't talking about that. Look out ahead of you at all the vendors. You said you were hungry."

She pointed as she crawled out of the truck. "Oh, yes, yes, yes! I want one of everything. Gyro. Turkey leg."

"Before or after you ride on the zipper?"

Her mind plummeted into the gutter. Ride on the zipper? Well, she'd like a ride on the cowboy after the zipper was undone. She quickly turned her head toward the Ferris wheel so he couldn't see high color filling her cheeks. "Not me. I'd throw up. I want two rides on the Ferris wheel."

He grabbed her hand and started up through the vendors and games. "Then let's get started. Gyro to start with, complete with onions?"

"Yes and sometime this evening you can win me one of those big teddy bears."

"Have you never been to a carnival?"

She shook her head. "I watched *Steel Magnolias* three times in one day last year and cried my eyes out every time. I loved the scene where they were at the Christmas festival. This reminds me of that only in the spring rather than winter."

"Are you going to eat snake too?"

She nodded, turned, and looked right into his eyes, not a foot from her face. "Yes, I am. What does it taste like?"

He let go of her hand and put his arm around her waist, tucking his fingers into her belt loops. "Something between fish and chicken. It's white meat. Tastes a little like frog legs."

"Never ate them either. Do they have them here?"

"Never know. The vendors change from one time to the next." He steered her toward a wagon painted in bright colors and advertising gyro sandwiches. He ordered two deluxe sandwiches and two Cokes at the window, then led the way to an empty table at the north end of the wagon. He pulled out her folding metal chair and moved his closer to her, leaving room for other folks if they wanted to sit while they ate. That put his thigh tight against hers and their shoulders touching.

She bit into the pita bread filled with meat, onions, and sauce and moaned. "This beats Chinese all to hell, and I love good Chinese."

She wasn't sure if it was the food or the sensation of his body next to hers. She would have given up the food in a heartbeat rather than move her leg, though, so the food did take second place.

Kent appeared from behind the wagon with two gyros in his hand. "Hey, Rye, I thought you were on your way to Duncan. Hello, Austin." He pulled out a chair and sat down at the same table with them.

"Evenin', Kent. Where's your family?"

"They had to stop at the turkey-leg wagon and get one each for the boys. Me and Malee like gyros so she sent me to get these and have them ready. Here they come now."

Austin looked over at Rye.

He raised an eyebrow.

The older boy pointed at Austin. "Hi, Rye. Who's that?"

Rye made introductions. "This is Austin Lanier. You remember Granny Lanier. This is her granddaughter. And Austin, this is Malee, Kent's better half, and his sons, Creed and Mason."

Austin looked at the turkey legs. "Pleased to meet you all. Are those turkey legs any good?"

"Best in the world. Mine's bigger than Mason's," Creed said.

Mason drew his back like a club. "Is not. You take that back, or I'll whip you all over this place with my turkey leg."

"You two stop fighting or you won't ride a single ride," Malee said.

Creed glared at Mason, who shook his turkey leg at his brother.

"I heard you was workin' out at Granny's house. How's it going? Need some help?" Malee asked.

"Thanks but I'm getting it under control," Austin answered.

Malee was a short, thin woman with stringy light-brown hair pulled back into a ponytail. She wore jeans and a knit shirt with a picture of Betty Boop on the front. Her brown eyes were too big for the rest of her face, and her lips were thin.

"Well, you need any help, you just call me. Boys are in school and I work but I'm free in the evenings and on Saturdays."

"Thank you."

Austin had never seen two huge turkey legs turn into nothing but bones so quickly. The minute Creed and Mason had swallowed their last bite, they began to run around the table begging their parents to hurry so they could go ride the Round-Up.

The two boys put their heads together behind hands, and Austin could see orneriness flowing like hot lava from their glittering brown eyes. It was the smiles on their faces as they discussed what they were about to get into that convinced her they were every bit as feisty as she'd heard.

Malee turned to Austin and said, "It was nice meeting you. I was serious about coming around to help. Call me if you need me."

Austin smiled at Rye as Malee and Kent walked away, Creed and Mason running off ahead. "They are going to give Kent and Malee fits when they are teenagers."

"Wouldn't be no different than now. I told you they were a couple of stinkers."

"I believe you!" Austin giggled. "And you want children. What if they turn out like that?"

"They won't."

"What makes you so sure?"

"Because I wasn't like that. Verline was Pearlita's friend. She and Kent's momma are distant cousins even though there's a lot of age difference. So Verline knew Kent and Oma Fay, his mother, all their lives and Pearlita was kin so she really knew them. I'm not making myself clear but what I'm trying to say is that Kent was just like those boys. Oma Fay let him do anything he wanted and never used a bit of discipline. I don't know how he turned out to be the man he is. Verline said that Malee straightened him out.

"Anyway, Oma Fay keeps the boys for Malee and Kent to work, and she's doing the same with them that she did with Kent. My mother had three boys in four years. I was four and Raylen was two when Dewar was born. She didn't have time or patience to let us run wild. So I intend to raise my kids like I was raised, not like Kent was."

Austin wasn't sure she understood the whole line of thought, but she did like to listen to his deep Texas drawl. That and his hard muscles right next to her was enough for her to stay right there all night and forfeit the rest of the festival.

"I see." She polished off the last of her gyro.

"What next?" Rye asked.

Please tell me you've had a change of heart and I'll find the nearest motel.

"I want to see all of it. Let's start right here and walk slow all the way down one side and come up the other one. Where are the snakes?"

"They usually keep them down by the courthouse in pens. They throw up a temporary goat fence pen for protection, but I guarantee you can hear them rattling even from that distance."

She stopped at a wine-tasting booth and they tried several

kinds of wines, none of which came close to Granny Lanier's watermelon wine. The next booth offered Indian tacos.

"Remind me before we leave to get a couple of those to take home for a midnight snack," she said.

Rye slipped an arm around her waist. "You have plans of working up an appetite before midnight?"

She wanted to weep. She would have loved to work up an appetite with a good bout of sex but Gemma was at her house. She had been thinking of her and the fact that Gemma's anger and sadness would be gone by the time Austin returned to the house and she'd be hungry.

"Person never knows what the evening might hold."

The next place displayed all kinds of costume jewelry. Austin's eye was drawn to a necklace made of big silver beads with a pendant of two crossed pistols over angel wings.

"You like that one?" Rye picked it up and fastened it around her neck. The cold metal and his ultra-hot hands combined to create hot, sizzling desire that started a fire in the pit of her heart and radiated out to the rest of her body.

Damn it, if I don't get my hormones in check, I'm going to have to find a booth that sells panties! They really should have one with this many sexy cowboys running around without wedding rings on their fingers.

She looked in the tiny mirror on the side of the display and nodded. "I'm buying it. I love it."

She would probably never wear it again after that night. Monday...Tulsa!

That thought almost put a damper on her mood, but she quickly put it out of her mind. She still had Saturday and until noon Sunday.

"Let me," Rye said. "It'll remind you of us at your first rattlesnake festival."

"Thank you, but I think I'll remember tonight forever."

I don't want to leave, she admitted to herself silently.

He removed the sticker price tag on the back of the crossed guns and paid the lady, and they continued on down the block, hand in hand. Little children were riding ponies in a circular pen not far from the courthouse. They passed hair-bow vendors that made Austin's biological clock set up a loud tick wanting a daughter so she could put big, fancy satin bows in her hair.

Now where in the hell did that idea come from? I've never thought about children. Barely even gave the idea of a husband a second thought. It's this place and all this family around me.

The next vendor sold sunglasses. To take her mind off the pretty pink satin bows, she tried on big, buggy orange glasses that made Rye laugh out loud.

She loved his deep laugh. It reminded her of her father's laugh when he was really tickled and not just chuckling at a joke. The last time she'd heard him laugh like that had been the day before he died. She couldn't even remember what had amused him, but something had sure set him off and it was her last memory of him.

When they reached the Ferris wheel, the line was short and the previous riders were getting out of their seats. Rye looked at her and she nodded. He handed the man the money and suddenly they were side by side in the rocking seat. She grabbed Rye's hand when the caretaker pushed the button and the wheel creaked to life. From the very top, she could see a swarm of people milling about at the festival. Did they look forward to this all year? Was this their big event of the spring?

Rye let go of her hand, slung his arm around her shoulder, and picked up her hand with his left one. "So what do you think, Miss Austin Lanier?"

"I love it. I might come back to Terral every summer just to do this. Look over there. You can see forever in this flat country."

When they reached the top, he kissed her with so much passion that she could've sworn several stars melted and fell from the sky.

His voice was husky when he said, "Grows good cattle and watermelons. Hell on wheels when it comes to tornadoes. There's nothing but mesquite and scrub oak to stop them, and they don't stand up too hot under that kind of wind."

"There isn't much that could stand up under a tornado. I've seen them uproot pecan trees that were three feet across the base," she said.

And those big, major Category 5 storms were nothing compared to the storm I've had in my heart since I came to Terral.

A helium balloon with ribbons tied to the end floated up so close to them that Austin reached out to grab it and rocked the seat even more. If the belt hadn't held her tight, she might have gotten a hold on the ribbon but it was inches beyond her grasp. The wind carried a little girl's wails, and Austin looked down to see a mother taking a little red-haired girl back to the vendor for another balloon. This time the mother tied it firmly to the girl's wrist and the child bounced around happily.

"It doesn't take much to excite a child, does it?" Rye said.

"Nor an adult woman who's never been to a local festival. Thank you for bringing me, Rye. I love it!"

She smiled at him and he returned the favor, their eyes melting the distance between them and their lips brushing in a sweet kiss as the ride came to an end.

"Now I want to go eat one of those fried pickles. They sound absolutely horrid."

He laughed and kept her hand in his as they stepped off the Ferris wheel platform. "And you want to eat one."

"Yes, I do. I've got a friend in Tulsa who'll never believe it when I tell her I ate fried pickles and rattlesnake."

Rye's mood changed instantly.

Austin had no idea what she'd said that chilled the evening. They went to the pickle stand, and she was amazed at the flavor of dill pickle rolled in batter and deep fried. It was so good she wished she hadn't eaten the gyro. She could get those in Tulsa any old time but she didn't know of a single place where she could buy a fried pickle.

He led her to the rattlesnake pens, and she shivered at the sight of long diamondback rattlers shaking their tails and standing up, looking at her with their beady little eyes.

"They look evil," she whispered.

He let go of her hand and crossed his arms over his chest. "Not so much. They're just snakes."

She wanted to bury her face in his chest, but his pretty green eyes were veiled and she couldn't see inside his soul anymore. She popped both hands on her hips and stepped right up into his face. "What's wrong with you? And don't be all chivalrous and tell me nothing because there is something wrong. You went silent and your jaws are working like you are chewing gum but you aren't. I know anger when I see it."

"Is this just a go-to-the-boondocks and go-home-and-laugh-about-it thing, Austin?"

She met him glare for glare. "What in the hell makes you think that?"

"You said that you wanted to eat awful fried pickles so you could go brag about it to your friend."

She took a step back. "And you got that boondocks shit out of that sentence?"

"Well?"

"That's a deep subject for such a shallow mind."

"Very funny. What did you mean by your comment?"

"I'm having a wonderful evening. I can't wait to go home and brag about it to my coworkers because they were all giving me shit about having to spend my vacation in the boonies. So yes, I want to go back and brag and say that they were wrong and that I've had the time of my life. And you aren't going to spoil my evening by reading wrong into what I said. I've loved this date, and you can pout if you want, but I'm going to have a good time. So where to next?" The gut that was never wrong said that Rye was a cowboy worth fighting for and with.

"I'm not pouting. Men don't pout."

"Bullshit is bullshit. You can call it rose petals and put perfume on it, but it will still be bullshit."

He chuckled. The anger left his eyes and he dropped his arms. "I can't believe you even know what bullshit is."

She took two steps forward and laced her fingers in his. "Granny had a hog lot and a pasture with steers for slaughter. I know very well what it is. I've stepped in it, had to wipe it off my shoes with a stick, and I've smelled it. And my sexy cowboy neighbor has bulls. When they shit in the pasture, the wind whips it across the road and I get a fresh smell. And you were pouting so don't change the subject."

The chuckle turned into laughter. "You are cute when you are mad. Your blue eyes flash."

"Oh, yeah? Well, the only thing that cures mad is more food. Now where is this rattlesnake?"

"How much can you eat? And I happen to know something else that cures mad."

"But you can't do it in the middle of a festival, can you? I want a plateful of rattlesnake and then I want a funnel cake when we pass that booth."

The grin stayed plastered to his face and his eyes twinkled again. "You don't have funnel cakes in rich-cat world?"

She pointed at him with her free hand. "That is enough."

He liked the way the other men looked at him with envy in their eyes when he walked down the sidewalks with Austin's fingers laced in his. He was suddenly ten feet tall and bulletproof and his chest was as big as King Kong's. But she wouldn't be staying and it wrecked his whole imaginary world. She'd said it was a great date. Maybe he'd beat out those hotshot corporate fellers' time yet. If only he hadn't had to be gone so much of the time she was there, he might have convinced her to stay.

She smiled back. "All settled then. Let's eat snake. And that is a sentence I never thought I'd say in my lifetime."

Her cell phone rang and she dug it out of her hip pocket without letting go of his hand. "Hello."

"Austin? Where are you? I hear horrible music in the background. Do you have the radio on the country music station?"

"I'm at the rattlesnake festival in Waurika with Rye. He's buying us some snake to taste. We've already tasted wine and it wasn't as good as Granny's watermelon wine, but the gyros were wonderful and you should try a fried pickle. It's hot and crispy and dilly. Reckon you could get our cook to make them? Wait just a minute." She reluctantly unlaced her fingers from his and motioned for him to bring a plate of snake over to her.

There wasn't a line so he paid for a plate and turned around to find her right behind him. She picked up a chunk of snake and popped it into her mouth.

"God, this is good! Mother, you should fly down here tomorrow and we'll come back tomorrow night so you can eat some of this stuff. It puts shrimp to shame."

Barbara gasped. "They *are* making a redneck out of you!"

"I'm afraid they are, Mother."

Barbara's voice went from shrill enough to call feral dogs down from the Canadian border to flatter than the Oklahoma countryside in Terral. "Leave it down there when you come home. It has no place in your field."

"It has a big place in my watermelon field. Oh, you meant my job in Tulsa field. I thought about dirt and you were talking about broad spectrum. Mother, you really should take a weekend and come down here so you can taste this and a fried pickle."

"No, thank you. I don't ever intend to set foot in that backwoods place again. Haven't been there since you were a baby. If

I'd had my way, you wouldn't have ever gone down there either. Verline could have come off her high horse and come to Tulsa if she wanted to see you and her son."

"I'm going now. We're going to ride in the teacups like little kids." She was having way too much fun to let Barbara spoil it.

"We are?" Rye asked.

She shoved the phone into her pocket. "Yes, we are. I saw them on television when I was a kid and always wanted to ride in them and on the ponies of a carousel. I don't see a carousel, so it'll have to be the teacups."

"Then teacups it is."

He'd stand on his head and spin around if it would keep her in Terral.

The line was a little longer than it had been at the Ferris wheel. The cups were filled to capacity, and about halfway through the ride, Rye and Austin took their place at the end of a row of a dozen mothers waiting with rambunctious preschoolers.

"Why are they looking at me funny?" Austin whispered to Rye.

"They're looking for your kids."

"Can't adults ride?"

"Yes, but those with reasonable intelligence don't usually."

"You know any of these people?"

"About half of them. Why?"

"Is it going to embarrass you to ride kiddy rides?" she asked.

"Not if I can ride beside you."

The mother in front of them with two little girls who wouldn't be still finally said, "You'd better enjoy this because as soon as it's over we are going home. I'm tired of your fighting and arguing."

"That's probably why I never went to a carnival. Mother would have been crazy with boredom in fifteen minutes," Austin whispered.

"Really? I can't remember a year when we didn't come to the snake festival. Daddy even had a booth selling tack for several years. Handmade bridles and usually at least one hand-tooled saddle. They're probably here tonight but I haven't seen them."

"Haven't seen who?" Maddie asked from a few feet away.

Rye nodded at his mother. "Hello, Momma. I was just telling Austin that we came to this thing every year. I can't remember ever missing a snake festival except the year I had chicken pox and had to stay home."

Maddie touched Austin's arm. "Hi, Austin. That year he pouted like a bitchy little girl for a week. Then the other kids came down with the pox and he got to go with his dad to the Mesquite rodeo and they all had to stay home. So don't let him make you feel all sorry for him. This your first time at this thing?"

Austin nodded.

Maddie was dressed in tight jeans, pink cowboy boots, and a pink shirt with a western-cut yoke of white lace. Her hair was dressed high on her head and held there with a comb shaped like a horseshoe. "Rye, have you seen Gemma? I thought she might come over tonight but I haven't seen her and can't raise her on the phone. I'm getting worried. She usually returns my calls in an hour."

Austin felt the blush creeping from her neck to her cheeks. She couldn't say anything but she wanted to relieve Maddie's worries so bad she had to bite her tongue to keep silent.

"Gemma's probably out with her friends. They may be up at the casino pestering Colleen," Rye said.

Maddie shook her head. "No, I called Colleen and she hasn't seen her either."

"I'm sure she'll call you soon," Austin said.

Her brow furrowed in a frown. "A mother worries no matter how old or young they are. Why are you in this line?"

"Austin never has ridden the cups and..." Rye shrugged.

"How did you talk him into ridin' a kiddie ride? Damn! I wish I had my camera. Gemma won't ever believe it without proof. Y'all comin' around for Sunday dinner? I had a mind to break a couple of horses in the afternoon. Raylen says he's better at it than Rye, but Rye has a touch with them."

"You tell Raylen to put his spurs on, and we'll see who can do the job best," Rye said.

"Sibling rivalry! It's very useful," Maddie whispered when she hugged Austin.

"I'll tell him and you be sure to bring Austin along. Strawberries are ready this week. You like shortcake?"

"I do," Rye said.

Maddie patted him on the back. "I wasn't askin' you, son. I know you can eat your weight in shortcake."

Austin's blue eyes were big as the full moon hanging right above the Ferris wheel. "That's a bunch of strawberries. But yes, ma'am, I love shortcake."

"Good. I'm off to find your father. I was seeing if there was any snake left when I saw y'all over here."

Maddie had disappeared into the crowd when Austin remembered that she'd be driving toward Tulsa on Sunday afternoon. Suddenly, she began to crave strawberry shortcake.

The ride stopped and all the children were turned loose, and then the vendor started filling up the big cups again. When Rye and Austin stepped forward to claim the last two seats, he looked around for children.

"No kids. We want to ride," Austin said.

He smiled. "You'll have to share with those four little girls."

Austin took a seat on the round bench and patted the spot next to her. Rye hesitated for a second before he sat down and the little girls all giggled.

"Are you a prince?" one asked.

"No, just a big, old cowboy."

"Are you a princess?" another one asked Austin.

"Afraid not, darlin'. I'm just a…" It was her turn to pause. What was she? Tonight she was a watermelon farmer out on a date with a rancher. But soon she'd be back in the rat race working her ass off for a promotion.

The third little girl leaned forward and looked her up and down several times as the cups began to move around in circles. "I bet you are Snow White all dressed up in cowgirl clothes, aren't you? Is he going to kiss you and wake you up?"

"Yes, he is. And then we're having strawberry shortcake. What do you think I should wear?"

"A fancy blue and yellow dress and diamonds in your hair."

Rye had an instant picture of her in fairy-tale attire and thought about how much fun it would be to remove each pin from her hair and unfasten every button on that fancy gown. He'd take his time and enjoy every single minute of watching the costume puddle up at her feet.

"I think that's a wonderful idea," Austin told her.

The little girls were so much fun that Austin wished the cup ride would last an hour. When it ended, they rushed ahead of Austin and Rye to tell their mothers that they'd ridden with Snow White.

Sucking lemons couldn't have wiped the smile from Austin's face. "Kids!"

"Where are you going to find a dress like that?" Rye teased.

"Don't worry about me. I'm Snow White. I can have the seven dwarves whip up anything I want."

It was eleven o'clock and the vendors were shutting down when they left the festival and drove south to Terral. He parked outside the house and walked her to the door.

"I had a wonderful evening, Rye. Thank you," she said. She wanted to invite him inside for a cup of coffee, a cold glass of watermelon wine, or a long session of steaming kisses and whatever they would lead to but Gemma's truck was still in the backyard.

Rye ran the back of his hand down her cheek and leaned in for a kiss. After his lips touched hers, she couldn't think of anything but throwing Gemma out to the coyotes and taking him to bed. One kiss led to another and that one deepened into a more passionate one that had her panting when it ended. She drew him to the porch swing and sat down in his lap. He wrapped her up in his arms and nuzzled the inside of her neck, his hot breath causing goose bumps the size of mountains all over her body. She pressed closer and closer to him, feeling the hardness and wishing that she had the nerve to make love with him right there. But Gemma could appear at the door any minute.

"This is very nice. Let's take it inside," he whispered. It was that or go home to a very cold, long shower and she'd been very receptive up to that point.

"Can't. Too big of a mess in there."

His fingers made their way up her bare back, unhooked her bra, and made long lazy circles on her back. She thought she'd melt into a pile of aching hormones if he didn't stop, and yet if he had, she would have wept. No one had ever sent her into such a sexual tailspin as Rye O'Donnell was doing right then.

His hands slowly made their way around to the front where he cupped a breast. The warmth of his hand on such tender skin made her moan.

"Cold?" he asked.

"No, hot as hell."

He chuckled. "I like your honesty. I don't care if it's messy in Granny's house. We'll shove it all to one side."

"Can't, Rye, much as I want to, I can't do it."

"Why?" He started at her knee and slowly made his way up to her belt buckle.

"Timing is wrong."

"I understand." He kissed her firmly, his tongue doing a mating dance with hers. "Then I'll see you Sunday. I'll pick you up at… What is that?"

"What?" She looked up at the golden glow coming from the kitchen window out onto the porch not six feet from them.

"Shhh!" He put his finger over her mouth. "Someone is in the house. I'll take care of it."

She tried to tell him that it was all right, but he was already sneaking across the porch before she could utter a word. He jerked the door open and barged in with her right behind him.

He stopped in his tracks just inside the door. "What in the hell… Gemma?"

She managed a weak smile on her tearstained face topped off by swollen eyes and an expression of pure misery. "Well, shit! Guess I'm busted."

"What are you doing here?"

"Don't throw a fit."

He sighed. "You promised me."

"Yep, but the heart wants what it wants, and it took awhile for it to change its mind and not want it anymore. I just spent four hours on the phone with him, and it's over this time. He's bringing all my things to Momma's tomorrow morning. I called her and she's not so happy either."

"And you knew?" Rye asked Austin.

"Hey, don't put me in the middle of the family squabble. I just gave her a place to stay while she sorted it all out."

"So that's why the timing wasn't right?"

Austin blushed when she realized what he'd thought she meant.

"What timing?" Gemma asked.

"You turning on that damned light," Austin said.

"I didn't hear y'all drive up. I didn't know you were out there."

"Okay, it's too late to do anything more tonight so let's all get some sleep. It'll look different tomorrow," Austin said.

Rye looked at Gemma.

"I promise I'll stay here until Momma says he's come and gone. I don't want to see him again, either, and I promise it's over. He really, really broke my heart this time. I couldn't go through that twice."

"It's not easy to believe you. You promised me the last time he acted up that it was over," Rye said.

Austin had never had a brother or a sister to give a damn what she did or didn't do. She made herself a promise right then that if she ever had children, she'd have more than one so they could have what Gemma and Rye had.

"Forgive me?" Gemma's eyes pleaded.

Rye opened his arms and she walked into them. "Want me to go bruise him up a little for you?"

"The answer right now is yes but it won't be in the morning because he's not worth you busting a knuckle on," Gemma answered.

Rye raised an eyebrow at Austin when he stepped back from Gemma. "Okay then, ladies, I'm going home now. Want to go with me, Austin?"

"Like I said, timing's not right."

"Don't let me stop you," Gemma said.

Austin rolled up on her toes and kissed Rye on the cheek. "Good night and thanks again for a wonderful night. I'll never forget it."

"Me either."

There was an awkward moment when he couldn't look away.

Her feet were stuck so tight to the kitchen linoleum that she feared she'd be standing there when eternity dawned. Finally, he turned around and walked out without looking back.

Gemma whispered. "I'll be damned!"

"What?"

"I can't believe it. Rye O'Donnell is in love."

"Hell's bells, Gemma! That is a very serious thing," Austin argued.

Gemma just grinned. "Let's make a pot of coffee and talk. I don't have any appointments tomorrow so I can sleep as late as I want. How about you? You got farmin' to do or is Saturday free for you too?"

"I'm free," Austin whispered.

"Where's the coffee and the filters?"

Austin pointed to the cabinet above the percolator. "I saw your mother at the festival. She was worried about you."

"I called her after I got things settled with the bastard. No, I shouldn't call him that. His parents were married when he was born. He could be a son of a bitch though because part of the problem is his mother. She is a bitch with a capital B. Nothing is too good for her precious baby and, by damn, his way is the only way. A woman is supposed to walk three steps behind him, figure out what he wants before he does, and have it ready thirty seconds before he asks for it—and never cross him."

"Sounds like he should catch the next plane to the Middle East."

Gemma made coffee and pulled out a kitchen chair. "Never thought of it like that but that would be a good place for him. Now tell me, what is going on with you and my brother?"

"Nothing. You ever hear that song called 'Strawberry Wine'?"

Gemma nodded.

"Remember that part where it said something about being caught somewhere between a woman and a child. Well, I'm not in that place. But I'm caught somewhere between watermelon wine and martinis, if that makes a lick of sense."

"It does."

"Okay, then let's talk about you. Where are you going to live?"

"With the folks until I can find an apartment in Wichita Falls. Tell the truth I wish I could just put in a shop in Ringgold."

"Then why don't you?"

"Population 100."

"Terral doesn't have a beauty shop. Folks have to go to Ryan.

Ringgold is closer and then there's all those people between there and Henrietta and from there to Nocona. You might have more business than you realize."

Gemma poured two cups of coffee and set them on the table.

"Oh, crap, I forgot," Austin said.

"What?"

"Out on the porch. I set them on the chair while…"

"While you were making out with my brother?" Gemma's eyes twinkled.

Austin gave her a mean look. "Indian tacos. If Rascal hasn't eaten them, I brought you some supper."

Gemma raced to the door and retrieved the Styrofoam containers, carried them into the house, and pulled out a chair. "You are a darlin'. I'll marry you if my brother is too stupid to ask you."

CHAPTER 11

GEMMA WAS GONE WHEN AUSTIN AWOKE THE NEXT MORNING. There was a note beside the coffeepot that said her boyfriend had wasted no time in getting her stuff to her parents' house that morning and she was going home to talk about the future. She thanked Austin for the safe house and the late supper, but most of all for the support.

Austin roamed through the house and decided to start in the garage again, but when she opened the door, she shut it quickly. That's when the realization hit her like a bitch slap in the face. She'd *have* to be in and out of the house for the next few months, so she did not have to deal with the garage today.

"So I can work on it a weekend at a time through the summer. And I can see Rye every weekend and maybe have dinner with the O'Donnells sometimes."

The battle began.

In this corner was common sense. If she came back every weekend for three months, she'd never want to sell the farm when fall came.

"But I don't want to sell it! Where in the hell did that come from? I can't run a farm and do my job in Tulsa too. I'm not Superwoman."

In the other corner her heart was pouting. It wanted more time with Rye to see where the relationship might go. *Out of sight; out of mind.* It kept repeating that phrase over and over, reminding her that they'd barely gotten a foundation laid in the two weeks she'd been there. He'd forget a few wild kisses and a couple of nights of passionate fumbling in no time.

Temptation begged to stay.

Ambition insisted that she throw her bags in the 'Vette and leave Terral behind in a cloud of dust.

She poured cold cereal in a bowl and topped it off with milk and carried it to the living room desk. She pushed aside the payroll checkbook. She really needed to be there on Fridays for payroll.

"But if I go for good, I could make arrangements for the bank to do a direct payment each week for the money going to Mexico and then give them their money in advance for the rest of the season. Felix will have the truck." The more she rationalized, the heavier her heart became.

When she finished her breakfast, she had another idea. She called her boss on his cell phone. He picked up on the first ring. He was in the office playing Saturday morning catch-up before going to his daughter's softball game in Oklahoma City.

They did the usual niceties including *Are you getting your grandmother's affairs settled?* and *How are things at the office?* Then she hit him with the bombshell. "I'd like to work four days a week until the end of the summer. This is taking longer than I thought in the beginning. There's a crop in the field and payroll to meet on Fridays for the hired help. I'll stay late at my job there every night Monday through Thursday to make up the time."

"I think that is doable. I'll see you Monday?"

"Yes, and thank you."

"Austin, you know you are being groomed for my job. Don't let us down by deciding to make a career move toward farming. I'm looking forward to having you back in the office."

She said goodbye and heard the guys talking as they rounded the end of the house on their way back to their trailer. She hurried out the front door and yelled at Felix. He waved and headed to the porch.

"What is it?"

"I've made arrangements to work four days a week in Tulsa and be here on weekends until the crop is harvested. You have the keys to the old truck. Is there anything else you'll need me to do before I leave this afternoon? I'll be back every Thursday night and stay until late on Sunday."

Felix removed his hat and leaned against a porch post. "I'm sorry that you are going, but we will take care of this place like it was our own. You will be here on Friday for our payday?"

"Yes, I will, and in time to take it to the bank."

He nodded slowly. "Our families depend on that."

"I'll be here. Would you take care of Rascal?"

"That old tomcat eats at our trailer a lot of the time anyway. He likes Lobo's tacos as much as he likes his morning eggs. And he wanders across the road to Rye's place pretty often. Rye took care of him all these months since Miz Verline passed on. You be careful. Does Rye know you are leaving today?"

"I'll get in touch with him. He knows I'm going this weekend but not this afternoon. If you have a problem, I'm sure he'll help until I can get back down here over the weekend."

Felix settled his hat back on his head. "We will see you next Thursday then."

"Thank you," Austin said.

Had it only been two weeks since she and Pearlita had the simple memorial for her grandmother? That day seemed like a lifetime ago, one that she should leave in the past and go on to a very different one that involved green John Deere tractors instead of black power suits.

She went back inside and called Rye's number and got the answering machine. "Rye, this is Austin. I'm going back to Tulsa today. I've made arrangements with my boss to take off a day at a time on Fridays so I'll be back next weekend. I'd like to get home in time to run by my office and get things in order for Monday morning. Tell Maddie I'm sorry I'll miss the strawberry shortcake. I told Felix that if anything happens to call you. You've got my cell phone number so please call me when you get this message." She paused. Did she tell him that his kisses were still hot on her lips after twelve hours or that she would miss him? "Well, I guess that's all. Talk to you later. See you next weekend."

She flipped her phone shut. "Shit! That sounded like a message I'd leave for my mother. And I'm beginning to cuss like Granny. Molly and Greta must be right. There's something in the water."

It was on the machine and she couldn't erase it so she neatly packed her things into the suitcase, adding her jeans and shirts to her black suits and pajamas. She dressed in hip-slung jeans, comfortable boots, and a western shirt and pulled her hair up in a ponytail. She tried to call Rye one more time but got his answering machine again.

"Rye, I'm on my way out of here. Wanted to talk to you in person before I left, but I guess you are off somewhere this morning."

Then she tried his cell phone and got nothing but left a message there too. "Rye, I've talked to my boss and would love to tell you the new arrangements. Please call me."

She drove slowly through Terral but didn't see his truck in front of the café or at the Mini-Mart. Turning north at the stop sign was almost as hard as watching her grandmother's ashes float down the Red River. She pulled off the side of the road in front of the big brick *Welcome to Terral* sign and sat there for several minutes. The Lanier gut said she was making a big mistake, that she shouldn't leave Terral. She fought with it for a few minutes but she pulled back out on the road and drove north, arguing with herself every single mile she drove away from Terral.

———

Rye was whistling when he came in the house at dusk. He and Kent had walked the fence line until noon, shoring up the sagging barbed wire. They'd had lunch together at the Peach Orchard and then worked all afternoon on the loading chute for the rodeo livestock. On April 23 and 24 he'd have to have them in Mesquite, Texas, for the first rodeo of the season. He'd bring them home after that weekend and then reload them the week of May 21 for the season. After that, he'd be in Mesquite two days a week. The bulls looked brawny and were mean as hell. They'd give any rider a run for his money.

Kent had left at five thirty to take the family to Wichita Falls for dinner at Long John Silver's and a movie. Rye had put the finishing touches on the chute and checked out the farm pond with intentions of taking Austin fishing down at the river that night. He'd already figured out which quilt to take and what picnic basket to fill up with snack food; found a cooler and filled it with beer, ice, and a bottle of watermelon wine; and had a shower when he saw the red blinking light on the answering machine.

He called Austin and smiled when it rang once, imagining Austin coming down the hall in her overalls and tank top, all sweaty after a long day of packing boxes. His pulse raced and desire flooded his body at the vision. On the second ring he could almost hear her swearing. By the third ring he was pulling back his mini-blinds to see if there were lights on in the house. Fourth: it was dark as midnight and her little red car was nowhere to be seen. Fifth: Verline's voice answered, "If this is a telemarketer, take me off your list. You ain't got a thing I'm interested in buying or hearing about. Anyone else, you know the drill. When it beeps, you talk. When I get the message, I'll call back."

Rye's smile vanished, leaving a frown in its wake. Maybe she'd gone with Gemma down to Ringgold. He dialed his folks' number and Gemma picked up.

"Hello. If you are calling to fuss at me, don't. I'm at home and Momma says I can stay here until I find a place. We've got an idea in the works that Austin set me to thinkin' about."

"Where is Austin?"

"I left her asleep this morning. We talked until way past midnight, and when I woke up this morning I was so excited that I drove down here to talk to Momma and Daddy about things. I'm thinkin' of putting in a beauty shop of my own right here in Ringgold. What do you think about that?"

Rye sighed. Right then he didn't care if she put one in front of the pearly gates and fixed hair for free to the ladies who had an appointment with Saint Peter. "Honey, that sounds great. You'd be closer to home and Momma would like that. You could even help with the horses in your spare time."

Gemma groaned. "What spare time? I'll have to fix hair from daylight to dark to pay the loan off if I borrow money for my own shop."

"I'll loan you the money. I don't think Austin is going to sell the farm anytime soon, and that's the only place up here I'm interested in buying."

"Ahhh! You are a good brother. Are you serious?"

"I am. You sure you haven't heard from her?"

"Not since last night. You two have a fight or something?"

"No, I just thought she might want to go fishing. She might have gone to play poker with Molly and Greta on a last-minute whim. See you at dinner tomorrow," Rye said. They only had this one last night together so surely she didn't go to a poker game. Unless she had decided to stay in Terral! His heart raced at that idea. Maybe she had gone to Nocona or Bowie to buy groceries for several weeks.

He hung up and looked at the flashing red light and the number four. He removed a beer from the cooler, popped the tab off the top, and pushed the button. Leaning on the kitchen cabinet, he listened to the first message, which offered him a great deal on a three-day trip to Branson, Missouri. Hotel, two shows a day, and dinner all for one low price.

"Does Austin like music shows?" he asked.

The second message wanted to sell him a time-share condo in Florida.

"What would she look like in a bikini?"

The third was a blank. Nobody talked.

He'd just taken a sip of beer when he heard Austin's voice telling him she was going back to Tulsa. His throat shut off and he had trouble swallowing. He listened to it all the way through. By the time it finished, he was gripping the can so hard that the sides were crushed and beer spewed out the top.

"Damn it all to hell! I thought we had at least one more day before she left." He threw the beer into the kitchen sink and stomped back to the window. The house across the street not only looked empty, it felt vacated. She'd said she'd be back on Friday but that was almost a week away.

He looked on the dresser where he'd emptied his pockets for his cell phone but it wasn't there. Then he remembered that the battery was nearly dead and he'd plugged it into the cigarette lighter outlet in the pickup and forgotten about it. He jogged out the back door to his truck and jerked the cords loose.

He listened to her two messages and dialed her cell number the minute they ended. She picked up on the first ring.

"Hi!"

"Where are you?" he asked.

"In traffic on the outskirts of Tulsa. I've got that dinner thing with my family tomorrow night, but I thought if I got up here early enough I could get my office in order tomorrow and the week would go easier. Did you get my messages?" she asked.

"I did."

"I'll be back late Thursday. I made arrangements with my boss to work late whenever I need to and to take three-day weekends all summer so I can be there to do the guys' payroll and have the weekends in Terral."

"I see."

"Are you mad? You sound angry," she said.

"No, I just wanted to see you before you left. I'm not mad. I'm disappointed. I thought we'd go get a pizza from the Mini-Mart and go fishin.'"

"Well, shit! I'm disappointed, too, but I'll be back Thursday."

He smiled at her cussing. "You could turn around and come back. You'd be home by midnight and we could forget fishin' and do something more fun."

"Ah, man! I'd rather do that anytime as drive in this traffic. Gotta go. It's too dangerous to talk and drive in this mess. Call you later."

CHAPTER 12

Austin's stomach was growling loudly when she hung up. She'd had a chicken sandwich from the McDonald's drive-through in Oklahoma City but had only eaten half of it. It was difficult to eat when all she wanted to do was cry.

A tour bus passed her and quickly pulled back in front of her little sports car. It had a picture of a bronc rider on the back in bigger-than-life full living color and the words "See Texas" across the side. That brought a picture of Rye to her mind and she sighed.

It was near dark when she pulled into the gated apartment complex where she lived and showed the guard her ID card. She parked her dusty Corvette in the garage, reset the security code when she had lowered the door, and went into the apartment through the back door. The spotless kitchen was decorated with shades of bright yellow against a black marble countertop, charcoal-gray tile floor, and stark white cabinets. Four modern chrome and black leather stools were drawn up to a bar separating the dining area from the kitchen. A matching glass-topped table with chrome legs and chairs with black padded seats took center stage in the dining area with the same decor flowing into the living room with its black velvet furniture, misty gray carpet, and bright-yellow throw pillows. A brass floor lamp illuminated an original oil of a sunset and the ocean hanging above her sofa.

Austin carried her suitcase to the bedroom and dropped it beside the king-sized bed that looked like an acre and a half after the twin-sized one she'd been sleeping on in Terral. She checked her answering machine. It looked like blinking lights on a Christmas tree. Holding her breath and hoping to hear Rye's deep voice, she hit the button and threw herself across the bed.

The first one had been left the day she went to Terral: her mother telling her that she was sorry she'd missed her. It went from there to telemarketers trying to sell her bogus extended warranties on her car, lesser insurance on her house since she owned it (which she did not), to more insurance on her life in case her children needed it for final arrangements, to political surveys to see if she was in agreement with all of the President's recent activity. But there was no message from Rye.

"Shit! He doesn't have my house phone. Just my cell phone."

She grabbed it but the batteries were dead. "Damn newfangled gadgets anyway," she grumbled.

She picked up the house phone and dialed Rye's cell number, and the call went to voicemail.

"I'm in my apartment. Please call me at this number," she said and unknowingly rattled off Verline's house number in Terral.

She stretched out on the sofa with the phone right next to her, shut her eyes and fell into an exhausted sleep. She dreamed of watermelon fields, watermelon wine, and Rye. They'd taken a bottle from the cellar and were picking their way through fully ripe watermelons on their way to the river to lie on the banks and watch the moon come up. They were older in her dream. White frosted the temples of Rye's black hair, and her dark tresses were streaked with silver. The happiness she had in the dream vanished when the telephone awoke her two hours later.

"Hello?" she said groggily.

"I figured you'd be up and on the road." Her mother's voice wasn't happy.

Austin sighed and looked at the clock. It wasn't quite ten. She wondered what Rye was doing.

"I'm not in Terral. I'm at my apartment. I decided to let the hired help bring in one more crop before I sell the place so they'll have a job. They have work visas and their families depend on their summer paychecks. So I've got all summer to take care of things in Terral. I made an arrangement with Harvey to take Fridays off," Austin answered flatly.

"Well, damn!"

"I thought you'd be happy that I'm home."

"I thought it would be over and done with today, and you'd be permanently home where you belong."

Where do I belong? Everything looks so sterile here and so cluttered there. Is there a happy medium somewhere in between the two places?

"Well?" Barbara quipped when Austin didn't answer.

"Guess I'm not," Austin said.

Was Rye already asleep or had he gone to his folks' house to talk to Gemma?

"I'm calling to tell you that your aunts couldn't get away so we're having the dinner next week instead of today."

She could've cried. She would have stayed in Terral until after dinner with the O'Donnells if she'd known. She would have had one more day with Rye and worked late on Sunday night to catch up at the office.

"You will be here?" Barbara asked when Austin didn't answer.

"I'll be here. I can leave early on Sunday and be back in time for supper. But I'll be leaving each week as soon as I get away from work on Thursday. I have to be at the Ryan bank on Fridays for payroll. Greta and Molly expect me at the Ryan drugstore at two for ice cream."

"I expect by the time you get that crop in you'll be damn glad to come home permanently. It's probably a wise decision because you'll see the contrast between Podunk and living right."

"Maybe so, but then maybe I'll decide I like Podunk better."

"I hope not! Have a good week. I've made plans for tomorrow, or I'd invite you over for lunch. See you in a week for dinner."

"I'll be there." Austin's heart whined for Rye O'Donnell.

She was in the shower when she heard her cell phone ringing again and hurried out to grab it. Standing there dripping water onto the hardwood floor in her bedroom, she answered breathlessly.

"Hey, girl, where are you?" Gemma asked.

"I came back to Tulsa. Didn't Rye tell you?"

"No, he called and wanted to know if I'd heard from you, but he didn't mention that you'd left. Then I can have your share of shortcake at dinner tomorrow?"

"Sure you can. Did you think about a shop of your own today?"

"I did. I told Rye and he said that he'd even finance it, and Momma said she and Daddy would help me get started. There's an empty building down beside the Chicken Fried Café a couple of miles south of Ringgold. It used to be a little used car place years ago, and they used the building for an office. It's a good size and there's parking room. Come back and help me decide on colors."

"I'll be there on weekends. Probably getting in late Thursday night and coming back about noon on Sunday," Austin said.

"That is wonderful! Have a good week, and we'll see you next weekend."

Rye turned on the television and surfed through the channels. Nothing, not even the bull riding, kept his attention. He popped the tab on a second beer, carried it out to the front porch, and stared at the empty house across the road. Finally he walked over there and sat down on the porch. Rascal meandered around the end of the house and lay down close enough that Rye could scratch his ears.

"Are you already missing her too?"

Rascal set up a noisy purr.

"I thought I had another day at the very least. Actually, I hoped for a miracle and that she'd stay on forever. I had big things planned."

Rascal arched his head back.

Stars twinkled in half the sky. The other half was a mass of black clouds rolling in from the southwest. Depending on how big the storm was and how slow or fast it moved, there was a good chance neither he nor Raylen would show off their bronc-busting powers the next day. He'd looked forward to a little rivalry between him and Raylen, just to show off for Austin. Now it would be work and not fun, so he didn't care if it poured down rain all day.

"Let's call her again." Rye pulled his phone from his shirt pocket, and the call went straight to voicemail.

"Why in the devil didn't I make sure I had her home phone number as well as her cell number? Maybe her cell phone is dead and she's recharging it? Maybe she turned the ringer off or maybe she's in the shower. What do you think, Rascal?"

Rascal jumped up in his lap. Rye scratched the cat with one hand and tried calling Austin one more time but got voicemail again telling him to leave a message at the beep. He was so engrossed in her voice that he didn't realize it was time for him to leave a message. "I was petting Rascal and didn't realize it was time to talk. This is Rye. I was checking to make sure you made it home all right. Call me when you have time."

He'd barely finished talking when his cell phone rang.

"Hello," he said breathlessly.

"What were you doing?" Gemma laughed.

"Nothing. The phone startled me."

"Hoping it was someone other than your sister?"

"You are nosy."

"And you thought it was Austin, didn't you?"

"Did you call for a reason or to tease me?"

"Momma says it's raining and the weatherman says it's a slow-moving storm coming from out around Amarillo so we won't be breaking horses tomorrow. We will have dinner, and I already talked to Austin so I get her share of the shortcake."

"Okay. I'll leave my spurs at home and be there in time for dinner."

"Aren't you interested in what she had to say? I called her to see if she was still coming to dinner and to tell her that I'm considering her idea about a beauty shop in this area."

"I talked to her awhile ago," he said.

"Good. My battery is about to go and I'm getting those annoying little beeps so we'll see you for dinner tomorrow."

———————

Austin had been in the shower when both phone calls came in. She was drying her hair when the house phone rang and she raced to the kitchen to grab it on the second ring, hoping to hear Rye's deep voice on the other end.

"Hello," she said breathlessly but it wasn't Rye. It was her mother.

"I've got the whole day free tomorrow after all. Let's do brunch and shop away the afternoon. I hear there's a sale on women's suits at Neiman's. I've been looking at a cute little red one that might be half-price today."

"I thought you were going to be busy."

"Ask me no questions. I'll tell you no lies. I'll pick you up at eleven. Dress casual since we'll be trying on clothes."

"I'll be ready."

She found Rye's messages on her cell when she went back to the bedroom and called him. He answered on the first ring.

"I need your house phone number. You never did give it to me," he said. "You've always called me on your cell phone or Verline's phone."

"I left it on your answering machine."

"You left Granny's number on my answering machine."

She giggled. "I'm sorry, Rye. Here it is." She rattled it off and wondered if it was an omen. Had she begun to think of Terral as home and automatically rattled off the phone there?

He wrote it down and memorized the numbers as she said them. "We've been playing phone tag for over an hour."

"I miss you," she blurted out.

That put a smile on his face and lightened the heavy rock lying where his heart was supposed to be. He jumped up from the sofa and danced around the living room, pretending the phone was Austin. "Oh, honey, I've been lonesome all evening. That house across the road is just as lonesome as I am."

She felt as if he'd kissed her with his words. "I'm so sorry I didn't see you before I left. It was tough leaving Terral. I thought I'd be ready to get back to Tulsa. I wasn't."

The rock was gone and his heart skipped two full beats.

"Good! I knew you were a farmer the first day you dropped seeds in the ground."

She yawned. "Can we talk about this more tomorrow? I'm so tired and sleepy tonight that I'm actually weepy."

"Yes, darlin', we can. You sleep late and I'll call in the afternoon."

"Good night, Rye. I wish I had a good-night kiss."

"So do I. Good night."

He said the words so softly that she touched her lips to see if they'd been kissed.

———

"Damn!" Austin exclaimed the next morning when her apartment door shut behind her. She hurriedly unlocked it, ran back into the apartment, and picked up her cell phone. She didn't intend to miss a single one of Rye's calls even if she was with her mother all day. She jogged to the car where her mother was waiting.

"Good morning. I'm glad for emergencies," Barbara said.

"Want to explain what you are talking about?"

"Not really because you are going to have a fit about it, but I suppose this is as good a time as any. I'm seeing a doctor, a surgeon."

She spit it out as if she was telling Austin about the new line of Chevrolets coming out in the fall.

"But…" Austin sputtered.

"Your father has been dead for years. I'm still young enough that I'd like to have a male companion, and James is a wonderful man."

Austin took a deep breath. "Okay, how long have you been seeing him?"

Barbara squirmed in the driver's seat of her Chevy Tahoe. "Why did you ask that?"

"Just wondered."

"I started seeing him six months after your father died. I knew you'd be a blister so I didn't bother to tell you until now. But now that's out of the way, we'll go to brunch and do some shopping," Barbara said and began to talk about how many cars she'd sold that week since her stock was back up.

Austin giggled.

"What's so funny? Selling cars is what makes my living."

"You are talking too much, which means you are nervous," Austin answered.

"If I'm talking, then you can't and I don't want to hear all that you are thinking about me having a companion all these years and not telling you."

"I was happy these past weeks in a strange kind of way. I thought I'd be sad after the memorial service and when I had to pack Granny's things. But it was weird how happy I was. I'm not mad at you. I want you to be as happy as I am."

You don't miss the water until the well runs dry. It felt like Verline was in the back seat of the shiny black Tahoe whispering in her ear.

Barbara didn't comment but changed the subject abruptly. "Your grandparents are finally tired of taking trips. I'm glad since they're both in their eighties now. I worry when they go to those faraway places that they'll have a heart attack over there. They were my age when they retired and gave me and your father the business. They were both fifty-two and still young, like I am. If this promotion doesn't come through for you, I've been thinking about retiring in the next five years and giving you the business."

You want to sell cars or make wine?

Austin turned around and made sure her granny wasn't sitting there in her overalls and boots.

"So?" Barbara asked.

"So don't expect me to make a decision like that on a moment's notice. I figured you'd run that business until you dropped dead after a record selling day."

"I planned on it but then…"

"But then you figured out how much fun James can be. Right? Is he about ready to retire? Oh, my God, is he about to propose to you? Or has he already done so?"

Barbara pushed back a strand of hair. "I'm not ready to hand you the keys today, but the place will be yours someday. I was younger than you are when your father and I took charge of it."

Wine, her heart whispered.

Cars, common sense said.

But what if it's neither or maybe both? she argued.

"Thank you for the offer but that's five years down the road…"

Barbara sighed. "That place got its hooks into you, didn't it?"

"Oh, Mother, you are getting worked up over nothing."

"It's my comeuppance. Your grandmother said that I took her son and someday I'd regret it. I loved him, Austin, with my whole heart but I could not live in that godforsaken place."

"I doubt there was much in the way of business down there that you all could have made a living at."

"We could have worked in Duncan or in Wichita Falls, either one, and been closer but…" She let the sentence dangle.

When there's a but there's a regret. Do whatever you do without a but, and you'll be happy.

Austin looked over her shoulder again but the back seat was still empty.

"Let's eat and shop," Austin said with as much excitement as she could muster.

They were walking into the mall when Austin's phone vibrated in her pocket. She picked it out to see a text message from Rye.

Call me when you wake up. I'm lonely.

Barbara went straight for the suit rack in her favorite dress shop, and Austin said she was going to look at shoes. She sat down in the back corner of the shoe department and sent him a text.

Shopping with Mother. Will call when I get home. Miss you!

She was trying on a pair of high heels when the phone buzzed again.

Miss you too! I want to hear your voice. Call me when you can.

They shopped until the stores closed in the mall, then made a trip through Walmart for their weekly staples like bagels, nonfat cream cheese, skim milk, and yogurt. When Austin got home, the little red light was flashing on the answering machine so she poked the right button and held her breath.

"Darlin', the day dragged by like a lazy old house slug. If every day is like this until Thursday, I won't live through them. Call me when you get home. I can't wait to talk to you."

She played the message through four times. His voice in her ear made her breath a little heavier, and she wished she could dart across the street and talk to him. Ask him what he thought about her selling cars or even simply find out what had gone on in his day.

Before she took the first bite of the fried rice, she called him. On the fifth ring his answering machine came on again. She called his cell and got his voicemail.

"Hi, this is Austin. We must be playing phone tag again. I'll be home all evening. Shopped with Mother. I just now checked the messages. I'm so sorry I missed your call."

The phone rang four times before she went to bed but none of them was Rye. She'd barely turned out the lights when the phone rang again.

"Hello?" she said.

"Austin, this is pure hell," he said bluntly.

"I know. I hate it, too, but it's the only way I can keep things going on two ends of the state," she groaned.

"I want to kiss you good night. I want to hold you, not this damned old cold phone," he said.

"Me too," she sighed. How was she going to leave next time knowing that Rye wanted to kiss her good night every night?

"Tell me about your shopping day," he said.

"You don't want to hear about dress racks and trying on clothing."

"I want to hear your voice. You can read the whole Bible or talk about accounting. I don't care what you say. I just want your voice in my ear as I fall asleep."

"Where are you?"

"On the sofa. Why? Where are you?"

"In bed with the lights turned out. I'm shutting my eyes and thinking about us being on the quilt beside the river. I can hear the tree frogs and the crickets," she said softly.

"You are killing me," he moaned.

"And you are running your hand up my thigh all the way to where my cutoffs end and oops, there it is right on the elastic of my bikini underwear," she said.

"And the other one is sneaking up on those bra hooks. God, Austin, I want you so bad," he said hoarsely.

"Now your lips are on mine, and I can taste strawberry short-cake and Coors beer. It's a wonderful combination. Your tongue is teasing my mouth open, and I run my hands over your rock-hard muscles. I touch the tat but it's not sticky like barbed wire. I can't even feel where it begins and where it ends."

"Your hands are like silk on my skin. I'm going to take off your shirt and taste you from nose to toes," he said.

She giggled. "If I'm going to sleep at all tonight, darlin', we're going to have to stop this phone sex before you talk about that or I'll be walkin' the floor all night."

"You could tell them all to go to hell, be here in five hours, and we could have the real thing. Wait a minute… your breasts taste faintly like that coconut bath oil you use."

"God Almighty, Rye! I'm so hot the sheets are steaming."

"Me too. Good night, darlin'. I know you'll be at work tomorrow. I won't call but I'll text through the day and save that coconut thought for tomorrow night."

Surprisingly, after going over the conversation again, she did fall asleep, almost as if in the afterglow of the real thing. She slept soundly and dreamed of Rye. The next morning she awoke with a start at seven thirty and realized that she hadn't set the alarm. She was about to be late to work for the first time in her life. Jumping out of bed with a shriek, she ran to the bathroom to take a quick shower and slap on makeup. Breakfast would have to wait. She had thirty minutes, and fifteen of that was the drive to work. She wanted to talk to Rye but there was no time.

She reached her office with one minute to spare and found a thick folder on her desk with a sticky note on the top from her secretary saying that she needed to look at it carefully before the morning's business meeting. She picked up a pencil and yellow legal pad to take notes and started reading. Her stomach growled and her cell phone rang at the same time. She pulled the phone from her purse hoping that it was Rye but it was her mother.

"Where are you?" Barbara asked.

"In my office playing catch-up so I won't be in the dark at the meeting that starts in a few minutes."

"Well, don't let me keep you. James and I are going down to Eufaula this evening and watching the sun set from his boat."

"Have fun," Austin said.

"I know you'll be busy this week, but don't forget about our dinner next week," Barbara said.

"How could I forget? You and my two aunts keep me well reminded."

"Don't get snippy. Terral does that to a person."

Austin leaned back in her leather desk chair and sighed. "Got to get back to work. Goodbye, Mother."

Austin had just finished looking over the notes for the morning meeting when her assistant appeared at the door with the week's itinerary.

"Thank you, Laura," she said.

"So you've got everything settled down in southern Oklahoma?"

"Nothing is settled, and I'll be working four-day weeks, so keep that in mind. We'll have to get five days done in four most of the summer."

Laura was a short brunette who loved too much blue eye shadow and miniskirts that were too tight and short to pass an office dress code, but she was the best help Austin had ever had. "It's a good thing you are here because Derk has been sucking up to the boss man. I think he wants that promotion that you are supposed to get. Something is different about you. You don't look the same."

Austin set her briefcase on her desk and gave herself a quick glance-over to make sure she hadn't done anything stupid in her haste.

"It's not your suit or your makeup," Laura said. "It's something about your face. You are smiling."

Austin smiled even bigger. "Are you saying that I don't smile?"

"Yes, you smile, but it never reaches your eyes. I'm saying that you look happy. Remember how I've told you that you need to get a life. Did you?"

"No, I didn't, but I did go to a rattlesnake festival and I rode those little teacup things with the sexiest cowboy in Jefferson County."

"Well, hot damn! That's a step in the right direction."

"Gotta run. Hold the fort down," Austin said and was almost to the meeting when her phone buzzed.

She looked at the message from Rye.

Are you at work?

As she walked, she answered: On my way to a meeting.

He wrote back: **Kick ass.**

She laughed aloud and hit the speed dial for his cell phone.

He picked up on the first ring.

"I needed to hear your voice," she said.

"Shut your eyes."

"I can't, Rye. I'm rushing from my office to the conference room. I'll fall on my ass rather than kicking ass," she said, laughing.

"Then shut one eye and imagine that I'm kissing you good morning," he said.

She stopped dead and shut both eyes. If anyone passed her in the corridor, they could think she was catching her breath before walking into the conference. The kiss that she imagined didn't make her have to change underwear but it didn't miss it far.

"Thank you, Rye," she whispered and opened her eyes to find two secretaries rushing past her.

"Keep that in your mind all day," he said.

"I really do miss you."

"Me too," he said.

Austin slid into her chair seconds before Derk strolled in with his million-dollar smile and overabundance of confidence.

"You're back!" His smile faded but his confidence didn't waver. "It's been hectic but I've kept the wrinkles ironed out."

"Good for you," Austin said.

He held up a palm. "No thanks necessary. Just doing what any good man would do."

She didn't miss the emphasis on the words *good man*. The gauntlet had been slapped down in front of her, and her competitive side picked up the challenge. She'd show him that a good woman could iron out wrinkles faster and better than a man could any day of the week. The room filled quickly after that, and Monday began with a rush that didn't look like it would slow down a bit until the weekend.

Her boss was giving them a rundown of the quarterly report in minute detail when she felt the phone vibrate in her pocket. She carefully pulled it out and read the message from Rye.

What are you wearing right now?

She bit the inside of her lip to keep from giggling and wrote back with one thumb. A business suit and spike heels.

Immediately he replied: **Cute black panties with the suit?**

She covered the giggle with a cough and took a drink of water. No one even noticed.

Hell, no. I had to throw them in the trash after that morning kiss.

She made one note before she got his reply: **Pretend I'm under the desk doing wicked things.**

She clamped her knees together so quickly that the stress sent a runner down her black hose, but he wasn't going to win the game.

Are you naked? she typed in while she pretended to listen.

Immediately he responded. **No!**

What are you wearing then? she asked.

A barbed-wire tat. Want to play with it?

Honey, I'd rather play with something else.

Okay, you vixen. I'm crazy with wanting you. Come home!

Will you meet me at the door wearing only a tat?

Yes, ma'am.

When she looked up, Derk was watching her with a wicked grin as if he'd hacked into her phone and read everything she'd written. She picked up her pen and tried to pay attention but it wasn't easy.

Barbara called at noon and her voice was happy. "Busy, are you?"

"Very." Austin talked and made notes for Laura at the same time.

"Just think how worn out you'll be making that drive twice every single week. You'll be making mistakes at work, and someone else will wind up with the promotion."

"Mother, stop trying to manipulate me. I'm thirty. I know what I'm doing." Austin rolled her eyes. *And after that text session this morning, I'd fight a hurricane to get to Terral this weekend.*

Laura covered her mouth to keep the high-pitched giggle from escaping.

"Well, I hope so. You are about to stagnate right where you are with no chance of going up the next ladder step because of a stupid watermelon crop."

"I've got a meeting in five minutes. If that's all you want to talk about, then we'll discuss it later."

"Oh, yes we will," Barbara said.

Austin put the phone back on the base and said, "Mothers!"

"Amen," Laura said. "Mine is out combing the countryside for a husband for me. I keep telling her I'm only twenty-five but she says I'm getting long in the tooth."

"Mine is scared to death I'll find a husband. She wants me to grow up to be like my aunts. A career woman to the bone marrow."

Laura picked up the notes and went back to her desk. "Ain't they wonderful?"

The day went by in a blur. Austin picked up takeout Chinese on the way home and remembered that she and Rye were supposed to have dinner at a Chinese place in Duncan on the night they went to the rattlesnake festival. Was that just three days before? Lord, it seemed like a year.

She set her briefcase and purse on the sofa, carried the sack with her supper to the bar, and propped a hip on a stool, intending to call Rye the minute she finished eating. She'd barely swallowed her first bite of rice when the phone rang. She picked it up on the second ring and said, "Hello."

"I just got in the house from a long day of plowing. How'd your first day back in the big business world go? I want to hear all about it. Don't leave out anything," Rye said.

His voice was both soothing and exciting. Austin shut her eyes and wished she was standing in his kitchen with a beer in her hand, watching his expressions as he talked.

"It was hectic as hell. I found out a man at work is kissing ass to get my promotion. Had dinner with my mother yesterday, and now she wants to give me the dealership within five years."

"Details." Rye carried the phone to the living room and melted into his recliner, wishing that Austin was sharing it with him, so close that he could hear her heart beat and smell her hair all freshly washed with that coconut shampoo.

"First you tell me about things in Terral. Are my watermelons coming up out of the ground? Are Felix and the hired hands doing all right over there? What about Gemma? I haven't heard from her since Saturday."

He talked first about the watermelons, the cat, and the hired hands. "Darlin', that is not what I want to talk about," he said.

"I know what you want to talk about but I'm telling you after that text session, I'm not sure my body can handle it."

"Ah, come on, Austin, tell me again what you want to play with that's lower than my tat." He laughed.

"Rye O'Donnell, I…" She stopped herself before she said "I love you but I really can't take any more phone sex."

"You what, Austin?"

"I'm going to take a long, cold shower and hope that cools me down."

"If you are as hot as I am, that won't do the trick. Three more days and then it's going to be more than phone sex or text sex."

"You'd better eat oysters all three days," she said and told him good night.

Hanging up was every bit as hard as turning north on Highway 81 out of Terral on Saturday afternoon. She held the phone to her heart and shut her eyes tightly.

One word played through her mind with country fiddles and Floyd Cramer's tinkling piano music in the background.

It was *wine*.

CHAPTER 13

ON TUESDAY, RYE SENT HER A TEXT MESSAGE WHEN SHE WAS having lunch with Laura. It said: **Which trash can?**

She giggled and wrote back: Boxers or tighty-whiteys?

Commando!

She groaned and Laura raised an eyebrow.

"That sexy cowboy has sex on the brain," she whispered as if Rye was in the next room.

"Then what the hell are you doing in Tulsa?" Laura asked.

On Wednesday she didn't hear from him until midafternoon when he called.

"I was lonesome and needed to hear your voice. I ate at the Peach Orchard and pretended you were sitting beside me," he said when she answered the phone. "Can we talk for a little while or are you too busy?"

"I'll take a fifteen-minute break," she answered and pushed her papers to the side of the desk. She slipped her shoes off and propped her feet on the desk. "I can't wait until tomorrow evening. Will you be there when I arrive?"

"I'll try to be. I've got to be out of town but you shouldn't beat me home by much. I left a key to my house under a flowerpot right beside the front door. Go on in and have a cold beer. I've already got a bottle of Granny's wine in the fridge," he said.

"I'll be there. If you get home before I do—" She paused. She'd said home, not Terral.

"What?"

"You can meet me at the door in nothing but that tat," she teased.

"Honey, are you sure you want to go there right now?"

She giggled. "No, sir! I do not! I can't waste any more panties."

"On that note, I'm going to hang up and call you tonight." He almost said "love you" before he hung up, but those words wouldn't quite come out of his mouth.

On Thursday Austin left work at exactly five o'clock and hit heavy traffic going out of Tulsa, then rain on the east side of Oklahoma City. It let up briefly near Chickasha but then came down in buckets from there to Ryan where she had about two minutes' reprieve before it hit again. She could hardly see the *Welcome to Terral* sign. The lights at the Mini-Mart let her know it was time to turn left, and the speed bumps in front of the school told her emphatically that she was going too fast.

She parked as close to the front porch as she could, grabbed her suitcase from the back seat, and hurried but was still soaked by the time she was inside Rye's trailer. She kicked off her high heels at the door and shed panty hose and clothing on the way to the bedroom. She unzipped the suitcase and took out a short, pink silk kimono robe and wrapped it around her body.

Food hadn't been a top priority on her list when she left Tulsa but now it was. She opened the fridge door to find a plate with a big square of lasagna covered with plastic wrap. A note on the top said to microwave for three minutes, that there was salad in the Cool Whip container and cut-up strawberries for shortcake in the Parkay margarine container. Beer was cold but if she wanted a bottle of wine, it was in the side pocket on the fridge door. It was signed, *Rye (but Maddie sent all the food)*.

Austin warmed the lasagna and ate the salad right out of the container. She opted for cold beer instead of wine and didn't leave a teaspoon of the strawberries or the juice in the margarine bowl. She put the dishes in the dishwasher and looked out the window at the rain, which was coming down even harder. The phone rang and she jumped like she did when she was a child and got caught doing something she shouldn't.

Racing down the hall to her purse, she stubbed her toe and swore in a bright array of blinding colors. She flipped open the phone on the fifth ring, just before it went to voicemail.

"Hello!"

"Is that any way to greet your mother?"

Disappointment washed over her worse than the rainstorm had done when she'd dashed from the car to the house. "I ran from the kitchen. Left my phone in my purse on the bed. Got a catch in my side," Austin said in short, clipped sentences.

"Just making sure you arrived safely. Is Romeo already there? Is that why you were in the bedroom?" Barbara's voice was cold disapproval mixed with smoking anger.

"His name is Rye. He's at a rodeo in Wichita Falls. He's riding a bull tonight. But he did leave me a wonderful supper of lasagna, salad, and fresh strawberries cut up and sugared for shortcake in the refrigerator, and I'm sure he'll be here to cook breakfast for me bright and early tomorrow morning."

"You'll gain fifty pounds by the end of summer."

"Last time I checked, they still made clothes in sizes with lots of X's so I'm not real worried about it."

"Don't be snippy with me. Verline's mother was obese, and you appear to have inherited her genes and attitude."

"You knew my great-grandmother? Everyone down here says I'm built like Granny. Tall and thin and can eat anything I want without gaining weight, but tell me about her mother."

"I met her one time right after your father and I married. There's James at the door. I'll see you on Sunday. Good night!" The line went dead.

A flash of lightning brought rolling thunder. The clouds couldn't be more than six inches from the roof to bring on such bright flashes or such rumbling thunder. Austin thought she heard the crunch of tires on the gravel driveway so she took her hands away from the sides of her face. It was probably a couple of teenagers used to using the driveway for a parking place since no one had been home all week.

The lights flickered and the electricity went out at the same time the next clap of thunder kissed the roof. She gasped when the front door opened and lightning lit up a man in a long denim duster standing between her and the door.

"Austin," Rye said softly as he threw the duster over the back of a chair.

She met him in the middle of the floor in a clash of passion that lit up the room brighter than the lightning flashes. His hands were under the robe and touching. His lips were on hers, hungrily trying to make up for five days without her. "God, I missed you so bad," he whispered as he carried her to the living room.

She unsnapped his shirt and ran her hands over all his hard muscles, thinking that there was no way she could ever leave again.

And that's when Verline's spirit interfered again! The phone rang and he groaned. No way was he answering that damned thing. She ignored it and threw her head back so he could kiss her neck. Delightful shivers danced up and down her spine.

The answering machine picked up. "Rye, guess you're still at the rodeo. I hope to hell there's still a key under the flowerpot. I'm coming home from Duncan tonight and the weather is horrible. I'm staying in your guest room. I'm just now on the outskirts of Terral but I'm not driving all the way home in this mess." Wil's voice came through loud and clear. "Don't wake me in the morning. I've been gone for three days and I'm sleeping until noon."

Rye groaned and picked Austin up like a bride, draped his duster over her body, and walked out the front door. By the time they were across the road and on her porch, they were both drenched but neither of them cared. There was plenty of heat from the passionate kisses they'd shared the whole distance.

She leaned down slightly and opened the door. After walking inside, he kicked it shut with his bootheel and tossed the duster on the floor. She fumbled with his belt but finally figured out how to loosen it, unzipped his pants, and wiggled until she was facing him with her legs firmly around his. She shifted her weight until he was inside her. He took a step and braced her against the wall and kept his lips on hers, their tongues twisting together in passion, and a sudden fury of thrusts that ended entirely too soon.

"Hot damn!" she mumbled. She'd never had sex anywhere but in a bed with the man on top. And it had never—not one time—brought about the kind of fire that still had her panting and wanting more.

"Yeah!" he said and carried her still wrapped around his waist to the living room where he collapsed on the sofa with her still sitting in his lap.

Until that moment she didn't know that a man could moan with a deep Texas drawl and just how damn sexy it was. With his lips still hungrily tasting hers, he ran his palms from her chin, up across her cheeks, and tangled his hands in her hair.

"You taste good and look beautiful," he whispered.

She couldn't say a word with his lips planted firmly on hers in kisses still so hot that she thought she'd melt in nothing but a puddle of whining hormones at the toes of his wet cowboy boots. She leaned back and looked up and their eyes locked in a flash of lightning and their lips met again in a clash louder than the thunder.

"Have I told you how much I missed you and how lovely you are in that robe?"

"Have I told you how much I missed you and how sexy you are with raindrops in your hair and scruff on your face? I've never seen you unshaven. I want more than a fast up-against-the-wall session after not seeing you for five days."

"Oh, honey, we are just getting started." He brought his lips to hers for another kiss. If the bulls got out tonight, they could swim the river and join a herd of wild longhorns. If Kent called to tell him lightning had struck his house and it was burning to the ground, he'd tell him to call later. He untied the belt of the robe and circled her small waist with his hands. "Your skin is cool silk. When I touch you, my brain goes to mush."

"I don't even have a brain, just an aching desire for you to keep touching my body." She shifted so that she could taste his neck and nibble on his earlobes. When she looked up, his eyes were dreamy and scorching hot at the same time. She stretched enough to brush a kiss against each of his eyelids.

Her touch, her lips, and her skin against his were satin sheets against rough, old callused hands. He had never taken a woman in such a fit of raw passion, never felt such a thing until he saw her standing there in a flash of lightning. He shifted his position, and suddenly she was under him on the sofa and her robe was wide open. She jerked the tail of his shirt from his jeans and peeled it from his shoulders. It landed on a table full of knickknacks when she tossed it and she giggled.

"What?" he asked.

"That bunch of animals won't be watching."

This time his touch was as gentle as a feather on her skin, making her gasp and arch her back for more. How could a cowboy's hands be so soft and gentle, yet so demanding at the same time? He worked his way down to her breasts, touching and feeling and tasting. When he touched her inner thigh, she opened up for him and gasped when he found erogenous places that had never been touched before. She grabbed his hair and pulled him back up for another kiss before she unbuckled his belt and unzipped his jeans. She flipped places with him and sat naked on his thighs as she removed his boots and peeled his jeans down from his hips and legs. They landed somewhere near the computer desk. She turned back around and stretched out on top of him.

Her hands were ice, fire, and cool satin all at the same time when they touched his skin. When she tugged his jeans off and kissed each toe, desire shot through his body like an IV of pure Jack Daniel's whiskey. As she worked her way up to his lips, lightning kept giving him flashes of her long hair and blue eyes that had gone soft and sweet.

When she was stretched on top of him, he wrapped his arms around her and rolled gently off the sofa onto the floor, pinning her beneath him. "This sofa is too narrow but there's lots of floor."

His hands were on that sensitive part of her ribs, right under her breasts. Another place she didn't realize could heat a woman up to the explosion stage. She arched her back against him and lost every sane thought. The delicious ache was back, even though she'd just had mind-frying sex with him. There were no watermelons, no bulls, no oil companies, no parents, and no decisions. Just a red-hot fire that only Rye could put out.

But Rye wasn't in a hurry. He'd waited all week for that moment, even though he'd figured it would be in his king-sized bed. He'd looked forward to playing all over her body. He nibbled on her earlobes, found the faint taste of coconut and pineapple on her breasts, made her shiver when he ran his tongue around her belly button, and slowly made his way downward.

Austin thought every fiber in her body would go up in flames when he brought her right up to the edge of passion with nothing more than his lips and tongue. She ran her fingers through his hair and said his name so slowly that it came out in five syllables. When she arched her back and tangled her fists in his hair, he looked up with a wicked grin and started scattering kisses on her hot, sweaty body as he made his way back to her lips.

After two kisses, she flipped over on top of him. She put one hand behind her on his tense thigh and the other on his chest and settled him inside. Then she began a fast rhythm that would end too soon so he traded places with her and slowed the train down a few notches. When he heard her call out his name in a throaty southern growl, he gave in to the desire and buried his face in her neck in a moan. He rolled to one side without letting her out of his arms.

Lightning continued to illuminate the room in bright flashes and thunder growled but Austin only saw and felt afterglow settling around them like a halo. She reached up and pulled one of Granny's quilts from the arm of the recliner and flipped it over them. She snuggled into his chest and shut her eyes.

Rye's heart and pulse still raced even after she snuggled up to his side. Nothing had prepared him for the feeling that lingered after sex was over. Nothing would ever be the same. He shut his eyes and dozed off with her in his arms.

An hour later she awoke. "Hey, cowboy, it's time to wake up and go home."

He opened one eye. "Why?"

"Because this floor is hard as hell and because we've both got a ton of work to do tomorrow."

"Date tomorrow night? I've got a king-sized bed at my place." He hated to leave, but Wil would be full of questions if Rye awoke him after dawn.

She kissed him on the shoulder. "Yes."

He stood and held his hand out to her. When she put her hand in his, he pulled her up and kissed her before he scooped her up in his arms and carried her toward her bedroom without breaking the kisses.

When they reached the bathroom, she slung out an arm and grabbed the doorframe. "Shower."

"Just you or both of us?"

"Just me. If you get in the shower, we won't leave this house until Sunday."

He laughed. "Sounds fine to me."

"Me too, but..."

"I like your butt just fine, and your boobs and your lips and your eyes." He gently set her on the floor in front of the big claw-footed tub and brushed a quick kiss across her lips. "I'll pick you up at six. Dinner, movies, and…"

"I'll be ready."

She waited until she heard his boots crossing the floor before she started the shower. Jesus, Mary, and Joseph and all the saints above, how in the hell was she ever going back to Tulsa after having sex with Rye O'Donnell?

CHAPTER 14

Austin looked down the furrows at the tiny plants turning the whole sandy field pale green. A sense of accomplishment filled her heart and brought a big smile to her face.

"Just look at them. Aren't they beautiful," she said.

"There will be lots of days between these first leaves and the final watermelon harvest but it looks good right now. There'll be spraying, plowing, weeding, and lots of praying for rain to make them full and plump. All the snow they got in this area last winter helped so we're looking for good things," Felix said.

"Snow is better than rain?" Austin asked.

"*Sí*! It puts the nitrogen into the soil."

She wanted to learn, wanted to be there when they cut the first melon from the vine and hauled the first load into town to the watermelon shed where the semis came and hauled them away to be sold in supermarkets everywhere. For the first time, she understood why her grandmother had farmed until her dying day and why she wanted her son to love it like she did.

"The boys and I will be working on the east end of the place today if you need us. Lobo is going to mow the yard this evening after work, and Estefan has the vegetable garden looking very good. We'll have green beans and little potatoes before long."

"Thank you, Felix," Austin said.

"We are grateful for work this year. We were worried that we wouldn't find anything and our families would suffer for it." He settled his straw hat on his head and left her standing at the end of the rows and rows of plants.

Will they have work another year? Verline's voice was back inside her head.

Granny, I love it here but my career is in Tulsa, Austin answered.

Verline didn't answer but Austin had the distinct feeling that she was still there as she drove into Ryan to do the banking business and meet Molly and Greta for ice cream.

"Sex. Two times! And ice cream all in twenty-four hours. Have I died and gone to heaven?" Austin talked to herself as she walked across the wide street from the bank to the drugstore.

Not heaven, honey. Terral! Verline answered.

"I didn't figure you'd give up without a fight."

I'm not fighting with you. It's your farm and your decision. Do with it what you want. But don't come whining to me when you are sixty years old and hate sitting behind a desk when you could be up to your elbows in watermelon juice making your own wine. And when you could have Rye and a dozen grandkids by then.

Austin darted the rest of the way across the street and pushed the door of the drugstore open. Molly and Greta both waved from the back.

"We saved you a seat, and they've got fresh strawberries so we ordered three sundaes with whipped cream, nuts, and a cherry on the top," Greta said loudly.

Austin pulled out a chair and was barely seated when the sundaes arrived. "How'd you girls know I'd be here?"

"You can't hide that bright-red sports car," Greta said.

"We parked about the time you went in the bank," Molly told her. "Now what's this about Rye O'Donnell coming to see you real late last night?"

Austin's face felt as if someone had just pushed her into a bonfire. "What?"

"Come on, honey, we're talking Terral and Ryan. Together they might have a thousand people if they padded the census more than a little bit. We got gossips that would put them television soap operas to shame. 'Fess up. What happened? Did he miss you? Was that the reason you went back to Tulsa? Was the fire gettin' too hot between you?" Molly fired questions more rapidly than a machine gun spits out casings.

"We saw you at the rattlesnake festival with him, and it looked pretty serious," Greta said.

Molly pointed at the ice cream with her spoon. "Eat your ice cream 'fore it melts and figure out a way to tell us meddling old women to mind our own business while you cool off. You are blushing so bad it looks like your face is about to catch on fire. I betcha Greta could light a cigarette off the tip of your nose."

Greta laughed. "That blushin' stuff must come from your mother's side. I never saw Verline blush in her life, not even when she got pregnant and…"

Molly slapped on the top of her hand with her spoon. "Shhh."

"Don't shush her. What about when Granny got pregnant?" Austin asked.

"Cat's out of the bag now, and it's a helluva lot harder to put the damn thing back inside the bag than it is to let it out. We might as well go on and tell her. Besides, she'll find the marriage license and her daddy's birth certificate and figure it out herself," Greta said.

Austin shook her head but the notion didn't fly out of her ears. "Granny was pregnant when she got married?"

Greta nodded. "And Verline didn't blush or fret about it neither. She was eighteen and Orville was nineteen. Verline's momma said that if she was the first one to get pregnant before she got married, then we'd take her to the river and drown her right then. And if drowning her would guarantee no other young girl would mess around before they got a ring, then we'd toss her off the bridge in a burlap bag tied to a rock. But it had happened back before Jesus was ever born and would keep right on until the end of the world. Wasn't the same story with Orville's momma. She had a fit. Swore that Verline didn't even know who the baby belonged to and wasn't about to let Orville marry a cotton farmer's daughter."

"Cotton?"

"Yes, honey, fifty years ago we raised cotton down in these parts more than anything else, and Verline was the only daughter of a cotton farmer. Orville's daddy was a big shot on the railroad and they lived down in Ringgold. His momma had come from Back East."

"Hampton, Virginia," Molly said. "And God Almighty, but that woman liked to put on airs. She even wore white gloves to church on Sunday. Said her ancestors come across the waters on the *Mayflower*. Lord, we didn't care if they walked across them waters but she took great pride in being a *Mayflower* woman."

"And this would be my great-grandmother?"

"Guess it would since it was your granddad's momma," Molly said. "Verline and Orville had only been married a few months when Verline's daddy dropped dead with a stroke out in the cotton fields. So she and Orville went to live on the property so she could help her mother. Orville had a real good job by then and he built that house for Verline. Grandma lived where the hog lot and garden is still at, down at the end of the property, in a house that was about the same size. She and Verline ran that place until she died. By then they'd already give up the cotton and started watermelons."

"And she adored your daddy. Not as much as Verline but she did love that boy. She died right after you were born," Greta said.

"Granny never talked about her."

"Verline always set her course for straight ahead and didn't dwell much on the past," Molly said. "Now enough about that. Tell us what Rye was doing at your house last night."

"A woman don't kiss and tell."

"If that didn't sound just like Verline. We tried to get her to tell us about s-e-x when she got pregnant so we'd have an idea what it was like. You know, back in them days folks didn't talk about such things. Not even women when they was all by themselves in a kitchen with the windows and doors closed. But she wouldn't tell us a thing."

Austin kept eating. If her grandmother had been as attracted to Grandpa Orville as Austin was Rye, then it was no wonder she got pregnant. Hell's bells, in those days they didn't tell girls a thing about birth control. Austin wasn't even sure they had such a thing back then. She stopped eating and thought hard... She hadn't used any protection last night. *Dammit!* She'd have to be more careful next time.

Next time!

That put some extra kick in her adrenaline.

"If you won't tell us what went on last night, at least tell us what went on up in Tulsa."

"Okay, it was a hectic week. I worked late every night so I'd be ready to leave yesterday. There's a man there named Derk who wants my promotion, and he's lobbying behind my back for it."

"Give it to him and move down here. We'll adopt you," Greta told her.

"My mother is terrified that I'm going to do just that. But I went to college for a business degree in management, and I've got a fantastic job with a promotion in line that's out of this world for a thirty-year-old woman."

"Can it make your little heart go wild at night? Can you wake up in its arms? Can you argue and fight with it and then make love to it?"

Austin shook her head.

"Then kick it out in the road and tell it to go to hell and live down here," Molly said.

Austin finished off the last of her ice cream and licked the spoon clean. "I'm not making a decision of any kind right now."

Greta poked Molly on the arm. "At least she's not turning us down flat."

"Where there's hope, there's a will." Molly grinned. "Now get on out of here. I understand you got a date and he's pickin' you up at six. Don't be sittin' here with us old women when you need to be gettin' all pretty, and don't forget to shave your legs."

Austin cocked her head to one side.

"Don't look at me like that. I'm not so old that I don't remember that menfolks like to run their hands up a nice slick thigh," Molly said.

"How did you know I've got a date?"

"Rye told Kent that they were callin' it quits at five o'clock because he's got a date with you tonight. Kent told his mother who called my neighbor because she's Kent's momma's cousin and told her. Then the neighbor came over and I was at the beauty shop gettin' my hair cut and curled up so she told Greta, who was waitin' for me to get finished so we could ride down here together. Greta called Pearlita but Kent's momma done already called her by that time and she already knew all about it. She's jealous as hell because she really wanted her great-niece, Pearl, to fall for Rye. Now she'll have to pick out one of the other O'Donnell men and Rye is the prettiest one."

Austin pushed back her chair. "Good Lord! Doesn't anyone have anything better to do than gossip?"

"Probably, but this is a hell of a lot more fun. Use some baby oil on them legs when you get done shavin' them. Makes them all shiny and Rye won't be able to keep his hands off them. We'll expect a full report next Friday unless you want to talk and then you can call us any old time," Greta said.

"Were you two wild in your younger days?" Austin asked.

"We were later bloomers than Verline but when we did bloom, honey, we made up for lost time," Molly answered.

"Tell me that story next week?"

"We'll tell you a story every week you make it for ice cream. Maybe not that one but we guarantee a good one," Greta said.

Austin dressed that evening in a pastel-plaid sundress that she'd bought when she and her mother went shopping. Barbara had declared that she was wasting her money because she'd never wear the dress but Austin purchased it and the pink knit cotton cardigan sweater that was shown with it. She straightened her hair, slapped on a bit of blush, and touched up her eye shadow.

All that was easy but then it came time to decide what shoes to wear. She had white leather flat sandals that were very comfortable, pink high heels that made her freshly shaven legs with baby oil on them look very shapely, and her cowboy boots. Rye knocked on the door and she had a high heel on one foot, a boot on the other, and carried the sandals in her hands when she opened it.

"Wow! You look handsome enough to..." she stammered.

"And you are beautiful enough to..." He met her halfway across the floor and wrapped her up in his arms. She dropped the sandals on the floor and wrapped her arms around his neck. When she leaned back, his eyes were closed and his lips were already zeroed in on hers. She shut her eyes and got ready for the jolt. She was not a bit disappointed.

Finally, she broke away but he kept an arm around her waist.

"Which one?" She pointed at her feet.

"Boots. Nothing sexier than a woman in cowboy boots and a pretty dress."

She kicked off the high-heeled shoe and went back to the bedroom for her other boot. He followed right behind her, slipping a hand up her dress and cupping her fanny.

"Checkin' to see if you are going commando tonight," he teased. "Are you?"

"I'm not tellin'. You'll have to find out for yourself. Just remember that I might be the whole time we are having dinner."

"Where are we going?" She gasped when his hand moved

under the elastic of her bikini underpants and she felt a callused hand on bare butt.

"Steak house over in Wichita Falls. Then a movie or maybe to a honky-tonk to do some dancing." He bent down and kissed her bare fanny.

The fiery heat of his lips on her left cheek made her suck air.

What if I'd rather just go straight to a sleepover in your big king-sized bed?

"Enough of that or we'll never get out of this room," she said.

"Yes, ma'am!" He teased her mouth open with another kiss.

She managed to get the other boot on between kisses and then he picked her up and carried her to the pickup, settled her into the seat, shut the door, and whistled all the way around the truck.

You idiot! that voice inside his head said. *You know down deep in your heart that she's never going to leave Tulsa. Pull them reins in and put a halt to this.*

He got into the truck and looked over at her sitting not three feet from him. He flipped the console back and patted the seat beside him. "Slide over here beside me."

When she was plastered next to his side, he put a hand on her knee, then slid it up to midthigh and let it rest there as he drove with the other one.

She threw her left hand up over the back of his seat and toyed with his hair.

"Next weekend starts the rodeo season with the Rodeo and Real Texas Festival in Mesquite, Texas. We'll be down there all weekend from Friday morning until Sunday morning," he said. Her hands felt like hot embers in his hair.

"Do you stay down there or drive back and forth?" She felt like someone had stuck a straight pin in her helium balloon. One minute it was flying higher than the clouds. Now it was tangled up in tree branches.

"We have reservations for the whole season at the Hampton

Inn right there beside the Resistol Arena. That way we can keep an eye on the bulls. Raylen and Dewar do some team roping and bronc riding."

"Do they bring horses from your folks' ranch?"

"Momma doesn't raise rodeo stock. Her horses are bred to race."

"You ride?"

"I ride bulls. But not at the Resistol Arena. It would be a conflict of interest for me to provide the bulls and ride my own animals."

"Why do Raylen and Dewar ride horses and you ride bulls?"

"I have no idea. Difference in brothers, I guess."

"What about Gemma and Colleen? Do they rodeo?"

He slowed down and swung right onto Highway 82 toward Wichita Falls. "Gemma rides bulls in the lady's division, but it's not a conflict for her to ride my bulls. Only for me to ride them. Colleen used to do some barrel racing, but she broke her leg a few years ago and gave it up. That does not mean that she won't be there to cheer on Raylen and Dewar and to check out the cowboys."

"Your parents go to the rodeos too?" His hand had moved upward a few inches. Austin couldn't stop him, but if it didn't stop, she was going to make him stop in Henrietta at a motel and forget about food.

"We've got a block of rooms on reserve from one year to the next. Momma loves it. Two nights a week from the end of May to the end of August."

"I thought you said it starts next weekend."

She was already missing him. She'd get into Terral on Thursday night and he'd leave Friday morning, returning Sunday morning after she'd already gone home to Tulsa.

"That's the Texas Festival rodeo. It's kind of like the hot-pepper popper appetizer before they bring out the steaks at dinnertime. Gets the folks in the mood for the summer. The schedule for the summer is in the glove compartment. It tells when it's just a rodeo and when it's a rodeo with a concert afterward."

She removed a stapled set of papers. "Looks like they have a concert once a month. Oh, my! Rascal Flatts and Tracy Lawrence are among the performers."

"Want to go? Gemma doesn't come down until Friday night because she's got appointments, and now that she's putting in her own shop down by the Chicken Fried Café, she'll be real busy on Fridays. Colleen works Friday night and comes down on Saturday morning. You could catch a ride with either one of them. We're home by early afternoon on Sundays."

"Sounds like fun. Maybe I could work things around to go. When does Gemma begin to work on her shop?"

"She's ordered the chairs and sinks and got a plumber coming to put everything in this week. She's painting the inside herself and putting a tanning bed in the back room. Folks in Ringgold and the surrounding area have to go all the way up to Ryan or to Bowie for haircuts and tanning right now."

"What is this Chicken Fried place?"

"It's a little café about two miles south of Ringgold. Serves breakfast and lunch and shuts the doors about three in the afternoon. Owner is about to retire. You want to go into the café business?"

"No thank you!"

Rye cut his eyes around at her. "You said that pretty damn quick."

"Yes, I did. Right now I'm up to my ears in snapping alligators. I've got a very good job at the oil company in Tulsa, and Derk is trying to edge me out of the promotion that I've worked my butt off for. I've got a watermelon farm that I'm having a devil of a time deciding what to do with because I can't hardly bear to sell off what's been in my family for decades, and besides, I love farming. So the answer is no, I do not want a café to run."

"This Derk the man who's trying to brownnose his way into your promotion?"

242   CAROLYN BROWN

"That's the one."

Rye chuckled. "Believe me, bosses know when a person is just kissing ass to get ahead. You'll get the promotion because you've worked hard for it."

"Thank you."

"You are quite welcome but that's just a fact, darlin.'" There was road construction and he had to use both hands to drive. She slipped her hand onto his thigh and squeezed. His body began to respond so he reached down and held her hand tightly.

He nodded toward a neon cowboy sign when they passed the Longhorn Inn on the left-hand side of the road right after a sign saying "The Baptist Church of Henrietta Welcomes You to Henrietta." "There's Pearlita's motel. Looks like she's got a full house tonight. Wonder what's going on?"

"I've been over here lots of times when I was a kid. Pearl would come to Terral and stay a night or two, and Granny would let me visit her. I wonder if they're having a fishing tournament." Austin saw a man sitting out in front of one of the rooms with a rod and reel.

"Probably so. Wonder what will become of the motel when she really retires or drops like Granny did."

"Pearl will probably inherit it. She's always been Pearlita's favorite, and she was named after her so she'll most likely have to make some decisions too."

"Pearl is Colleen's friend. She's been to the house a few times. I can see her being your childhood friend. She's sassy like you."

"I'm Verline Lanier's granddaughter and she's Pearlita's great-niece. We didn't have a chance at being all syrupy sweet."

"What does Pearl do these days?" Rye tapped the brakes to slow the truck down to the right speed to go through town.

"She works over in Durant, Oklahoma, at a bank. She's got a degree in business finance, but I don't know what it is that she does actually. I think she teaches a couple of classes at the college at night but that was news from five years ago. Could be that she doesn't do that anymore."

Rye loved the sound of Austin's voice. Even when she wasn't making those little sexy noises as he undressed and kissed her.

"That must mean you two don't stay in close touch?"

"We wouldn't have even known each other if my grandmother and her great-aunt hadn't been friends. And if Granny hadn't been trying to find someone to keep me company while I was here. Pearl was... How do I explain Pearl?" She pondered.

Rye gave her a few minutes to think about her old summer friend.

"Kent's boys, only worse!"

"You're shittin' me!" he exclaimed. Pearl hadn't seemed like that to him when she visited Colleen.

"No, that's the best way I can explain Pearl."

"Examples?" he asked.

"One comes to mind instantly. We must've been about eight and Pearl came to stay a couple of days. Granny was busy with the watermelons, and it was so hot that we could almost fry eggs on the metal cellar door. Yes, we tried. Granny caught us after we'd wasted a dozen eggs. Actually we didn't waste them; we fed the half-raw things to an old stray cat that had come up. We thought if we tamed her, she might lead us to where she had kittens."

"How'd you know she had babies?"

"Her boobs were sagging. But that wasn't the story I was about to tell. I just wanted you to know how hot it was. It had been a dry summer so the river wasn't very deep or wide. We begged Granny to let us go exploring on the riverbanks, and she said that we could but not to get our clothes wet."

He chuckled. "How you get around that?"

"We went skinny-dipping. Two little girls out there in the river splashing and having a big time. Granny threw a fit when she found out."

"You tell her?"

"No, our hair was wet. She never thought we'd go all the way to the river. She figured we'd go about halfway and turn around and come back to the house. She fussed and fumed the whole time she washed the red mud from our hair. But that was Pearl. The two of us could get into the most amazing trouble."

"Did you stay in touch when you went back home every summer?" He would have rather gotten a room at the Longhorn than eaten supper. Hell, he could have Austin for supper, midnight snack, and breakfast the next morning. But explaining to Pearlita what he was doing in her motel with Austin Lanier would make him stutter and blush at the same time.

Austin shook her head. "No, we were just summer friends."

She remembered that last summer they'd spent a couple of days together. Fifteen years old. Pearl was dating. Austin wanted to date but Barbara said she was too young. There was a really hot Mexican boy working in the melons, and Austin and Pearl had both drooled over him. That had been a lifetime ago.

Rye had made reservations at the steak house and asked for a secluded table. The waiter seated them at a corner table with a burning candle in the middle. He laid menus in front of them and took their drink orders. When he returned with two beers in frosted mugs, Austin ordered a filet mignon, medium-rare baked potato, and house salad. Rye asked for a rib eye with a loaded baked potato and a house salad.

The waiter disappeared and Austin slipped a boot off under the table and ran her toes up the inside of Rye's thigh.

"Be careful. There *is* a tablecloth, and I will crawl under the table and have my way with you," he said.

The wicked twinkle in his eye said he wasn't teasing and he'd really do it so she dropped her foot and grinned at him. "You were evil with those text messages."

"So were you."

"We should've eaten oyster stew and gone to bed in your king-sized bed," she teased.

"Too late now. We've already ordered, but I'm game for forgetting about the movie and going home," he said.

"Me too," she whispered and blew him a kiss across the table.

Stars twinkled like diamonds on a bed of black velvet when they left the steak house. A red rosebush in the flower bed in front of the restaurant put off a fresh intoxicating smell. Parking lot birds hopped around chirping to one another about their latest find, whether it was a dropped french fry or a chunk of dinner roll.

"It's a beautiful night," Austin said.

Rye pulled her close to his side. "Not as beautiful as you, and it's about to get even better."

"Thank you. Let's go home and have a glass of wine. I'm too damn full to make love right now, and the night is young. Think we could put a movie into the DVD player and fool around until our food settles. You got anything interesting?"

He laughed out loud. Austin was so damn blunt that it was refreshing. After a meal like they'd just eaten, it would take at least an hour of fooling around before either of them would want weight put on their stomachs. And as hot as it made him to think about her cute little naked fanny sitting on him, he rather liked the idea of fooling around. "How about *8 Seconds*?"

"What's it about?" She slid into the passenger's seat and he shut the door.

"Bull riding. You've never seen it?" He put both arms around her and kissed her hard before he pulled his seat belt around his broad chest.

She shook her head.

"Then you have to see it. I've still got a bottle of Granny's watermelon wine."

"Is it a guy movie with blood, guts, and gore?"

"It's based on a true story about Lane Frost, a real bull rider, and all the trials he went through on his way to fame."

"Now you've got my interest if it's a true story. Is he pretty?"

"Well, I wouldn't think so but he was a damn fine rider."

"Was? As in he doesn't ride anymore?"

"I'm not saying another word. You can decide if he's any good or not."

"But I don't know a thing about bull riding. Will you tell me what's going on?"

"Of course I will, darlin'."

When they reached the house, she kicked off her boots, poured a glass of wine for each of them while he started the movie, and curled up on the sofa. His boots joined hers and he sat down beside her, a glass of wine in his right hand, his left arm thrown across the back of the sofa with his fingertips barely touching her shoulder.

He kissed her once but when the show started, she got so involved in it that her facial expressions mesmerized him. Halfway through the movie, she looked up at him and asked, "Do all rodeo men commit adultery?"

"Not all of them."

"Right now I don't like Lane Frost so well."

He picked up her hand and kissed her fingertips, nibbling on each one a few extra seconds. "It's life, Austin. Bad things happen. You either get over them or let them take you into the gutter."

By the end of the movie she'd forgiven Lane and cried when he rode his last ride. She buried her face in Rye's shoulder when the credits started to roll. "He didn't really die, did he? Please tell me he's still alive and he and his wife have a dozen kids on a ranch like this one."

"Can't," Rye said with a lump in his throat. No matter how many times he watched the movie, he was always stunned at the end.

"How can you ride bulls after that?" She sniffled.

"Just get on the old boy and hope I can make it eight seconds."

She was going to sell the watermelon farm and never look back. She might not even come back to Terral when she left that week. She could make arrangements for payroll through the bank over the phone. Her heart would break if what happened to Lane ever happened to Rye. She might as well nip the whole thing in the bud right then as watch it blossom only to have him die before her eyes.

He picked her up and carried her back to his bedroom, laid her on the king-sized bed, and stretched out beside her, just holding her hand and looking deep into her eyes. He shifted until they were face-to-face, pressed against each other. He teased her mouth open with his tongue and tasted the sweetness.

His kisses sent surges of desire through her body but Austin was determined to take it slow and enjoy every single minute of making love with him in a king-sized bed instead of on the floor. She unfastened his shirt a button at a time and peeled it from his body. Running her hands over his back as he tasted her neck and her breasts, and started down toward her belly button as he undressed her. With the touch of his lips on her skin, she forgot all about Lane Frost and her determination to never see Rye again.

"You taste like honey and warm butter all mixed together," he mumbled.

"Mmmm" was all she got out.

She couldn't have spoken intelligent, understandable words any more than she could have suddenly become fluent in an obscure dialect from a remote mountain tribe of Russian people.

"Your skin is so, so soft," he said as he ran his tongue back up her midsection toward her neck.

"Oh, my God!" she yelled.

He rose on his elbows and looked at her, writhing beneath him, rocking from one side to the other. "What?"

"Get off me. I've got to stand up," she yelped.

"Why?"

She pushed him and he rolled off the bed, hitting his head on the nightstand on the way down. Her foot hit the floor and she tried to stand but stumbled over his leg and landed halfway out in the hall, still yelling and screaming like a half-dead coyote.

He rubbed his head and brought back a hand streaked with blood. "What in the hell?"

"Charley horse!" she panted as she pulled herself up by the doorframe.

"Well, thank God."

"Thank God? My leg feels like it's in labor and about to deliver an elephant! That's real sympathetic of you."

He looked up at her standing on one leg, naked as the day she was born and sexy as hell even with a cramp in her leg. "No! Thank God it's not something horrible that I did to turn you off."

"Darlin', you could never turn me off! What is that on your head? My God, you are hurt, Rye."

She limped over to the bedside table and turned on the lamp. The light showed the lump on the side of his forehead and a puncture wound that was oozing blood down across his cheek.

"We need to take you to the hospital right now. Is the nearest one at Nocona or do we go to Duncan? Ouch, ouch! Dammit! It's not gone yet." She hopped around on one leg while trying to pull on her underpants.

He felt the lump as he stood up. "I'm not going to a hospital over a bump on the head, Austin. See, I'm not even dizzy. It's bumped out, which means it's not a concussion."

He headed toward the bathroom with her right behind him, her underpants dragging along on one ankle. He flipped on the light and leaned in close to the mirror. A quick swipe with a washcloth showed that it was a hole put there by the corner of the nightstand. He'd had a tetanus shot last year when he got tangled up in some rusty barbed wire so he was good there.

With a little hop, she was sitting on the vanity with his head between her palms. "I'm telling you that could be dangerous."

"And I'm telling you I'm caught up on shots and, look, it's almost stopped bleeding. It's not dangerous but it damn sure spoiled that mood, didn't it?"

She bit the inside of her lip to keep from giggling. Greta and Molly would love that story but she couldn't tell it. They'd set the phone lines on fire telling Oma Fay and she'd tell Kent and Rye would never speak to her again.

"Proved to me that there was more ways for a bull rider to get killed than eight seconds on the back of a bucking bull," she said.

It started as a chuckle and built into a roar that had them both wiping tears. She held her ribs. He sat down on the edge of the tub and held the washcloth against his wound. When it settled into soft laughter, she got the hiccups and blushed.

"Mother says I can't hiccup, sneeze, or burp like a lady."

He patted her leg with his free hand. "Shall we try again?"

"Hell, no! My leg still hurts."

"Then get dressed and I'll take you home."

"Not until I see that head better and bandage the wound. You can't go to bed like that. What if you bumped it in the night? What have you got in the medicine cabinet?" She didn't wait for him to tell her but opened the doors and checked for herself. "Besides six boxes of condoms?"

"Man has to be ready."

"Iodine. Spray antiseptic. Triple antibiotic ointment," she said as she lined the bottles and tubes up on the cabinet. "Band-Aids."

"Just slap a Band-Aid on it."

"I'm the nurse tonight. You are the patient. Put your hands over your eyes and close them as tight as you can."

"The nurse at my doctor's office isn't naked while she treats me," he said.

"I'm fixin' to spray this stuff so you'd better close your eyes."

He did.

She sprayed.

He yelped.

She blew on the burn.

Her warm breath created a fire in the rest of his body that made his wound feel like a warm candle compared to an out-of-control Texas wildfire.

"Okay, now the ointment and then the Band-Aid. What are you going to tell Kent when he asked what happened to your head?"

"I don't know. What are you going to tell your momma on Sunday when she asks about that big, old hickey on your neck?"

She spun around to look in the mirror, and sure enough, there was a bite mark the size of Rye's sexy mouth right there below her ear. She'd have to wear high-necked blouses all next week to cover the thing up or else Barbara would demand details.

"That I was in bed with a sexy cowboy and he was making wild passionate love to me when I got a charley horse in my leg. And that if that hadn't happened, I'd have a matching one on the other side, and when she starts breathing again, I'll ask her if she'd like to see the one on my inner thigh."

"Okay, then I'm telling Kent the truth."

"You wouldn't!"

He smiled. "Kiss me and I'll be good."

She leaned forward and he wrapped his arms around her naked body. His lips met hers in a searing passion that almost, but not quite, made them forget the bedroom fiasco.

"Promise you won't tell Kent. I don't think I could face him," she said.

"And you think I could face your mother if you told her that story about the hickey?" He teased her mouth open for another fiery kiss.

"I'd better take my sore leg home and you'd better get some sleep. We've both got hard work tomorrow and it's past midnight. Walk me to the door. I can find my own way across the road."

"I'll walk you home. Granny Lanier would resurrect and tack me to the cellar door if I wasn't a gentleman."

He pulled his boots on after they were dressed and she carried hers as they walked across the dew-kissed grass in his yard, the rough dirt road, and then the sweet wet grass in her yard. He kissed her at the door so hard that she forgot all about the cramp in her leg and pulled him inside the house. He backed her up against the bar separating the living room and kitchen and continued to erase all memories of a failed attempt in his bed. Finally, she broke away and using her forearm brushed every knickknack off the bar. Ceramic animals met their death when they landed on the floor in a clatter. She peeled his shirt over his head, and he removed her dress and set her up on the countertop. She lay back and motioned toward him.

They'd had the foreplay and the teasing so he shed his clothes, peeled off her panties, and stretched out on top of her. She was more than ready so he slipped inside and she groaned. The cabinet top was hard as a rock but she couldn't say a word, not until that deep, aching need was satisfied and she was wallowing in the afterglow again, pressed up to his side with his arm thrown around her.

They'd had a king-sized bed, big enough for sumo wrestlers to roll around on, and it was a disaster. They'd had a room full of knickknacks and barely enough floor room to have sex without bumping into something, and it worked fine. Now tonight they'd had a cabinet top not even as wide as a twin-sized bed and managed not only to have sex but to get comfortable in each other's arms afterward.

Austin would bet her underbritches on the fact that her grandmother was meddling from the other side of eternity to fix things the way she wanted them to be.

CHAPTER 15

Rye finished work on Saturday afternoon and rushed home with intentions of having a quick shower and calling Austin. His sister's little red pickup sitting in the driveway was the last thing he wanted to see, but there it was, bigger than Dallas. He slapped the steering wheel but that didn't make the truck disappear.

Grumbling, he opened the front door to the smell of home-made bread permeating through his house and Blake Shelton singing "Austin" on a CD. Colleen had an apron tied around her waist, her black hair pulled off to one side in a ponytail, and she was grating cheese.

"Hello, brother. I had a weekend off and thought you might like a home-cooked meal tonight. We're having chicken parmigiana with my made-from-scratch spaghetti sauce, which is simmering on the back of the stove, hot Italian bread, and warm apple pie with ice cream for dessert. I've got a salad chilling and wine in the bucket so go get a shower and get ready for a big supper. The rest of the family will be here in a few minutes. Momma is bringing the dominoes so we can set up two tables on the deck, but you and Raylen don't get to be on the same team. You cheat." Colleen prattled on while she placed chicken cutlets in a pan and covered them with grated cheese.

"I'll call Austin and we can make it two tables of four."

She pointed the knife at him. "Family only tonight, darlin'. No dates for any of us."

Rye ignored her, took his phone from his shirt pocket, and hit speed dial for Austin's number. He got the answering machine in his ear, a chill in the room, and a hateful look from his sister. "Hi, Austin. Guess you're still out on a tractor. Call me when you get this message, please."

"What happened to your head? Have you gone plumb crazy or what?" Colleen asked.

"You want the real story or the funny one?"

"Well, I damn sure don't want to be entertained. You've been runnin' around like a chicken with its head cut off ever since that woman came to town. What are you going to do when the new wears off and she's left this area for good? Tell me that instead of a funny story."

His face was flushed. She'd never seen him act like he'd been doing the past few weeks. He couldn't keep his head on straight and Raylen even did a better job at breaking horses the weekend before. That city chick had sure messed him up. Later he'd thank his sister for interfering and saving his sorry neck. When he found a suitable girlfriend, one that would be happy on a ranch and wouldn't throw a hissy fit every time he walked in with cow shit on his boots, he'd look back and tell her that he'd been wrong.

"This is my life and my business."

"Evidently it is but I damn sure don't have to like it. How is Oma Fay doing? Is her MS getting any worse?" Colleen changed the subject.

"You'll have to ask Kent. She's still able to take care of the boys after school until Malee and Kent get home from work so I guess she's doing all right. I'm going to take a shower. If Austin calls, tell her that I'll talk to her in a little while."

Colleen didn't answer so he left the door open and set his phone on the bathroom vanity so he could hear it. He towel dried his hair, wrapped a towel around his waist, and padded barefoot down the hallway to his bedroom. He chose a pair of faded jeans and a worn T-shirt from his closet. The phone still hadn't rung when he went back to the kitchen.

"She didn't call. Maybe she's gone back to Tulsa. I don't see her little red car over there," Colleen said.

"She parks it in the backyard."

Colleen shrugged. "I hear trucks pulling into the driveway. Momma and the rest of the family must be here. Go on out on the porch and play nice. I'll make the iced tea and get the bread from the oven," Colleen said.

He walked out on the porch and saw Austin parking one of the tractors beside the house. She shaded her eyes with her hand and waved back when he held up a hand.

Gemma grabbed him in a fierce hug. "Isn't it exciting, Rye? I'm moving to Ringgold! You are never going to look like this again when I get here with my scissors. We're having a family fest tonight to see what I'm going to name my very own shop, so put your thinking cap on. Hey, did you invite Austin? She should be here because she was the one who came up with the idea in the first place."

"Haven't yet."

"It's family only," Colleen said from the doorway.

"Bullshit! I'll call her myself," Gemma said.

"I won't play nice. I didn't plan for dates or friends," Colleen said.

"Stop your bickering and let's eat," Maddie said. "I've been craving Colleen's chicken all day."

Rye shot his sister a mean look. She'd planned this all day and hadn't called him because she knew he'd invite Austin.

Colleen bounced the look right back at him.

"You can't babysit me twenty-four seven," he muttered as he led the family inside.

"But I can this night," she whispered.

Gemma dropped her purse on the sofa, fished her phone from it, stepped out onto the deck, and called Austin. "Hey, girl, what are you doin'?"

"Just got off a tractor. I smell horrid and there's enough dirt in my socks to plant a hill of watermelons. Everything all right? No one died, did they? Is Rye sick?"

"Everything is fine. He doesn't look dead to me. Colleen decided to make dinner here tonight and surprise him. Come on over and have supper with us. You were the one who helped me make this decision, and we're naming the shop tonight. You should be here."

"I'm wiped out tired. Thanks for the offer, but I think I'll pass for a long soak in that big old claw-footed tub."

"Okay, then get your bath and when you get done, I'll bring a plate across the road. There's tons of food here, and there's no need for you to eat a sandwich or open a can of soup," Gemma said.

"Thank you," Austin said.

Disappointment could have been tattooed on her forehead or, better yet, on her neck, right across the hickey that had gotten darker and darker as the day went by. She'd entertained all kinds of scenarios as she drove the tractor up and down the fields that day, plowing up the center lanes to cut out any weeds and keep the dirt soft. They all involved a bed with Rye in it and not a blessed one of them involved two sisters, two brothers, and a mother and father.

"I'll give you an hour and then I'll bring food," Gemma said.

Austin shed clothes all the way down the hallway to the bathroom, where she sat down naked on the edge of the tub and poured bath salts into the water as it shot from the faucet. She barely heard her phone when it rang the second time. It was on the fifth and final ring before it went to voicemail when she flipped it open and said, "Hello."

She could hear noise in the background before Rye said a word. Dewar said something and Raylen laughed.

"Rye?"

"Colleen decided to do a surprise dinner for the family at my house. I'm sorry. There was nothing I could do about it, and I can't get out of it. I saw you getting off the tractor and everyone is filling their plates right now. Can you take a fast shower and come on over?" he asked.

"I'm tired. I think I'll pass."

Chicken! Verline's voice said from inside her head. *You should get a shower, dress up all pretty, put on perfume, and walk over there. Kiss Rye right smack on the lips when you walk in the door and be sure to pull your hair back so that hickey shines. That'll teach that girl a thing or two. I'm shocked that she's being so tacky but not as much as I am at you for being a wimp.*

"Ah, come on," Rye said in his best "aw-shucks" voice.

"Come over and have a beer with me when they've all gone. By the way, Gemma already called and said she'd bring over a plate of food. What am I having?"

"Chicken parmigiana and apple pie," Rye said. He'd rather be eating bologna sandwiches on the porch with Austin.

Colleen yelled across the kitchen, "Hey, Rye. It's ready to serve up. Grab a plate. Oh, I forgot to tell you that my friend is coming around after work. She should be here at ten, and I told her we could use your two spare bedrooms tonight so we don't have to drive back until morning."

"What was that?" Austin asked.

"It was the last straw. I'll bring your food over in about ten minutes. Leave the door open and I'll feed you while you soak. How's that for sexy?"

"Don't you dare! It's an important day for Gemma, and I will not be the cause of it not being a great evening."

"Okay, then I'll be over as soon as we eat and decide what to call her new business. Get that full-sized bed ready because I'm too big for a twin bed and I'm too damned tired for the floor."

"Rye!"

"Feed you in the tub or spend the night? Your choice."

"Maybe I want both."

"It can be arranged, darlin'."

"Can your whole family hear what you are saying?"

"Frankly, darlin', I don't give a shit what they hear. My sister is not going to control my life. I'll let her have control of the evening until after supper but that's as nice as I intend to play."

Colleen yelled again. "Rye! Hang up the phone and come eat supper."

"On my way," Rye answered.

"Who are you talking to?" Austin asked.

"Enjoy your bath. I'll be there in an hour."

"So," Gemma said at the supper table, "I was thinking about Cut & Curl."

"I was thinking about Gemma's Place," Maddie said.

"That sounds like a café, and people would be coming in expecting a hamburger instead of a haircut," Colleen said. "Do something exotic."

Rye raised an eyebrow. "In Ringgold?"

"What do you think, Daddy?" Gemma looked at Cash.

"You going to cut men's hair as well as fix up the womenfolks?" She nodded.

"Then call it Petticoats & Pistols. That way they'll know they are all welcome. We'll make a hitchin' rail out front and you can decorate it all up like a cowboy joint," Cash said.

Gemma clapped her hands. "I like it. Anybody got anything better? Goin' once. Goin' twice. Sold to Daddy. He gets the honor of naming my beauty shop."

"Just seemed like the way to go to me." He beamed. "Now that that's over, I call Gemma and Dewar on my domino team."

"That leaves Momma, Colleen, and Raylen on the other one," Rye said.

"Are you goin' to be the referee?" Cash grinned.

"No, I'm not going to be here. I made plans for the evening with Austin. We were going out to dinner and maybe dancing but Colleen surprised me with this wonderful meal so I called Austin and now we're staying in over at her place. I'm taking her dinner from the leftovers, and we're watching a movie over there."

Colleen shot daggers across the table. "That's not very nice."

"I thought it was very nice. I didn't forsake you for dinner or the naming of the new business," Rye told his sister with a big grin on his face.

"You aren't even yourself lately. You used to be the serious O'Donnell child. Now you run around grinning and whistling. You are going to fall hard." Colleen shook her finger at him.

"Well, I like her. You go on, son. We can play dominoes without you. I'm goin' to whip Dewar all over the place," Cash said.

Colleen set her jaw. "My friend?"

"Your friend and you are more than welcome to stay here."

"Rye, are you really serious about Austin?" Maddie asked.

"I'll answer that tomorrow... maybe."

"That's a hell of an answer," Dewar said.

"It's a hell of a world. I'll see you all on Sunday."

———

Austin lazed in a hot bath until the water went cold and her skin looked worse than Greta's. "We are not horny sixteen-year-old teenagers. We can stay away from each other," she said as she let out half the water and turned on the hot water again.

Might as well be. Thirty-year-old women with any class at all don't go around with hickeys on their necks. Verline's voice was as clear as if she were standing in the bathroom with Austin.

"Oh, hush," she said.

"Who are you telling to hush? You got company?" Rye asked from the doorway.

"No, I was arguing with Granny again."

He peeled off his clothes until there was nothing left but his socks. "I put your supper in the fridge. You want me to go get it and feed you?"

"No, food can wait. Come right in. The water is fine." She crooked a finger at him.

He peeled off his socks and crawled in, facing her. He leaned forward at the same time she did and their hungry lips met in a passionate clash.

"I wonder if we will ever feel any different," she said.

"Don't think so. It's fire and ice every time I kiss you."

He ran a hand up her leg and she winced.

"What?"

"I haven't shaved and they're all prickly."

He picked up a long leg and set her foot on the edge of the tub. Then he covered the leg with the shaving cream sitting on the straight-back chair beside the tub and picked up the razor. With slow, deliberate motions he carefully shaved her leg, stopping to kiss her every few seconds. Then he dropped it back into the water and ran his hand from ankle all the way up. She smiled at him and propped up the other leg.

No one had ever shaved her legs before, and it was as intoxicating sexually as drinking a whole bottle of champagne. By the time he got the second one done, every bone in her body was jelly and she felt like she'd just walked out of a spa.

"My turn," she said.

"You're not shaving my legs," he protested.

"No, I'm getting out of this tub and giving you a bath, and you can't touch me until I'm finished."

"That ain't fair," he said.

"Life ain't fair. Now hush. It's my turn."

She got out and wrapped a towel around her body, tucking the ends in under her arm to keep it there. She wet his hair with warm water poured ever so slowly from a plastic cup and then lathered it with shampoo, working it in with her fingertips.

"That feels so damn good I may never leave this tub," he said.

She kissed him on the neck and nibbled on his earlobe.

"No fair. You are touching!" he said.

"Darlin', I said you couldn't touch me. This is like a water lap dance. Be still and enjoy it."

She took her time rinsing the shampoo from his hair and then put conditioner in it, rubbing his scalp and dark hair until it was slick and soft. When she rinsed that out, she picked up a washcloth, soaped it heavily, and started on his back. He was moaning by the time she pulled the plug, and he started to stand up but she put a hand on his shoulder.

"Not yet, cowboy."

She turned on the hot water to warm up the bathwater again and put the plug back in. "Now I do the front."

She washed each arm and his chest, playing in the dark swirls of hair with her fingertips. Then she dropped the washcloth and soaped her hands. His eyes widened when they quickly sank beneath the water, and her blue eyes widened when she found him hard and ready.

She smiled and kissed him on the lips. "When we get done, we'll take this show to the bedroom. Now your right leg, please?"

Instead of propping up his leg, he pulled the towel off her with one sweep of the hand and pulled her into the tub with him with the other. She hardly realized she was in the water before he'd turned her over and was making love to her in the warm water. The sensation was even greater than when they'd made love against the wall.

"Oh, my! Don't stop!"

"I couldn't if I wanted to," he said.

"Mmmm," was all she could get out before his lips found hers again.

"That was amazing," he whispered as he collapsed on her.

The water made them almost weightless, and he decided right then that he was installing a big Jacuzzi so they'd have more room.

"I've never…" she started.

"Me neither," he finished.

"I love it in water," she panted.

He grinned. How could he tell her goodbye every Sunday?

She wrapped her arms around his hips and ran a finger over the scar. "You never did tell me how you got this."

"Bull got me one time when I was about twenty. Took an even dozen stitches to get it sewed up, and I couldn't ride again that season. What made me mad as hell was he ruined a brand-new pair of Wranglers," Rye said.

She giggled.

"It wasn't funny."

"I know, but it is now. Rye, I don't know if I could watch you ride after seeing the scar and that movie."

"Yes, you can. I've ridden for twelve years since then and nothing's happened. Paid my dues early on." He rose up out of the water like a god—no, like a wet cowboy. That was a helluva lot sexier than any god.

She couldn't take her eyes off him dripping on the bath mat with the water sluicing off his skin and his dark hair all shiny wet. She finally blinked and stood up.

"Damn, you are somethin' else, girl. All wet and glowing after sex. You make my mouth go dry."

She looked down. "Looks like something else is affected too."

He wrapped a towel around his waist and held out one for her.

"Sex makes me hungry as hell. You sure your sister didn't poison my supper?"

"I didn't tell her I was bringing anything over until it was all cooked."

"She doesn't like me." Austin started toward the kitchen.

Rye reached out, drew her close to his side, and kissed her on the forehead. "I don't want to talk about Colleen. Gemma decided to name her new joint Petticoats & Pistols. Daddy is making a hitching rail out front, and she's doing up the inside in cowboys and cowgirls."

Austin heated the food in the microwave while he pulled his jeans on and fastened them. No underwear. He really was commando!

He pushed her hair back and kissed the hickey. "What is that mark on your neck, young lady?" he teased.

"This handsome, sexy man that I know put a hickey on my neck. But hey, he looks worse than I do. I knocked him off the bed. He hit his head on a table and has a Band-Aid on his forehead. I bet he told his sister that surprised him with this wonderful food that he hit his head on a loading chute."

The smile got even wider and his eyes twinkled. "So you think I'm sexy, do you?"

"You plumb take my breath away, Rye O'Donnell. You have since I first laid eyes on you." She took the food out and set it on the table.

It was as if she and Rye had grown up next door to each other and just that spring found the physical attraction that had been lying dormant for years.

"So tell me how many sexy men have you..."

She held up a palm. "Don't even go there or I'll ask you the same thing—and remember I saw all those condoms in your medicine cabinet."

He grabbed her hand and kissed her fingertips. "Never been to bed with a single sexy *man*. That's a promise."

"You are incorrigible," she said, laughing.

"Well, I'm damn glad. I thought all this time I was corrigible and it's worried me so much that I can't sleep at night. I even asked the doctor if I could have some penicillin to cure the corrigible but he said the only cure for it is lots of sex with a beautiful dark-haired gypsy woman. And that she had to live so close to me." He picked up the fork and fed her a bite.

"I'm a big girl. I can feed myself."

"I didn't say you couldn't, darlin'. But it's a whole lot more fun this way."

CHAPTER 16

GRANDFATHER AND GRANDMOTHER DRANK MARTINIS. AUNT Clydia had white wine. Barbara fixed a margarita and Aunt Joan had a Tom Collins.

"You got any beer?" Austin asked when she arrived.

"I don't keep beer," Barbara said.

"Too bad. Then I guess I'll have Gentleman Jack, neat."

Barbara's quick intake of breath made Austin smile. If Jack Daniel's was enough to make her suck air, then wait until she told them her really big news. She'd made up her mind and nothing was going to change it.

Her heart was in Terral.

The watermelon plants had brand-new little melons growing on them now, and she figured she knew a tiny measure of how mothers felt when they went off to war, leaving children behind. It was hard to be in one place when the heart was in another. Running back and forth had worked fine until she made up her mind, but now she knew how she wanted to spend the rest of her life, and it wasn't working in an office.

Grandmother touched her arm. "Your mother tells me that you've been spending lots of time in southern Oklahoma at that strawberry farm your other grandmother left you."

"Watermelon, not strawberry. I've got almost two thousand acres of melons. I can't wait until the last part of June when some of them are ready to harvest so I can start making wine. I've been studying all of Granny's old recipes." Austin could hear the excitement in her voice as she reached for the short, squatty glass of Jack Daniel's.

"I'll buy it from you. We'll have it appraised and I won't even quibble over the price," Grandmother said.

Austin looked at her mother and aunts and saw a picture of herself in twenty-five years. In her grandmother she could see herself in fifty years. The Watson women had been popped out of the same mold for more than a century, according to Grandmother. They were all tall, slim dark-haired women with blue eyes.

"Why would you want a watermelon farm?" Austin asked.

"I don't. I'll turn around and sell it at auction. If I lose money, it'll be a tax write-off. If I make money, I'll give the profit to the local library and that will be a write-off. You need to concentrate on your job and promotion, not be exhausted from running back and forth to that hellhole," Grandmother said.

Austin sipped her whiskey. It warmed her from her mouth to the bottom of her stomach, not totally unlike Rye's kisses, only they went even deeper and heated her up much, much hotter.

"Thank you for the offer but my farm isn't up for sale," Austin said.

She'd chosen a simple black dress that evening with a double strand of oversize pearls that hung below her breasts. Her black heels were four inches high and open-toed to show a fresh pedicure of bright-red polish that matched her fingernails. Her hair was straightened, layered, and needed trimming but she hadn't had time to even think about calling Gemma.

"Why? You are going to sell it eventually anyway."

"Thank you for the offer." Austin politely moved to the other side of the room and backed up against the stones surrounding the cold fireplace. Aunt Clydia was telling Grandfather about the possibility of being appointed a judge. She'd gone from prosecuting lawyer to DA in her part of the world, and now there was a nomination for a judgeship. His smile said it all. He was very proud of his daughter.

Barbara and Joan were discussing something in the business line; at least they were until Grandmother joined them. Now they were talking in quiet whispers and being obviously careful not to look at Austin.

Another sip of whiskey brought back the warmth and made her think of the amazing sex she and Rye had had the past weekend. She wished she was back in that jam-packed house rolling around on the bed or, hell's bells, even the floor with him.

"Dinner is served, ma'am," the cook said from the doorway leading into the dining room.

Everyone set their glasses on the bar and migrated that way with Austin bringing up the rear. Light from the cut-glass prisms on the chandelier made the crystal water glasses and the wine-glasses sparkle. Steam rose from bowls of spiced tomato soup, and the waiters stood ready to refill glasses when they were emptied.

Grandfather sat at the head of the table with Grandmother on his right and Barbara on his left. Clydia had the other end of the table with Joan on her right and Austin on her left, which put Austin across the table from her mother.

"It's been a long time since we've all set down to dinner together. This is nice." Clydia smiled.

Everyone raised a glass and said, "Hear, hear!"

Austin picked up her knife and carefully buttered a breadstick, bit off a piece, and remembered the delicious stuff that Rye served with steaks.

Grandmother looked at Austin. "You look exhausted, my dear. By the summer's end you'll be ready for an asylum."

"I like it in Terral. It's peaceful. You should all fly into Dallas for a weekend and drive up there to see for yourself," Austin said.

"No thank you. I don't have that kind of time. I'm stretching it by promising to fly up here a couple of times a month to spend time with the family," Clydia said seriously.

"What in the devil is that?" Barbara blurted out.

"What?" Joan looked around quickly and then realized her sister wasn't staring at her but at Austin.

Barbara pointed. "That horrible mark on your neck. Good God, that's so low class it's..." she stammered.

"It's a hickey," Austin said.

Grandmother slapped her hand over her mouth, but it didn't keep the gasp from being heard all the way around the table.

The cook giggled.

Clydia shot her a look that froze her laughter in midair. Austin wondered how a person could make noise stop once it was out in the air. She might just get to be a judge with that kind of power.

"So you really have been down there in that hovel sleeping with the neighbor?" Barbara said.

"Didn't sleep with him when I got this hickey. Got a Charley horse in my leg before we could have sex. I started flailing around trying to get untangled from his long legs and arms and knocked him off the bed. He bumped his head on the nightstand and it bled. It was just too damn funny to have sex after that. So I got the hickey without getting screwed."

"Good God! You..." Barbara was speechless after three words.

Grandfather held up a hand and said, "Tell us more about this fellow. Other than making a mark on your neck, what does he do?"

"He's a rancher and owns rodeo bulls. He lives across the street from my property, and I like him a lot. His name is Rye O'Donnell."

"He lives in a trailer house," Barbara said petulantly.

"Yes, he does. And he's got a tattoo of barbed wire around his arm too."

"You are sure you didn't have..." Grandmother couldn't make herself say the word.

"Not when I got the hickey. Don't ask me about later on or about last night." Austin grinned.

"What are you saying?" Joan asked. She wasn't smiling.

Grandfather was.

Grandmother had taken her hand from her mouth and her eyes were big as saucers.

The two waiters' jaws were clamped so tight they couldn't smile for fear Aunt Clydia's glare would melt them into a pile of ashes right there on the white carpet.

"I'm saying that tomorrow morning I'm going to my office and packing up my stuff in a box. Derk can have the promotion. I'm going to move to Terral and raise watermelons. I hate getting in the car and coming to Tulsa. I want to stay down there among all that clutter and drive a tractor every day or else mow the lawn or visit with Molly and Greta on Friday after I make my weekly trip to the bank. I don't want to be here. I don't give a shit about the job I've been doing. I just want to go home."

"This is your home. It's where you were born and lived your whole life," Joan said.

"But Terral is where my heart is."

"You let that man talk you into this, didn't you?" Barbara said.

"Rye doesn't even know I made this decision. He isn't expecting me until Thursday. I didn't even know I was going to make it until a few hours ago. The closer I got to Tulsa this week, the more I wanted to turn the car around and go home and make sure my watermelons are growing right and that Molly and Greta haven't died while I was gone."

A smile turned up the corners of Barbara's mouth. "You are making a very foolish decision, but when it falls in a heap around your ears, you can always come home and run the dealership for me. If you go through with this crazy notion, I will not give you the business but I will hire you as manager. At least you'll have a job when you get tired of living in squalor."

"If the economy goes belly up and you don't have a job, I'll return the favor. You can come to Terral and help me make watermelon wine."

Barbara's eyes narrowed to slits. "You're even talking like those rednecks."

"Thank you."

Clydia held up a palm. "Enough! Austin, you have played the shock-value card enough for one night."

Austin laid her napkin beside her plate. "I have packing to do, so I'm leaving. Y'all enjoy the dinner and please don't let me ruin anything else. I'll call you tomorrow when I get home, Mother."

She marched out of the house with her head held high, but her temper had gone far beyond the boiling point. How dare they treat her like a child when they'd treated her like an adult since the day she was born!

On the drive home her phone rang. Dreading another fight with her mother, Austin almost didn't answer it. On the fourth ring, she checked the ID to find that it was her boss, and her first thought was that her mother had wasted no time! He offered her a three-month sabbatical to think things over before she absolutely made it final.

"Thank you but I want a clean break. I want to move to Terral without thinking about coming back to Tulsa."

"I want you to be happy, Austin. Derk can step right into your office and the promotion. I'd rather leave knowing you were taking care of my job, but he's capable."

"Thank you. I'll be in and clean out my office tomorrow morning then."

She pulled into her garage and said goodbye. When she opened the door into her apartment, she flopped down on the sofa and stared at the ceiling for a long, long time. Was she being too rash? Was her mother right? Would she grow to hate the town, the people, and the hard work? Was she severing the ties too completely? Should she take the sabbatical and give it some time?

When no answers came floating down from the crystal light fixture in the recessed ceiling, she threw her hand over her eyes. Granny's face appeared as if it were on the other side of a dense fog.

Good decision. Don't worry about tomorrow. It will take care of itself. Be happy today.

Granny's face faded and the misty gray fog disappeared, then Rye materialized. He didn't say a word but the expression on his face said it all. In the background Gemma was dancing around like a sugared-up six-year-old after a day at the rattlesnake festival. Colleen had folded her hands over her chest and was shaking her head back and forth. Dewar and Raylen were both patting Rye on the shoulder.

Austin moved her hand and her eyes sprung open. "Guess Colleen and Mother will have to learn the hard way. If this works between me and Rye, that's great. If it doesn't, I'm still going to grow watermelons and make wine. He's not the reason I'm leaving. He's just the icing on the cake. But hey, I can eat cake without icing too."

Her cell phone rang, and she dug around in her purse until she had it in her hand and answered on the third ring without looking at caller ID.

"Hey, girl," Gemma said. "Are you busy? I'd like to run something by you."

"Not a bit. What's on your mind?"

"It's about the rodeo this weekend. There's a post-rodeo concert with Tracy Lawrence. I'm scheduled to ride Saturday night. I know you don't get home until Thursday night, and I've got appointments on Friday so I can't leave until Friday afternoon. Want to go with me? You can room with me and Colleen or else I'll call down and make arrangements to add a room to our block for the summer."

"I'd love to go but I think I'd rather have a room of my own. No offense but…"

"None taken. Colleen is a great person. She'll see the light. It just takes her awhile."

"How'd you get to be so smart?" Austin asked.

"They saved the best 'til last. I promise we'll get you home in time to drive back to Tulsa on Sunday."

Austin grinned. She wasn't telling Gemma before she told Rye.

"That will be great," she said.

CHAPTER 17

RYE FIDGETED WHILE HE WAITED. AUSTIN WAS COMING HOME to Terral for good. She'd even left her car behind in Tulsa and flown to Dallas. He'd arrived an hour early and looked through the shops. He bought a long-stemmed red rose wrapped in crinkly clear paper and tied with a bright-red ribbon. Then he waited in the baggage check area. Time crept by so slowly that he wondered if the clocks had stopped, but every so often the boards with arrival and departure times would shift. Finally, her flight number and time fell into place and the line after said that it would be right on time.

Ten more minutes and her plane should be setting down. He picked up a six-month-old magazine, but nothing in it held his attention for more than five seconds. Fifteen minutes passed before he saw a stream of people coming up the corridor. She wasn't among the first ones and he feared she'd changed her mind. When she'd called the night before, she was excited about the plans but she'd had time to sleep on it, time for her mother and aunts to convince her not to make such a foolhardy change in her life.

Rye caught a flash of a tall woman with dark hair, and there she was, waving at him with one hand, dragging a small suitcase on wheels with the other. He stood up and waved back and everyone in the Dallas/Fort Worth airport disappeared. She covered the distance in long strides and walked into his open arms.

He swung her around in circles and kissed every inch of her face. He set her down and kissed her long and passionately, then picked her up and swung her around three more times. When he set her down, he gathered her into his arms and kissed her again, this time longer and more lingeringly and with more heat.

"I can't believe you came home for good. I'm so happy I could jump up and down like a little kid at Christmas," he whispered in her ear as he hugged her tightly to his chest.

"I missed you too!" She laid her head over his heart and heard the steady rhythm. That was Rye. Steady. Dependable. Truthful and still sexy as hell!

He tipped up her chin with his fist and kissed her again and then handed her the rose. "Welcome home."

"Wow! Kisses and a rose and you... What a homecoming!"

"That's just the beginning of the story. Let's go to baggage claim and get your things."

"No need. Got it all right here."

He raised an eyebrow.

"There's still three months on my apartment lease so I just brought a few things. Later, I'll have it all packed and put into storage closer to Terral."

He looped her arm through his and picked up the handle of the suitcase. "Then let's go home, Austin Lanier. Have I told you in the last ten minutes that you are beautiful?"

"No, but flattery gets sex in the bathtub or on the counter. Hey, we haven't christened the kitchen table yet." She smiled. She wore the jeans and lace blouse from the Red Barn and had topped it off with a suede vest that tied in the front that she'd picked up when she and her mother had shopped.

"Anytime you want to give it a try, I'm game, but remember that table is at least fifty years old." He hugged her tighter to his side.

"But what a way to kill it, right?" She giggled.

"Hungry?" He changed the subject.

"For you or food?"

"Either one can be arranged."

He'd found a short-term parking spot close to the entrance of the terminal, so he draped an arm around her shoulders and led her outside to his truck. He opened the door and helped her inside, then rounded the tail end and settled into his seat. He'd barely slammed it shut before she flipped the console unit up and wiggled her way into his lap, her long legs straddling him like he was a saddle.

"I want an appetizer of you and then food." She kissed him long and hard, unbuttoning his shirt the whole time, feeling his rock-hard muscles and abs. "I'm not ever leaving again."

"Promise."

"Oh, yeah! Now let's go find some fast food and go home."

"It's not fast food but we could get a beer at Chili's Grill & Bar." He sank his face into her hair and inhaled deeply.

"Sounds wonderful. I want a beer in a bottle and chips and picante, and when I'm done with fajitas, I want one of those chocolate cake things that are absolutely sinful."

He grinned and kissed her so long that she was panting when he broke away. "Whew!" She fanned her face with her hand. "Gotta stop or else figure out a way to have sex in the airport parking lot."

She shifted back into her seat.

He couldn't wipe the grin off his face. She'd said *home* more than once so she must mean it! No more counting the hours until she got back from Tulsa. No more phone calls that left him pacing the floor with hot desire.

"How about you, Rye O'Donnell? You wanted my farm. Are you glad that I'm not selling or disappointed that you won't ever get that land now?" She strapped in her seat belt.

Oh, honey, there's more than one way to get that land. But I'm not nearly as interested in three square miles of dirt as I am in you, he thought.

He said, "I'm not a bit disappointed."

Her phone rang at the same time he started the engine and she fished the phone out of her purse, checked to see who it was, and answered, "Hello, Mother. I'm on the ground, and Rye and I are heading toward a Chili's for supper."

"Good. When you get tired of playing farmer down there in the hinterlands, call me. I've hired a decorator to redo an office for you at the dealership," Barbara said.

"Don't spend too much money," Austin said.

"There's the doorbell. James and I are having dinner with some friends."

"Have fun." Austin flipped the phone shut and put it back in her purse.

"Spend too much money on what?" Rye asked.

"An office in the dealership. It's her hope that I'll hate this place by the time we bring in a watermelon crop and will need a job so she's creating a managerial position in the dealership for me. Since I used poor judgment and left a gravy job in the oil company, I am no longer deemed responsible enough to own Lanier Chevrolet, but I won't be allowed to live in a cardboard box out by the Goodwill store. I told her that if the car business went belly up I'd give her a job."

Austin had left an apartment full of her things and a mother with an office waiting. Things weren't nearly as simple as Rye had hoped they might be but, hey, the watermelon crop wasn't in, and if she'd come home to him, then she might stay home with him if he gave her plenty of reason.

"What are you grinning about?" she asked.

"Your mother on a tractor? I've never seen her but somehow I don't think high-heeled shoes and a fancy suit would last long out there in the watermelon fields."

Austin giggled. "She wouldn't be caught at a dog fight in overalls, much less covered in sweat and dirt. And riding on a tractor? That is a funny vision."

"I'm glad you are home, Austin. I can't begin to tell you how much I miss you when you are gone. I feel like I've known you forever," he said.

She'd wondered after the first few times that she talked to him why she was so drawn to their conversations on the phone. Why she felt so energized and happy when she talked to him. Ten years and she'd never met the man who'd been such a big part of her grandmother's life. Then she met him in the café. Was that fate and if it was, why?

Hell's bells, I betcha Granny fixed that too! She's been having a grand old time making sure the timing was right for us. That's why she didn't want her ashes scattered until Easter—so I'd be here for the first of the planting. And that's why she doesn't want us to have sex at his house. She wants us to settle into the place across the road. Sly old girl, aren't you?

"You look pretty serious over there. Regrets?" Rye asked.

"No regrets."

"*Cháchara*?" He chuckled.

"I've got lots of time to take care of the rest of the junk. Tomorrow I will call a company for one of those roll-off dumpsters. When it arrives, the scoop shovel can take care of the *cháchara*."

"Set up a couple of tables out in the yard and put all the junk you don't want on them. Put a sign that says 'free' in great big letters on it, and you'll be surprised how little of it gets into the dumpster."

"Is that where Granny got so much junk? Did she go to free sales?"

"She loved garage sales and the Red Barn. My grandmother is the same way. I'll take you to her house sometime. It looks just like Granny Lanier's."

"You are kidding me."

"No, I'm not. They've both got their own quirks but they are a lot alike. Like planting the first seeds of each row by hand."

"Yes, she did have her ways and she was superstitious as hell."

"So is Grandma," Rye said.

"We made good time getting out of the airport traffic. We shouldn't even have to wait for a table."

"Good because I'm really hungry. Mother says I'll be calling Omar the tentmaker to design my clothes if I stay in Terral."

What stuck in his brain was "if I stay in Terral." She must have a few doubts hiding in the shadows of her subconscious to say that, but he would erase them if it took every damn bit of the energy he had left in his body.

"Granny was tall and thin and never watched a thing she ate. A couple of years ago, the doctor told her that her cholesterol was slightly elevated and if she'd be careful she might never have to take medicine for it. Know what her response was?"

Austin nodded. "I will eat what I want and die when I'm supposed to."

He parked the truck and unfastened his seat belt. Turning toward Austin, he ran the back of his hand down her jawline. "I wouldn't care if Omar did make your clothes."

Her nose wrinkled in disbelief and she said, "Really?"

"Really." He leaned in and brushed a soft kiss across her lips. "You'd be beautiful in a burlap bag tied up in the middle with a piece of frayed-out rope."

"I already told you that flattery will get you anything you want, including a bump on the head or bathtub sex." She quickly unfastened her seat belt and opened the door. She met him in front of the truck and he laced his fingers in hers.

They devoured the first basket of tortilla chips and went through two bowls of salsa before their meal arrived. She was on her second beer when she realized he was still nursing his first one and raised an eyebrow.

He read her expression and held up the mug. "I'm driving. One is my limit. You don't have a limit."

"I love this stuff. Never drank it, so it's not an acquired taste. Must be a dormant gene that's surfacing."

"You never drank beer? Not even in college?"

She shook her head. "I always had a martini and my limit was one."

"When did you have your first one?"

"At your house. My dad loved a good cold beer, but Momma said she wouldn't kiss him with beer on his breath, so he didn't drink them often. Guess that's my dormant gene. Did Granny like beer?"

"Honey, your granny loved beer. Coors was her favorite. That and Jack Daniel's, neat. Two fingers."

"That I knew. It's pretty damn good too. I had one yesterday just to see. Granny told me that it was sipping whiskey, not the kind that you throw back down your throat like they did in the old western movies."

Rye stuffed a flour tortilla with grilled beef, peppers, and onions, added a bit of guacamole and a spoonful of salsa. "She's right. It is sippin' whiskey. It's meant to be savored, not tossed back. Kind of like sex with you," he teased.

"Then that must be the reason I like it so well!"

———

They talked all the way home just like two old friends, but when he parked in the front yard, friendship stopped and something far deeper began. The kisses started at the pickup door with a slow brush across Austin's lips. They intensified so much with each step that by the time Rye and Austin reached the porch a step at a time, she was panting, he was breathing hard, and red-hot desire could have been written in the stars overhead.

She was pressed against the wall but didn't break the kiss as she reached around behind her, opened the front door, and walked backwards into the house. She kicked the door shut with her bootheel and unfastened his plaid western shirt starting at the top and working her way down through three buttons before sinking her hands into all those muscles and groaning.

He slipped his hands under her blouse and whispered, "I love touching you."

Her lips found his again in the darkness.

He didn't tell her that he liked a woman her size, that tiny women scared the bejesus out of him. She didn't tell him that she had never been so turned on in her life or that she didn't care if she got another leg cramp. She peeled his shirt from his broad shoulders and tossed it at the sofa. "Sit down and let me get those boots off."

He pulled her down to the sofa with him and removed her blouse and bra before he let her remove his boots. She sat on him backwards, put one hand under the heel of the boot and one on the toe and had them both off in seconds.

"You're pretty damn good at that."

"I'm learning," she said.

His fingertips danced up and down her bare back, sneaking around the sides for quick touches of the sides of her bare breasts and loving the way she gasped. The past was gone and he wanted to be a big part of her future.

She stood up and led him down the short hallway to her grand-mother's bedroom, fell back on the full-sized bed, and dragged him down with her.

He didn't know when her boots had been left behind, but when he pulled her jeans down over her hips, they were already gone. Moonlight flickering through lace curtains on the window made her red toenails sparkle. He kissed each one individually, taking time to make her moan before making his way back up to her lips.

"Don't make me wait. I've thought about this moment all day. I was scared to death that the plane would have to land somewhere between Tulsa and Dallas and I wouldn't be able to do this." She ran her hands over his body and felt tension and desire bottled up there as much as she felt it in her own body.

"Yes, ma'am, but I do not intend to hurry. I've thought of nothing else all day too." His breath was warm against her already-hot skin.

He started a rhythm that produced shivers, purring noises, and long, sensual kisses. Keeping things from going too fast was the hardest job he'd ever done, but he made it last until she finally dug her nails into his back and pleaded. After which he rolled to one side and drew her close to his side.

They slept until midnight in the soft glow of moonlight and that special light reserved for cowboys and the women who brand them. She awoke first to find his strong leg thrown over her body, one arm under her and the other over her, her breasts pressed into his chest and his face buried in the crook of her neck.

That uncanny feeling that tells a person when someone is staring at them awoke him. He opened his eyes slowly and hugged her tighter.

"Round two?" He kissed her neck right where the hickey still shone.

"Too tired. Time for you to go home. We've both got a big week ahead of us and rodeo on the weekend."

"Wake me early and I'll make breakfast," he mumbled.

"Rye, I'm going to live in this town for the rest of my life. You are going home."

"Okay! Okay!" He rolled off the bed and grabbed his jeans.

She pulled the sheet up under her arms and stood toe to toe with him. "Don't get huffy."

He hugged her close to his bare chest and kissed her on the forehead. "I'll see you tomorrow, and I'm not huffy."

"I'll cook supper, so plan to eat here."

"And go home before daylight?"

"Probably before dark."

He groaned. "I know I've said it a lot but you really are killing me, Austin Lanier."

CHAPTER 18

Tuesday night Kent and Rye spent until past dark working on a new loading chute for the rodeo bulls and getting them into the corral. He called Austin in the middle of the afternoon to tell her they wouldn't be finished by suppertime. She answered the phone from the seat of a tractor and told him she and the guys were plowing weeds that day. She was about to call him to say that she wouldn't have time to cook but they could grab a basket of fish at the Peach Orchard. By the day's end they were both too tired to do anything but talk on the phone ten minutes before they fell asleep.

Wednesday night Austin worked until after ten o'clock, the last two hours by the light of the tractor headlights. Felix said it was important to get the whole crop fed and sprayed if they wanted to make some real money at harvest. Austin didn't have a high-paying office job anymore, and she didn't want to touch the savings accounts Verline had left for her. She wanted to prove to her mother that she could make a watermelon farm work from day one and to show her granny that she hadn't put her trust in a quitter. Rye called at eleven from the motel in Mesquite.

"I wanted a kiss before I left but you were nowhere in sight," he said.

"Me too, but I must've been at the end of the row on a tractor. I'll see you Friday night. Gemma called this afternoon and said she had another room put on the block for the season so I can go any weekend I want to."

"You could have stayed in my room."

"Yes, I could and I might. But..."

"I know," he said.

"Thank you."

"So do you go every week this early?"

"No, just this time when I bring down the stock. After this, only weekends. Kent takes care of the place for me while I'm gone. When I'm in Oklahoma, I pay a groundkeeper to feed and take care of the bulls."

"I see." She yawned. "Your house looks vacant and I miss you!"

"Now you know how I felt when you were in Tulsa. I miss you too. Are you already in bed?"

"Yes, I am. You?"

"Oh, yeah. What are you wearing?"

"You won't laugh at me?"

"Promise."

"Absolutely nothing."

"You are killing me graveyard dead."

"Well, you sleep in the raw. I decided to try it and it's wonderful."

He chuckled. "When you get down here, darlin', I'll show you how wonderful it is. Now, go to sleep. Dream of me."

"Good night, Rye." She didn't tell him that every time she shut her eyes she dreamed of him.

Thursday night she went to bed at ten and was asleep when her head hit the pillow. At midnight she awoke to every hair on her neck standing straight up. She rolled over to look out the window on the other side of the bed and found Rye lying next to her, propped up on an elbow. "I missed you so bad that I drove home for the night. I'll go back tomorrow morning. I just want to spend the night beside you."

"Oh, Rye! That's the sweetest thing you've ever said."

He grinned and his eyes twinkled in the moonlight. He gathered her in his arms and snuggled against her back. "I'm not here for sex tonight, darlin'. I just want to hold you until morning and wake up with you in my arms. Don't tell me to go home."

"To hell with what people think. Hold me." She snuggled deeper into his arms and shut her eyes. She awoke the next morning to the smell of coffee and bacon, and to the noise of rattling pots and pans. She smiled and slung her legs out of bed.

Life was truly good!

He left right after breakfast and enough kisses to keep her until she could make it to the motel and rodeo that night. She drove the new truck into Nocona to the feed store to fill the order for more fertilizer and spray. Next spring she was putting a couple of feeder steers and some hogs back in the lots east of the house and maybe even getting a few of those baby chickens to grow up into fryers. She got back in time for Felix to mix up the right amounts for the tanks and check the spraying apparatus to make sure the filters were working properly. Then it was lunchtime so she wolfed down two sandwiches, half a bag of corn chips, and the rest of a container of guacamole dip. She did the payroll and headed to the bank.

When she walked into the drugstore, Molly waved from the first table at the back of the place. "Hey, girl, we wondered if we'd see you today. We're havin' a dip of each kind. What do you want?"

"Yes." She nodded.

"Yes, what?"

"Yes, whatever you said."

Greta told the waitress and scanned Austin from head to toe. "Good-lookin' tan you got there. Better be sure to use lots of that sunscreen shit. You don't want to grow up and have as many wrinkles as me and Molly got. We didn't have that sunscreen stuff when we was your age or we might still look like movie stars. Oma Fay said that you came home for good. Darlin', do you have any idea how hot the summer is down here out there on a tractor or bringing in a crop? This ain't play. It's real work."

"I thought you wanted me to come home."

Molly nodded so hard that all three of her chins wiggled. "We do, but we don't want you to get Rye's hopes all up and then leave him high and dry. Farmin' ain't pretty shoes in an air-conditioned office. It's dirty work."

"I know how hot it's getting and how dirty it is. But it will get cooler come winter and I can wash the dirt off at night."

"Good. Now tell us about Rye. Is he any good in bed?" Greta asked slyly.

Austin smiled. "I still don't kiss and tell. Right now he's in Mesquite at the rodeo where he'll be every single weekend until August. We both work so hard all week that we don't have time to see each other and then weekends he's at the rodeo so there's not much to tell."

"So go to the rodeo. Dance a little, both vertically and horizontally." Molly winked.

Austin giggled. "You two make me laugh. Last time I did a dance like that I got into big trouble."

"Tell us," Molly said.

"Only if you don't tell Oma Fay."

Molly crossed her heart and held up two fingers.

"Okay then. I had a big hickey when I went home for Mother's Day, and Mother spotted it. I thought she was going to pass out right there under the crystal chandelier. She told me it was low class."

Greta giggled. "It is but hell, it's damn sure fun gettin' them, ain't it?"

"Except when you get a cramp in your leg and have to get up and jump around like a one-legged chicken at a coyote convention. And when you kick your partner out of the bed and he hits his head on the nightstand and makes a bump and it bleeds."

Greta put her spoon down and slapped the table so hard the salt and pepper shakers rattled. She laughed until her wrinkles were flooded worse than the Red River in the springtime.

"Did that really happen?" Molly got the hiccups.

"It did and you can't tell."

"Oh, Greta, we've got secrets. Now when Oma Fay calls with

something really big, we can say that we know something we can't tell because it's a secret that Austin trusted us with. And she'll think we know they went to bed and we ain't tellin'. Ain't life wonderful? We're so damn glad you moved back to Terral that we could…" She paused.

Greta finished for her, "That we could piss in our boots and call it lemonade."

Austin got the giggles at that. "Okay, girls, I've got to get this finished. I've still got to iron my jeans and Gemma is picking me up at five to go to the rodeo. Think I ought to see if I can get this hickey renewed?"

"Good God, don't ask us a stupid-ass question like that, girl," Molly said. "You know the answer before you even ask."

———

Gemma knew all the back-road shortcuts to get to the Resistol Arena in record time. It reminded Austin of getting around in Tulsa where she knew which streets to avoid, which ones had more red lights, and what parking lots to use as a detour to get from her apartment to the oil corporation building in the center of Tulsa.

Gemma made a right-hand turn on Rodeo Drive, a left one into the Hampton Inn parking lot, and hooked a spot not far from the front doors.

"Impressive," Austin said.

"I've been doing this since I was sixteen. Daddy let me drive down here in the summer to get my big-city training. Passed my driving test the first time out, which is better than most Ringgold kids do. We have no red lights, few stop signs, and very few curbs in Ringgold so it's not easy to get any training. We all start driving when we can see over the pickup steering wheel, but passing the test is another thing." Gemma got out of the truck, opened the back door, and removed her suitcase.

"Are you really riding tonight?" Austin pulled her suitcase from the other side of the back seat of the truck.

"Yes, I am and I get to ride in the opening ceremonies. You'll like that. It's quite a production."

Austin looked for Rye when they rolled their suitcases into the Hampton. He'd said that he'd be busy with the stock and couldn't see her until after the ceremonies but she'd hoped he would surprise her.

It didn't happen.

"We're going to have to rush more than I like. Momma's waiting to leave until we get here so she can show you the ropes this first night. It won't take me twenty minutes to get into my finery for the opening ceremonies. I'll take my riding britches with me and change in the restroom." She led the way to the front desk where room keys waited.

"Call Momma's cell phone when you get ready. I'm not going to wait on you since I've got to find Daddy and make sure my horse is ready for the ceremonies."

"Horse?" Austin managed to sneak in a word.

"He brought my horse this week. He'll bring her back home on Sunday since this is the only week I ride in the opening ceremonies and there ain't no way I'd leave her down here all summer. She'd get fat and lazy. See you after I ride. Keep your fingers crossed. I really want to win tonight."

"Why?"

"I need the points for the championship rides," she said. "Here are our rooms. Mine is next down the hall and Momma's is right beside that."

"Okay, then I'll see you later." Austin was suddenly nervous. She was out of her element completely.

Business, she knew.

Watermelons, she was learning.

Rodeo? It was a foreign language.

She opened the suitcase in her room, hung her clothes in the closet, used the bathroom, hoped her nervous bladder didn't act up right in the middle of Gemma's ride, refreshed her makeup, brushed her hair, and then called Maddie.

"Hi, kiddo. It don't take you long to get ready. I'll be in the hallway by the time you open your door."

Austin picked up her purse and found Maddie already in the hall with a smile on her face. She wore a bright-pink satin-trimmed shirt, snug fitting jeans with a silver laced belt set off with a rhinestone buckle, and pink boots.

"You ready? We'll walk over to the arena. Cash is already there. He's a clown tonight. Can't wait for you to see him in his cutoff overalls. The man never did have much meat on his legs, and now that he's past fifty, they are even skinnier. He makes a real good clown."

Austin followed half a step behind Maddie. "What does a clown do?"

"They distract the bulls or broncs while the cowboys get away and they generally entertain. Cash loves it. He used to ride the broncs until he got too slow. It about killed him to give it up but then he found out he could clown and he's really good at it. Makes enough to pay for the hotel rooms and puts him back into the excitement of the rodeo."

Two people were in the elevator when the doors opened. A little girl dressed in jeans, a pink shirt emblazoned with rhinestone longhorns on the front, and scuffed-up cowboy boots and her mother, who was dressed for a rodeo but didn't take Austin's eye like the little girl did. The little girl looked up with bright blue eyes set inside hot-pink and silver face paint and smiled at Maddie.

"Nanna," she whispered.

"No, but I'd love to be," Maddie said.

The mother smiled. "You would remind her of my mother. She's only seen her a couple of times. My father is military, and they've been stationed in Germany ever since she was born."

"How sad. They are missing a princess growing up," Maddie said.

"Yes, they are but such is life," the mother said as the elevator doors opened.

"I want a whole house full of those, and I can't get a single one of my kids to cooperate." Maddie sighed.

"Girls?"

"Either or both. I'm just ready for grandchildren. It's not a long walk and our seats are reserved." Maddie pointed at a building when they left the hotel. "That is the 8-Second Club. Cash paid the dues for the family, so make Rye take you there to eat after the rodeo."

"Rye made me watch a movie by that name the other night. I don't know anything more about rodeos than what I saw in that movie. I'm feeling a little out of place."

"Like maybe you need your spike heels instead of them boots," Maddie said, laughing.

"Yes, ma'am. Exactly. Like I'm the clown and trying to be something I'm not."

"Going to the rodeo is like going to the opera. Either you love it or hate it. After tonight you'll catch the bug and want to be here every weekend or you'll never come back."

"I love the opera. Get emotional every time I go."

"Then you know what I'm talking about. Loved it the first time you sat in the balcony and didn't understand a word of the songs but felt the emotion down to your toenails, didn't you?"

Austin nodded.

"So did I. Cash hates it."

"How about your children?"

"Gemma said she'd rather spend the afternoon in an outdoor toilet as go back. Raylen and Dewar snored through their first visit and never went back. I got Rye to go twice, but it's not for him. But Colleen, now there's a girl who loves it as much as I do."

Austin sighed. Wasn't that just the luck?

The excitement was a living, breathing entity that wrapped itself around Austin's shoulders like a mink coat on a bitter-cold day. From the moment she walked through the gates and up into the stands surrounding the arena, her heart raced. The smell of dirt, horses, and bulls and the noise of the crowd surrounding her all mixed together to stir her emotions even before she looked up to see Rye coming across the arena with his tall Texas swagger that made her blood boil.

The walk across the arena was the longest walk Rye had ever made. It was Austin's first rodeo and he was scared shitless that she'd hate it. He remembered when his mother made him go to an opera in Dallas. He thought he'd die of boredom before that woman stopped singing. Give him some good old country music any day of the week. He swore he'd never go back to another one of those bellowing banshee affairs. And now Austin was sitting in the same kind of spot. If she hated the smell of dirt, hot sweaty bulls, and cow shit, he wouldn't make her ever go to another rodeo, but it would break his heart.

When he sat down beside her and brushed a kiss across her cheek, his palms were sweaty. "So?"

"So what?" she asked.

"Do you like it?"

"Don't know. I haven't seen anything yet except a dirt corral and a bunch of people."

"I'm so glad you are here," he whispered.

"Welcome to the Resistol Arena," a big booming Texas voice said from the judges' stand. "And welcome to the Mesquite Championship Rodeo. Get ready to see the meanest bulls in Texas, the wildest broncs, and the cowboys and cowgirls who intend to tame them tonight. And now please welcome our judges for tonight's performance with a big round of applause."

Catcalls and hand clapping went on for a full minute before

the announcer could be heard above them. "Sounds like a good crowd tonight. So I'll ask everyone to stand while tonight's singer, Colleen O'Donnell, does a fine job of our National Anthem and then we'll have a moment of silence for all our troops."

"Colleen?" Austin asked as she stood and put her hand over her heart.

"She went to Nashville for a year. Might've made it but she hated the city life," Rye whispered.

Colleen's soulful rendition of the song brought tears to Austin's eyes, and she could have sworn even the bulls bowed their heads for a moment of complete silence. Rye slipped his arm around her waist and peace settled around Austin like angel wings.

"Thank you," the announcer said. "Once again, welcome, and now we'll begin our opening ceremonies for tonight."

"What's going to happen?" Austin asked.

"Just watch."

The first horse to come from the far side was a big, black beauty that stepped high. A lady in a sparkling silver shirt and tight jeans rode standing up, her boots in stirrups at the front of her saddle, one hand on the bottom of the American flag, the other on the top edge. The motion sent it fluttering back behind her as she controlled the horse's speed with her feet.

The next horse was just as black and beautiful, and Gemma rode on his back with the Texas state flag in her hands. She wore red sequins and black western-cut jeans. Her belt buckle was the Lone Star state flag done completely in sparkling jewels. She smiled at the crowd as they clapped and stood up when the flags passed in front of their part of the bleachers.

"Oh!" Austin exclaimed. "I love it!"

Rye didn't even know he was holding his breath until he let it out in a whoosh.

She looked over at him. "What?"

"I was afraid you'd hate it as bad as I hate opera."

She kissed him smack on the lips right there in front of his mother. "Darlin', it is spectacular. I love it. When do the bulls come out of the chutes? Can we really do this every weekend all summer?"

Colleen joined them, sitting beside her mother. "She looks beautiful tonight, doesn't she?"

"Yes, she does." Rye was grinning from ear to ear but it didn't have a lot to do with his sister. "Be nice if she can stay on that bull long enough to rack up some points."

"How does that work?" Austin kissed him again in front of Colleen just to prove to Verline that she wasn't afraid of any of the O'Donnell women.

Colleen gave her a dirty look but explained, "There are three judges. Two in the box and one back by the bull chutes who'll break any ties with his points. Fifty is a perfect score from each judge. Twenty-five is for her performance. Twenty-five is for the bull. Forty is a good high score from each judge. Serious riders want a mean bull because he gets points for power, speed, and drop in the front end, kick in the back end. If he can change directions, that's even better. She needs the points to get seeded."

"What's that and what would get points taken off?" Austin asked.

"Seeded means the rider is ranked among the top forty-five bull riders. She'll get to go to the PBR's major league tour and then have a shot at the season finale held in Las Vegas. She's been close before and this could be her year," Rye explained.

"What about her new beauty shop business?"

"If she gets a shot at that tour, the business will have to wait," Maddie said.

"Things that would go against her are touching herself or the bull with her free hand. That's instant disqualification. She'd lose points for poor body position or lack of control," Rye explained.

"Is she riding one of your bulls?"

"She got the draw for Lucifer." Rye nodded.

"Is he mean?"

"I've only seen two riders stay on him the full eight seconds."

Austin grabbed his hand and held on tightly. "Don't you worry about her?"

He draped the other arm around her shoulders and slid in closer to her. "She's a good rider. Hey, you want to ride the mechanical bull when this is over? You could get a taste of riding."

"Good Lord, Rye," Colleen said. "Boots and jeans don't make her riding material."

Austin shot a look at Colleen. "I'd love to ride the bull."

"Better not eat first. You'll have trouble keeping it down," Colleen said.

"Why don't you join us for supper and watch me ride? I'll bet you a hundred dollars I can stay on it for the full ride at top speed," Austin said.

Colleen reached across her mother with an outstretched hand. "You are on, lady."

"You ever ride the mechanical bull before?" Rye asked.

Austin shook her head. "But I'm taking a hundred dollars from your sister tonight. You want to bet against me, I'll take your money too."

Rye shook his head from side to side. "No bets from this corner of the house."

The opening ceremonies ended and the bull riding began. First the men rode. Two of them managed to stay on the full eight seconds and had a total of eighty points each. The third judge, the one on the back of the bucking chute, had to break the tie with his points on both of them. Austin could smell the excitement in the rolling dust from the middle of the arena, the bulls' snorts and kicks, and the tension that lasted eight seconds on the clock and eternity in real time.

"It's a good thing I never went to one of these before now. I'd be one of those groupie girls like in that movie," she told Rye.

"You mean like Rosalee?" Colleen asked.

"Colleen!" Maddie exclaimed.

"Well, she was. Remember when she used to call the house and even stalked him?"

Austin smiled even though she was so jealous she could have bitten nails. "I might have had to whip her cute little ass if I'd been a groupie back then."

"What makes you think it was cute?" Colleen asked.

"Must've been cute if Rye looked at it," Austin shot back at Colleen.

The announcer's voice stopped any more talk. "And now coming out of chute six on Lucifer, the biggest, meanest bull in the great state of Texas, is Gemma O'Donnell. If this girl don't land the big silver buckle at the PBR rodeo this winter, I'll be one surprised cowboy. Give it up for our own Texas cowgirl, Gemma O'Donnell."

The crowd went wild, whistling and stomping the bleachers until Austin was sure the real Lucifer wrapped his long tail around his ears to keep out the noise.

When the gates opened, Austin sucked in a lungful of air and held her breath. When the bull rolled to one side, his nose practically touching his tail, with all four feet off the ground, she let it out in a whoosh. With one hand up in the air, Gemma leaned back and kicked the bull to make him work harder. Three seconds into it, Austin was on her feet. Five seconds and she was yelling as loud as Colleen and Rye. Eight seconds later, a rider went out to help Gemma get off the animal, which was still pitching and bucking.

"Let's hear it again for a near-perfect ride," the announcer said.

Gemma hopped down off the horse and raised both hands until she heard the points. Then she settled her hat and headed around the edge of the arena to sit with her family. It took several minutes to get there because she had to stop along the way for hugs and pats on the back.

When she reached the family, Rye wrapped her up in a bear hug. "You done good, sister."

"Was there ever any doubt? I had a visit with Lucifer beforehand. I told the sumbitch if he didn't get out there and be the meanest critter in Texas, I was going to drown his sorry old speckled hide in the Red River at the end of the season."

Raylen and Dewar were off their game that night. Neither of them did a bit of good on their broncs, but they both declared they'd do better the next week.

"Okay, you want to stay and watch it to the end or go over to the club and get something to eat?" Rye asked.

"I want to eat but first I've got a bull to ride," she said.

Gemma looked at Colleen, who explained.

Gemma grinned as big as her brother. "I've got twenty out that says Austin can stay on it the full eight seconds."

"You put that kind of trust in me?" Austin asked.

Gemma nodded. "If you say you can ride it the first time out, then I reckon you got your reasons for saying so. Don't make me lose twenty dollars. How much did you bet, Rye?"

"I didn't."

"Chicken!" Gemma said.

"I don't have a doubt in the world that Austin can ride that bull. Hell, I'll even let Colleen operate the machinery so we know there's no favoritism. She'll give her the hardest ride possible so if Austin stays on, Colleen can't do anything but pay up with a smile," Rye said.

"You got a deal," Colleen said from three feet behind them as they headed toward the club.

"Ride first. Eat later." Austin hoped like hell her training at horseback riding, ballet lessons, and skiing paid off.

"You sure you've never been on a mechanical bull?" Colleen asked.

"Cross my heart."

"Then what makes you so stupid?" Colleen asked.

"Maybe I'm just looking forward to a trip to Cavender's Western Wear Store in Nocona on your hundred-dollar bill," Austin replied.

Maddie, Colleen, Gemma, Austin, and Rye all headed for the bull without stopping to lay claim to a table.

"Mind if I borrow them spurs?" Austin looked at Colleen.

"Be glad to loan them to you. You know you get extra points for spurring him or for drinking while he's bucking. Want me to get you a beer?"

Austin nodded. "Longneck. Coors. Now Gemma, you tell me the rules."

"They're the same as the arena. Eight seconds. One hand up all the time. One hundred points possible. If you get a perfect score, you get three free pints from the club. Your choice of beer. We'll have two judges, neither of which can be Rye, or me, since I've got a bet on your ass. So I'll find a couple of waiters to judge."

Gemma motioned for a couple of waiters.

Colleen returned with the beer and a pair of gloves.

Austin rolled up slightly on her toes and wrapped an arm around Rye's neck.

"Kiss for good luck," she said as her lips met his in a crashing hot, deep kiss right there in front of Colleen. "Don't worry, darlin'. I've had lessons in horseback riding, ballet, and skiing plus I've ridden something meaner and tougher than that bull."

"Oh?" He raised an eyebrow.

"Yep, and to top all that off, I've ridden a helluva sexy cowboy and stayed on more than eight seconds," she whispered in his ear.

"You'd better get ready to give up that hundred-dollar bill," Rye told Colleen.

"There's never been anyone stay on the back of a bull eight seconds when I'm running the controls. Don't expect one bit of sympathy," Colleen said.

Austin wrapped the rope around her left hand and held on.

She held the beer in her right hand and settled onto the back of the mechanical bull. She took a long swig of the beer and yelled, "Okay, let her rip."

Colleen moved the control from bottom to top in two seconds and Austin spurred, swilled beer, and rode the ton of metal for the full eight seconds, putting on enough of a show that the waiters were clapping and whistling by the time it was over. When it stopped, she crawled off, hoped her stomach didn't spew the beer all over Rye when she got to him, and held out her hand to Colleen, who promptly laid a hundred-dollar bill in it.

"You cheated. There's no way you have never ridden before," Colleen grumbled.

Austin shoved the bill down into her bra. "Never have. Never been to a rodeo until tonight. But I'll be honest. I watched close and I've done a lot of skiing and horseback riding. And when I was younger I took ballet and gymnastics. It's all a matter of balance."

Gemma patted her on the back. "Shit, girl, you ought to be riding the real thing."

"No, thanks. Doubt I'd ever get back on that one. He was pretty dang tough. Did I get enough points for my three pints or not?"

One of the waiters handed her three tickets. "Darlin', I'd let you ride anything I've got any night of the week."

"Sweetheart, I've got my own personal cowboy that I have trouble keepin' up with."

Rye drew her close with one arm and kissed her on the top of her head. "You were damn good. I don't think you needed any lessons from me, though," he whispered.

"I was damn good but it was the kiss that brought me good luck. My stomach is starting to settle. I could eat a steak the size of a turkey platter."

"Whoever is feeding this woman better have a big bank account. She always could out-eat any hired hand Verline had on the place," a woman said from behind them.

Austin spun around to see Pearl right behind her. "Pearl! What are you doing here?"

"Checking out the hot guys in tight jeans." She laughed and hugged Austin tightly. "Hell, girl, you did better than me on that bull and I been tryin' to tame him for five years."

"Want to have dinner with us?"

Pearl was a short woman with shoulder-length curly red hair worn the same way she did when she was fifteen. She was slightly top heavy with a tiny waist and rounded hips. She had full lips and green eyes with golden flecks dancing in them.

"I'm here with a friend. Can't exactly say it's a date like you'd think of a date but he's picking up the tab for a beefsteak tonight. Introduce me to… Oh, my God, is that you, Colleen?"

"It is. Haven't seen you in a helluva long time," Colleen said.

"Old home week," Rye said.

Austin laid a hand on Pearl's shoulder. "We're going to find a table. I'm hungry and I just stayed on that bull for eight seconds. Come around the watermelon farm and see me sometime."

"Aunt Pearlita told me you'd inherited the place and had given up your fancy job to run it. Tell the truth, I wasn't even shocked. Is the phone number still the same at the house?"

"It is. Call me," Austin said.

Rye led her away to a table with Maddie and Gemma right behind them. Colleen lingered behind with Pearl to play a few minutes of catch-up.

"Tomorrow night we eat before rodeo because I'm not riding and because right after Tracy Lawrence is going to perform and I'm dancing the leather off of a bunch of good-lookin' cowboys' boots," Gemma said.

"And what do we do all day tomorrow?" Austin asked.

Rye raised an eyebrow.

"Harry Hines Boulevard," Gemma said.

Rye groaned.

"You can go play golf with your father or shoot the breeze with your buddies here at the club. We are shopping," Maddie said firmly.

"What time and Harry who?"

"It's this amazing string of stores where we buy purses, jewelry, and bling-bling clothes for the season. You can get anything from swords to lingerie," Maddie said. "It's actually a street, not a place but that's what we all call it. You're going to love it."

CHAPTER 19

THE ELEVATOR WAS FULL SO RYE AND AUSTIN DECIDED TO take the stairs up to their hotel rooms. The kissing started on the stairwell. By the second floor Austin was backed up to the wall with her arms around his neck. He had a handful of jean-covered butt cheek in each hand and was wishing they'd taken the elevator. When they reached the third floor, she was panting. By the fourth he was laughing and had her black silk bra hanging out of his hip pocket like a flag. His shirt was unbuttoned and pulled out of his jeans.

At the top floor her belt was undone and the top button of her jeans opened. They looked both ways for family traffic before they rushed into his room and tore the rest of each other's clothing off. Austin had doubts that they could have sex anywhere but in Verline's house, but evidently it was okay in the hotel because no one called, the bulls didn't get out, and neither Wil nor Ace needed a place to get in out of the rain. It was one of those fast and furious sessions like the night she'd wrapped her long legs around his body and he'd taken her up against the kitchen wall.

"Whew!" Austin exclaimed as she pulled the sheet up under her arms. The cold air coming from the ceiling right above the bed chilled her sweaty body.

Rye slipped one arm under her and one over her. "Which was better? The concert or this?"

"Oh, honey, there's no comparison. Tracy Lawrence is good. Sex with you is damn wonderful."

Before he could say another word, his cell phone lit up and started ringing.

Got that one past you, didn't I, Granny? she thought. *You must've*

been planting watermelons out on heaven's back forty and didn't real-
ize the rodeo and concert were over.

He looked at the clock. "If that's Gemma at two o'clock in the morning, she's in big trouble. Yes?" Rye answered the phone with one word that had ice hanging from it. He listened intently forever in Austin's time, then said, "I'm so sorry. I'll take care of it. You take care of that child and call me tomorrow when you know more."

Chill bumps popped up on Austin's arms and she dreaded hearing the news. "What?"

"One of Kent's boys fell out the window in his bedroom. They have no idea what he was doing but when he fell, he hit his arm on a big rock right below the window. They took him straight to Nocona but it's a compound fracture and they sent him to Children's Hospital in Oklahoma City. Kent was calling from there. They're taking him into surgery, and Kent won't be able to do chores in the morning. I'll have to leave really early," he explained.

"I'm not sleepy but I will be at that time of the morning. Let's go now. Besides, the traffic will be horrid early in the morning."

"You sure?" Rye asked.

"Absolutely. I'll leave a message for Gemma and your folks at the front desk. Without traffic we can be home in a couple of hours, maybe less." She hopped out of bed and dressed as she talked.

"It makes sense."

"I'm going back to my room. I'll have my things together in fifteen minutes and meet you in the lobby. We can be home before daybreak."

Sure enough, when he stepped out of the elevator, Austin was at the front desk checking out and leaving a note for Gemma. Traffic was light and they were through the congested part of Dallas in record time. When they turned back to the west in McKinney, it thinned out even more. They were on the south side of Montague with home about half an hour ahead when Rye saw the red, white, and blue lights flashing in his rearview mirror.

He immediately checked the speedometer but he was barely going the limit. He looked over at Austin who'd already spotted the lights. Her seat belt as well as his was firmly fastened. He eased off the gas and pulled into a parking spot right beside the courthouse, thinking that the officer would breeze on past them. But he nosed into the parking spot right beside them and a policeman came running down the sidewalk from the courthouse in front of Rye's truck with a drawn gun. The one in the car got out slowly, gun in his hand, and pointed at the driver's side window.

"Roll down the window. Put both hands outside the window and open the door with your right hand."

"You too!" the other one said to Austin.

"What is going on, Officer?" Rye asked.

"Do what I say. You and the woman with you. Get out easy and don't make any sudden moves. Now put your hands on the truck and spread your legs."

"What did I do?"

"Do what I say right now!" the officer barked.

Handcuffs came right after a frisk job. Then the officers marched Rye and Austin across the lawn and into a cell together.

"Now back up to the bars and I'll take off the cuffs. You have the right to remain silent…" He read them their rights as he unlocked the cuffs.

When he finished, he said, "You are both under arrest for drug trafficking."

Rye couldn't believe his ears. "What!"

"We've got you both dead to rights. The drug dog has already hit on your truck. Get comfortable. Come daylight, we'll book you formally in front of the judge."

"Who do you think I am?" Rye asked.

"You've got a dozen names that you go by but your real name is John Jones. That's the one your fingerprints match. Tall, dark-haired, green eyes, cowboy dresser, black truck with Oklahoma tags. Numbers match. Drug dogs don't lie. Tomorrow we'll have the Oklahoma State Bureau down here to tear that truck apart for drugs."

Rye pulled out his billfold. "This is my driver's license. I am Rye O'Donnell. I own a ranch in Terral, Oklahoma. This is Austin Lanier who operates a watermelon farm in Terral."

"John has lots of identities."

"Bring a fingerprint kit in here. I can prove I'm not John Jones."

"Who am I supposed to be?" Austin asked calmly.

The fact that she wasn't screaming and yelling surprised her. Two months before, she would have been mortified, but she'd ridden a bull for eight seconds, spent two wonderful nights in Rye's bed, and been shopping on Harry Hines Boulevard. Jail was just another candle on the cake.

"You are his wife, Loretta."

"Actually, I like that name, Rye. Can I keep it?"

He shot her a look that made her laugh harder. "You got Loretta's fingerprints on file too?"

"Oh, yes, and yours are going to match hers perfectly. Tall, dark-haired, good-lookin' broad with big blue eyes."

"And what did I do?"

"You've been running drugs with your husband up and down I-35 from Dallas to Wichita, Kansas, for five years."

"Then why are we in Montague and not on 35?"

"Thought us backwoods cops wouldn't catch that tag number, I suppose. Little detour cost you though. Now we've got you."

Austin sat down on the bench and pulled out her cell phone.

"You have to surrender that to me."

"I'm entitled to one phone call," she said.

"Not until you are formally arrested. Give it." He stuck his hand through the bars and she handed it to him. "Now give me everything in your pockets and all your jewelry. Both of you." He turned to the other officer and said, "Get me two envelopes and a pen. We should've done this before we put 'em in the cell."

They put their valuables into the envelopes and watched the officer label the outside.

"If you lose that necklace, you will be very, very sorry. I just bought it on Harry Hines Boulevard, and if one silver bead is damaged, I'm taking it out of your hide," Austin said.

"Darlin', where you will be spending the next forty years, they don't let the ladies wear necklaces," he said seriously.

The officers left and Austin started to giggle.

Rye slumped down on one of the two narrow benches and put his head in his hands. "What a mess!"

Austin sat on the bench right next to him and grabbed his hand. "You really know how to give a girl an exciting weekend. Rodeo, bull riding, concert, two fantastic nights of passion, and now jail."

"Don't be sarcastic."

"Sarcastic, hell! I can't wait to tell my mother. I was just about to wake her up from a dead sleep and tell her I'm sitting in a tiny little town's jail because you and I just became the new Bonnie and Clyde. That we are going to rob the bank in Nocona soon as we can chew our way out of this jail cell. I bet that hickey wouldn't look so damned bad anymore if I could've made that call."

"You are amazing."

"Why? Just think of the stories I can tell Molly and Greta this week. I'm calling Molly first thing when we get out of here before you can tell Kent." She threw a long leg over one of his legs and one over the other and straddled his lap.

He brushed a soft, sweet kiss across her lips. "What?"

"Here's the way it goes. Whatever you tell Kent he tells Oma Fay who calls Pearlita and then she tells Molly and Greta. They feel like shirttail kin since they never get any firsthand news so they can lord it over Oma Fay and Pearlita, so this time I'm giving them the whole jail story before you have time to tell Kent. It's a hell of a lot better than anything Oma Fay knew first about us before now."

"Austin Lanier, I'm in love with you." There, he'd said it and she could never say that it wasn't a memorable night when she first heard the words.

She smiled and her blue eyes sparkled. "Rye O'Donnell, I don't only love you. I'm in love with you too."

He pulled her face to his in a long, lingering kiss. His heart was thumping around like he'd been on a bull eight seconds. She'd said that she loved him, that she was in love with him. Hell, he didn't mind being in jail. He could spend the rest of his life with her in his lap and her lips on his.

"What are we going to do?" he asked.

"I can think of lots of things," she murmured in his ear. "I'm wearing black lace underpants. Want to see if you can get them off before the guard comes back to check on us?"

"You are killin' me again. Look up there. Even in a town this small there's a camera on us," he said.

"Think Mother would disown me if we made a porn film right here with nothing but a bench?"

He laughed and hugged her tightly. "If she took the dealership away from you because of a hickey, I reckon she might."

"I do love you, Rye, and I don't really give a damn if they can see us making out." She pulled his face down for a long kiss.

"I love you too, Austin," he murmured.

"Greta and Molly will have to know that you told me you loved me the very first time in a jail cell. I have to share."

"Honey, I'll stand on top of the water tower in Terral with a bullhorn and tell the whole world." He laughed.

"Okay, kiss me again and hold me while I rest my eyes a little bit."

He gave her one that came close to steaming up the camera

lens, and she could have sworn she heard Verline giggling as she cuddled down into his shoulder and shut her heavy eyelids.

Rye tried leaning back but the wall was too hard, so finally he leaned to one side and rested his cheek on the top of her head and fell asleep. There was going to be some almighty embarrassed police officers the next day when they found that they did not have John and Loretta Jones in their jail cell.

An hour later the police officers rattled the jail-cell door and Austin jerked awake with such force that she butted Rye's forehead.

"We're going to fingerprint you both now." The tall, bald one had an apparatus in his hand.

"How do you want to do this?" the other shorter, rounder one asked. He was probably the one who fed the dog powdered-sugar donuts.

"Make her stick her hand out the bars. She was talking about escaping and whispering so low we couldn't hear it on the cameras. She's probably got a plan."

"I demand my phone call or I'm not giving you jack squat," Austin said. "This has gone beyond funny into ridiculous. So if you want to avoid a court scandal, you'd best give me a cell phone and let me have my call."

"Ah, give her the call," Tall Man said.

"You are the senior officer." Short Fellow pulled his own phone from his shirt pocket and handed it to her.

Austin poked in the numbers and waited. It was still an hour before daybreak. She hoped that Molly wasn't asleep.

"Hello, Greta. I'm ready. Just honk when you get to the front yard."

"Molly, it's not Greta. It's Austin and I need your help." She went on to tell Molly what had happened.

When she finished, she handed the phone back to Barney and cooperated while they fingerprinted her. They wouldn't know who she was but they'd damn know who she wasn't when they ran them.

"Okay, Loretta, why did you call Molly?" Rye wiped at the blue ink on his fingers with a wet toilette.

"Well, John, darlin', it's like this: if anyone can get us out of the joint, Molly can. She'll bring one of those automatics that shoot a million bullets an hour and bust us out. They don't call her Mugsie for nothing, you know. Call me Loretta Bonnie from now on. And you are John Clyde." She resumed her earlier position curled up in his lap. "I figure I can get about thirty minutes before Mugsie busts in here and breaks us out. Go to sleep. We'll need it when we're on the run."

The end was rather anticlimactic. Half an hour later, Molly and Greta hit the police station with enough force to give two policemen weeklong migraines, demanding that they let them see Austin, who could hear the commotion through the shut door into the jail's front office.

By then the fingerprints had shown that the police definitely did not have John and Loretta Jones in custody. And a more careful investigation of the truck showed the only place the drug dog would hit was the license tag. They'd pulled a single print from the bumper that matched Loretta Jones'. When they checked the VIN of Rye's truck against the truck tag, it came up wrong, proving that someone had switched car tags with them in Texas.

They put out a "be on the lookout" warning on the real truck tags only to hear back in five minutes from a hotel owner in Duncan. Police surrounded the room to find an elderly couple who owned the black truck and had been to the rodeo in Mesquite with their grandchildren.

Molly and Greta were so excited to be there when the officers finally let Rye and Austin go that they insisted on treating them to breakfast at the Dairy Queen in Nocona, only nine miles up the road.

"I'm so sorry I had to call you this early. Other than my mother's and Rye's, I couldn't remember another phone number except yours and I figured you'd find me a lawyer," Austin said when they found a booth in the Dairy Queen.

"Honey, this is the best day of our week. We can't wait to call Oma Fay when we get home," Greta said.

"Hell, I got to yell at a policeman. I almost made him wet his britches," Molly said.

Greta threw an arm around Molly. "We done good for a couple of old women."

"You sure did," Austin said.

Under the table, Rye gently squeezed Austin's thigh.

"Did Austin tell you that she's thinking of changing her name to Loretta and she's going to start staking out banks to rob?" Rye asked.

Molly's eyes glittered. "I'll drive the getaway car and Greta can be the watchdog."

"Don't call me a dog."

"It's better than calling you a bitch."

Rye burst out laughing.

Austin couldn't remember the last time she'd laughed so much at something that should've made her mad enough to burn the watermelon farm and catch the next flight to Tulsa.

CHAPTER 20

AFTER THE JAIL INCIDENT, AUSTIN SETTLED INTO A BUSY BUT comfortable rut where she worked hard all week, watched watermelons grow, and went to Mesquite on weekends. She talked to her mother several times a week, to Rye every day, and to Molly and Greta on Fridays. Summer was wetter than normal so the melons were full and ripe by the end of June, and that weekend the harvest was so busy that she could not get away to go to the rodeo.

Rye caught up to her on his way out of town that Thursday evening at the watermelon shed just east of town. She'd been driving the converted old school bus back and forth from the fields all day to the shed. Dust and sweat beads had combined to give her a dirt necklace. Her hair hung limp with the humidity, and her cutoff overalls looked as if they'd been dusted with red powder.

He gathered her into his arms, planting kisses all over her face.

She giggled. "I'm so dirty. You'll be filthy when you get to the hotel."

"I don't care." He kissed her eyelids and the tip of her nose, nibbled on her neck and ran his hand up her sweaty back. "I hate to go without you. I love you so much."

"And I hate to stay home. I love you too. Now go before I tear up."

"Don't you dare cry. If you do, I'll shoot the bulls and never leave you again." He hugged her tighter.

"Never miss the water until the well runs dry. Now I know what they're talking about," she said.

"Oh, I'm a well and I've run dry?"

She leaned into his chest, listening to his heartbeat and wishing she was going with Gemma that night. Visions of him in that big king-sized bed at the hotel didn't help matters.

"For this weekend. Don't be finding a groupie and forgetting me."

He tipped her chin up and kissed her hard. "Darlin', a man doesn't eat bologna when he can have sirloin."

"What if he's starving?"

"I've only got an appetite for you."

"Don't forget that."

He brushed another kiss across her lips and then deepened the next one into something usually reserved for the bedroom instead of right out in public in broad daylight. When he broke the kiss, he asked, "Think that might whet your appetite?"

"Hell, no! That made me forget watermelon wine, and now I'm hungry for good old bedroom sex."

He chuckled and got into his truck. "I'll call you tonight after the rodeo."

"Tell Colleen not to gloat too much. I'll be there next weekend."

"She's comin' around. She just doesn't like being wrong."

Austin leaned in the window and kissed him one more time. "Drive safe."

When he rolled up the window and drove away, she groaned, hopped up in her melon-hauling wagon, and fired up the rattling engine. Granny had bought three school buses at an auction and then set about making them into something better than a pickup truck for hauling melons from the fields to the shed. School buses set up high to get over rough roads to pick up kids in backcountry places, so getting in and out of watermelon fields was no problem. The hired help had cut the windows out of the bus and taken the back doors off. Each year they busted a bale of hay on the floor to cushion the melons, but the buses weren't air-conditioned so the work was hot and backbreaking.

Austin shifted gears and pushed back a few hairs that had stuck to her cheek. Next week, if she had time, she intended to make an appointment with Gemma to get her hair trimmed. She passed Lobo on the way to the shed and waved. When she arrived at the field, she parked and hopped out. Felix and Jacinto already had half a mile of melons cut and ready to toss. On the other end of the field Hugo and Estefan were loading a bus.

"It's a wonderful crop this year." Felix picked up the first melon and threw it to Jacinto who threw it up to Angelo in the bus. He handed it off to Austin who stacked them carefully to prevent busting.

"I'm glad"—Angelo paused to translate from Spanish to English—"that you are"—another pause—"staying to make the farm run."

"You will all come back next year, won't you?" She suddenly had a panic attack. What if they didn't want to work for her another year? How would she go about getting help?

"Sí. We will be here. We were worried that we wouldn't have jobs next year, and we like it here. Our family has been coming to this place for more than forty years. Way before I was born."

Her panic attack eased and she continued handling each melon as if it were a newborn baby. "I'm glad that this will be done in a few weeks. I hate being away from Rye."

"What did you say?" Angelo asked.

"I was talking to myself," she said, laughing.

"Sometimes I do that too. I talk to my wife at night before I go to sleep," he said.

"You must miss her so bad." She couldn't imagine being away from Rye four months out of every year.

"Sí. I miss her and my three children, but this is a very good job and it takes care of us all year in my small village. I am happy to have it."

At dark they called it a day. Austin had lost count of how many trips she'd made back and forth to the watermelon shed, and she was bone-tired when she kicked off her boots and went into the house. She had dozens of melons waiting in the garage to run through the colander, but a shower was the first thing on the agenda.

She unhooked her overall galluses and was halfway down the hall when she heard the crunch of tires in the driveway. She redid her overalls as she headed back up the hall and heard people talking. She opened the front door and was struck speechless.

"Hello… Damn it to hell! Look at you!" Barbara said.

"What the hell?" Joan's eyes widened.

"You look like shit," Clydia said.

"Well, I've damn sure accomplished something tonight. I've got all three of you cussin'. Come right in." Austin threw open the door. "Don't wrinkle your nose. I'm still working on the mess. I just came in from the fields, so you'll have to open a bottle of wine and wait for me to take a shower before you tell me what the devil you three are doing in Terral."

"We all met in Dallas to shop for a long weekend. We decided to drive up here and take you back with us to do some shopping," Barbara said.

"I'll be back in ten minutes. Have you had supper? I was about to make a sandwich."

"We ate at a little German restaurant over in Muenster," Joan said.

"Go on and get your shower. You actually stink, girl," Clydia said.

"Yes, I do and my boyfriend hugged me in this condition before he left this afternoon." She grinned. "Wine is in the fridge. Glasses above the sink."

She washed the grime from her hair and body, used a blow-dryer and a brush on her hair, applied a bit of makeup, and then wiped most of it off because it was too light for her new brown skin. She donned a pair of denim shorts she'd found at the Red Barn, a bright-blue knit shirt, and her best cowboy boots and headed back to the living room.

The sisters were sitting around the kitchen table with a bottle of watermelon wine and three glasses. Joan looked up and swallowed quickly.

"'Bout choked on that, didn't you?" Austin said.

"You look worse now than before," Clydia said.

Austin opened the refrigerator and took out a can of cold Coors. "Yeah, but I don't stink now. You got something to say, Mother? If so, go ahead and spit it out because then it's my turn."

"I can't bear to see you like this," Barbara said. "Didn't you bring anything decent from Tulsa to shop in?"

"I'm not going shopping. I usually spend my weekends in Dallas with Rye at the rodeo, but it's harvest time and I'm working all weekend. And I'm happy in my new skin so get used to seeing me like this."

"What do you mean, harvest? Don't you have hired hands that do that work?" Clydia asked.

"Six of them, but I work too. It's my farm and I want to know what goes on."

Clydia downed the rest of her wine and poured another. She was dressed in navy slacks and an ecru top. Her necklace was a two-carat diamond solitaire on a thick gold chain with earrings to match. "This is good stuff. And you are planning to make it just like Verline did?"

"I've already got two batches in the refrigerator with plans to put another two in there tomorrow."

"Well, save me a couple of bottles. It's damn good."

Barbara looked around the kitchen. "God, this place hasn't changed in thirty years, but it's changed you."

"Thank you. I wish Rye hadn't already left. I'd love for you to meet him."

Austin looked out the front window. "Oh, Mother, you've rented a Caddy and not a Chevrolet. Saint Peter is going to give you demerit marks for that."

"He's going to tell you to go straight to hell, do not pass go or collect any money at all for moving down here," Barbara snapped.

"Maybe so, but if it's like Terral, I reckon I'll feel right at home," Austin shot back. "Why are y'all really here?"

Clydia set her wineglass down and said, "Your mother wanted us to come help rescue you. She's given you long enough to come to your senses. She thought if we came down here and took you to the city, did some shopping, and saw a play or a concert, you'd see the difference and change your mind."

"It ain't happenin'," Austin said.

Joan frowned. "Even your language is different. You talk like these people. Barbara is right. This place changed you."

"Thank you for noticing," Austin said.

Barbara whined, "You really aren't coming back to Tulsa, are you?"

"No, Mother, I'm not. I'll visit in the winter probably since that's my slow time, but from Easter until after July 4 there's no way I can get away."

"You really are happy down here. I hate that."

"I am, and I'm sorry that you don't like it."

"I'm not coming down here very often," she declared.

"You are welcome anytime. When I get around to cleaning out the house, I'll even fix up Granny's old room for you."

"I'll stay in a motel. I'm not staying in Verline's bedroom. She'd haunt me," Barbara said.

"She might at that," Austin agreed, remembering all the times when she could swear Verline was meddling in her life. She sat down, reached across the table, and touched her mother's hand. "It's good to see you, Mother. I've missed you but not Tulsa so much."

CHAPTER 21

RYE SWAGGERED INTO THE HYATT REGENCY IN HIS STARCHED jeans, freshly polished cowboy boots, silver belt buckle, and a crisp yellow-and-green-plaid western-cut shirt. His black hair was combed straight back, and he carried his best Stetson hat in his hands. He crossed the lobby and went straight for the restaurant on the other side of the bar. Everything was quiet for a Saturday morning, but then it was only ten o'clock.

He'd called for brunch reservations and ordered a pot of coffee and waited. Being early gave him the advantage. He'd finished off one cup of coffee and had just poured another when he saw them step out of the elevator. He'd recognize them anywhere because they looked like older models of Austin, but which one was the mother and which were the aunts was a toss-up.

They were all dressed in black slacks and muted colored tops. Their hair was cut in different styles, and two of them had a few more wrinkles around their eyes. Austin had mentioned that her mother was the youngest one by several years, so he took a chance when the waitress led them to his table. He stood up, shook his jeans legs down to stack over his boots, and stuck out his hand.

"Miz Lanier, I'm Rye O'Donnell. It's right nice to meet y'all."

Barbara admired his firm shake and appreciated his manners in holding the chair for each of them before he sat back down. "It's nice to meet you, also. I've heard a lot about you from my daughter."

He picked up the pot. "Coffee?"

"Yes, please. We're all coffee drinkers, and I haven't had any at all today," Clydia said. "I can see why Austin is attracted to you."

"You'd be Clydia?" he asked.

"Yes she is and I'm Joan. Fill it to the brim. I'm not a pansy like these other two. I drink it black."

Rye filled it up. "You sound like my kind of woman."

"I could be if I was thirty years younger. Now tell us why we are here?"

"I wanted to meet you all. I'm lonesome for Austin, and she's dog-tired with the harvest, but it won't be but a few weeks until she can play with her wine-making all fall. By the time it's planting time again, she'll be antsing to get back out in the fields. But right now I'm down here alone and y'all are here so I thought we'd meet and have brunch," he said.

"So she's behind this brunch?" Joan asked.

Rye shook his head slowly. "No, ma'am. She is not behind this. She doesn't even know that I sweet-talked the desk lady into putting the call through to your room for me. I'll tell her all about it later. By the way, have you had the pancakes? They are wonderful."

"You've stayed here before?" Barbara asked.

"Couple of times. Shall I order pancakes for all of us, or would you like to do the all-you-can-eat bar?"

"I'll have the pancakes. The way we've been eating, I'll have to spend two hours a night in the gym this next month," Clydia said.

"Y'all are all like Austin. Always fussing about weight and never gaining a pound, I'll bet." Rye smiled.

"Austin is like Verline and her father. They could eat elephants, and it wouldn't affect the scales," Barbara said.

"Believe me, we have to watch our weight," Joan said. "But I'm having pancakes."

"They bring warm syrup and serve them with raspberries," Rye said. "More coffee?"

Clydia held out her cup and he poured. "Tell us about yourself, Rye."

"I'm thirty-two years old. I own a cattle ranch right across the road from Austin's watermelon farm. I also ride bulls and pretty often take home the purse from that. I raise Angus cattle and own rodeo bulls. I make a few dollars hauling them to the rodeo, which is why I'm in Dallas this weekend and every weekend in the summer months. The Resistol Rodeo Arena is in Mesquite, and I have a contract with them to provide stock for the events. Want to go to the rodeo tonight? You can be my guests," he said.

All three heads shook from side to side without hesitation.

"And you ride bulls as well as raise them?" Barbara asked.

"Yes, ma'am. Make a little on the side doing that. Been close to making enough points to go to the pro bull rider events a few times."

"Has Austin seen you ride?" Joan asked.

"Not yet but she will. She rode the mechanical bull a few weeks ago. Blew my sister's mind right out of the place when she hung on for the full eight seconds and even downed a bottle of beer while she was riding. Everyone in the place clapped for her."

Barbara gasped. "She did what?"

"Guess she didn't tell you about that, did she?" He grinned.

The pancakes arrived and the waitress set a pitcher of warmed maple syrup in the middle of the table and switched the empty coffeepot with a full one.

"Thank you," Rye said.

"You are very welcome," she said.

"We want to hear more about Austin's bull riding," Joan said.

"Well, my sister Colleen dared her to ride. My sister, Gemma, rides the real bulls. Austin let Colleen handle the controls so she wouldn't say that the handler gave her an easy time. And Colleen didn't. She probably overworked the mechanical bull but it looked like Austin was a pro. She said later it was because she had had horse riding lessons and was a skier and had danced the ballet. She said it was all a matter of balance."

Clydia smiled.

Rye could have kissed her. It was the first sign that he was getting anywhere with the ice queens of the big city.

"What else has my child done that I don't know about?" Barbara asked.

"Oh, no! You're not getting me to talking anymore, Miz Lanier. Austin is probably going to throw things at me as it is for telling you about the bull. And this old cowboy ain't takin' no more chances," he drawled.

"Are you telling me that you are in love with my daughter?" Barbara asked.

"Yes, ma'am, I am," Rye said without hesitation. "If her father was alive, I'd have a visit with him and ask if I could have his blessing on courting her. I suppose I ought to ask you for the same blessing."

"And if I don't give it to you?" Barbara asked.

"I'm going to do it anyway. She's thirty. I'm thirty-two. I just happened to be old-fashioned that way. So you can either give me the blessing or keep it in the family vault. I couldn't any more keep away from her than I could live without breathing."

Barbara sighed. "Terral raises passionate men, doesn't it?"

"I don't know about Terral, but the O'Donnells do," Rye said.

"You have my permission to court my daughter. I don't like it because I don't want her to waste her life in that town, but being hateful about it will only drive her away from me and she's all our family has in the way of another generation."

"Thank you. Maybe someday your family tree will expand."

Joan giggled. "Wouldn't that be a hoot? A bunch of little farmers and ranchers. Mother will have a cardiac arrest and leave all her fortune to charity."

Rye chuckled. "I'm not a bit interested in anyone's fortune. Just in Austin Lanier's heart."

Austin was waiting on the front porch when he got home the next day. She wore a white eyelet-lace sundress with spaghetti straps and no shoes. Her hair flowed about her shoulders and was even lighter after hours of working in the broiling sun.

She stepped off the porch and met him halfway from the truck to the house. He picked her up and hugged her so tight that she could hardly breathe. "I'll help you and make Kent help too. You can't miss another weekend with me. I was too lonely down there."

"Me too!" she said.

He set her down, tipped her chin up, and kissed her. "Let's go cuddle on my big bed."

"Let's stay here in my small bed and do more than cuddle."

"Why don't you want to go to my house?" he asked.

"Think, Rye. Every time we try to do anything over there, something happens. At this house we could stay in bed twenty-four hours and the phone wouldn't ring, the bulls wouldn't get out, and no one would come visiting."

His dark brows knit together above his eyes.

She giggled again. "Darlin', it's Granny Lanier. She's going to be sure we stay on this side of the road."

He laughed with her and scooped her up in his arms. He carried her up to the door and she opened it. When they were inside, he kicked it shut with his foot. "I wouldn't put anything past her, and I'll move my big bed over here anytime you want me to. Hell, I don't care which side of the road we're on."

When he set her down on the kitchen floor, she undid two buttons on his shirt and ran her hands inside across his broad, muscular chest and raised her lips to his for another passionate kiss. "I missed you, too, but if the melons aren't in, I'll have to miss another weekend. Tell Raylen to take care of the stock for you and stay home with me."

"If you keep touching me, I'll tell the stock to starve and stay home with you," he said.

"No, you will not let those bulls starve," she said. "But that's another day and right now I just want to make love with you and not think about watermelons or bulls."

He slowly unzipped her dress while setting her on fire with kisses filled with so much emotion that she could hardly breathe. His hands roamed over her silky-smooth skin, finding new places to ignite her desire.

She unbuttoned the rest of his shirt and rolled on top of him, shedding the dress on the way, and pressed her bare breasts against his chest.

He picked her up again and carried her to the bedroom. "Have I told you today that I love you?"

"Yes, six times on the text messages and three times on the phone. But that's not enough so I'd like to hear it again."

"I love you, Austin," he whispered seductively in her ear.

"And I love you, but right now I'm interested in your body. I'm hot enough to burn down the whole town of Terral, Baptist church, school, and all."

"Then I reckon we better put that fire out. You got any ideas," he teased.

She pulled him over on top of her and said, "Yes, I do."

It was dusk when she awoke from the sleep reserved for two people in love who've had too much mind-boggling sex. She opened her eyes to see him propped up on an elbow and staring down at her.

"Good morning."

"Good evening," he answered. "I should've told you before, but we were interested in something else. I took your mother and aunts to brunch at the Hyatt yesterday morning."

"I know."

"And?"

"Aunt Clydia thought you were simply delicious. Mother wanted to know if we'd both sell out and come to Tulsa. She offered us the dealership. Straight up. No payments. No strings. And she offered to buy us a house."

His heart stopped. Was she going to ask him to give up ranching to sell cars? "What did you tell her?"

"That I wasn't interested in a good city boy, that I'd keep my bad boy with a tat and a John Deere tractor, and that I was keeping him in Jefferson County. No way was I taking him to Tulsa for all those women to try to take him away from me. I'd have to beat one of them until she was cold if she made a pass at you. So I'm sorry if you are disappointed that you don't get to go to Tulsa and live the life of luxury. I'm too happy to leave Terral."

CHAPTER 22

THE WATERMELON CROPS WERE IN, AND THE GUYS WOULD BE going back to Mexico the next week. Rye had already cut two cuttings of hay from his fields, and he and Kent spent the day moving the big, round bales into long rows against the back fence.

That morning he'd thrown a pound of bologna into the cooler with their water and soft drinks and a loaf of bread and some chips into a paper bag. He and Kent had eaten lunch under the shade of a pecan tree. The summer might be mild according to statistics, but July 1 was still only slighter cooler than a barbed-wire fence on the back forty acres of hell.

Rye wiped sweat from his face and neck with a red bandanna. "We'll get at least one more cutting, maybe two if we get the right early fall rains."

"Hand me that loaf of bread. Ain't nothin' better than a bologna sandwich out in the fields," Kent said.

"How's Mason's broke arm coming along?"

"Didn't slow him down a bit. It'd take more than one broke bone to put that boy out of commission. He's got the cast off and he's already throwing a ball."

"You are payin' for your raisin'," Rye said.

"Yep, I am but it's going to be your turn one of these days and pretty damn soon from the way you look at Austin. Just keep in mind, the longer you wait, the higher the interest."

"What does that mean?" Rye asked.

"It means exactly what I said. If my boys are leading me around by the nose ring at thirty, just think what yours will do when you are lookin' forty smack dab in the eye."

"I'm only thirty-two," Rye said.

"Yeah, well by the time you get married and have two or three, you'll be forty, and the interest on raisin' gets higher with each passin' year. So why don't you ask Austin to marry you and get ahead of the game?"

Rye spewed cold Coke five feet. "What made you say that?"

"You love her. She loves you. Time is a-wastin', my friend," Kent said with a broad grin. "Now chew on that like a hound dog with a ham bone."

"What if this is just a passing fancy and I'm part of it?" Rye whispered.

"What if she's just waitin' on you to do the askin' and you let the moment slip right through your fingers? You've been in love with her since the first time you laid eyes on her down by the river."

Rye nodded. "I'll chew on it."

"Good, now hand me that bologna and some more bread. You better get to chewin' on something for the body instead of just for the heart or you're going to be left suckin' hind tit. I've already had more than my share while you been sittin' there thinkin' about Austin."

Rye made himself a sandwich and opened up another Coke. Kent was right. He loved her and she loved him, but what if they married and she decided she wanted to be in Tulsa after all?

———

Austin sat on the porch steps and watched the big moving truck back into the driveway. If Oma Fay had seen it come through town, she was probably already blazing the phone lines getting the word out that Austin had finally thrown in her secondhand boots and was on the way back to Tulsa now that the harvest was over.

She looked down at her boots while the driver maneuvered the truck so that the back doors would open up close to the porch.

"Still got 'em, Oma Fay, so don't send the vultures out to buy my watermelon farm until you get the whole story."

The driver rolled down the window and yelled, "Mornin', ma'am. You'd be Austin Lanier? Where's your help?"

"They'll be here in about five minutes," she said. "Want a glass of tea while we wait?"

He got out of the truck and headed toward the porch. "I'd love some sweet tea. I could relocate down here. It's peaceful."

"Yep, it is. I'll be right back. I'd ask you to have a seat but I expect after that drive you'd rather be standing," Austin said on her way into the house.

"You got that right." He grinned. He was middle-aged with a sprinkling of gray in his dark hair; medium height, medium build, and bowlegged as if he'd ridden a horse his whole life.

She filled a quart jar with ice and tea and found him leaning against a porch post smoking a cigarette and talking to her hired hands when she returned. "I see you've met the guys."

The man nodded. "Felix introduced me. By the way, I'm Paul. Soon as I finish this smoke and polish off half that tea, we'll get started."

"We'll bring out the boxes and put them on the porch while you take a break," Felix said.

Paul nodded and turned up the tea. When he finished drinking far more than half, he set the jar on the porch and started helping the men bring box after box out to the front yard.

"Y'all sure you don't want me to haul that stuff for you?" he asked.

"No, we are taking everything to the old barn to store for Miz Austin," Lobo said.

"It'll take several trips in trucks. Once we unload this stuff, I'll have enough empty room at the back of my truck to take them in one load for you. Since you are helping me for free, I'll be glad to do that for you for free," Paul said.

"Then we'll take your offer," Felix said.

At noon the front yard was full of boxes and furniture.

"It's dinnertime," Austin said. "I'm calling the Peach Orchard and telling them to feed you all today and put it on my bill. Felix, take both trucks and Paul with you. When you get back, it won't take long to unload the truck. Lord, where did all this..."

"Cháchara!" Felix grinned.

Austin smiled.

"But it was her junk and I'm not ready to get rid of it," Austin said.

"Someday you might like to have it so don't get in a hurry," Felix said.

"What is this Peach Orchard?" Paul asked.

"You like fish?" Austin asked him.

"Love it."

"Calf fries?" Lobo asked.

"You got to be kiddin' me. They really make them there?"

"Yes, they do. You can even buy a T-shirt that says so if you want," Felix told him.

"Well, hot damn!" Paul said excitedly. "Let's go. If you'd have told me that, I mighta hauled all this fancy stuff down here for free."

"Just my luck. I've already paid you," Austin said.

"No, honey, you paid the company I work for. For calf fries and decent sweet tea, I wouldn't have charged you a dime," he said.

"You goin' with us, Miz Austin?" Lobo asked.

"No. You guys go on," she said. Hopefully, Rye would stop by on his lunch break. With harvest, rodeo, and wine, she hadn't seen him in three days. They'd talked on the phone each night, and once he'd tooted his horn when he was on his way to Nocona for a tractor part, but that didn't net even one kiss, much less a trip to the bedroom.

Rye's heart stopped.

His breath caught in his chest.

The world stopped turning.

He stomped the brakes so hard that his truck slung gravel halfway to Galveston, and he only missed running smack over Granny's old sofa sitting out in the yard by turning the steering wheel hard to the right.

One minute he had been driving along listening to Blake Shelton sing "Delilah"; the next he was out of the truck and stomping toward the porch, his boots crunching the driveway gravel with each step.

Austin dropped the tray of ice on the floor and ran to the door when she heard the commotion. It sounded as if there had been a wreck right in her front yard. She met Rye blasting through the front door.

"Want a sandwich?" she asked.

"Hell, no!" he growled.

"Well, good afternoon to you too," she said curtly.

No hug.

No kiss.

"What are you doing?" His voice was hoarse and cold.

"I might ask you the same thing. Why were you trying to sling all my gravel to the river? What's got you all in a twist?"

"You!"

"What did I do?"

He pointed to the tat around his arm. "I should've listened to the barbed wire."

She popped her hands on her hips. "Honey, there ain't a piece of barbed wire mean enough in the world to keep me out of a pasture I want to crawl into, and you'd best start explaining that comment."

"You are leaving. This house is empty."

"You've got shit for brains. I'm not going anywhere. I closed up my apartment in Tulsa a month early. That truck out there has my things in it, and I'm moving them in here. Granny's stuff is all going up to that room at the back of the implement barn up by the garden. Someday I might go through it a box at a time, but right now I don't have time. I've got wine to make and a wedding to plan if the hotheaded sexy rancher from across the road ever gets off his lazy ass and asks me to marry him."

She wore cutoff overalls, a red tank top, and her hair in a ponytail. Her cowboy boots were worn at the heels and scuffed at the toes. Her blue eyes danced and sweat trickled down her neck. She was so damn beautiful that he couldn't believe what she'd just said. He shook his head but the words didn't disappear.

"Well, I'm talking about you, Rye O'Donnell."

"My ass is not lazy."

"Yes, it is. And honey, if I have to, I'll get the wire snips and take part of that damned barbed-wire tattoo off your arm. I intend to get to the other side and make a nice warm nest in your heart."

Had someone told her four months before that she'd be standing in her grandmother's kitchen proposing to the man from across the street, she would have never believed them. But there she was, vulnerable as she waited on his response and hoping she didn't have to really get down the wire snips and make him bleed when she removed a section of his barbed wire.

Rye dropped down on one knee and took her hand in his. "Austin Lanier, will you marry me?"

"Do you mean it, or are you just protecting your tat?"

He pulled at her hand and she joined him on the floor.

"I love you. Have since the first minute I laid eyes on you while you were taking care of Granny's ashes down at the river."

"Aha! I knew my gut wasn't wrong."

"What?"

"I knew you were back there. I could feel it in my gut. And this is supposed to be romantic so…"

He smiled. "I've planned something far more romantic but that truck out there scared the bejesus out of me."

"Yes, Rye, I will marry you. I've loved you almost as long as you have me."

He gathered her into his arms and kissed her long, hard, and passionately.

"When?" he whispered.

She snuggled into his chest a few moments longer and then leaned back. "As soon as you buy me a wedding band. A big, wide gold band that I won't have to take off to squeeze watermelons for wine-making. How soon can you do that?"

"Tomorrow morning," he said.

"Then tomorrow morning, it is." She wrapped her arms around his neck and brought his lips down to hers.

CHAPTER 23

WIL CLAPPED A HAND ON RYE'S SHOULDER. "GRANNY LANIER meant for me to have her granddaughter, and you slipped across the road so fast I didn't have a chance."

"Yes, I did." Rye grinned as he hugged Austin up closer to his side in the reception line.

"Heard y'all moved into the house and you're bringing Felix and his family up from Mexico legally to work for y'all."

"That's right," Rye told Wil. "We're hoping to get this bunch settled in by next spring and maybe one more family the year after that. We're going to build a bigger house down the road a little ways."

"But on Granny's side of the road," Austin said.

"Why?" Wil asked.

"Because that's what she wants, and she isn't nice when we don't do what she wants." Austin laughed.

"Well, be happy and come visit my ranch sometime," Wil said and moved away to the food tables.

"Sneakin' off to the courthouse like that wasn't fair." Ace was next in line. "You knew you had to act fast or else I'd steal her away from you."

"Wasn't takin' no chances," Rye said.

Austin was beautiful in a white lace dress that barely touched the tops of her new white cowboy boots. Rye wore a western-cut black suit and eel boots polished to a shine. Pictures had been taken. Food was being served from long tables in the Terral community room. The yard was full of tables set up under tents, and people were standing in line to congratulate the bride and groom.

Molly and Greta were happy because they'd been the first to

know about the courthouse wedding the month before, which put them on top of the gossip game. They'd actually planned the reception at the community room in Terral, sent invitations, and ordered a cake and food before they even told Austin it was in the works.

Pearlita was serving wedding cake. Colleen and Gemma were taking care of the groom's table.

"Happy?" Rye whispered when he kissed her for the hundredth time since they'd awakened that September morning on their one-month wedding anniversary.

"Of course I'm happy. I love you, Rye."

"What was that?" Barbara walked up behind her.

"I said I love his cowboy ass." Austin laughed.

"What happened to my child?" she moaned to her sisters, one on each side of her.

"She grew up," Clydia said.

"Don't worry, Momma. In between making hay, making wine, and making love we plan on making lots of children. You can come to Terral and spoil them all you want," Austin said.

"You called me Momma... I don't know if I like that," Barbara said.

"It'll get you ready to be called Granny in a while," Austin told her.

"I'll come around and spoil the babies when they come along if she doesn't," Clydia said. "That way, I can have grandchildren without all the fuss of a husband and kids of my own."

"Oh, no you don't. They are *mine*," Barbara said.

Austin winked at Clydia. "You are all welcome anytime."

"Look at the time." Barbara pointed to the clock on the wall.

"What?" Austin asked.

"Time for your dance out by that stage thing in the yard, and then I get to dance with that handsome cowboy you married while you dance with his father," Barbara said. "You've got to learn to share, Austin."

Austin slipped her hand in Rye's. "Not very often, Mother. But you do deserve to dance with him since he's your son now." She tugged on Rye's hand. "Let's go show 'em how it's done, darlin.'"

The whine of Raylen's fiddle met them when they walked across the lawn. Rye pulled Austin close to his side as Grandpa began to sing "Rye Whiskey."

"Welcome home, Austin O'Donnell," Rye said.

Austin wrapped both arms around his neck, and the kiss went on and on until the whole crowd began to whoop and holler.

The song finished and Colleen stepped up to the microphone. "Hey, y'all. Everyone havin' a good time?"

Applause answered her.

"I've got a toast for the bride and groom. Got to admit I didn't really like Austin at first. Figured her for a city slicker that wouldn't get her hands dirty and who damn sure wouldn't stick around when the going got tough. She proved me wrong so here's a toast to my new sister and to my brother who was a love-drunk cowboy from the minute he laid eyes on that woman." Colleen held up a bottle of beer.

"Where'd she get that beer? I'd do anything for a cold Coors," Austin said.

Rye wiggled an eyebrow. "Move back across the street into my trailer."

"Hell, no! I'm not living in that trailer. I like sex too much to live on that side of the road, and you promised me a yard full of mean boys. How would we get them over there?"

He picked her up, swung her around, and buried his face in her hair before setting her back down.

"I really do feel like a love-drunk cowboy," he said.

"I intend to see to it that you always do," she said and sealed that vow with one more kiss.

Summertime on the RANCH

A Spikes and Spurs novella

CHAPTER 1

BECCA SCOLDED HERSELF FOR LEAVING THE DOOR OPEN.

Now Dalton's pesky dog had snuck into the watermelon wine shed. If he scratched off a hair and it landed in one of the containers of juice, she intended to strangle the shaggy critter and hang him out on the barbed-wire fence to show all the other ugly mutts in southern Oklahoma what happens when a dog hair got into her wine.

She crammed the air lock down on the bottle, wiped the outside, and hurried over to the door. "Get out of here!" she yelled as she pointed outside. Austin had trusted her with the wine shed for a whole week, and she was not going to let her boss and best friend down.

Tuff rolled over on his back and looked up at her with big, brown eyes. "I said, go!" She stomped her foot, but the dog just wagged his tail. "Who names a raggedy-ass mutt, Tuff, anyway?" She grabbed a broom, and his tail flipped back and forth so fast that it was a blur.

"He ain't afraid of a broom." Dalton's deep Texas drawl startled her. "I use one just like that to scratch his tummy out in the barn, and he's named after Tuff Hydeman who is a world champion professional bull rider." He gave a shrill whistle and Tuff jumped up from the floor and stood at attention. "Come on, boy. We won't stay where we're not wanted."

"Shaggy from the old Scooby-Doo shows fits him better," Becca said.

"Now, you're just hurting the poor little fella's feelings," Dalton said. "Don't pay no attention to what she says, Tuff. She don't know jack squat about a good rodeo dog like you."

Becca popped her hands on her hips. "I've been to rodeos, and I grew up on a ranch. Don't tell me that I don't know nothing about cattle dogs."

Dalton Wilson's confidence oozed out of him, but then there wasn't a woman in the whole universe who wouldn't jump at the chance to walk down the aisle with him. Sweet Lord, the cowboy looked like sex on a stick.

Dalton flashed a brilliant smile that softened his square jaw. "You should never judge a book by its cover." He gave another shrill whistle and Tuff pranced toward the door, head and tail held high as if he was marching up to the judge's stand to receive the biggest trophy in a prestigious dog show.

In Becca's opinion, he was still as ugly as sin on Sunday morning.

Together, Dalton and Tuff strutted out of the shed. One sexy cowboy that Becca was determined not to let get under her skin or in her heart, and a wiry dog that shared DNA with steel wool.

"Dammit!" Becca swore under her breath. "I've probably joined all the women in the universe in admiring him, but the difference is that I'm stronger than they are, and I can damn well fight off his charms."

Becca McKay lived up to her Irish heritage with her flaming-red hair and mossy-green eyes. She loved Irish coffee and Irish food and had a little of the Irish accent, just like her daddy who'd been born in County Cork. When it came to music and the southern accent in her voice, she was her mama's daughter, and she was country through and through.

Becca had covered songs by Tanya Tucker, Reba McIntire, Dolly Parton, and a whole host of other female country artists from the time she could hold a microphone at county fairs, family reunions, or anywhere anyone would let her sing. With stars in her eyes, she'd gone to Nashville right out of high school, intent on making a career as a country music recording artist. By Christmas, she figured she would have a contract, and all the folks back home in Ringgold, Texas, would be listening to her sing on the radio.

Yeah, right.

At Christmas, she was working for one of the dinner theaters in the evenings and singing on street corners just to make rent for the one-bedroom apartment she shared with four other girls. Ten years later, she was working at Tootsie's Orchid Lounge as a bartender at night, in a winery during the day, and living in the same walk-up apartment. At least by that time, she was sharing the place with only one other girl, who was just as desperate as she was to get a toe in the door as a country singer.

The previous December, she had been on her way home from Tootsie's sometime after two in the morning when the high heel of her boot stabbed a piece of paper. No matter how hard she shook her foot, it wouldn't let go. Finally, she leaned against the brick wall of a building and removed it with her fingers.

The streetlight illuminated the paper enough that she could identify it as the last page of a contract that had no signature. The next morning, her grandmother, who lived just over the Red River from Texas in Terral, Oklahoma, called to tell her that she had fallen and twisted her ankle. Could Becca come home for a few weeks to help her out? Everything seemed like an omen—the contract with no name on it suggested that she would never sign with a record company, and her grandmother, who never asked for help from anyone, seemed to say that Nashville would never really be her home.

Becca gave notice at both her jobs, handed her set of apartment keys to her roommate, and drove west, watching her hopes and dreams fade away in the rearview mirror. Grammie McKay, Irish to the bone and with a thick Irish accent, got her the job with Austin O'Donnell's wine business. Grammie's ankle healed, and she was getting around really well these days. Becca enjoyed her work, but Terral, population less than four hundred, sure didn't provide many opportunities for her to sing.

"Maybe that's a good thing," she muttered as she closed the door to the wine shed and went back to squeezing the juice from the first watermelons of the season.

The door hinges squeaked, and Becca flipped around, ready to yell at Tuff if he'd figured out a way to get inside again. She might not like Dalton's dog, but her pulse jacked up a few notches at the thought of seeing Dalton a second time that morning. She was already visualizing him in those faded tight-fitting jeans, scuffed-up cowboy boots, and his dusty old straw hat as she turned away from the watermelon she was cutting into chunks. In her mind's eye, she could see his dark hair curling on his chambray shirt collar, and his bright blue eyes twinkling as he teased her about his worthless dog.

"Rodeo dog, my butt," she muttered.

"You callin' me a dog, darlin' girl, or have you given up singin' and gone to ridin' bulls?" Grammie McKay's accent jerked the picture of Dalton right out of Becca's head.

"No, ma'am," she answered. "I was fussin' to myself about that mutt of Dalton Wilson's. Seems like every time it gets a chance, it comes lookin' for me."

Grammie sat down in a lawn chair. This morning she wore a bright-green sweat suit that brought out the glimmer in eyes that were almost the same color as Becca's. Her red hair, now sprinkled with gray, was twisted up in a knot on the top of her head. "There'd be something wrong with a lassie who doesn't like a dog, so maybe you better examine yourself instead of poor old Tuff. Pooch can't help the way God made him anymore than you can help the way the good Lord made you. What's really eatin' on your heart this mornin'? Are you afraid you can't run this wine-makin' business for a spell all by yourself?"

"Nothing like that, and Lord knows Austin and Rye and those precious children of theirs need a vacation. I'm glad Austin trusted me enough to leave me to do the job for a week." Becca admitted that much, but she sure didn't want to talk about the way the cowboy who lived across the dirt road affected her. Dalton Wilson was known all over southern Oklahoma and north Texas for his bad boy reputation, and Becca sure didn't need that in her life.

"Then is it Dalton and not his poor, old ugly dog that's gotten your knickers in a twist?" Grammie asked.

Becca dragged a lawn chair across the room and sat down beside her grandmother. "I don't have time for a one-night-stand kind of guy. Dalton is a love-'em-and-leave-'em cowboy, and I refuse to be just another notch on his bedpost."

"Ahhh, darlin' girl." Grammie smiled. "That does bring back memories. That's exactly what my mama told me about your grandpapa. She said, 'Greta, that boy will break your heart, and you'll be nothing but a notch on his bedpost.' It takes a brave and determined woman to tame a wild boy, but once you get the job done, they make mighty fine husbands, fathers, and lovers," she said with a sly wink. "And I'd be living testimony of that. I tamed Seamus McKay. Not to say it didn't take a while, but by the time we had your daddy, he had come through the fire and was pure gold until the day he died."

"Fire?" Becca asked.

"Do you think that tamin' him was easy? I had to light a few blazes under him before the job was finished. Dalton might be wild as a March hare right now, but maybe he hasn't met the right Irish woman, someone willin' to strike the match like I was with my Seamus."

"Well, I hope he meets her soon and quits crossing the road to this part of the O'Donnell property," Becca smarted off.

"Better think hard about what you ask for, Miss Greta Rebecca McKay." Grammie used her full name, which meant she was dead serious.

Dalton gave his best cowboy boots one more swipe with the brush, settled his good straw hat on his head, and headed for the door that Saturday evening. Tuff whined and thumped his tail against the wooden floor. Dalton stooped down to scratch the dog's ears and whisper, "If I get lucky, I'll be back right after breakfast. If I don't, I'll see you before dawn. Hold down the fort. I left the cartoon channel on for you." He lowered his voice to a whisper. "And thanks for this morning, ole boy. You done good, sneaking into the wine shed so I could see Becca. That woman has gotten under my skin, and I'm running out of excuses to go over there and talk to her." He patted the dog on the head one more time. "You're a good wingman, Tuff, but the Broken Bit don't let us cowboys bring our four-legged buddies with us."

Dalton was whistling as he got into his truck and drove west through the tiny town of Terral. He'd grown up in Bowie, Texas. Strangely enough, Becca had lived in Ringgold, just twenty minutes up Highway 81, and he'd never met her until she came to work for Austin last December.

Dalton had known from the time he could take his first steps that he wanted to be a rancher. By the time he was a freshman in high school, he was on the payroll at his grandfather's ranch a few miles south of Bowie in Fruitland. When he graduated, he went to work full time for his grandfather, and then two years ago, he met Rye at a rodeo. Rye was looking for a foreman. Dalton was wanting to spread his wings, so he took the job in Terral, Oklahoma, when Rye offered it to him. The only bad thing about jumping over the Red River to live in Terral was that Dalton sure had to endure a lot of teasing during the Texas-Oklahoma football weekend. Dalton was a die-hard Texas fan, and there was no way he'd ever turn his back on the Longhorns.

He had turned on the radio even before he adjusted the air conditioner. Good country music would get him in the mood for some two-stepping and beer drinking that evening, and maybe, like he'd told Tuff, he would even get lucky and not be home until after breakfast.

There's not a woman in the world who can satisfy that itch you've got for Becca. His father's voice popped into his head just as Blake Shelton began to sing "Honey Bee" on the radio.

He ignored his late father's advice and sang along with Blake. Dalton had always thought love at first sight was a bunch of over-fried bologna. Rye had told him all about how he'd been down-right love drunk when he first met Austin, and Dalton had thought he was crazy. Now, he wasn't so sure, because he was feeling what Rye described for Becca.

"And she's not even my type," he muttered when he turned south. "She's too tall. She's a redhead and everyone knows they've got a temper. To top it all off, she's got those green eyes that I could drown in."

A mile down the highway, he glanced over at the new casino that had gone up three years ago. Sitting right on the edge of the Red River, it drew people in from all over north Texas and pro-vided a few jobs for the folks around the little town of Terral. He almost stopped there to have a drink or two and blow a twenty-dollar bill at the slots, but that would put him late getting to the Broken Bit, which would mean all the ladies would already be taken. Besides, he wanted to flirt with a cute little brunette and maybe get lucky enough to get Becca off his mind.

He crossed the river bridge into Texas and drove another five miles to Ringgold. There he made a right-hand turn on Highway 82 and headed toward Henrietta. In another ten minutes, he pulled into the Broken Bit's dimly lit parking lot. Judging by all the pickups and cars and the loud music that seemed to be raising the roof a few inches, the place was booming—just the way he liked it. He got out of the truck, locked it, and shoved the keys into his pocket.

"Hey, Dalton," a feminine voice called out behind him.

He turned around to see Lacy Ruiz not ten feet away. "Hey, girl. You just now getting here?"

"Yep," she answered. "You want to save me the last dance?"

A broad grin covered his face. Lacy was his kind of woman—short, brunette, a good dancer, and he had spent enough nights with her to know that she made a mean western omelet the next morning.

"We'll have to see about that," he said as he pulled a ten-dollar bill from his pocket and gave it to the man at the door for both their cover charges. "Never know what might happen between now and closin' time."

"Ain't that the truth, but we could be each other's backup plan," she suggested.

"Sounds good to me."

She disappeared into the crowd of folks doing a line dance. The female vocalist was doing a credible job of the band's rendition of "Any Man of Mine," by Shania Twain. Dalton followed Lacy inside, slid onto the last empty barstool, and ordered a longneck Coors.

"How about you, Dalton?" Tessa, the bartender, grinned. "You goin' to ever walk the line like the song says, or are you going to go to your grave still chasin' women?"

"Haven't decided," Dalton answered. "All the good ones like you are done taken."

"Honey, I'm old enough to be your mama," Tessa told him. "And there's plenty of good ones still out there. I just doubt you'll ever find the one for you in a place like this."

"You're here," he said.

"Yeah, but my husband and I met at a church social. It wasn't until we'd been married twenty years that we bought this place, and for your information, we'll both be in church tomorrow morning," she told him.

"So will I," Dalton said.

"Sure, you will," Tessa giggled.

"What's that supposed to mean?" Dalton asked.

"You'll sow wild oats tonight. Tomorrow mornin', you'll be sittin' on the back pew praying for a crop failure. You can't fool me, cowboy," she said. "I hear that Austin and Rye are off on a vacation and have left you and Becca McKay in charge of the place for the next week. You might want to put those wild oats on the back burner tonight and be a responsible foreman."

"You givin' me advice now, Miz Tessa?" he asked.

"Yep, I surely am." Tessa headed off to the other end of the bar.

The lady singer stepped back from the microphone and took her place behind a keyboard, and the male singer started singing Travis Tritt's "T.R.O.U.B.L.E." The lyrics had just said something about looking at what just walked through the door when Dalton caught sight of a tall woman with flaming-red hair in his peripheral vision. He turned to look and almost dropped his beer when he saw Becca coming straight toward the bar.

"You are a genius, Travis," Dalton murmured.

Becca crossed the room, weaving her way among the line dancers, and sat down on the barstool right next to him. He waited until she ordered a beer and then tossed a bill on the counter when Tessa brought it to her.

"I'll buy your first drink tonight in exchange for the last dance of the evening," Dalton said.

"Good God!" Becca exclaimed. "Where did you come from?"

"Been right here the whole time." He grinned.

"I'll pay for my own beer," she said.

"Too late." Tessa pocketed the bill. "Don't forget that you owe him the last dance."

"I never force a woman to dance with me." Dalton turned around to face Becca. Damn, but she was beautiful in her tight jeans, that cute little dark-blue lace shirt with the pearl snaps, and those fancy cowgirl boots. Her red hair floated on her shoulders, framing her face like a halo, and even in the dim light, her green eyes glimmered.

"I pay my debts, cowboy." Becca took a long drink of the beer and then held it up toward him. "Thanks for this."

"You are so welcome. Want to pay for it right now? I can teach you to two-step." He arched an eyebrow.

"Darlin', I've been in Nashville for the past ten years, and besides I was two-steppin' when I still had a pacifier in my mouth." She took another drink of her beer and motioned for Tessa. "Set this back until I finish showing this smartass how to dance."

"You might ought to let me just dump it and start all over with a cold one," Tessa teased. "It might get warm before you get him taught."

"You got a point there." Becca slid off the barstool and headed to the dance floor.

Dalton finished off his beer and set the empty bottle on the bar. This was his lucky night even if he had to make his own breakfast in the morning. Tessa could be wrong about meeting the right girl in a bar, he was thinking.

You met her five months ago, the pesky voice in his head reminded him.

He didn't even bother to argue but simply held out his hand toward Becca. He'd wondered what it would be like to hold her in his arms, and he was not one bit disappointed when she moved in close to him.

"Lesson number one," she said, "is not to hold a woman too closely on the first dance."

"Darlin', I know how to two-step," he whispered into her ear.

"But do you know how to dance with a woman who's almost as tall as you are?" she asked. "I hear that you prefer short little gals with dark hair."

"So, you've been asking questions about me?" He avoided answering her question. Truth was, he had not danced with many tall women, but oh, sweet Jesus, he did like the way Becca fit into his arms. He was tempted to tip up her chin and kiss her when the male vocalist in the band started singing "Tennessee Whiskey," but he didn't dare push his luck.

"Don't have to ask questions about a rounder like you, Dalton," she answered. "The news just floats around this part of the world like dandelion fluff in the springtime. Everyone knows who and what you are."

"And that is?" Dalton asked.

"They'd call you a player in the big cities, but in this part of the world I think you're just referred to as a bad boy," she told him.

"Do you like bad boys?" he asked.

"Only on Saturday night when I'm in the mood to dance, and honey, I might dance the last two-step with you to pay for that first drink, but when this place closes down, I will be going home alone, so let's get that straight right now," she told him.

"I bet you can't cook up a decent breakfast for a hungry old cowboy anyway," he teased.

"You won't be finding that out in the morning." She smiled up at him.

His heart melted. His pulse raced. She didn't say that he'd *never* find out, but she said *in the morning*. Someday, he hoped, this woman would make his breakfast every single morning—or maybe he'd make the morning meal for her. He'd sure be willing to do that if it meant he would get to wake up with her in his arms.

CHAPTER 2

"You do not come into my kitchen with that grumpy face," Grammie said on Sunday morning. "This is the Lord's day, and He expects us to be happy."

If Becca had still been in Nashville, she wouldn't even have been up that early on Sunday morning. She would have worked a double at Tootsie's on Saturday, gone home long after two o'clock when the place was cleaned up, and fallen into bed to sleep until sometime in the afternoon. The old cuckoo clock in the foyer had struck twice, telling everyone in Jefferson County that it was two thirty, when she had taken a quick shower and tried to go to sleep, but the sun was peeking over the far horizon when she finally drifted off.

Becca groaned as she threw her legs over the side of the bed and padded barefoot to the kitchen. "I've had less than three hours' sleep."

"And that, darlin' girl, would be your own fault, not our Lord and Savior's, so get a cup of my good, strong black coffee and wake yourself up." Grammie pointed toward the half-full pot on the countertop.

Becca yawned and poured a full cup of the thick, black stuff her grandmother called coffee. Without a little cream and sugar, it was strong enough to melt the silver plating off the spoon, but that morning, she needed an extra boost, so she took it straight up.

"Muffins are on the table, and we'll be heading to church soon. Jesus, Mary, and Joseph! You can't be goin' to church wired to the moon," Grammie said as she slathered butter on a blueberry muffin and handed it to Becca.

Poppa McKay had died when Becca was eight years old, and

Grammie had left Ireland to live closer to her only son who lived in Ringgold, Texas. In the past twenty years, she'd left some of her Irish slang behind, but when she blasphemed, she did it with the whole family, and *wired to the moon* was another way of saying that Becca was hungover.

"I only had three beers all night," Becca argued and then bit into the muffin.

"Your eyes are tellin' me a different story, but I'm not fussin' at you. I remember when I was a young woman and spent my Saturday nights at the local pub." Grammie's eyes went slightly dreamy. "I met my Seamus at that pub, and we had fifty good years together." She blinked and sat down at the table. "My mam didn't let me miss church just because I was still sleepy. No, ma'am. Not one single time. So, eat your breakfast and get all prettied up. We'll sit on the front pew, so you won't be fallin' asleep."

"Grammie!" Becca gasped.

Greta giggled. "I'm just funnin' you. We'll sit on our regular pew about halfway back in the church. I figure that's a safe place for you. The devil can't drag you through the back door with all those folks around you."

Becca reached for a second muffin. "What makes you think the devil even wants me?"

"Honey, he wants all of us. We just got to outsmart him, kind of like I did my Seamus back in the day." Greta stood up and headed out of the kitchen. "I'll be waitin' by the door with my purse and Bible in my hand at a quarter of eleven."

"Yes, ma'am, but that's two hours from now," Becca said.

Greta stopped in the doorway. "Us older ladies take a little longer to get beautified than you young'uns. What gravity ain't got a hold of, wrinkles have. Finish your coffee and then go make yourself pretty for that cowboy you been runnin' from since Christmas. If you run hard enough, you'll catch him." She giggled as she disappeared down the hallway toward her bedroom.

"I'm not sure I want to catch him," Becca muttered as she finished off the last of her coffee and then pushed back her chair. She put the dirty plates and cups in the dishwasher and went to her room. Six outfits later, she finally decided on a sundress the color of her eyes and a pair of strappy high heels that matched it. She was sitting on a ladder-back chair in the foyer when her grandmother appeared with her white patent-leather purse slung over her arm.

Greta pointed at Becca's feet. "I'm pea green with jealousy over those shoes, darlin' girl. You might be named after me, but you got those long legs from your mama. I bet Dalton's old heart throws in an extra beat this morning when he sees you walk past him."

Becca stood up and slung an arm around her grandmother's shoulders and tried to veer her away from Dalton. "Grammie, I've seen pictures of you when you were my age. You were stunning."

"Don't you be tryin' to butter me up so I won't talk about Dalton Wilson." Greta shook a finger toward her. "I might be old, but I ain't stupid."

The old folks around town kept saying that they were in for one hot summer, and Becca believed every word of it when she opened the door and a blast of hot air rushed across the porch to meet them. Hot summer. Hot cowboy. Hot everything—or so it seemed.

Nothing in Terral was more than ten minutes away, not even the new casino that had been built out at the edge of the Red River. To go from the ranch and watermelon farm to the only restaurant on Main Street, the churches, or the convenience store up on the corner of Apache Avenue—the street most folks called Main—and Highway 81 took half that time. Driving the four blocks from her grandmother's place to the church took about three minutes. Becca's little compact car wasn't even cooled down when she turned into the gravel parking lot. That old saying that if you blinked while driving through the two blocks that were downtown, you'd miss it was the unadulterated, guaranteed truth.

As luck would have it, Dalton arrived at the same time as Becca and her grandmother, and he rushed over to be the perfect gentleman and help Greta out of the car. Becca opened her door, slung her long legs out, and turned to look over the top of the car—and locked eyes with Dalton.

"I just asked this handsome young man to sit with us," Greta said.

He arched an eyebrow toward Becca.

"And what did he say?" Becca's eyes didn't leave his.

"That he'd be glad to attend church with us this mornin.'" Greta flashed her brightest grin, deepening the wrinkles around her mouth. "If you two kids are real nice and sing pretty, maybe he can even go home with us for Sunday dinner. I put a pot roast in the oven, and it will be done by the time services are over."

"I can be the best cowboy in the whole state for a Sunday dinner like that." Dalton grinned. "Here, Miz Greta, take my arm. Those steps going up to the church are pretty steep."

You can worm your way into my grandmother's heart, cowboy, Becca thought as she followed them into the sanctuary. *You can dance with me, and even have dinner at Grammie's house, but I refuse to be another conquest in your line of one-night stands.* She felt like a little puppy trailing along after her two masters as the three of them made their way into the church and down the center aisle.

"This is where I like to sit." Greta stopped in her tracks about the middle of the church.

"Yes, ma'am." Dalton stood to one side.

Becca bit back a groan when she realized she would be sitting between her grandmother and Dalton. Three of Greta's friends had already sat down on the other end of the pew, and like always, there was only room for two more people to sit comfortably. Adding a big, strapping cowboy like Dalton would squeeze them together, but there was nothing she could do but sit down.

Dalton wedged himself into the space that remained, but with the end of the pew on one side and Becca's body on the other, there was very little room for him.

"There's no sense in you two bein' crowded up like this," Greta whispered. "Go on and find yourselves a seat up closer to the front."

"I'm fine." Becca's voice sounded a little high in her own ears, but then her heart was thumping and her pulse racing. Dalton looked like the cover model for a western romance novel in his tight jeans, plaid shirt, and polished boots. She took a deep breath, hoping to put out all the sparks dancing around them, but whatever shaving lotion he had used that morning sent her senses reeling.

"No problem here." Dalton smiled.

"No leaning on each other and falling asleep," Greta warned with a shake of her finger. "Or yawning, and if you snore, there will be no Sunday dinner."

"Yes, ma'am," Becca and Dalton said in unison.

The congregation sang two songs, and since there was only one hymn book available, Becca had to share with Dalton. Their fingertips touched and the contact sent unholy pictures flashing through her mind of him in tangled sheets. She checked out the window on the south side to be sure there were no black clouds shooting lightning streaks toward the church.

The preacher took his place, adjusted the microphone, and said, "It's been laid upon my heart to preach from Corinthians about love."

Sweet Jesus! Becca rolled her eyes toward the ceiling.

Greta elbowed her in the ribs and whispered, "Pay attention and stop checkin' to see if there's cobwebs on the ceiling fan."

Somewhere between the part about love being kind and not seeking its own way, Becca's eyes got heavy. She leaned on what she thought was the arm of the pew and planned to rest her eyes for a minute, but a movement startled her. Several folks around her chuckled, and for a split second she wondered if she had, indeed, snored. She jerked her arm away to find that she had really propped it on Dalton's shoulder. Then she felt a weight in her lap and looked down to find Tuff had stretched his wiry body out across both Dalton's and her laps. The dog had slipped into the church through the open doors and made himself comfortable.

"I guess we have a four-legged visitor." The preacher laughed with the rest of the congregation. "I suppose if God knows the very hairs on our head and when every sparrow drops, then He surely won't mind if Dalton's dog attends the rest of the service—as long as he doesn't snore."

A few more chuckles echoed through the building. Becca was wide awake by then with a dog's head planted in her lap. Tuff's big, brown eyes were looking right at her face, and damned if it didn't look like he was smiling.

Dalton was always welcome to Sunday dinner at his grandpa's place in Fruitland. Nana Wilson usually fried up a mean batch of chicken after church, and her biscuits were the best in the whole world. He had a standing invitation, and if he wasn't there by noon, Nana put a plate back for him. Very seldom did he miss at least running by to say hello to them on Sunday. He figured they would understand his absence if it had to do with him going to church and dinner with a woman, but he still planned to give them a quick call on his way to Greta's place. They'd be elated since they had gone past throwing out hints and were making serious comments about how it was time for him to hang up his wild ways and settle down. They wanted to see a few great-grandchildren before the end of their time, and since Dalton was their only grandchild, that responsibility fell on him.

The preacher finally asked Eli White to deliver the benediction. Mr. Eli stood to his feet, bowed his head, and began to thank God for everything from the good watermelon crop that was coming in to the ladies who cleaned the church. He spoke slowly in a monotone, and if it hadn't been for Dalton's growling stomach, he might have really snored by the time Eli finally said, "Amen."

"Thank God that's over," Greta muttered as she stood to her feet. "Another minute on this hard pew and my hips and knees would have rebelled."

"I'd carry you out to the car if that happened." Dalton grinned.

Tuff must have realized the service was over because he jumped down and meandered down the center aisle toward the door.

"Poor thing must've been worn out," Greta said. "It's four miles out to the ranch, and that's a long way for him to walk just to get to church. He's a good dog to feel his need to be here."

Dalton didn't tell them that Tuff had hitched a ride in the back of his truck like he did every Sunday morning. Lots of times, he just curled up and took an hour-long nap, or else ran around the town, checking out the female mutts and hiking his leg on every bush he could find.

"His fur is kind of soft. I figured it would feel like steel wool," Becca admitted as she got to her feet. "You're not going to make him walk all the way back to the ranch, are you?"

"Naw," Dalton drawled. "I'll park under that big old pecan tree in Miss Greta's yard, and he can sleep in the truck bed. I thought you hated him."

"I don't hate Tuff," Becca protested. "I just don't want any of his hair to get loose and taint my wine."

Greta hung back and talked to her friends. Dalton ushered Becca outside with a hand on the small of her back. She could feel the burn all the way through her body, and her palms were sweaty when it was her turn to shake with the preacher.

"I'm glad to see y'all sitting together this mornin'," the preacher said and then dropped her hand. "And Tuff was such a good boy. You can tell him he's welcome at services anytime. I shook hands with him a few minutes ago, and I believe he's headed out to your truck."

"I'll tell him." Dalton stuck out his hand next. "Good sermon this morning."

"It's that time of year when young folks are planning summer weddings, so they need to think about what it truly means to be in love." The preacher winked.

"Yes, sir," Dalton nodded. "See you next week."

"Did you really listen to the sermon?" Becca asked. "Or were you just saying something nice."

"It was all about what it's like to fall in love, right?" Dalton stopped beside her car and opened the door for her.

"So, Dalton Wilson, how many times have you been in love?" She slid behind the wheel.

"I might have to take my boots off to count that far," he answered.

"I mean in real love, not lust," she said.

"Well, in that case…" He closed his eyes as if trying to count. "That would be one time." No way was he admitting that the time was right now. The woman was Becca, and it had been love at first sight. "How about you? Give me a number."

"Lust a few times. Love, never. I was too busy concentrating on getting a music contract to let a man into my heart and life," she said.

"You going back to that anytime soon?" he asked.

"No." She shook her head. "I gave it my best for ten years, and it didn't work. It's time to leave that dream behind and move on."

"To what?" he asked.

"Right now, making wine. I'm enjoying the work, and I've even entertained notions of putting in a vineyard of my own," she answered.

"There's lots of good sandy land to do that around here," he suggested.

"Hey, are you two about starved?" Greta yelled as she started down the stairs.

In a few long strides, Dalton was beside her and had looped her arm in his. "Here, Miz Greta, let me help you, and yes, I'm starving. I didn't have time to eat breakfast, so I might be just about to embarrass Becca."

"I love a man with a good appetite." Greta smiled up at him.

"That's great, because I *love* good home cookin'," he told her.

When Greta was settled and her seat belt fastened, Dalton went to his truck and followed them to the house. After he'd first met her at the watermelon farm, he'd driven around town until he spotted Becca's little dark-blue car with its Tennessee license plate. That was another thing he'd never admit because it made him sound like a stalker.

Greta was out of the car and headed toward the porch by the time he got parked. He saw her lips moving, but he couldn't tell what she was saying. From Becca's expression and the way she rolled those big, beautiful green eyes, it was something that she didn't really agree with.

"Hey," Becca waved. "I'm supposed to tell you that it's too hot for Tuff to spend the afternoon in the back of the truck, and you're supposed to bring him inside. I hope he's housebroken."

"Of course he is, and he appreciates the offer." Dalton gave a shrill whistle and Tuff bounded out of the back of the truck. Tail wagging and head held up, he marched right up on the porch and lay down in the shade. "He says that if he could have a bowl of water, he'd be right comfortable out here."

"I believe we can manage that," Becca said. "Come on in."

The redbrick house had a wide-enough front porch to support a swing at one end. A white chaise lounge with bright-green pillows sat on the other end. A gentle summer breeze spread the scent of the red roses that grew across the front of the place.

Dalton followed Becca inside, removed his hat, and hung it on a hall tree right inside the door. "Nice place," he said.

"We like it just fine. Daddy wanted Grammie to buy property down in Ringgold, but she checked the property taxes, and they were cheaper in Oklahoma." Becca kicked her high heels off and slid them up under a ladder-back chair. "It's only a five-minute drive down to Daddy's ranch, so it's not that big a deal unless it floods and they close the river bridge."

"Becca, darlin' girl, you can come on in here and make the salad," Greta called out.

"I'm glad to help out." Dalton followed her into the kitchen.

"Where's Tuff?" Greta asked.

"He opted to protect the house from the front porch," Dalton answered as he rolled up his sleeves.

"Good dog, that one," Greta said. "Never know when we might get one of them salesmen or Bible-thumpin' folks knockin' on the door. Tuff has my permission to bite either of them on the arse."

"If you will point me in the right direction, I'll set the table." Dalton rolled up his sleeves. "Been pettin' Tuff, so I'll need to wash up. All right if I do that in the sink?"

"Sure thing," Greta said. "My Seamus always got cleaned up in the kitchen sink. Brings back good memories."

Dalton washed his hands all the way to the elbows and then turned to look for a towel. Becca was standing right behind him, towel in hand. He took it from her and started drying the water from his arms.

"My turn." She hip butted him to one side. "Can't be tearin' up the lettuce with the smell of dog on me either. Plates are right there. We'll need salad bowls, too, and you might as well get dessert dishes down. Grammie made a pecan pie for dessert."

"I've died and gone to heaven," Dalton groaned. "Pecan pie is my favorite, right next to apple, cherry, and peach cobbler, and banana cream."

"In other words, you like pie?" Becca finished washing her hands. Dalton gave her the towel and took down the plates. Thank

God, Nana had raised him by the goose and gander law. She always said what was good for the goose was good for the gander and insisted he learn a little about cooking and keeping house as well as how to work cattle and build a barn. "I love pie of any kind, cake of any kind, and ice cream and homemade fudge, and I could go on and on. I have a sweet tooth that is never satisfied."

Becca giggled. "That sounds like a pickup line."

Greta laughed with her. "And the next thing you should say is 'And you're the sweetest thing I've ever seen,' right?"

"I'll have to remember that." Dalton grinned as he set plates and cutlery in the proper places.

When everything was ready, Greta told Dalton to sit at the head of the table and she sat to his left, leaving the place to his right for Becca. "I'll say grace," she said, and gave a twenty-second grace for the food. "Eli already blessed everything in the whole bloody county, so that's enough even if it is Sunday." She passed the platter with the pot roast, potatoes, and carrots over to Dalton.

"This is one fine meal," he said as he heaped his plate and handed the platter to Becca. "Thank you so much for inviting me."

"You're very welcome. It's nice to have a man at the table." Greta took out a good portion of meat and vegetables when Becca was finished. "Us McKays are not a bit bashful when it comes to eating. We like our food, and we're not ashamed to take seconds, so don't hold back, Dalton, but do remember that we have pecan pie for dessert."

"Yes, ma'am." He tried to eat slowly so he could spend more time with Becca, but he was so danged hungry that he'd finished off his plate in record time.

"After dinner, me and my friends are going down to the casino to see if we can turn twenty dollars into a hundred," Greta said as she reached for a second helping. "There's movies in the entertainment center. You kids can pick out one and watch it while I'm gone, unless you've got somewhere you need to be, Dalton."

"No, ma'am." He grinned and picked up a second hot roll. "I'd love to settle in and watch a movie with Becca."

"Just don't fall asleep." Greta grinned. "My granddaughter can be a real practical joker."

"Oh, really?" He arched an eyebrow toward Becca.

She shrugged. "Fall asleep and find out."

CHAPTER 3

GRAMMIE WAS A SNEAKY ONE.

Becca was *not* going to watch a movie with Dalton that afternoon. She intended to curl up on the porch swing and read one of the romance novels her mother had given her last weekend. Or she might go down to Ringgold, saddle up her horse, and go for a ride across her folks' ranch. She had fended off all the real cowboys, wannabe cowboys, and cowboy singers in Nashville, but she had to admit she was attracted to Dalton. The chemistry between them was way too strong to spend a whole afternoon alone with him.

Or is it? She pondered.

Dalton Wilson could be like chocolate. If she had too much of it and got downright sick of the taste, she might not want to ever look at it again. If she spent some time with the man, she might possibly find all kinds of things about him that she didn't like.

Grammie was also more than a little controlling.

"I've got the perfect movie for y'all to watch this afternoon," Grammie said as she rifled through the drawers in her entertainment center. "Here it is. It's an old one, probably popular when y'all were just kids."

"What's the title?" Becca set a glass of sweet tea on the end table and then plopped down on the sofa.

"It's got Patrick Dempsey in it, and it's..." She held up the movie to show them that it was *Lucky 7*, "...and Kimberly Williams, and it's all about a girl who thinks..." She stopped and smiled. "Y'all just watch it. I'll be back in a couple of hours. It won't take us long to lose twenty bucks at the casino." She picked up her purse from the coffee table and left the house when the sound of a car horn blasted out in the front yard.

"You ever watched this?" Dalton sat down on the other end of the sofa.

"Nope." Becca said. "Grammie loves chick-flick movies, so you can bet your bottom dollar this is not an action film. You can sneak away if you want to."

"Naw," Dalton grinned and put the disk she handed him into the player. "I don't reckon one love movie will hurt me."

Becca picked up the remote, hit the play button, and then read the back of the container that held the movie. Oh, yes, sir, Grammie was playing matchmaker for sure.

"Mind if I take off my boots?" Dalton asked.

"Not one bit." Becca propped her bare feet up on the coffee table. "Grammie says this is what a coffee table should be for, not for doilies and fancy flower arrangements."

"Smart woman." Dalton removed his boots, set them to the side, and stretched his long legs out. "What do you like, Becca? Do you prefer fancy fixin's or do you follow after Greta?"

"A little of both," she answered and focused on the movie that showed a bagel shop right close to the beginning. She missed grabbing a bagel on the way to work each morning the way she had done in Nashville. She hadn't even minded driving a little bit out of the way over to Abbot Martin Road to get a fresh one.

"So, this girl is going to be waiting for her seventh boyfriend to really fall in love, right?" Dalton asked after the very first flashback scene to where a young girl was visiting with her dying mother. "Tell me that your mother is alive and well, and that you aren't waiting for number seven."

"My mama is Trudy McKay, and she is very much alive," Becca answered. "I'm not waiting for any particular number."

Dalton wiped his forehead in a fake dramatic gesture. "Whew! I was afraid I'd have a long wait if I had to go on home and wait until you went through six boyfriends."

She started to smart off with a quick comeback, but a scratching noise distracted her. She stood up, crossed the room, and found Tuff with what looked like a big gray rat in his mouth. The ugly critter was wagging his tail like he expected praise for bringing the dead varmint to her. She quickly closed her eyes so she wouldn't have to look at it anymore, slammed the door, and yelled, "Dalton!"

In what seemed like the blink of an eye, he was right beside her. "Are you all right? What happened? You're as pale as a ghost."

"I hate rats," she said.

"Where is it?" Dalton looked around the foyer. "Which way did it run? I'll catch it and get rid of it for you."

She pointed. "Tuff has it on the porch."

Dalton opened the door just enough to peek outside. "Tuff has brought you a present, but it's not a rat. Come on over here and take a look. He was raised with cats, and he loves kittens."

Becca eased across the room, and sure enough, there was a little gray kitten fighting with Tuff's tail as it swished back and forth on the porch. "Ohhh, isn't it the cutest thing. Where do you think he stole it from?"

"I'm sure he filled out all the adoption papers and everything is legal." Dalton slung open the door and picked the gray ball of fur up by the scruff of the neck. Tuff ran into the house, stopped, and looked back over his shoulder. He whined and the kitten let out a pitiful meow.

"Is it going to try to scratch my eyes out?" Becca reached her hands out.

"Don't know, but evidently, he didn't want this one to be raised as an only child." Dalton pointed to a yellow-colored kitten just about the same size as the gray one sitting on the porch. "Or else he thought you and Greta each needed your own pet." He opened the door again.

Becca picked the kitten up as it entered the house like it owned the place. It flopped over in her arms like a baby and started purring. "These have to belong to someone. We can't keep them. We'll get attached and then have to give them back."

"Tell you what." Dalton put the gray kitten in her arms with the yellow one. "Tuff and I are going to take a little walk around the block. I bet we find the owner, and I'll ask if they want them back. How's that?"

"Thank you," Becca answered, but it was too late. She'd already lost her heart to the two little critters.

———————————

Dalton whistled and Tuff came out of the living room with his head hanging and tail wagging. "You did good, ole boy, but we've got to be sure that the owners of those two babies don't want them back. We need to go for a little walk and find out where they came from."

Tuff barked once and followed Dalton back to the sofa. Dalton jerked his boots on and nodded toward Becca. "Don't name 'em until I get back."

Tuff ran on ahead of Dalton when they stepped off the porch. Two houses down the street, he stopped, sniffed the air, hiked his leg on a bush, and then sat down.

"This isn't going to work," Dalton told him. "You know very well where you stole those kittens. What if there's a third one, and we want to take it home with us?"

The dog stood up and slowly made his way to the end of the block. He sat down at the end of the porch steps of the last house on the block and yipped twice.

"Is this the place?" Dalton walked up to the door and knocked.

"Hey, Dalton, what's up?" Frankie, one of his hired hands, asked as he rounded the side of the house.

"You got some kittens around this place?" Dalton asked. "Tuff has dragged a couple down to Greta McKay's house."

"Had five out in the storage shed. Gave three away last week and been tryin' to get rid of the other two ever since. Their mama got killed on the road. If Miz Greta don't want them, I was goin' to ask you if you'd like to have them for barn cats. Their mama was a real good mouser," Frankie said. "Come on inside. Want a beer?"

"Thanks. A cold one sounds good, but I'd better get on back to Miz Greta's. Becca and I've got a movie on pause. I just didn't want her to get attached to a couple of kittens if you weren't giving them away," Dalton said. "See you at the ranch in the morning."

"I'll be there bright and early," Frankie said. "Hey, have you heard from Austin and Rye? Are they havin' a good time?"

"Haven't talked to them, but Rye said he'd call in this evening to check on things," Dalton said.

Frankie waved and went on inside. Dalton turned around and headed back down the block with Tuff right at his heels. "You done good, boy, but next time scratch on the door and ask if you can take another man's property."

Tuff barked a couple of times and tore off down the road like the devil was chasing him. When Dalton reached the house, the dog was sleeping under the porch swing. "I guess you figure you've done your good deed for the week, right?"

The dog didn't open his eyes, but his tail thumped a few times. Dalton raised his hand to knock, but Becca threw the door open with the kittens still in her arms.

"What did you find out?"

"Frankie says he's glad to get rid of them," Dalton answered. "Do you think you should ask Miz Greta about them before…"

Becca butted in before he could finish his sentence. "I already did. She said she and her friends were going down to Bowie for ice cream. She's going to pick up kitten food and litter while she's there."

"If you love cats so much, why haven't you had one before now?" He followed her into the living room, kicked off his boots for the second time, and sat down on the end of the sofa.

"I lived in an apartment in Nashville that didn't allow any pets, not even a goldfish. With four of us in a small apartment and all of us scrambling for jobs and hoping for a contract, we didn't have time for pets anyway, and then my last roommate was allergic to everything that had fur." She handed the gray kitten to him. "Meet George and this right here is Dolly. Grammie and I already named them."

He took the kitten from her. "Hello, George. I betcha you got your name from those two singing 'The Blues Man.'"

"How'd you know about that song?" Becca asked.

"My grandpa loves anything by George, and Nana is real partial to Dolly Parton." He laid the cat up on his shoulder.

———————

A big, old sexy cowboy holding a kitten that wasn't as big as one of his rough hands melted Becca's heart. She kept stealing glances over at him. Could it be that beneath bad boy exterior there was a man who wanted to settle down someday? Grammy had said that when she met *her Seamus*, as she always referred to him, he'd been a player too. The only time Becca had gotten to spend a month with them in Ireland, he'd been such a loving husband to her grammie that Becca couldn't imagine him ever even looking sideways at another woman.

"I wonder how they got so tame." Becca was talking about the cats, but her mind was still on her grandfather and Dalton and the business of taming them.

"Frankie and his wife have a bunch of grandkids that are always popping in and out of their house. I imagine they played with them and got them ready to give away to good homes." Dalton leaned his head back on the sofa and closed his eyes.

He and the kitten both were sleeping soundly within a few seconds. Dolly curled up in Becca's lap and put a paw over her little nose. For several minutes Becca looked her fill of Dalton. Women were already falling at his feet so rapidly that it was a wonder he didn't have one of those take-a-number-and-wait machines attached to his porch post. If those ladies could see him now with a kitten on his shoulder, the poor old Terral police would be having to break up catfights.

She only meant to rest her eyes for a second, but in minutes she was sound asleep. She didn't even hear the front door open or Greta fussing about having to haul in supplies. She did wake up when Tuff licked her, starting at her chin, going up across her cheek, and not stopping until he reached her hairline. Becca came up off the sofa wiping at her mouth, then stopped dead in her tracks and looked around to see if she'd thrown the new baby kitten off on the floor.

Tuff made a hasty retreat to hide behind Grammie's recliner when he got a taste of hair spray. Dalton opened his eyes slowly to find that both cats were now on his shoulder and tangled up together.

"Awww, look at the wee babies asleep with Dalton. It's a good man, yes, it is, that animals love," Greta said in a high baby-talking voice. "I've been thinkin' about gettin' us some kittens for a while now." She reached out and picked up the gray one. "Come with Grammie, darlin' kit-tee, and I'll show you the new litter box and fix you a bowl of kit-tee food." Her accent got thicker with every word. "It's been a while since I've had babies in the house. We're all going to have a good time, aren't we?" She kissed the little gray kitten right on the nose. "Not to worry, Dolly, I'll be right back to get you, darlin' baby."

"Well, that worked out well. Do I dare put my boots on, or have you played some kind of practical joke on me?" Dalton asked.

"I slept as long as you did, and we never did get back to the movie," she said. "We could finish it now since Grammie is taking care of the babies."

"Yes, I am, and what's this about not watching the movie?" Greta plucked the yellow kitten from Dalton's shoulder.

"We got so involved with the kittens that we forgot to watch the rest of it," Becca admitted.

"Well, that's for another day," Greta told her. "The girls are coming over to play cards this evening, so you can't watch it now. We set up our table in here."

"I should be getting home." Dalton pulled on his boots again. "Rye and I just keep a skeleton crew on weekends, so I should help with the evening chores. If you're not playing cards, you could come drive the truck for me."

Listening to four old women drink wine and argue over gin rummy or go with Dalton? She chose the lesser of the two evils and smiled at him. "If you'll give me five minutes to change into jeans, I'll go drive for you."

He nodded. "Take ten, and after we get the chores done, we'll drive down to Bowie for some ice cream."

Was ice cream a date? Becca wondered as she hurried to her bedroom and changed into jeans and a T-shirt. Would he expect more than a friendly handshake or a kiss on the cheek when he brought her home? Or worse yet, would she be disappointed if he didn't kiss her good night? She ran a brush through her long hair and reapplied a little lipstick.

"It's not a date," she muttered as she headed down the hall.

Grammie was sitting in her recliner when she reached the living room. Both kittens were in her lap, and she was singing to them. She stopped when Becca entered the room and winked. "They're good kit-tees. They both used the litter box and ate some of their special food, and now they're sleeping. The girls are going to love them, but Dolly and George are going to love me more than anyone."

"Why haven't you gotten a pet before?" Dalton stood up and rolled the kinks out of his neck.

"I don't know," Greta answered. "I guess it's because I had to leave my old mama cat behind with my best friend in Ireland when I moved to the States. I missed her real bad, but I felt like I would be dishonoring all the years she caught mice for me if I brought in another cat. But Tuff brought these to me, so in a way, it makes it all right."

"I'm glad," Dalton said. "I'll tell him you said thank you."

"And the next time I make a ham, I'll save him the bone," Greta said. "Now, you kids get on out of here. You've got chores to do and ice cream to buy. I won't wait up for you, Becca." She threw a sly wink her way.

"We won't be that late," Becca said. "I've got to be up early in the morning to get some more watermelons squeezed and ready to start into wine."

"You could bring home a bottle of that so we can celebrate our new babies," Greta suggested with a raised eyebrow.

"I'll see what I can do." Becca smiled.

"We could bring a bottle by on our way to Bowie for the ladies who are playing cards with you," Dalton offered.

"You are such a sweetheart." Greta flashed her brightest smile at him.

"You are spoiling her," Becca whispered as they left the house.

"She spoiled me with a good dinner and a great nap. Do you realize that I haven't even kissed you, and we already slept together?" he teased.

"We slept, as in close our eyes and snore. We did not have sex," she told him.

"Don't know about you, but we did in my dreams." He chuckled as she opened the truck door for her.

She'd heard of hot flashes in older women, but Jesus, Mary, and Joseph, they couldn't be as hot as the heat filling her body as she watched him strut around the front end of the truck. She might need enough ice cream to fill a bathtub just to cool down after the pictures his comment painted in her mind.

CHAPTER 4

To get to know someone really well, spend some time working beside them.

That's what Grammie had told Becca more times than she could remember. Seeing Dalton's gentle nature with the cattle as he fed them that evening just added to the feeling that she'd had when she watched him sleep with a kitten on his shoulder. He had a soft heart, and for crying out loud, he'd even named some of the bulls.

"Hey, that does it for this job." He crawled into the passenger seat of the ranch work truck. "You about ready for ice cream?"

"What I'd rather have is a big, juicy bacon cheeseburger," she answered.

"A woman after my own heart," he grinned. "Got a particular place in mind?"

"Dairy Queen in Nocona," she answered.

"Then drive us back to my truck, and we can be there in twenty minutes," he told her.

"Fifteen if I drive." She smiled.

"A cowboy always drives his lady wherever she wants to go," he said.

"Oh, so I'm your lady?" She shifted the truck into reverse and turned it around in the pasture.

"You could be," he answered.

"Why not your woman? Or your one-night stand? Or the red-head that you got lucky with?" she asked.

"A cowboy's lady is so much more than any of those things you just said," he answered.

"How so?" she asked.

"I respect all women. That's the way I was raised, and it's the cowboy code. But a cowboy's lady goes way beyond plain old respect. She's put on a pedestal," he answered.

Put that in your corncob pipe and smoke it, Grammie's voice popped into her head.

Becca ignored the comment and asked, "And how does a lady feel about her cowboy."

"One hundred percent the same as he feels about her," Dalton answered. "Just park right beside my truck, and we'll make the switch and go to Nocona."

Becca didn't have a corncob pipe and she didn't smoke, but she sure thought a lot about what he'd said. That was exactly the example she had seen in her grandparents, both maternal and paternal, and in her own parents.

She put the truck in park, turned off the engine, and was about to open the door when it swung open. Dalton held out his hand to help her out of the truck, and she slipped her hand into his outstretched one. Men had opened vehicle doors for her since her first date when she was sixteen, but in that moment, even though she was wearing jeans, she felt as if she had a crown on her head and was truly royalty. Not a single man she'd ever known had made her feel so special.

"Aren't you the perfect gentleman?" she said.

"Honey, I'm thirty years old, but my mama and my grandmother both would take a switch to me if I didn't treat a woman right." He kept her hand in his all the way to his truck where he helped get her settled into the passenger seat.

Her phone rang as she was buckling her seat belt and trying to watch him walk around the front of the truck to get behind the wheel. "Hello, Grammie," she answered.

"Are y'all done with chores?" she asked.

"Yes, ma'am. Do you need me to come on home?" Becca crossed her fingers like a little child, hoping that the answer would be no. She really was looking forward to that cheeseburger.

"Lands, no, child," Greta said. "If y'all are still going to Bowie for ice cream, I want you to go to Walmart and get me a couple of baby blankets and some cat toys."

"We're going to Nocona for cheeseburgers," Becca said.

"Then go to the Dollar General there. I'm sure they'll have what I want. Go on and get half a dozen blankets so we can keep the babies with a fresh one every day. One more thing, I checked these babies. George is a girl so her new name is Loretta, so buy pink blankets," Greta said. "Is this a date?"

"I have no idea, but probably not." Becca smiled at Dalton as he started the engine.

"If he kisses you good night, it's a date. See you later, and I *will* wait up for you," Greta said.

"Greta need something?" he asked.

"George is a girl and has been renamed Loretta. She wants us to bring pink baby blankets and some cat toys," Becca answered.

"Didn't even think to see if we had boys or girls." He chuckled. "If we can't find what she wants in Nocona, we'll drive down to Walmart in Bowie. Who would have thought she'd fall in love with those kittens? Tuff did a good thing when he pilfered them from Frankie."

"Looks like he did," Becca agreed. "I thought one of them might belong to me, but I'm beginning to doubt it."

"When and if you ever get a place of your own, I'll have a visit with Tuff and tell him to bring you a kitten of your very own," Dalton said as he backed the truck out of the drive and headed west toward town. "Got a particular color in mind?"

"I don't think Tuff is that good." Becca laughed.

"Never underestimate the powers of a dog trying to please a lady."

There was that word again—lady. For some crazy reason, the old animated movie *Lady and the Tramp* came to Becca's mind. She stole a glance over at Dalton and decided in a split second that he definitely didn't look like the dog in the movie, but Tuff dang sure did. A picture of her and Dalton sharing a plate of spaghetti like on the movie poster flashed in her head. Thank goodness they were having cheeseburgers, or she'd never get the blush off her cheeks. No amount of blinking seemed to make it disappear.

"I'm not sure I want a kitten when I get my own place. I might want a puppy," she said.

"What kind? A Pomeranian that you can carry in your purse?" he teased.

"Nope, I was thinking about a cocker spaniel," she said.

"Good dogs." He nodded. "They make excellent pets and they're easy to train."

Maybe Tuff will fall in love with Lady, which is what I'll name my dog, and then we'll have our own real-life movie right here in Terral, Becca thought with a big smile.

Don't you ever accuse me of matchmaking when you're thinking like that, Grammie's voice was back in her head.

"You were smiling one minute and then frowning the next," Dalton said. "Who are you fighting with?"

"Grammie," she answered honestly.

"About what?"

"My dog that I haven't even gotten," she said. "When I get one, I want a female."

———————————

Dalton was already trying to figure out where he might buy her a cocker spaniel for Christmas if things worked out between them. Suddenly, that old movie he had seen as a kid popped into his mind. "*Lady and the Tramp.*" He said aloud and snapped his fingers.

"What?" she asked.

"I was thinking about the old movie *Lady and the Tramp.* Did you see it when you were a kid?" he asked.

"Of course," she smiled. "Mama has every Disney movie ever made. She bought them when I was a little girl and says she's saving them for her grandkids."

"Did you know they made a new one of those a couple of years ago? We should rent it or buy it and watch it some evening."

"I didn't know, but I'd love to see the new one. Do you realize how much that Tuff looks like the Tramp?" she asked.

"Not until you mentioned a cocker spaniel, and that movie popped into my mind because that's what breed Lady was. Don't go tellin' Tuff that he looks like a movie star or he'll want to go to Hollywood, and he's a damn good cow dog," Dalton told her.

"You should never stand in the way of his dream," Becca scolded, but couldn't keep the grin off her face.

"He told me he knew he wanted to work on a ranch when he was just a puppy," Dalton protested.

She shook her finger at him. "I'm living proof that a person, or a dog in this case, can change their dreams."

Dalton loved bantering with Becca. Women who he picked up at the Broken Bit on the nights he was lucky didn't want to do much talking. They were more interested in shedding clothing, starting at the front door and leaving a trail all the way to the bedroom or the living room sofa, or once even on the credenza right there in the foyer. Not that he didn't have a good time with each of them... Hell, it was more than just good; it was almost always a great night.

This thing with Becca went way beyond that, though. Who would ever have thought that Dalton Wilson would be having a wonderful time flirting with no thought of getting lucky that night? Maybe his nana was right about him settling down. He glanced over at Becca, and yep, whether he believed it or not, he'd fallen in love with her at first sight. With his past and with her dream of a recording career just shattered, though, he would have to take things slow. Dalton was a patient man. He could take his time and follow the rainbow to its end when he knew there was a pot of gold waiting on him.

Only a few vehicles were parked in the Dairy Queen lot when they arrived, so he snagged a spot close to the front door. The stars had begun to pop out in the sky by the time they were inside and had ordered. Since there were few other customers, the waitress brought their order pretty quickly, and Becca dived right into the double-meat-and-cheese bacon burger.

"This is one thing I missed in Nashville," she said between bites.

"They don't have Dairy Queen in Tennessee?" Dalton asked.

"Yes, they do, and their burgers are good, but not as good as these. Maybe it's because I'm home when I have one here," she answered.

"You weren't home out there?"

"Home isn't a place. It's a feeling," she told him. "I was always scrambling out there. Here I'm just Becca McKay, someone who sings sometimes at church and entertains sometimes at a Watermelon Festival, but I'm not doing it to follow a dream of being a famous singer. I'm singing for fun."

"Well, I for one am glad that you feel at home in this part of the world. Austin says that you're the best help she's ever had in the wine shed, and she hopes you don't get the itch to go back to Nashville." Dalton ate slowly so that they could spend more time together.

"I love working there. One of my part-time jobs in Nashville was working in a winery," she told him. "Like I told you before, I wouldn't mind having a vineyard of my own and trying my hand at creating my own label someday."

"What would it be named?" he asked.

"I haven't gotten that far," she answered.

"I've got a name for you." He grinned.

"Spit it out," she told him.

"Southern Lady. That sounds classy like you." His grin got bigger.

"Thank you, and I do like that for a label," she said and then pointed at the huge Coca-Cola clock hanging on the wall of the burger joint. "The Dollar General closes at eight. That means we've only got thirty minutes to round up the stuff for the kittens."

"Then we'd better get going." He slid out of the booth and waited for her, then ushered her to the door with his hand on her back. Walking beside a woman like that wasn't anything new to him, but the heat radiating through his hand damn sure was. This must be an extension of that love-at-first-sight thing Rye kept telling him about.

The Dollar General was right next door to the Dairy Queen, so it only took a couple of minutes to walk over to it. When they were inside, Becca latched onto a cart and pushed it right back to the baby section. Dalton followed behind her and located a rack with packages of three baby blankets in each.

"Pink," she reminded him when he picked up the first one and it had a blue striped one in it.

He hung it back and riffled through the rest of the packages until he found two that had all pink ones. "Will this do? Some are striped and some are plaid."

"If it's got pink on it, Grammie will be fine with them," she answered.

"Well, well, well!" Lacy Ruiz came around the end of the aisle with a cartload of merchandise. "So, this is why you…"

"We're buying these for…" Dalton started to try to explain, but then he figured that telling his old standby with the credenza in her living room that they were buying blankets for cats would sound totally crazy. "A gift for a couple of new babies."

"Yeah, right." Lacy started at Becca's toes and slowly let her eyes travel up to the top of her red hair. "I guess I'll lose my five dollars."

"I'm Becca McKay," she introduced herself. "How are you going to lose five dollars because we're buying blankets for new babies?"

"Lacy Ruiz," she nodded. "We've got a pot goin' at the Broken Bit about what kind of woman will finally rope Dalton, and I sure didn't bet on it being a tall redhead. I guess there's more than one way to get a cowboy to the altar." Her eyes shifted from Becca's stomach to the blankets in the cart. "I've got several things to get before the store closes." She paused and patted Dalton on the cheek. "I just can't see you as a daddy. I guess this will keep you away from the Broken Bit, but if it goes south, darlin', you know where I live."

"Sweet Lord!" Becca gasped when the woman had gone.

"I expect they'll all be disappointed in nine months." Dalton shrugged. "Let's go find the cat toys now."

"Why didn't you tell her we were buying these for kittens?" Becca asked.

"You think she would have believed me? That sounds like a lame excuse," Dalton said.

Becca giggled. "It does, doesn't it? I guess I'd better tell Grammie about this as soon as I get home. I bet that hussy is calling everyone she knows on her cell phone right now, and I sure don't want to have Grammie yelling at me because she heard it first from one of her friends."

"So…" Dalton dragged out the word. "Are you going to marry me and make a decent man of me?"

"Nope." She shook her head slowly as she tossed half a dozen cat toys into the cart. "I'd never rope a guy in by getting pregnant. Marriage should be for love, not necessity, and there should never be regrets."

"How did you get so smart?" he asked.

"It's the Irish in me." She started toward the checkout counter. "Grammie says we're born smart."

"I believe it." Dalton's eyes glanced at Becca's flat stomach behind the waistband of her jeans, and he wondered what she'd look like pregnant. If they ever did establish a permanent relationship, their children would be tall for sure. With him standing at six foot two inches and Becca almost kissing six feet, there was no way they'd be short. Would they have dark hair like his or red like hers? Would their eyes be blue or green, or maybe even brown like his maternal grandfather's?

"Earth to Dalton." She poked him on the arm.

"Sorry, I was off in another world," he said.

"What world would that be?" she asked.

"I've got to deliver some rodeo bulls down to a ranch rodeo in Haskell, Texas, on Friday." He said the first thing that came to his mind. "Want to ride along with me? We'll be back by suppertime."

"Depends on what's going on in the wine shed," she answered.

At least she didn't say no, he thought as he pushed the empty cart away from the counter for her.

The trip back to Terral seemed to go by in a flash, and suddenly, they were parked outside Greta's house. There wasn't a full lover's moon hanging in the sky, but it was a three-quarter one with stars dancing around it. He could think of all kinds of come-on lines, but not a single one of them seemed appropriate for a woman like his Becca.

My Becca, he thought. *Someday, maybe—if I'm as lucky as Rye was when he fell for Austin at first sight.*

He got out of the truck, helped her out, and carried the bag of their purchases to the door for her. "I had a great time today, and thanks for helping me with chores."

"Thanks for supper." She locked eyes with him.

He dropped the bag on the porch and tipped up her chin with his fist. Her eyes fluttered shut, and her thick lashes fanned out on her cheek. He wanted to kiss her eyes, but that could come later. Right then, he craved the taste of her full lips.

When the kiss ended, he politely picked up the bag and put it in her hands. "Good night, Becca." His voice sounded strange in his own ears.

"Good night, Dalton," she whispered.

"I'll call you tomorrow," he said.

"Okay," she said.

———

"I guess it was a date," she muttered as she took the blankets and toys into the house.

"So?" Greta raised an eyebrow.

Becca held up the bag. "Six pink blankets and toys. Where's Loretta and Dolly?"

"I made them a special bed out of a laundry basket, and they're sleeping soundly in my room," she answered. "I'm not talking about the baby stuff. I got a phone call from Mavis a while ago. She says that you're pregnant. Am I going to be a great-grandmother, and is Dalton the daddy?"

"Gossip travels faster than the speed of sound." Becca plopped down on the sofa, removed her boots, and propped her feet on the coffee table. "We were buying baby blankets when Lacy Ruiz came into the store... No, that's not right." She drew her brows down and then snapped her fingers. "Lacy Ruiz...that's her name. Do you know her?"

"Oh, yes," Greta nodded.

"She got the wrong impression, and did you know there's a bet about what kind of woman Dalton will finally wind up with?" Becca asked.

"I'm not surprised. That boy has a reputation like my Seamus had before he fell in love with me," Greta said. "So, you were buying baby blankets and Lacy got the wrong idea. Did you tell her it was for our new kittens?"

"Think about it, Grammie," Becca said. "Would you have believed a story like that?"

Greta's giggle even had an Irish accent. "I don't guess I would. It does sound a bit like bull coodle. I guess when you don't swell up like you've swallowed watermelon seeds, they'll realize that Lacy's full of…"

"You're in America, Grammie," Becca told her. "You can say bullshit."

That made Greta laugh even harder. "The one way you could get around this mess is to marry the boy, you know, and let him make an honest woman of you."

"We've only been out on one date, and it could hardly be considered a date," Becca gasped.

"Then he did kiss you good night," Greta raised an eyebrow. "Did it send a shot of heat all the way to your toenails?"

"I don't kiss and tell," Becca answered.

CHAPTER 5

MONDAY WAS A LONG DAY FOR BECCA. THE HARVESTERS brought a pickup load of melons to the shed, and she spent the whole day squeezing the juice from them. She wanted to get all of them ready for the next step, so she didn't go home until after eight that evening. Dalton called and said that he and the hired hands had been hauling hay all day, and since it was supposed to rain the next day, they'd be working by the headlights of the trucks until the job was done.

"Watermelons and hay," she said.

"We must love it, or we wouldn't stay with it, right?" he asked.

"Ain't it the truth," she sighed.

"I'm at the barn with this load, so good night. Maybe I'll have time to come by the wine shed tomorrow," he said.

"Good night." She looked forward to seeing him. Lord only knew how often she'd thought of him that day, but maybe it was better if they both had a little space after that steaming-hot kiss they had shared the night before.

His voice sounded almost as tired as she felt that evening. She was glad to see a note from Greta saying that she'd gone to the movies with her friends and wouldn't be home until late. The kittens came tumbling out of the living room, purring and rubbing around Becca's ankles as she made her way to the bathroom and ran water in the old claw-footed tub.

"Sorry, Loretta and Dolly," she said as she slipped out of her clothing and sank down into the warm water. "Cats don't like baths, so you have to just sit there and talk to me. So, how was your day?"

Loretta meowed pitifully.

Dolly gave Becca a dirty look, picked up a pair of socks in her mouth, and carried them out into the hallway.

"Well, my day was crazy. I juiced a whole truckload of melons, checked the progress of all the wine in the place, and loaded the rinds in the back of the work truck to take to the chickens over on the ranch. I saw Dalton from a distance once and got a hot flash just looking at him with no shirt on out there in the hayfield. I'm glad you can't talk, because I have no doubt you'd go tell Grammie what I just said," she told the kittens.

Tuesday morning went just fine except that it poured down rain most of the time. Becca stopped working long enough at noon to prop her feet up and eat a sandwich she'd brought from home. She had tossed the plastic baggie and the napkin in the trash and was headed back across the room to begin scooping out more melons to juice when she heard the first bump against the wooden door.

Her heart skipped a beat and then raced ahead with a full head of steam. Dalton had arrived, and she hadn't seen him up close since he had kissed her good night on Sunday. Would things be awkward between them?

The second bump was followed by a bellow, and the walls of the metal shed rattled. That wasn't a cowboy—it was a bull! If he knocked the door down, the old saying about a bull in a china shop wouldn't begin to describe the damage he could do. Becca grabbed her cell phone and called Dalton.

"Do you have a bull out of the pasture? I've got one trying to get into the wine shed," she said.

The noise of another loud bellow echoed through the roar of the rain beating down on the metal roof, and then a big horn poked right through the wooden door.

"That sounds like Big John," Dalton said.

"Well, you'd best come get him or he's going to be Dead John," Becca said. "I keep a five-shot thirty-eight in my purse, and if another horn comes through the door, I'm going to start shooting until it's empty. Then I'll reload and keep it up until he's ready to go to the dog-meat factory."

"Don't shoot," Dalton said. "I'm on my way. The crazy bull loves watermelon. He was probably headed to the field and caught a whiff of what's in the shed."

The call ended and the horn disappeared from the door. Becca picked up a butcher knife and deftly halved a melon, scooped out a little of the middle, and then stuck it up to the hole in the door. "I'm willing to share if you'll back away from the door and let me open it."

Her original plan was to toss the melon out into the yard and then slam the door, but when she peeked out, the bull took a step forward. "Oh, no! You will not come inside, and you aren't eating this on this side of the road."

The animal lowered his head and rolled his eyes. She stomped her foot, glared at him, and took the first step out of the shed. She held the melon out so he could smell it, and then jerked it back. "You can follow me to your pasture, or I'll take it back inside and you can do without."

She had dealt with cattle all her life, and Big John didn't scare her one bit. If he turned malicious and came at her, she could always throw the melon down and run like hell. Rain soaked her to the skin, and her long, red hair was hanging limp before she had taken half a dozen steps, but the bull followed behind her like a lost puppy.

Dalton drove up in the ranch work truck about the time she made it to the middle of the dirt road. He rolled down the window a few inches and yelled, "Are you crazy? Big John is the meanest bull at the rodeos. He could kill you in a split second."

"Not as long as I've got a watermelon in my hands. Turn the

truck around and show me which pasture to put him in." She took another step, and her foot sank down in mud that came up over the top of her shoes. Not even the rain could mask the sucking noise when she pulled the shoe out and kept walking. There was no way she could go across the cattle guard with the bull, but she saw where he had broken down the fence on his way to the watermelon field.

"Okay, Big John," she told him. "We're going in the same way you came out. If you rip up a leg on the barbed wire, I'm not going to feel a bit sorry for you."

The bull threw back his head and bellowed louder than ever before.

"If you want this watermelon, then you can quit your belly-achin' and get over one little strand of barbed wire," she told him.

Dalton drove across the cattle guard and headed toward the gate into the pasture nearest the gap in the fence. He stopped the truck and Becca saw a flash of yellow. She cradled the chunk of melon like a baby and wiped the rain from her eyes. "You've got a rain slicker and I'm wet to the hide," she grumbled. "Thank God, you don't have a camera."

Dalton opened a gate and she carried the watermelon through it with Big John right behind her. When she was twenty feet into the pasture, she set the watermelon down on the ground and slowly backed out through the gate. Big John lowered his head, and Becca could have sworn the bull sighed.

Dalton slammed the gate shut and started to take off his slicker. She shook her head. "No sense in both of us being soaked."

"At least, come up to my house with me and let me throw your things in the washer and dryer," he said.

"All right." She wiped water from her eyes and glanced at the house, a good twenty yards away. "But I'm not getting in your truck. It's only a little way, so I'll walk. I'm not ruining the seats."

"They're well-worn leather. I can dry them with a towel with no problem," he argued. "And it's warmer in there. If you get a cold from enticing my prize rodeo bull home, Greta will kill me and never ask me to Sunday dinner again."

Becca walked through mud puddles over to his truck and climbed inside when he swung the door open for her. Water dripped from her hair, her clothing, and her body and saturated the seat while he drove up to his small house. She left a puddle behind when she stepped out into the still pouring rain. A quick glance at the driver's seat told her that it didn't look a bit better than hers.

"You're going to need a lot of towels to clean that up," she said as she headed toward the porch.

Tuff came out from under a lawn chair and shook from head to toe. Any other time she might have fussed about the spray, but what were a few more drops when she was already saturated?

Dalton rushed up the steps, slung open the door for her, and apologized for Tuff. "I would have brought him along to help corral Big John, but the bull hates him. He's the only critter on the ranch that Tuff doesn't have his bluff in on. Let me show you to the bathroom."

Becca dripped water on the hardwood floor all the way from the living room down the short hall. The place was even cleaner than Grammie's house, and that woman had never met a speck of dust that she couldn't conquer. The aroma of his woodsy shaving lotion lingered in the bathroom. She was surprised to see a big, claw-foot tub on one side of the tiny space and a walk-in shower on the other.

He pointed to a hook on the wall. "You can use my robe until we get your clothes washed and dried. Toss them out in the hallway, and I'll put them in the washing machine. In an hour, you'll be all dry and ready to go back to the watermelon shed."

"You don't have to wash my things. I can do that," she said.

"I don't mind. I'll put on a pot of coffee. You could use

something warm to take the chill off that chilly rain. Crazy, isn't it, how that even in the summer, the rain can feel cold?"

"Yep," she agreed.

"Big John doesn't like most people. I'm surprised he didn't just run you down and take that melon away from you," Dalton said.

"Maybe I'm a bull whisperer," Becca suggested.

"I can believe it after what just happened," Dalton nodded. "Just follow your nose to the kitchen when you've taken a shower." He finally closed the door and left her alone.

The air conditioner kicked on, and cold air flowing down from a vent in the ceiling sent shivers up and down Becca's body. She turned on the water in the shower and quickly slipped out of her clothing.

"Of all the days for me to wear faded blue cotton underpants," she groaned as she peeled them down from her hips. When she was completely naked, she threw her jeans, socks, shirt, and underwear out into the hallway and fought the urge to cuss when the panties landed a foot from the rest of her things.

She stepped into the shower and was surprised to find a bottle of lavender-scented shampoo and matching conditioner. "Well, that proves he keeps things ready for the women he brings home with him," she muttered as she worked some of the shampoo into her hair.

When she'd finished, she slid back the glass door, stepped out of the shower, and wrapped a towel around her long hair and used a second one to dry her body. Then she slipped on the white terry robe and wondered how many other women had worn it while they had breakfast with him. Just as he'd suggested, she followed the smell of coffee down the hall and into the kitchen.

"Have a seat." Dalton motioned toward the wooden table with four chairs around it. "Have a cookie while I pour coffee. Cream and sugar?"

"Nope, just black, and thank you." She felt very vulnerable wearing nothing but a robe that could be opened with only a tug on its belt.

"Your stuff is all in the washer. The cycle will be done in a few minutes and we'll throw them into the dryer. I'm not sure what to do about your sneakers. I sprayed them off in the sink, but…"

"I've gone barefoot before." She pulled out a chair and sat down.

He brought two mugs of coffee to the table and sat down across from her. "Me too, but that was when I was a kid. If your feet weren't so small, you could wear my rubber boots."

"Only little part of my whole body. I've been told lots of times that someone who's six feet tall shouldn't wear a size six shoe." She picked up a cookie and bit into it. "Are these homemade?"

"My nana believed that a boy should be just as at home in the kitchen as the barn. If I'd had a sister, she would have made her haul hay and work cattle, but I'm an only child," he answered. "When I can't sleep, I bake."

"So do I." She took a sip of her coffee and then set the mug back on the table. "I like to cook, but I really love baking."

"We should have a cookie evening," he suggested. "How about tonight?"

"I've got plans for the next couple of nights," she answered, "but Thursday is free. My place or yours?"

"Mine," he replied. "I'll have everything ready. You bring a bottle of wine, and we'll make sugar cookies. According to Austin and Rye, they go really good with watermelon wine."

"Grammie has an amazing recipe for sugar cookies. I'll bring a copy with me," she said.

What am I doing? she scolded herself. A week ago, she wouldn't have given Dalton the time of day, and she really didn't like Tuff. How could things have changed so fast?

"I've got one question before we do this," she said.

"Shoot." He grinned. "But I assure you, I keep a full pantry, so when I'm in the mood to cook, I've got what I need."

"How many women have worn this robe?"

"One, and that's you. I don't share my toys with others very well," he answered.

"Then why is there lavender-scented shampoo in your shower?" she asked.

"My mama likes it, and last week she was down here helping me get my spring cleaning done," he answered. "I don't bring women to the ranch, Becca. I'm not a saint, and probably seventy percent of what you've heard about me is pure truth, but when I spend the night with a woman, it's not at my place."

"Why?" she asked.

"Because someday I will settle down, and this will be my home until I can have enough saved for my own ranch. I wouldn't want my wife to feel the ghosts of girlfriends past every time she turned a corner," he answered.

"That's pretty nice of you," she said and picked up a second cookie.

———————

Dalton grinned as he pushed back his chair and stood up. "I'm just a nice cowboy. The washer just quit. I'll throw your things over into the dryer."

He had just gotten her stuff into the dryer when his phone rang. He slipped it out of the hip pocket of his jeans, saw that it was Rye, and answered on the second ring.

"Hey, how's things in Florida?"

"Hot and humid and the kids are loving every minute," Rye answered.

Dalton leaned his back against the washer. "How about you?"

"I'd rather be ranching"—Rye chuckled—"but it's not too bad. I love seeing the expressions on Austin and the kids' faces, and the food is really good. Everything under control there?"

"Yep, and you'll never guess what happened today. Big John broke through the fence…" He went on to tell Rye the whole story, ending with "and I couldn't believe that Becca did that. She's sitting in my kitchen now while her clothes are drying."

"You've got a woman in your house?" Rye asked.

"I told you before you left that it was love at first sight," Dalton said.

"I didn't believe you," Rye said. "I remember that feeling. I'll just hope that you can convince her you're ready to settle down. I can't wait to tell Austin. Believe me, she'll do all she can do to help you out. She and Becca have become good friends these past months."

"Thanks," Dalton told him. "Anything you want me to do more than what we're doing?"

"Just be sure the rodeo stock gets down to Haskell on Friday. I'll be home Sunday evening, so I'll go pick them up on Monday," Rye said.

"I might take Becca with me to control Big John," Dalton said, chuckling.

"Tell her to take a couple of watermelons along." Rye laughed. "It's our turn to line up for a ride. Talk to you later. Austin says to tell Becca hello."

The call ended, and Dalton headed back to the kitchen. "Austin says to tell you hello."

"Are they having a good time?" Becca smiled up at him.

He refilled their coffee mugs and sat down. "Yep, but Rye says he'd rather be ranchin'."

"I can understand that for sure," Becca said. "Amusement parks are not my idea of a fun week. I'd rather stay home and make wine, or maybe go to a nice quiet beach and listen to the ocean waves coming in and going out."

Damn! This girl was really after his heart in every way. "Me too, or maybe take a trip up into the mountains when there's snow on the ground, build a roaring blaze in a fireplace, and just sit in front of it with a good cold beer."

"That sounds pretty amazing too," she agreed. "Put on some good slow country music in either one of those places, and I'd love it."

He made a mental note to have music playing while they made cookies on Thursday evening. "Was it a cultural shock to come home after spending ten years in Nashville?"

"Not as much as it was going to Nashville after being raised in Ringgold," she answered. "I got used to it after a while, and coming home, well...it's home." She raised a shoulder in half a shrug.

"Reckon you'll sing at local events?" he asked.

"Maybe," she answered. "Making the decision to give up on my dream wasn't easy, but as time goes by, it's becoming something of the past. Does that make sense?"

"More than you'll ever know." He nodded in agreement.

"What makes you say that?" she asked.

"I wanted to be a champion bull rider as well as a rancher. It took about eight years and a few broken bones for me to realize that I'm just not that good," he said. "Not that I'm sayin' you're not good enough to make it in country music, but when I finally figured out that I wasn't cut out to ride bulls, I put that dream behind me and put my all into ranchin'."

"And chasin' women?" She raised an eyebrow.

"Bull ridin' gets more ladies than plain old ranchin'," he replied. "I've sown my wild oats in both arenas—ranchin' and rodeoin'. I'm lucky that I didn't have to reap a harvest from that, but I'm thirty years old now, and I'm finding that all that glitters is not gold."

"Seems like there was an old song that said that same thing," she said.

Dalton nodded again. "Yep, and every word of it is true. The dryer just dinged."

"I'll get my things and get dressed." She pushed back her chair and headed out of the kitchen.

His robe only came to her knees, and her hips curved out from her small waist where she'd roped the belt tightly. She whipped the towel from her hair, and just looking at her long legs, her bare feet, and all that tangled, damp hair made his heart throw in an extra beat. He'd love to untie that robe, watch it fall into a puddle at her feet, and then scoop her up in his arms and carry her to his bed.

If he was lucky, maybe that would happen someday.

She carried her clothes straight to the bathroom and emerged five minutes later, fully dressed except for shoes. Her long hair had been brushed and drawn up into a still damp ponytail. She reminded him of one of those Greek goddesses that had stepped forward in time to the twenty-first century. He might not be able to untie the belt or slip the robe off her shoulders at the moment, but the muddy yard gave him every excuse to carry her to the truck.

The rain had finally stopped. They stepped out onto the porch, and without asking permission, he took a step forward, picked her up like a new bride, and said, "No need for you to get your feet muddy."

"I don't think I've ever been..." She gasped.

"Then, darlin', you've must have been dating the wrong guys."

CHAPTER 6

On Tuesday Becca hit the ground running and didn't stop until it was almost dark. She was dragging by the time she made it back home. She plopped down on the sofa the minute she got into the living room. Both kittens climbed the arm of the sofa like it was a tree and walked across the back until they reached her. Then they used her ponytail for a batting toy.

"Did you see Dalton today?" Greta asked.

"Nope," she answered. "He's been in the hayfield all day. They got a second cutting on one of the big pastures. He texted me a few times. Grammie, I like him a lot, but..."

"Honey, you listen to your heart. If it tells you to walk away, then do it. If your heart tells you to stick with it, then do that. Ain't a one of us old ladies or any of your young friends can give you solid advice on love. I like the cowboy. He's got a helluva bad reputation when it comes to lovin' and leavin', but..." Greta shrugged.

"But what?" Becca pushed for more.

"But he looks at you like my Seamus looked at me. It might sound crazy to you, but it means something to me. Now, get on in there and dip you up a plate full of corned beef and cabbage. You look like you're on your last leg. A little nourishment will be good for you." Greta pointed toward the kitchen.

"Yes, ma'am." Both kittens had already climbed to Becca's shoulder and were curling up to take a nap. She set them on the floor and headed toward the kitchen. "Hey, did I tell you that Dalton can cook, and that he makes great cookies?"

"My Seamus liked to help me in the kitchen. His meat pies were the best in the world. I never have been able to make pie crust as good as his." Greta raised her voice.

Becca dipped up a bowl full of food and carried it to the living room. "We're making cookies on Thursday night."

"That's a good thing," Greta said. "You need to spend time with him, so your old heart knows what to tell you to do. How would it know whether this is a real thing or just a passin' fancy if you avoid him like you've done since you got here?"

"I needed time to figure out whether I was going to go back to Nashville to give it one more year," she answered. "Besides, I'd heard that all he was interested in was a good time."

"You still yearnin' after that dream of singin'?" Greta asked.

"No, I'm pretty content now where I am," Becca said. "Why? Are you wantin' me to get out of your house so you can flirt with some old guy?"

"Bloody hell, no!" Greta gasped. "I love havin' you here, and I gave my Seamus my whole heart. Ain't nothin' left to give another man."

Becca wanted that kind of thing for her own—someday. She wasn't in a hurry to find it by any means, but she didn't intend to settle down to a permanent relationship with anything less than what Grammie had had with *her Seamus*.

―――――――――

Wednesday crawled by like a snail in a foot of snow on the way to a funeral. Every time Dalton looked at the clock, only thirty seconds had passed. Thursday was even worse. He helped the hired hands repair fence all day, and yet time seemed to stand still.

Finally, the day ground to an end. He rushed home, took a quick shower, shaved, and then got into his truck and drove into town to pick up Becca. Without a doubt, he'd just spent the longest three days of his life, and if he could avoid it, he'd never go that long without seeing Becca again. He'd proven that *out of sight, out of mind* was a crock of bullshit.

She was sitting on the porch when he arrived. She was wearing a cute little dress with strings for straps, and a pair of sandals. Strands of her hair had escaped the messy knot on top of her head. Just looking at her made his mouth go as dry as if he'd just bitten down on a green persimmon. She picked up her purse and a paper bag and started toward the truck. He jumped out of the truck and rushed around to open the door for her. A whiff of her perfume—something with a hint of vanilla—sent his senses reeling.

"You sure are gorgeous tonight. Maybe we should forget all about cooking and go out to dinner at a fancy restaurant," he suggested.

She handed the paper bag to him. "I'm cooking tonight, and then we're making cookies. My mouth has been watering for sugar cookies all day."

"What are you cooking?" He set the bag in the back seat.

"Chicken Alfredo. And I'm making a salad and I've got a loaf of Grammie's homemade bread to go with it," she said.

"And the wine?" he asked.

"It's in my purse. Two bottles. One for supper. One for dessert." She smiled.

"I always wondered why women liked big purses." He shut her door and rounded the front of the truck. When he was behind the wheel, he adjusted the AC and shifted the gear into reverse.

"The bigger the purse, the more wine we can bring home," she teased.

"You think two bottles is enough?" he asked.

"Depends on how much you drink. I'm Irish. I can hold my liquor, wine or even good beer. How about you?" she threw back at him.

"Is that a challenge?" he asked. "Because if it is, honey, I've got about five kinds of whiskey, a bottle of coconut rum, one of tequila, and two of vodka, and a six-pack of cold beer in the refrigerator. We can do shots, or even make a vodka watermelon if we run out of wine."

"Oh, I do love a booze melon," she said. "It's crazy that I was raised right here in watermelon country and never had a vodka melon until I went to Nashville. Let's stop by the watermelon field where the sugar baby melons are grown. They're the best ones for wine and for vodka melons."

"What's the prize for the one who's still sober enough to drive you home at the end of the evening?" he asked.

"A kiss good night." She was definitely flirting.

"I don't shave for a second time in a day for less than at least a thirty-minute make-out session if I'm the winner," he shot back at her.

She stuck her hand across the console. "If I'm the winner, I get to name the time and place for that make-out session."

———

Becca knew she was playing with fire, but Grammie had advised her to get to know him. What could be better than making out for thirty minutes? Besides, she'd missed him the past three days, and she'd never felt like that about any man in her past. With her work, time for dates was scarce, and there had only been one relationship—if six dates, one weekend in bed, and a couple of quick lunches could qualify as such.

They stopped by the watermelon field closest to the wine shed on the way back to the ranch, and Dalton insisted that he knew the difference between a sugar baby and the other types of melons. "You sit right there, and I'll put a couple in the back of the truck. You can decide which one you want to juice up with vodka."

"Thank you," she said.

He thumped around on a few melons. Each time he cocked his ear to listen for a hollow sound. When he was satisfied that a couple of smaller ones would be perfect, he cut the vine with his pocketknife, tucked each one under an arm, and carried them out of the field. He gently laid them in the back of the truck and then crawled in behind the wheel. "Those should do the trick. After a bottle of wine, I bet we'll be loosened up enough to dance."

"We're not going to the Broken Bit, are we?" she asked.

"No, darlin'." He reached across the console and laid a hand on her shoulder. "We can dance in the living room and not have to bump into anyone else."

That fire she'd thought about earlier seemed to be getting hotter and hotter. He drove across the road, parked the truck, and helped her out of the passenger seat. Then he picked up the bag of groceries in one hand and one of the melons in the other. "I guess you'll have to open the door for me this time, but you've got to promise not to tell my mama or my nana. They'd tack my hide to the smokehouse door if they found out I wasn't a gentleman."

"My lips are sealed," she said as she threw the door open and then followed him inside. She set her purse on the kitchen table and unloaded the things she needed to make supper from the bag. "I should have asked you whether you even like Alfredo."

"Love it." He uncapped a bottle of vodka, set the lid on the side of the watermelon, and used it as a pattern to draw a circle. Then he carefully cut a plug from the melon and inverted the bottle into the hole without spilling a single drop. A few air bubbles floated up to the top of the bottle and the vodka began to slowly seep into the meat of the melon.

"This is not your first rodeo, is it?" she asked.

"Nope, and I really like for the vodka to infuse into the melon for twelve to twenty-four hours. If we decide the wine is enough for our bet, then we can have this tomorrow night." He raised an eyebrow and grinned, "Or maybe for breakfast in the morning?"

"I don't think I'll be around at breakfast, but you think there's going to be a tomorrow night?" she asked.

"I can always hope," he answered. "Now, what can I do to help with supper? I'm starving."

"You can make a salad and slice the bread while I put the Alfredo together. The wine is chilled, and I see you've already set the table," she replied.

"Did that when I came in for a lunch break," he admitted. "Today was the slowest day in history. I began to think it was like the preacher said about a thousand years being as one day."

She found a large cast-iron skillet under the cabinet and dumped the chicken she'd cooked the night before into it. "I agree. Do you know what *wait* is?"

"It's misery," he said.

"No, it's a four-letter word." She giggled.

"Amen to that, and Nana would wash my mouth out with soap for saying those kinds of words." He finished making salads in two small bowls and put them on the table. Then he got out a sharp knife and sliced half the loaf of bread.

When he reached for two wineglasses, his hip bumped against hers. "Sorry about that."

"I'm not," she muttered as she whipped around and laced her arms around his neck. "Did you feel some electricity between us?"

"Honey, I feel the chemistry between us every time we're in the same room," he admitted as his lips found hers in a long, steamy kiss. "I've dreamed about kissing you all day," he whispered when the kiss ended.

"Did it live up to your expectations?" she asked.

"One hundred and fifty percent." He gave her a quick peck on the forehead, picked up the glasses, and took them to the table.

Every nerve ending in her whole body hummed with desire. Good old common sense told her that more than sharing a few kisses was out of the question. That didn't mean she didn't want to forget about wine, vodka-infused watermelon, and even supper and slowly undress him on the way to the bedroom.

The noodles took longer to cook than the sauce, but the Alfredo was ready in fifteen minutes. She carried the skillet to the table and set it on a hot pad. A fancy bowl would have gone better with the pretty table Dalton had set, but the cast iron would keep the food hot longer.

He pulled out a chair for her and then poured the wine. "Are you going to say grace, or am I?"

"It's your house, so it's your call," she told him. "Do you always pray?"

"Yep," he answered as he took her hand in his. "I grew up in a household that said grace before every meal, and it just don't seem right not to give thanks."

"Me too." She bowed her head.

He said a simple prayer and then held up his wineglass. "To us."

She picked up her glass and touched his. "To us."

By the time supper was over, they'd finished the first bottle of wine. As Becca had bragged earlier, she could hold her liquor as well as any good Irishwoman, but she'd never had good, aged watermelon wine. When she got up to help clear the table, the room did a couple of spins. She finally got it under control by holding on to the counter for just a minute.

"All right," Dalton said when he put the last plate in the dishwasher. "Great supper. Good wine. Amazing company. Now let's make cookies and pop open that second bottle of wine. I've got a confession. I thought wine was for sissies until Rye introduced me to watermelon wine. I liked it from the beginning, but I like this stuff even better." He thumped the watermelon on the counter, removed the empty vodka bottle, and put the plug he had cut out of the melon back in place. "And one more confession... I talk a lot when I get a good buzz going."

The door is open. Don't lose the opportunity. Grammie's voice was loud and clear in Becca's mind even if she did have a little buzz going on in her own head. *If he's got a mind to talk, then ask questions.*

"So, you are a happy drunk, not a mean one?" she asked.

He chuckled as he got out the ingredients to make sugar cookies. "I usually stop drinking after a little buzz. I don't like to be drunk, and I hate hangovers." He laid his phone on the counter and touched the screen. "A little music," he said as Garth Brooks sang "The River."

The lyrics said something about standing on the shoreline and letting the waters run by. Becca nodded in agreement when Garth sang about rough waters. "What made you choose this song?"

"I like that line that says I'll never reach my destination if I don't try," he said. "I like you, Becca McKay." He leaned over the container of flour and kissed her on the tip of the nose. "I have to try to make you like me back, even if I have to do what the song says and sail my vessel until the river runs dry."

"I don't think you'll have to try until the *Red River* is completely dry," she whispered.

"Good." He grinned. "I was worried about that."

"You are a charmer," she said.

"Nana told me when I was just a little boy that good looks would take me far in life, but charm would get me whatever I wanted," he told her.

"And has it?" She measured out the flour and then cut a stick of butter into it.

"Until you came into my life," he said. "I thought you were immune to my sweet-talkin.'"

"I had to get the past out of my system before I could..." She paused and locked eyes with him. "Are you just tryin' to get me into bed, or are you serious about a long-term relationship?"

"Darlin', I'm as serious as a cowboy tryin' to hang onto a buckin' bull for eight seconds," he said.

That might not sound like a declaration to some women, but Becca sure understood what he was saying.

"Okay, then," she said. "I believe you."

"Thank you for that. I don't lie, Becca. I will tell you the truth, even if it hurts me to do it," he said as he put the first pan of cookies into the oven.

She refilled their wineglasses and took a sip. "I'm pretty much the same. That might have been part of my problem in Nashville. I wasn't willing to do anything for a contract. If I couldn't get one with my singing, I damn sure didn't want one if it meant I had to fall on my back or drop down on my knees."

Dalton chuckled. "You are pretty straightforward, aren't you?"

"Yep, it's the only way to be," she said. "And speaking of that, I'm tellin' you right now, this is some damn fine wine, and it's hittin' me harder than whiskey usually does."

"This must be Austin's good stuff. Did you get it from the top shelf?" he asked.

"Yes, I did. I wanted to bring the best," she answered.

He removed the pan of cookies and slid the second batch into the oven. "Like 'em warm?"

"Honey, I like 'em hot," she said, giggling.

"Let's take them to the living room." He lifted twenty cookies off the pan with a spatula and put them onto a plate. "You carry the wine, and I'll bring this."

"Don't you dare drop them on the floor," Becca cautioned. "I've looked forward to warm cookies and cold wine all day."

"If I do, we'll just sit down on the floor and eat them. You don't have to worry. My floors are just that clean," he told her.

"Did you see that episode of *Friends* when Joey and Rachel and Chandler eat cheesecake off the floor? This reminds me of that night, only they were stone-cold sober." She picked up the wine and took short steps all the way to the living room where she set the glasses on the coffee table and then sank down into the sofa.

"And we are not." Dalton sat down beside her and draped an arm around her shoulders. "I'm not sure if it's the wine or if I'm slap happy because you're here. After almost six months of wanting this to happen, now it is, and I could be drunk on that and not the wine."

"You are a charmer for sure." Becca reached for a cookie, took a bite, and then sipped the wine. "Very good together. Do we really have to wait until tomorrow night to get into our vodka melon?"

"It takes at least twelve hours for it to infuse, but if you want to have it earlier, you are welcome to spend the night," he told her.

Before she could answer, someone knocked on the door and then came right in without being invited. Becca hoped like hell it wasn't his mother or his grandmother. Either of them seeing her half-lit would not bode well.

"Well, well, well? So, it's true. You're not pregnant. If you were, you wouldn't be drinking wine." Lacy stopped inside the door and popped her hands on her hips.

"What the hell are you doing here?" Dalton asked.

"I came to tell you that you were having twins, only not by the same mama, but I guess you'll only be getting one little dark-haired baby in about seven months." She pointed down at her flat belly.

"Oh, no!" he said loudly. "If you're pregnant, it's not mine. I haven't been with you since before Christmas."

"Are you sure?" She raised both eyebrows. "Run along home, Becca McKay. He lives by the cowboy code, and he'll marry me because it's the right thing to do."

"She's lying," Dalton whispered. "She's trying to cause trouble. I swear to God, I haven't been with her since right after Thanksgiving."

Becca shook off his arm and stood up. "You clean up this mess before you text or call me again."

"You're too drunk to drive," he said.

"I don't plan on getting behind the wheel. I'll sleep it off in the watermelon shed," she told him as she went to the kitchen, picked up her purse, and headed toward the door. "Forget about me going with you to deliver the rodeo animals tomorrow."

"I'll swear on a Bible, take a DNA test, whatever it takes, Becca. Trust me," he said.

With tears running down her cheeks, she staggered down the lane and across the dirt road. She was almost to the watermelon shed when she heard a vehicle. Her hands knotted into fists. If it was Lacy, she might drown the bitch in a five-gallon bucket of watermelon juice and swear to God that she had nothing to do with it. The truck came to a stop and Dalton got out and tried to take her hands in his, but she wasn't having any of it. She might be able to forget the past and her dreams, but evidently his wild oats were going to follow him around forever.

"I'm so sorry, but I mean it. If she is pregnant, it's not my baby," he said.

"We both need to sober up before we talk," she said. "Go home, Dalton. You shouldn't even be behind the wheel."

"Can I call you tomorrow?" he asked.

"I suppose," she nodded, "but not until you get back from Texas."

CHAPTER 7

GRETA CAME THROUGH THE DOOR LIKE A CATEGORY 5 tornado. "Get your drunk arse up and go get in the car. You're comin' home with me right now, girl. There ain't no way you are sleeping in a lawn chair all night."

"I'm not drunk. I'm barely buzzed, and I'm perfectly fine sleeping right here," Becca argued.

Greta pointed toward the door. The expression on her face said that she wasn't about to repeat herself and she wasn't taking no for an answer. Becca slowly got to her feet and stumbled that way. She didn't have the energy to fight with her grandmother, especially when the odds were against her. Not once in all of her twenty-eight years had she won an argument with her grandmother.

When they were in the car and on the way home, Greta glanced over at her and said, "What in the hell happened?"

"Nothing," Becca growled. "And I'm going home with you, so you win."

"Don't you sass me, Rebecca McKay," Greta told her. "I told you that spending time with that cowboy would prove if you should be with him or not, one way or the other. Evidently, it's not."

"Yep," Becca agreed.

"If he can't trust you, then you don't have a foundation to build on anyway, so it's best to end it before it even gets started," Greta said as she parked in front of her house.

"Yep," Becca said a second time. "Whoa! Wait a minute. Him trust *me*? Evidently, he called you because you came to get me, but it wasn't *me* who's..." She paused and glared at her grandmother.

"I know what I said, and it's exactly what I meant. You should have stood up for him when Lacy came bursting in accusing him of something that he says couldn't be true. Bloody hell, Becca. That woman's like a doorknob on a public loo. Everyone has given it a turn with her, and if he said he hasn't been with her in more than six months, then why didn't you believe him?"

Greta parked in the drive, got out of the car and marched up to the porch. She didn't even turn around to see if Becca was all right. Becca sat there a couple of minutes, then she slung the door open, got out, slammed it shut, and stomped to the porch, carrying guilt on her shoulders like a heavy blanket in the middle of a July heat wave. She went straight to the bathroom, brushed her teeth, and met Greta in the hallway when she came out.

"You can be mad at me, but that don't make me wrong." Greta picked up the kittens and carried them to her bedroom.

"No, but I don't have to like it." Becca muttered as she closed her bedroom door. She dropped her dress and underwear on the floor, kicked off her sandals, realized that her feet were dirty and padded back to the bathroom.

She stood under the warm shower for several minutes, letting the spray beat down on her back. Her grandmother was right. Becca should have popped up on her feet, glared down at Lacy, and then showed her to the door. "Hindsight, and all that shit," she said as she stepped out and picked up a towel.

When she got back to her bedroom, she pulled on a pair of underpants and her lucky sleep shirt, fell into bed, and practically passed out. When she opened her eyes, the sun coming through her window was attempting to burn holes in them. With a moan, she buried her face in the pillow. Her head felt like rock music was blasting away with the bass turned all the way up. She couldn't remember the last time she'd had a hangover and vowed never to touch watermelon wine again if this was the price she had to pay for it.

She crawled out of bed, dressed in jeans and a T-shirt, and stumbled into the kitchen with her hand over her forehead.

Greta poured her a cup of hot tea and set it before her. "Drink this while I make you a good Irish breakfast to cure that wine hangover."

"I couldn't eat a bite of food," Becca groaned. "I don't get drunk. I don't have hangovers. And on wine, Grammie? Have I lost my Irish wings?"

"No, darlin', not until you have a morning like this after good Irish whiskey. Austin has figured out a few secrets, like how to make her top-shelf wine more potent. Did y'all drink a whole bottle?" Greta asked.

Becca held up two fingers.

"Bloody hell, Becca. No wonder you were *fluthered*! Me and the girls share a bottle and all four of us get downright giggly." Greta set about making breakfast for two. "'Tis a good Irish breakfast you need, and another cup of tea, and then you'll be ready to go to work."

"Grammie!" Becca groaned. "Not a full Irish breakfast. I'm just two steps away from heading for the bathroom right now."

"When you eat every bite of what I'm making, you will be cured. The black pudding, beans, and fried tomatoes are already done. Do you know how much trouble it is to get good black pudding in this part of the world? I have to go all the way to Saint Jo to get it, so you won't be wastin' a bite of it. Do you hear me?" Greta shook an egg turner at Becca.

"Yes, ma'am," Becca groaned.

"I just need to finish up the bacon, sausage, and eggs. Then I'll pop the toast in the machine, and you can begin to eat," Greta said. "Besides, I've been starving for a breakfast like this. I love it even when I don't have a watermelon wine hangover."

Becca sipped her tea and hoped that she would be able to get a few bites down. Black pudding wasn't something she enjoyed even when she was sober, but if Grammie said it would cure her aching head, she would force it down.

"Have you thought about what an opportunity you missed last night?" Greta asked as she put half a dozen pieces of bacon into the skillet.

"I can't think at all," Becca answered. "My head hurts too bad."

"Then drink some more tea," Greta told her.

"Why would Lacy do that?" Becca whispered.

"Because Dalton is showing signs of being ready to settle down, and she wants him." Greta turned the bacon and cracked two eggs into another skillet. "He'd be a good catch, and besides all that, she's probably got a bet going about how long it will take her to get him in front of the preacher. She'll make some money and have a good husband too."

"That's just wrong!" Becca narrowed her eyes and set her jaw.

"Sin is sin. One ain't no more wrong than the other. You not letting him explain or believe him was just as wrong as what she is doing." Greta finished making two plates and carried them to the table. "Eat and then you'll feel all better."

"Do you think she's really pregnant?" Becca cut up her eggs, dipped a corner of a piece of toast in the yellow, and put it in her mouth.

"Maybe she is, but if she is, then it's not Dalton's. Think about it: why would he get careless after all these years. He said he hasn't been with her in six months, and I believe him," Greta cut off a piece of the black pudding. "Cowboys have a code. If she is pregnant and the baby is his, he will marry her, but if it's not, then…" Greta shrugged. "Y'all need to talk."

―――――――――――

Those last four words were still rattling around in Becca's mind when she reached the wine shed that morning. Just like Greta had promised, the tea and all that breakfast did make her feel much better. Her head still felt slightly like one of the round watermelons she sliced open to juice, but that was minor compared to the way she had felt when she first woke up.

She gave the bottles of wine on the top shelf of the winery a dirty look as she flipped the strap of a bibbed apron over her head. The hired hands had already unloaded a pickup load of melons into the shed, and there would be at least that many more arriving after lunch. If she'd gone with Dalton on his stock delivery, she would have been working long hours over the weekend to catch up.

She figured more watermelons were coming in when she heard the hinges on the door squeak. "Just stack them over against the wall."

"Hey," Dalton said.

His deep Texas drawl made her drop the butcher knife on the floor.

"Hey." Her eyes locked with his across the room.

"You ready to talk?" he asked, but he didn't take a step forward.

"How did you get back from Haskell so quick?" she asked.

"I didn't go," he answered. "Didn't plan to take the bulls myself from the beginning. I just thought it would be a good little trip for the two of us, but…" He blinked and took a deep breath. "Need some help?"

"Doin' what? Apologizing for not trusting you, or juicing melons?" she asked.

"I was thinkin' of melons," he said. "Are we going to talk about last night or pretend it didn't happen?"

"I think we'd better talk about it." She picked up the knife and carried it over to the sink. "I'm not a big believer in sweeping things under the rug." She motioned to a couple of green lawn chairs over in the corner.

He waited for her to sit down, and then he eased down in the chair beside her. "I visited with Lacy this morning on the phone. I didn't go to her place or invite her to come to mine. Everyone in town knows that I live out here on the ranch in the original old house, but until last night she'd never been in my place."

"I believe you," Becca said. "I shouldn't have reacted the way I did."

"Actually, you had every right to react that way. I also talked to my grandpa and my dad this morning. They both reminded me that I was just reaping what I'd sown. I've chased women since I was a teenager, and they told me time after time that the day would come when I would have regrets about being so wild," he confessed.

"Grammie read me the riot act, too, only she said that we shouldn't even consider having a few dates because I didn't trust you," Becca told him. "In her opinion I should have kicked Lacy's arse out of the house when you told her that the baby couldn't be yours."

"She's not pregnant," Dalton said. "She got angry when she saw us buying baby blankets, and she wanted to break us up."

"What a bitch!" Becca said.

"She might be, but it worked for her last night anyway," Dalton said. "Now what do we do?"

"I'm sorry for the way I acted," Becca said. "Everyone has a past, no matter how good or bad it is. The important thing is to leave all that where it belongs and go forward."

"Is there a forward for us?" he asked.

She had loved being with him on Sunday and then again last night. She had swallowed her pride and apologized.

"I sense by your hesitation that you don't know," he said. "Anything I can do to change your mind?"

"You could ask me out on a date that doesn't involve wine, and we could take it one step at a time, if you're willing for that," she said.

"Becca, will you go out with me tonight? There will be no wine and no drinking, but I can promise you supper and a nice quiet evening where no one will barge in on us." He smiled for the first time.

"I'd love to go with you. What can I bring to help with supper?" She returned his smile.

"Not one thing. I make a real mean ham-and-cheese sandwich, and I've got just the hideaway spot for us to visit." He stood up. "We could leave from here when you get off work at five."

"I probably should go home and get cleaned up if this is a date," she told him.

"If you want to, you can lose the apron. If not, then you look pretty damn gorgeous in it." He extended a hand to help her up.

Her fingers tingled the moment they touched his. One date, and then she'd make a decision and never look back with regrets whichever way it went. After the way she'd acted the night before, he deserved that much. When she was on her feet, he pulled her to his chest and kissed her—long, hard, and passionately.

Well, maybe two dates just to be sure, she thought when the kiss ended and he walked out of the winery without saying another word.

CHAPTER 8

BECCA WASN'T SURE WHAT TO THINK WHEN DALTON CAME TO get her for their date. He was driving the beat-up old ranch work truck. When he had told her she should just take off her apron, she hadn't expected that they would go to a five-star restaurant or a dinner theater, but she did think maybe he would spring for his fancy club-cab vehicle.

"Where are we going?" she asked as she fastened her seat belt.

"Somewhere secluded and so quiet you can hear the tree frogs singing," he answered. "Do you trust me?"

"Yes," she answered.

"I promise you're going to love it, and before you ask, I've never taken anyone, male or female, there before. It's my hidden place where I go to think," he told her.

"I feel special," she said.

"Darlin', you are far more than just special," he whispered softly before he closed the door.

This wasn't her first rodeo when it came to pickup lines. She had worked in bars all over Nashville and fended off lots of guys when they brought what they thought was a game good enough to sweet-talk her into bed. What Dalton said didn't affect her as much as his tone, and the way his warm breath caressed her neck when he spoke.

He drove through Terral, passing the elementary school on the right, Mama Josie's café on the left, and then he crossed Highway 81, and drove through a cattle guard with HT welded onto the gate.

"What does that stand for?" she asked.

"Hard Time Ranch," he answered. "The owner is a friend of

mine, and he doesn't mind if I cross his property to get to my hidey hole down by the river."

She envisioned a place where they'd have to crawl back into a cave of some kind and hoped to hell there were no spiders or field rats in it. "The river, huh?" She pulled her phone from her purse, found the song they'd listened to the night before, and played it.

"Yep, and I do love that song," he answered. "We're going to the river to sail our vessels. I've got them ready in the back of the truck, along with our supper in a basket."

She turned around and looked out the back window, but all she could see was a big basket and some chunks of wood. Maybe he was speaking symbolically instead of having a real vessel to sail.

The truck rattled and groaned when he drove down a rutted path toward the river. She was amazed when they passed a herd of white-tailed deer and a wild hog with a dozen little piglets following behind her. They flushed a covey of quail out of the path, and she watched them fly away, and then a bobcat with a couple of kittens watched them go by.

"Aren't they the cutest things ever? I wonder what Grammie's new babies would think of one of those," Becca said.

"I'm not sure you could tame one of those any better than a cowboy can a wild Irish lass with a temper." Dalton grinned.

"So, you think I'm a wild lass?" she asked.

"I saw a little of that in you last night, and truth is, I kind of liked it," he admitted.

"I'm glad you like me just the way I am," she said, nodding.

He braked and brought the truck to a stop. "Honey, I wouldn't change a single thing about you. We'll walk from here. It's not far. I'm taking my boots off. I like to feel the sand beneath my bare feet like when I was a kid."

She kicked off her shoes and tossed them in the bed of the truck along with his boots. He shoved the wood and some string down into a paper bag and picked up the basket. "See that willow tree over there with the limbs hanging in the water?"

"It's beautiful," she gasped.

"That's where we'll have supper. Would you bring the quilt? I've kind of run out of hands." He pointed toward the cab.

She reached over the side and picked up the patchwork quilt. This just might be the most interesting date she'd ever been on in her entire life. The river was peaceful, flowing along, just like it had been since the beginning of time. A pungent aroma filled the whole area, and the willow branches swayed in the warm evening breeze.

When they reached the huge tree, Dalton set the basket and sack down and parted the thick limbs. "Welcome to my secret place, Becca McKay."

She carried the quilt inside the opening and spread it out on the sand. "It's lovely, Dalton. Thank you for trusting me enough to bring me here."

He picked up her hand and kissed the knuckles. "Thank you for trusting me, period. Have a seat and we'll have our supper, and then we'll go sail our vessels."

"Are you serious?" She eased down on the quilt.

"Yep, I brought homemade sailboats and string so we can guide them down the river. Sometimes I fish right here, but tonight, I want us to float our little boats and think of that song about the river." He sat down and opened the basket. "Another confession. I haven't dated much. Last time I actually asked a woman out was probably for my senior prom in high school."

"Really?" she asked.

"I want us to be open and honest with each other," he told her.

"I've dated a lot, but I've never been picked up in a bar," she told him.

"Then we've had two different lifestyles." He handed her a cold bottle of root beer and then laid the rest of the food out between them on the quilt. "The sugar cookies from last night and the bananas are for dessert."

Supper was a ham-and-cheese sandwich, a small bag of potato chips, and sweet pickles that they ate with their fingers right out of the jar. Every bite tasted better to Becca than if she had been eating filet mignon in a five-star restaurant.

"I can see why this would be your favorite place," she said. "It's so quiet that I really can hear the tree frogs."

"Sometimes they argue with the owls and the other birds roosting in the trees for center spot," he said.

At that moment Becca could feel peace surrounding her heart, much like the drooping branches of the weeping willow tree circled around her and Dalton.

"If this works out between us, we should come here once a week and leave all our troubles, arguments, and disagreements in the river," she said.

Dalton leaned over the food between them, cupped her face in his hands, and brushed a sweet kiss across her lips. "That's what I do when I float my little boat down the river. I put all my worries on it and give them to the current."

"Then why the string to control the boat?" She touched her lips to see if they were as hot as they felt and was surprised to see that they were actually cool.

"Because sometimes I'm not quite ready to let go of my worries, but when I am, I drop the string," he answered.

"What worries are you going to put on your boat today?" she asked.

"I'll tell you mine if you tell me yours," he replied.

"You first." She nodded toward him.

"My first worry is that this will be our one and only real date."

You kissed me on Sunday. According to Grammie, that makes it a real date, she thought.

"My second is that my wild past will always hang around to haunt us both."

Not if we work at squashing it every time it rears its ugly head.

"My third is that I won't have the courage to tell you how I feel about you, and make you believe me."

I think I already know because I'm listening to my heart.

"Now, it's your turn," he said.

"You cited three, and that's a lot to put on one little boat. My worries are number one"—she held up a finger—" that if we did enter into something serious, you'll get tired of me and break my heart." The second finger went up. "That I might regret not giving Nashville one more year." The third finger shot up. "And that you'll never bring me back here again."

"I would never get tired of you, darlin'"—he took her hand in his—"and if we get really serious about each other, I will love you so much that Nashville will never enter your mind again." He brought her hand to his lips and kissed each knuckle. "And Friday or Saturday night can be our official weeping-willow-tree date night. Are you ready to sail our vessels down the Red River?"

"This is crazy to think about this right now, but I just remembered that Austin scattered her grandmother's ashes on this very river. Do you think she'll destroy our worries for us?" Becca put all the trash and leftovers back into the basket and then stood up.

"Rye told me that the first time he laid eyes on Austin, she was at the edge of the river giving it her grandmother's ashes, and it was love at first sight," Dalton said. "I bet her granny will be glad to drown our worries for us."

Dalton got to his feet and picked up the paper sack. In a few long strides they were beyond the willow tree, and he took two small pieces of wood from the bag. He'd drilled a hole in the top of each one that held a tiny paper sail affixed to a dowel rod.

"They really do look like little sailboats," Becca said.

He tied a long piece of twine to each of the dowel rods and handed one to her. She set her boat in the water and mentally loaded it down with her worries. Dalton did the same, and soon the river gently took them both downstream. Within a few minutes, the strings got tangled up together and tightened in their hands.

Becca took a deep breath and let go. Dalton held on for just a second longer and then turned his vessel loose. The strings were so tangled up with each other that the little boats floated side by side on down the river, forever touching each other.

"Think that's an omen?" she asked.

He slipped an arm around her shoulders. "I hope so. We've known each other almost six months, Becca. We've worked for the same folks and gone to the same church, so we know each other pretty well. I don't know where the future will take us, but I hope that those little boats with their strings all tangled up together mean that wherever our life journey takes us, we are together in it. I would never rush you, but will you be this old cowboy's lady?"

Without hesitation, she wrapped her arms around his neck and whispered, "Yes, Dalton, I will be your lady."

Keep reading for a taste of one of
Carolyn Brown's earliest romances!

Secrets
IN THE
Sand

Coming soon from Sourcebooks Casablanca

CLANCY MORGAN DIDN'T PLAN TO GO TO THE TISHOMINGO
Alumni reunion but changed his mind at the last minute. The
banquet part of the evening was almost over when he arrived, so
he stood in the back of the room and scanned the room from the
shadows. Evidently, one of his classmates from ten years before
had done the same thing, because a woman stood over behind a
huge fake tree just inside the double doors leading into the ballroom. Clancy's dark brows drew down until they were almost a
solid line above his chocolate-brown eyes. Something about her
silhouette looked familiar, but it had been a while since he'd seen
most of his former classmates, and he couldn't make out her face
in the dim lighting. Perhaps she hadn't been a member of his grad-
uating class, but was someone's wife, or else their plus one.

A vision popped in his mind of a girl who used to stand like
that with one hand on her hip. He shook the memory out of his
mind. Angela wouldn't show up to a noisy ten-year high school
class reunion, not as shy as she had been.

"And now, please welcome Dorothy Simpson, the valedictorian
of the class of nineteen fifty-three, and the woman who keeps this
alumni association going," intoned the master of ceremonies from
the podium. "Isn't she wonderful?"

The crowd applauded as a frail, elderly woman made her way to the front. Clancy sneaked in and sat down at the first table with an available empty chair.

"Dorothy Simpson is probably the only living member of that class," Janie Sides Walls whispered to him.

Clancy smiled and applauded dutifully with the rest of the alumni. When he looked back to see if the mystery woman was still standing in the shadows, she was gone. Nothing was there but the doors swinging to and fro, as if she had seen enough...and left. Clancy wished he had gone over just in case she had been Angela.

"Damn," he mumbled under his breath. "Now she's gone, and I'll probably never see her again."

Dorothy leaned in close to the microphone and held up her palm for them to stop the applause. "Thank you all, but really, I'm just good at delegating, and I managed to live to be eighty-five. I always told that Emily Jacobs that I'd be famous someday."

Everyone laughed and clapped even harder than ever.

"Welcome to the Tishomingo Alumni Banquet and reunion," Dorothy went on, "a place where we're all seventeen or eighteen again. Ever realize that when we come to these affairs, we're all seniors in high school again? Too damn bad that we don't look like we did then."

Clancy laughed with everyone else, but he couldn't get Angela Conrad off his mind.

———————————

Angel was aware that he had spotted her. She had felt the questions in his soft brown eyes, but she wasn't ready to face him. Before the evening was over, he would know who she was if she had to sit in his lap and tell him herself. But for now, she had to get ready. The sound equipment was in place, the microphones set up, the amps ready to bring the house down, and the rest of her band members were in the bus.

Angel slung open the door, stomped up the steps, and slumped down on the short sofa on the far wall. She crossed her arms over her chest, sucked in a lungful of air, and let it out slowly.

"Did you see Clancy?" Bonnie asked.

All of the members of the band were blonds, except Angela. Patty and Susan were the same height, but Bonnie stood at just under six feet tall when she wore her cowboy boots.

"Yes," Angel answered. "Looking just as egotistical and full of himself as ever. And he's even sexier than he was ten years ago."

"Methinks me hears a note of love gone wrong. Hey, sounds like a good title for our new song. Maybe I just got the inspiration for the *Billboard*-breaker song that we've needed all these years to take us straight to the top in Nashville." Patty pulled on her boots and twisted her straw-colored hair up in a twist.

Susan tossed Angel's cowboy hat across the bus. With her honey-blond hair and round face, some folks said that she could have been Miranda Lambert's sister. "Right. Just when we've decided to give up touring."

Angel caught her hat and laid it beside her. She stuck out her tongue at her friends, stood up and peeled faded jean shorts down over her hips and tossed them beside the hat. She jerked her knit tank top over her head, threw it in the direction of her shorts, and slipped on a black silk kimono-style robe.

"Hey, girls, I want to thank you again for tonight. Only real friends would play a two-bit gig like this, and I appreciate it. Means a lot to me." She sat down in front of a built-in vanity, complete with mirror and track lighting, and slapped makeup on her face, covering a fine sprinkling of freckles across her upturned nose. She outlined her big green eyes with a delicate tracing of dark pencil, then brushed mascara on her thick lashes. She flipped her dark-brown hair around her face with a styling comb and sat back to look at her reflection. Not bad for a backward girl who'd been scared of her own shadow ten years ago.

She wondered if anyone would recognize her. Not that Angel had planned on attending this reunion any more than the other nine that had already gone by. But then she had received the letter from the class president and decided—without exactly knowing why—that she'd come to this one. Some of the alumni might doubt she'd even been in their class when they saw her onstage, but after tonight they'd go home and drag out their yearbooks to find her name and picture. And there she would be in big glasses, which she'd since replaced with contacts, and wildly curly hair, which she still couldn't tame.

Tonight, Angel was going to put away the past and forget about the pain. The self-help books she'd read and her therapist both told her to face her fear. Tonight she was doing just that. Tomorrow she was going to wake up a brand-new woman, ready to face whatever life might bring her, and she was never going to think about Clancy again.

She forced a smile at her reflection and then reached up and peeled the letter from the class president off her mirror. The committee had asked for a brief paragraph listing her accomplishments in the decade since she'd finished high school. Her short biography would be published in the alumni newsletter that would be sent out the next week. They had also asked for a contribution of some kind to the reunion. Angel had written back and offered to bring her band and play for the dance—free of charge.

"Better jerk them jeans on, darlin'." Mindy came out of the small bathroom and looked at Angel in the mirror. "Clancy Morgan's eyes would pop out of his head if you got to gyratin' your hips in nothing but that cute little lacy bra and underpants. I can't wait to see his face. Be sure you do something so that we know which one of the guys is the man who broke your heart."

"Oh, hush." Angel giggled as she stood up and took her freshly starched white jeans from a hanger and shimmied into them. Then she topped them with a sequined vest with flashing red and white horizontal stripes on the right side and white stars on a ground of blue on the left.

"Lord, all I need is a couple of pasties with tassels." Angel checked her appearance in the mirror one last time.

"Hey, we're playing a gig for a bunch of high school alumni. We ain't doing a show for Neddie's Nudie Beauties. Time to go, ladies. Ten minutes until showtime." Allie, the shortest one in the band and the one with the lightest blond hair, crossed the floor and pushed open the bus door to lead the way.

"Y'all look wonderful," Angel was proud of her five friends in her band. They wore identical black jeans and black denim vests with the state flag of Texas embroidered on the backs.

"We clean up pretty good," Susan agreed. "You'd never know we were plain, old working women the rest of the week."

The band members laughed and headed for the ballroom.

"Let's give the equipment one more check before they open the doors between the banquet room and this ballroom," Allie said. "Testing." She blew into the first microphone, which produced an ear squeal, and she nodded toward Bonnie, who was adjusting the amplifiers.

"Smoke machine is…ready," Mindy said from the side of the stage.

Allie turned a knob or two, double-checked the timer, then sat down at her drums and gave a warm-up roll with the sticks. "Ready to rock and roll," she growled into the microphone beside her.

"Ready," Susan breathed into her microphone, and drew her bow across her fiddle, creating a haunting sound that made Angel's blood curdle, just as it did every time they played.

"Then let's knock 'em dead." Mindy stretched her fingers and warmed up on the keyboard with a few bars of Miranda Lambert's "Hush, Hush."

The double doors from the banquet room swung open into the ballroom, and people wandered in, not quite sure this was where they belonged. Clancy Morgan and several companions found a table right in front of the small knockdown stage Angel toted around in the equipment trailer behind the bus. Even its slight elevation of twelve inches gave the band an advantage, which was better than being stuck back in a corner of a room on the same level as all the dancers.

"Dark in here," Angel heard a man say. "These itty-bitty candles on the tables don't give much light."

"You didn't complain about that ten years ago at the prom." His wife giggled. "Matter of fact, you wanted to blow the candles out so the ballroom would be darker."

"Yeah, but back then you were fun to be with in the dark," he teased.

The woman pouted.

Angel thought she recognized him—wasn't he Jim Moore?

The alarm on Allie's watch went off, and she did a roll on the drums and pushed a hidden button with her foot. The smoke machine emitted trails of white fog across the stage, and a rotating strobe picked up every flicker of candlelight from the tables. When the smoke began to clear, there were five Texas state flags facing the darkened room. Then, from somewhere behind a huge amplifier, Angel stepped out, all aglitter in red, white, and blue sequins.

"Good evening, ladies and gentlemen," she said in a deep, throaty voice. "I'm Angel—and this is the Honky Tonk Band. There's Allie on the drums." She stepped aside, and Allie stood up, bowed, and gave the audience fifteen seconds of a percussion riff.

"And Patty on rhythm guitar." One of the flags turned around to reveal a blond woman, even taller than the drummer and built like an athlete. Patty bowed, and struck a chord and waved to the people, hoping for an enthusiastic crowd. Lord, but she hated to play to a dead bunch, and these alumni sure didn't look as lively as the folks they'd played to last night.

"Bonnie, on steel." The second flag turned, and Bonnie made the guitar slung around her neck whine like a baby.

"Susan, on the fiddle." Angel waved to her left, and a short woman with red hair perched a fiddle on her shoulder and let them hear a tantalizing bit of a classic country tune.

"And over here is Mindy on the keyboard." The final flag turned slowly to face the alumni of Tishomingo High School.

"Hi, ya'll," Angel said huskily into the mike as Mindy made the keyboard do everything but sing.

"And this is Angel!" Dorothy stepped up to the microphone. "You might remember her as Angela Conrad. She and these gorgeous band members have agreed to play for us tonight for free. Let's make them welcome and get ready for a show. These ladies will be at the Arbuckle Ballroom in Davis next Friday night for their final gig, so we're lucky to get 'em. Angel says she's tired of working all week and the weekends, too. So, give them a big hand to let them know how much we appreciate them playing for us." She started the applause and the audience followed suit as she left the stage and grabbed a young guy's hand, led him to the dance floor and nodded to Angel to start the party.

"Wind 'em up, girls," Angel whispered. She grabbed a mike and started off the evening with a surefire crowd pleaser. Mindy tinkled the keyboard keys and Allie kept a steady beat with the brushes on the drums. Angel strutted across the stage, sequins flashing in the strobe lights, and the long diamond drops that dangled from her ears glittering in her dark-brown shoulder-length curls.

Before long, there were at least twenty couples in the middle of the floor, dancing in one way or another. Several were doing something between the twist and the jerk, and an older couple was executing a pretty fine jitterbug. Angel kept looking down at the table where Clancy Morgan sat alone while his friends tried to keep up with the beat on the dance floor. Evidently Melissa—if he had married her—couldn't accompany him tonight. Or maybe he hadn't married her. Now wouldn't that be a hoot?

Angel put her left hand on her hip and struck a pose, and memories from that summer ten years ago flooded Clancy's mind, again. What had happened to the Angela Conrad he'd known? She was supposed to marry old Billy Joe Summers and raise a shack full of snotty-nosed kids. She was supposed to work in a sewing factory, supporting Billy Joe's life-threatening drinking habit. She wasn't supposed to be on a stage, belting out songs by famous artists.

Patty started a strong rhythm and Angel stepped off the stage and mixed with the people in the dancing crowd, singing into a cordless mike. Then she sat down on the table right in front of Clancy, wiggled her shoulders, and sang to him as she looked right in his eyes. He wanted to say something, but what could he say? Words wouldn't turn him from a jerk into a decent guy, so he just sat there without saying a word, shaking his head in disbelief.

She looked something like the old Angela, except she wasn't wearing glasses. She leaned toward him far enough that he could see down the front of her vest, and a red heat stirred inside him as he remembered her body against his. She kept singing while the girls provided backup on the stage; then suddenly before he could blink, she was back on the stage.

"Hey, Mike Griffin, pull that woman up a little closer. You sure danced closer than that when we were in high school," Angel teased in the middle of another song, a more romantic one, while the band played the break.

She glanced at the table to her left and saw that Clancy still had a bewildered look on his face, as if his eyes couldn't believe his ears. Angel could still list his every accomplishment. Quarterback from tenth through twelfth grade, taking the team to the state championship all three years. Debate champion, too, winning the regional trophy during his senior year.

Angel would bet dollars to doughnuts that if Clancy had to hop up on the stage right now and speak, he'd be as awkward as he'd been that summer night just before everyone was leaving for college. He couldn't hide his feelings then, and he obviously still hadn't learned how. Because his long face told her he was having a hard time dealing with her putting on a show for the alumni organization. In fact, his ego appeared to be *severely* deflated.

"We'll have a fifteen-minute break while we grab something to drink." Allie pulled her microphone close to her face. "See y'all in a quarter of an hour."

———

Before Clancy could make sense of his thoughts, Angel had gone out the side door, surrounded by her band. He stretched out his long limbs, amazed that he'd sat still for an hour and a half while memories and her presence tormented him. He smiled and nodded at several of his old friends as he made his way to the doors leading out to the balcony, where he could see the bus parked in the lot behind the ballroom. It was black with gold metallic lettering, that sparkled in the light from the streetlamps. The word *Angel* had a crooked halo slung over the capital *A*, and *The Honky Tonk Band* had little gold devils with pitchforks sitting on each of the *o* letters.

He remembered the nights when she'd sung along with the radio in his new red Camaro, and he hadn't been able to tell which was the real singer and which was Angela. Who would have ever thought she'd be running around in her own bus with a band of women who looked like candidates for the Dallas Cowboy Cheerleaders?

Tonight had been crazy. Clancy hadn't even thought about Angela showing up. She was almost the one voted most likely *not* to succeed. Although hardly a day had gone by in the past ten years that something didn't make him think of Angela Conrad, he'd long since learned to disassociate himself from what had really happened that summer. It was as if it happened to someone in a book, and he'd just read about it. He hadn't really sat on the creek bank with her late into the nights and let the minnows nibble their toes. He hadn't actually walked away that last night, knowing she was crying. No, it couldn't have been him. It was someone else in a novel or a movie, and he just remembered the details too well.

———

"Whew." Allie dabbed her face with a tissue. "Pretty lively crowd for a bunch of has-beens."

"Hey," Angel giggled nervously. "I graduated from this place. I belong to that crowd."

"Yeah, like I belong at the pearly gates of heaven," Susan's blue eyes twinkled. "You outgrew them years ago. Don't let these hicks make you think you still belong to their world."

"Thanks." Angel pretended to slap her cheek. "I needed that."

"Well, I can see why you were so stuck on that Clancy. He fills out them Wranglers pretty damned good," Patty sighed. "And those big, wide shoulders about gave me the vapors." She fluttered her long eyelashes. "Maybe you oughta give him another chance, Angel. Lord, handsome as he is, I'd give him a chance if he wasn't already wearin' your brand."

"Hell," Angel snorted. "He never wore my brand. He's free for the taking if you're interested. I don't think he's still married. If he is, his wife didn't come with him. But stand assured, he's about as trustworthy as those two little devils painted on the side of this bus."

"No, thanks," Patty said, putting on fresh lipstick. "You can keep him. Then tame him or kill him, but don't give him to me."

"Me neither," Mindy gulped in the hot night air and looked up at the starlit sky to see if there might be a stray cloud with a few raindrops to spare. "Hey, look up on the balcony when you come outside, Angel. Clancy's up there staring down here like he can't believe his little eyeballs."

"Yeah? That's nothing new. He always did look down on me." Angel was suddenly tired. Her bones ached like they'd never before during a performance…and so did her stupid heart. "Another hour and a half and we'll take this bus home and park it. Then I'll forget about Clancy Morgan and get on with life. I was here for closure, and I've got it."

"Sure, you do." Bonnie chuckled. "You'll forget Clancy when you're stone-cold dead and planted six feet down. Women don't forget first loves, and they *never* forget a first love who did them dirty."

CHAPTER 2

ANGEL FLIPPED THE LIGHT SWITCH JUST INSIDE THE MASSIVE doors of her office and slipped off her shoes. She padded across the thick ivory carpet and plopped down in an oversize blue velvet chair behind an antique French provincial desk. She tossed the alumni newsletter on the desk, laced her hands behind her head, and tried to calm down.

She'd gone to the reunion to give her former classmates a dose of comeuppance. She had planned to leave with a smile on her face and never think about any of them again. Several former acquaintances had made a point of stopping by the stage between songs and saying hello to her, but Clancy left just after the last song without a word. But then, what could he say? He'd made his choice ten years ago, and there was no room for a change of heart.

Angel got up and went to the window. Patty was the last one leaving the parking lot. The other girls had already left in the early-morning darkness. Next Friday they would be playing at a honky-tonk just south of Davis, Oklahoma, and then a new band called The Gamblers would pick up the bus and have it repainted with their logo. It was high time for the Honky Tonk Band to go out with a flourish and retire. The girls enjoyed performing, but they needed their weekends these days. Allie was married and her husband, Tyler, complained that he never saw her on weekends. Susan lived with her boyfriend, Richie, and they needed more quality time together.

Bonnie was engaged and planning an October wedding, and Mindy was in the middle of a divorce. Besides, none of them were getting any younger. Angel sighed, thinking about how she could catch up on all the work at the farm when she stopped touring, and she had this oil business to run as well.

She thought about Tishomingo again. Main Street had changed a little in the past ten years. The courthouse was new, and the café where she and her grandmother had an occasional burger had a different name these days, and there was a new chiropractor's office on the corner of Main and Broadway. Blake Shelton's businesses were where a clothing store and a drugstore used to stand. She'd looked upstream at Pennington Creek when they'd crossed the bridge over it into town and noticed that it hadn't changed at all. The same trees still shaded the sandbar below the dam, and the memories of what had happened night after night on a blanket in the privacy of those trees were so real, she could almost smell Clancy's aftershave.

Angel picked up the newsletter and began to read. Each page had a classmate's name at the top and a summary of their accomplishments in the past ten years. Apparently almost everyone had sent in the questionnaire, whether they could attend the alumni banquet and the dance or not. She found her own bio and reread it.

Because of previous engagements, I'm not able to attend the banquet. However, my band and I—Angel and the Honky Tonk Band—will play for the dance free of charge if you would like. Let me know at the following address. Angela Conrad. She'd added a box number in Denison, Texas. But no one knew that she had rented the box for one month just for the return answer to her letter.

She scanned down the letter to what Clancy had written. Since leaving high school, he'd graduated from the University of Oklahoma with a bachelor's degree in geology and chemistry and a minor in education. Then he'd enlisted in the air force and had been stationed in Virginia for most of his four-year career and had gone to graduate school for a master's in education. Just recently he'd come back to Oklahoma and started teaching in an Oklahoma City high school. Under *Marital Status*, he had marked an X beside *Divorced*.

So, he probably had married Melissa after all. But what had happened? By small-town society's rules, Mr. and Mrs. Clancy Morgan were supposed to be living happily ever after. Suddenly, Angel wished she had subscribed to the Tishomingo weekly newspaper. Then at least she would have known who'd married whom, who had children, and so forth.

When her granny had driven their old green pickup truck out of Tishomingo that long-ago fall day, Angel hadn't even looked back in the rearview mirror for one last glimpse of the place where she'd lived since she was three years old. She hadn't left anything behind but heartaches, and she didn't need to look back at the fading lights of town to recapture them. They would be with her forever.

She looked through the newsletter to see what Billy Joe Summers was doing these days. She hadn't seen him at the dance even though she'd scanned the ballroom several times to see if there was a six-foot, five-inch gangly man standing shyly on the sidelines. Billy Joe had always been nice to her, and that awful night on the sandbar when she'd sat with her feet in the warm water, it had been Billy Joe's name that Clancy had mentioned so scornfully.

"Hello again, Mr. Henry." Angel picked up a worn teddy bear sitting on top of her filing cabinet and held him, just for old times' sakes. Mr. Henry had listened sympathetically to all her tales of woe in the years since she'd been given him for her fifth birthday...and here she was, still feeling sorry for herself.

She wondered how her memories of Tishomingo could still be so vivid. After all, she hadn't ever wanted to go back, even though she and her granny had lived there for fifteen years, since the day she'd turned three years old. Angel had spent her babyhood in nearby Kemp, and although they visited her great-grandpa at the farm there a couple of times a year, she couldn't recollect anything about it.

When Angel had turned eighteen, her great-grandpa Poppa

John had died and left his twenty acres to his only child—Angel's grandmother. After his estate had been settled, Angel and her granny had left Tishomingo and gone back to Kemp. And it hadn't happened a minute too soon, in anyone's opinion. Memories flooded her mind. "Don't stay out late, Angela. We've got to pack in the morning," her granny had reminded her. "Got to be out of the house before midnight or pay more rent, you know."

"I know." Angela had gone out the front door and walked west toward the dam. All summer she'd gone swimming every evening in Pennington Creek, and it was a good thing August had arrived, because her bikini was beginning to look as worn-out as her jeans. Most times it seemed like just a hop, skip, and jump from her house to the swimming hole, but that evening the walk took forever.

Angel had shimmied out of her shorts and shirt, tugged the top of her bikini down and the bottoms up before she sat down on the sandbar and waited for Clancy. She picked up a twig and drew an interlocking heart in the sand. She put her initial in one heart, Clancy's in the second one, and wrote *baby* in the part that interlocked. She loved him, and he loved her. The secret that they had been hiding all summer would come out as soon as she told him her news. Sure, they were young, but she had a scholarship, and he didn't have to go to Oklahoma University. The important thing was that they would be together.

She soaked her feet in the lukewarm water while she waited. Clancy wouldn't be there for another half hour so she thought about all the scenarios lying ahead. She'd known the first time they'd accidentally met each other in this very place that she was flirting with big trouble, but she'd been in love with Clancy Morgan since kindergarten. If he would just touch her hand or kiss her one time before she moved away, she could survive forever on the memories. That he didn't want anyone to know they were dating stung a little, but now their secret would be out in the public. Clancy was a good guy. He would do the right thing.

ABOUT THE AUTHOR

Carolyn Brown is an award-winning *New York Times* and *USA Today* bestselling author and a RITA finalist. She is the author of more than one hundred novels and novellas, and her books have been translated into nineteen foreign languages.

She was born in Texas but grew up in southern Oklahoma where she and her husband, Charles, a retired English teacher, make their home. They have three grown children and enough grandchildren to keep them young.

When she's not writing, Carolyn likes to plot new stories in her backyard with her tom cat, Boots Randolph Terminator Outlaw, who protects the yard from all kinds of wicked varmints...like crickets, locusts, and spiders. Visit Carolyn at carolynbrownbooks.com.